WHO WE USED TO BE

CAITLIN WEAVER

Storm
PUBLISHING

Ebook ISBN: 978-1-80508-929-2
Paperback ISBN: 978-1-80508-931-5

Cover design: Eileen Carey
Cover images: iStock

Published by Storm Publishing.
For further information, visit:
www.stormpublishing.co

To Lauren, Kim, and Cari, who've been there for everything.

ONE

DANA

Six days before

Dana's heart raced as she opened the car door. She was ten minutes early for her meeting, and hoping it would come off as polite, not desperate. She straightened the gold buttons that ran down the front of her navy dress and smoothed her long, dark hair that she'd pulled into a demure low ponytail, trying to shake the dread sitting in her chest.

Inside, the bank's lobby smelled of lemon cleaner, instantly dragging her back to childhood visits, where she would sit in the lobby sucking on the peppermint candies provided by the receptionist while she waited for her mother. But today there wasn't time for memories. Instead, she headed past the front desk and straight into the president's office.

"Dana, good to see you," Harlan Sinclair said, rising from behind his imposing mahogany desk. Harlan had been in charge of the shop's account—the business her mother had started—since the day Haven and Hearth opened decades ago.

"Harlan." She forced a smile. She noticed the boxes stacked

against the walls. "You're really leaving, then? The place won't be the same without you."

"Afraid so," he said, settling back into his chair. "New management takes over next week." Harlan lifted an eyebrow. "The place won't be the same, period."

The local, independent bank had recently been acquired by a larger company, and would be closing for remodeling. As part of the acquisition, Harlan had accepted a retirement package.

Dana sighed. "No, I suppose it won't."

Harlan gave a resigned smile, then his face brightened. "How's Cora?" he asked.

Dana hid her grin. "Oh, you know my mother," she said. "Busy riling everyone up over at Shady Pines." Dana and her husband, Eric, had recently moved her mother to one of Atlanta's poshest senior living facilities. So far Cora had lodged complaints about the food (under seasoned), the housekeeping (lacking), and pickleball courts outside her window (noisy).

"Cora was never short on opinions," Harlan said with a soft laugh. "I'll have to get over and see her one of these days."

"She'd like that," Dana said.

He shifted in his seat. "So, Dana, how can I be of assistance? I figured it was important when you asked to meet on a Saturday."

Dana felt a flush creep up her neck. "Yes, thank you for that," she said. "It's a bit... time sensitive." She felt a stab of guilt as she thought of the growing stack of unpaid bills she'd shoved into a desk drawer back at the shop. *It's only time sensitive because you let everything go for so long,* she chided herself. With humiliation, she thought of how she'd even missed the last payroll for SueEllen, her full-time employee, who'd been working at the home goods shop since Dana was a teenager. Dana had blamed it on a glitch with the payroll system. She had to remedy the situation—fast. Squaring her shoulders, she summoned her sunniest smile for Harlan. "I'd like to extend

Haven and Hearth's line of credit," she said, trying to project confidence.

Harlan nodded slowly and sat back in his chair. He paused as though gathering his words. "I was afraid you might say that," he said.

Dana's flush deepened and she felt her stomach drop at the grave note in his voice.

Harlan fished a pair of Clark Kent reading glasses from his breast pocket and opened a manilla folder in front of him. The numbers on the pages he flipped through were too small for Dana to read. Peering at her over his glasses, he gave a tight smile. "If it were up to me, Dana, I'd do what I could. But as of next week, well, I won't be the decision maker. And the new management team, well..." He sighed and took off his glasses. "I don't see them deciding in your favor."

A cold sweat broke out on the back of Dana's neck as her heart raced. She had been counting on that extension—without it, she couldn't pay her bills or SueEllen. "Why not?" she asked. "I've done it before."

"Yes." Harlan nodded. "Three times. But with the guidance we have from the new team based on today's interest rate environment, it's just not going to happen again. I'm sorry." The corners of his mouth turned down slightly.

Dana closed her eyes. Her mother, she knew, would never have taken out a loan to begin with. Cora had always kept enough in the coffers to weather a downturn. But Dana had told herself it was just a temporary bridge until business picked back up.

She opened her eyes and leaned forward. "What are my options, then?"

Harlan gave her a sympathetic smile. "I'm afraid there aren't many. We could potentially refinance, but given your recent profit statements, I doubt the bank would agree."

"So, I just have to... repay?" Sweat trickled down her back. Dana wished for something to fan herself with.

"Yes, repayment will start in January."

Dana inhaled deeply. It was October tenth, and already Halloween decorations had sprung up around the neighborhood. January was less than three months away.

Harlan leaned forward and placed his elbows on his desk. "I'm sorry, Dana, I really am. If there was anything I could do to help, you know I would. Your mother—Haven and Hearth—well, it's a neighborhood institution."

Dana blinked to keep her tears at bay. Cora had turned the business over to Dana only three years ago, and already Dana was on the brink of losing it.

Dread rolled over her. She had to find a way to fix this before her mother found out. More importantly, she had to admit to Eric just how dire things actually were.

"I understand," Dana said, pushing her chair back and standing. She held out her hand and Harlan took it and held it between both of his for a brief moment.

"Give my best to Cora, will you?" he asked.

Dana nodded, then fled his office before she could start to cry. How was she going to tell Eric? Or her mother? And, more imminently important, how was she going to make it through the damn neighborhood block party today? Safely in her car, she allowed herself to bury her face in her steering wheel and cry. After five minutes, she sat up, wiped her eyes, blew her nose and rummaged in her handbag for her makeup. As she reapplied mascara, she gave herself a firm look in the rearview mirror and told herself she could do this. Then she started the car and headed home.

Pulling into her driveway, the street was already busy, and she could smell the savory aroma of chili in slow cookers set up on a row of folding tables on the sidewalk, mixed with a sickening combination of sugar and diesel fuel coming from the ice cream truck the neighborhood association had chipped in for.

Children with sticky hands darted through the crowd with their faces painted, chasing each other and tossing footballs. Dana's neighbors milled around in the warm October sunshine, a month that, in Atlanta, usually felt more like summer than fall. Dana had known most of her neighbors for decades; Pinecrest Drive, with its close proximity to the main street that housed Haven and Hearth and a handful of other local shops, wasn't a street with much turnover. The neighborhood moms maintained a text thread where they regularly traded favors and helped each other out when babysitters canceled at the last minute or someone ran out of eggs in the middle of a recipe.

Getting out of her car, Dana tried to push her financial worries out of her mind and headed to the table where Eric had set out a bowl of her famous rum punch. She helped herself to a generous cup, then took a long sip.

"Hey there," came a voice. "Thirsty?"

Dana lowered her cup to see Padma, her best friend and next-door neighbor. She flushed. "Something like that," she said.

Padma eyed her. "Everything OK?"

For a brief instant Dana considered telling her about the meeting with Harlan, then brushed it away. This was not the time. "Just trying to keep up with Mel," she said, nodding to Melanie Curt, their across-the-street neighbor, who stood a few feet away clutching a wine tumbler bearing the slogan "Mommy's Sippy Cup" and laughing too loudly.

Padma grimaced. "No one should try to keep up with Mel," she said. She pulled her heavy, dark hair off her neck and tugged at the collar of the white T-shirt she wore tucked into flowy linen pants. "Ugh, it's October, when is it actually going to be sweater weather?"

"Hon, it's sixty-two degrees, are you sure you're not just having a hot flash?" Dana said, tilting her head. At fifty-two, Padma was six years older than Dana.

"Oh, believe me," Padma said, "if I were having a hot flash, I'd look like I'd just rafted Class Four rapids." She raised her formidable eyebrows, her forehead crinkling. Padma was one of the few women Dana knew who hadn't had Botox. Then again, she had the smooth, plump skin of a twenty-year-old, while Dana's pale, freckled face stayed perpetually dry and flaky, no matter how much expensive moisturizer she used.

"Afternoon, ladies." Dana's husband, Eric, approached, and more than one of the neighborhood moms followed him with their eyes. While Dana felt increasingly invisible with age, Eric only seemed to look better. His thick brown hair was only beginning to gray, and instead of slackening like hers, his body had tightened over the last year thanks to his new trainer and intermittent fasting routine.

"Hi." Dana greeted him with a peck on the lips. "Are the kids here?"

"Last I saw, Izzy was policing the kids in the bouncy house, making sure no one gets hurt," Eric said.

"I think Maeve's with her," Padma said.

Dana laughed and tucked her dark hair behind her ear. "How did we end up with such *responsible* kids? I was nothing like that at their age." She shook her head, recalling the high school keg parties she attended with her cheerleader friends, where she spent most of the night worrying her mother would find out and ground her for life.

Padma frowned. "I know, I worry about them trying to be so perfect all the time. Like, now is the time to screw up a little bit, you know? When the stakes are low."

"Well, at least Ian has that covered," Eric said with a disapproving frown. "That kid doesn't have a drop of ambition in his body. If he's not careful he'll end up—"

"Ahem." Dana cleared her throat and nodded frantically at their son approaching Eric from behind.

"Um, hey," Ian said. He wore his usual blank expression, and Dana couldn't tell whether he'd heard his father's remark. She hoped not.

"Hi, honey," Dana said. She reached out to push his wavy light brown hair out of his perpetually sleepy hazel eyes, the same color as his father's. "Having fun?" she asked, gesturing around at the crowd of neighbors.

He shrugged. "Can I take the car?"

"Did you clean up the kitchen from breakfast?" Eric asked.

"I didn't eat breakfast," he pointed out.

"But it's your weekend for kitchen duty. The chart's on the fridge."

Padma flashed Dana a sympathetic smile and stepped away.

Ian was the polar opposite of his sister. While Izzy was an honor roll student, Dana felt relieved when Ian brought home Cs. Izzy ran varsity cross-country, was on student government, and already had a target list of prestigious—and expensive—colleges she planned to apply to next year. Ian, on the other hand, mostly played video games and hung out with similarly apathetic friends.

"I'll clean later, I promise," he said to Eric.

Eric gave a curt shake of his head. "It doesn't work like that," he said.

Dana bit her lip and thought about trying to intervene, but she knew she'd only get a lecture from Eric about how Ian had to learn that actions had consequences.

Ian narrowed his eyes and gave a loud sigh. "Never mind," he said, stalking away.

"So typical," muttered Eric. "He wants what he wants when he wants it."

Dana shrugged. "Every seventeen-year-old does," she said lightly.

Eric pursed his lips. "Not his twin sister."

Dana tried to smile. "Izzy is exceptional," she said. "I'm not sure we should be holding anyone to her standard—especially Ian."

Eric's jaw tightened. "He has to learn how to operate in the real world—where you don't just get to do whatever you want all the time. You're always making excuses for him."

Dana looked around at their neighbors. "Do we have to do this here?" she murmured. "Why don't we save it for Tuesday?"

"Tuesday?" Eric frowned in confusion.

"Regina?" Dana said softly. Regina was their couples therapist—or would be. Tuesday was their first session. Dana was surprised Eric had even agreed to go when she'd suggested it. She felt a flicker of worry now at the growing tally of topics she was already mentally scheduling for their first appointment.

A strange look came over Eric's face, then he nodded, his eyes flickering away. "Right. Regina."

Dana held out her hand. After a brief hesitation, Eric uncrossed his arms and took it.

TWO

PADMA

Five days before

Padma stood in the kitchen clad in her scrubs, sipping coffee and watching a couple on the TV in the living room argue about the budget for their kitchen renovation.

Lars came downstairs, dressed in a fitted light blue button-up shirt and slim cut navy trousers. "They'll end up getting the farm sink," he said, nodding at the TV. "They always do." Even after years of living in the US, he still spoke with a slight Swedish accent, the English words rolling around in his mouth like a ping-pong ball. Padma found it as sexy as she did his bright blue eyes and silvery blond hair.

"Speaking of," she said, "maybe we should get a new sink."

Lars held up his finger. "No more renovations, you promised!"

Padma laughed. Her world revolved around her work as an ER doctor, but her one indulgence—much to Lars's chagrin—was home improvement. She treated open houses the way others treated trips to department stores: "just to look." In their twenty years of marriage, they'd moved three times and renovated twice. Despite everything they'd done to perfect their current home, Padma still felt the occasional itch to move—but now, she couldn't imagine living anywhere but next door to Dana.

"Fine," she sighed, filling her travel mug with coffee. "At least not until Maeve goes to college."

Lars rolled his eyes, then pointed at her thirty-ounce mug. "Please tell me you're not actually going to drink that much coffee today."

Padma yawned and shrugged. "Probably not. But I like knowing I *could*."

"Emotional support coffee." Lars nodded, and she laughed. "You finish at five?" he asked, and she nodded. "Then you have your meeting?"

Despite the fact that Padma had been attending her Monday AA meeting religiously for years, Lars always asked her about it. Sometimes she wondered whether it was his way of reassuring himself that she was still committed to not drinking, even after twenty-four years of sobriety.

"Yes," she confirmed. "I'll be home after my meeting. Maeve should be home from orchestra practice around the same time."

Lars nodded. "Have a good day, my love." He leaned forward to kiss her and she inhaled his familiar scent of fresh soap and pine sap. Despite all their years together, she still felt a small thrill at the feeling of his hand cupping the back of her head and his neatly trimmed beard brushing her cheek.

"You too," she said.

Padma pulled into the hospital parking lot and sat in the car for an extra four minutes, scrolling through Zillow. Then, hefting her backpack, which contained mostly snacks—she never knew whether she'd have time to eat lunch when she was on a shift—she headed into the hospital.

The ER was in full swing when she grabbed a spot at one of the computer terminals where the doctors sat—"The Fishbowl" they jokingly called it, for its central location and surrounding plexiglass walls—and pulled up the list of patients.

"Welcome to chaos." The doctor next to her nodded with an exhausted smile, just as the red phone nearby sounded with a loud siren ring, indicating an ambulance en route.

It was the kind of day where time vanished and Padma's emotional support coffee sat untouched, forgotten and cold. Hours later, her stomach growled, a reminder she hadn't had a moment for herself. When she finally broke free, she headed to the break room where she'd stashed her backpack with its selection of nuts, protein bars, and a couple of apples. She sighed, and gave the bag a small pat. "Sorry, not today, buddy," she said.

Her eyes drifted to the vending machine. A few months ago, Toby, the Director of Emergency Medicine, had swapped the usual snacks for healthier options—trail mix, dried fruit, electrolyte water—after the nurses complained about the lack of choice.

Bypassing the healthy options, she headed out of the break room into the nearby stairwell and up two flights. Checking her watch, she hurried down a long hallway until she arrived at another set of vending machines, ones she knew were stocked with the salty potato chips and Dr. Pepper she was craving.

"Hey, Toby," she said as she approached. The other figure in front of the machines startled and looked at her, a guilty expression sliding over his ruddy face.

"Oh, hey, Padma," he said, glancing down at the Doritos and Diet Coke he held. "I really shouldn't be eating this." His hand went to his rounded midsection.

"Spoken like a true doctor," she said cheerfully, sliding her credit card into the machine and making a selection. Padma had always liked Toby because, like her, he struggled to take the medical advice he doled out to others. He loved fast food, hated all forms of exercise, and drank Diet Coke like it was an Olympic sport. Padma had tried to embrace the things that were supposed to be good for you—salads, Pilates, juice fasts—but none of those habits ever stuck. She blamed her parents. In their eagerness to assimilate to American life, they'd abandoned cooking the vegetable rich Indian meals they'd grown up with. Instead, her childhood was filled with boxed mac and cheese, chicken nuggets, and endless hours of American TV.

"Takes one to know one," Toby shot back, grinning and smoothing his thick, silver hair which he wore slicked back from his face like a mobster.

Padma laughed and retrieved her potato chips and Dr. Pepper from the machine. Ripping open the bag, she popped one in her mouth, letting out a sigh of satisfaction as the salt and oil coated her tongue.

"Busy morning," Toby observed. "But that's Monday for you."

Mondays were typically the busiest days in the ER, always with a rush of people who'd put off seeking care during the weekend.

"I didn't want to miss the game," a man had told her once as she'd informed him he was having a heart attack and prepared him to receive a stent.

"Yep," Padma replied to Toby. "But I know you wouldn't have it any other way."

Toby laughed and cracked open his Diet Coke. "I do thrive on chaos."

"We all do." Padma twisted the top off her Dr. Pepper and took a long swig. As a doctor, she knew the sugar wouldn't actually hit her bloodstream that fast, but still she swore she could feel it pumping through her veins almost immediately. She loved that first sip of soda almost as much as she'd once loved that first sip of alcohol. "How're the kids?" she asked. Toby had two college-aged boys, who Padma still pictured as the sticky-faced toddlers they'd been back when she started at the hospital all those years ago, coming around to visit their dad at work sometimes so—according to Toby's wife, Monica—"the kids won't forget what he looks like."

Toby hadn't been head of the ER then, of course, but he'd been older and a more experienced doctor than Padma. He'd recognized an all-too-familiar quality in her: singular ambition, often at the expense of other things. She'd been lucky to have him as a mentor and friend all these years.

"Jason graduates this year, can you believe it?" Toby shook his head and brushed an orange Dorito crumb off his chin. "And Andrew just told us he's going pre-med." His eyes shone with pride. "Monica nearly lost her mind. Why spend your life at a hospital when you could major in computers and go make millions in Silicon Valley, she wanted to know." He gave a wry smile.

Padma shrugged. "She's not wrong."

"Don't I know it," Toby sighed. "God, I can't wait to retire."

Padma snorted. "You'll never retire."

Toby paused and looked around, then lowered his voice. "End of January," he said. "But no one in the department knows yet, so keep it between us."

"What?" Padma's jaw dropped. "But it's already October!"

"Honest to God," he said. "Monica made me turn in the paperwork. Said she'd leave me if I didn't."

Padma knit her eyebrows together in skepticism. "She'll never leave you." She loved Monica, whose thick Long Island accent matched Toby's and who complained vociferously and proudly to anyone within earshot about how much Toby worked. "Besides, you'll drive her crazy at home all the time."

"We're gonna travel," Toby said. "Hawaii. California. Maybe one of those river boat cruises in Europe."

"You hate the water," Padma pointed out. One year they'd had the department's annual summer barbecue at someone's lake house, and Toby had refused to even venture onto the dock.

He shrugged and grinned. "Whatever Monica wants, Monica gets. You know she's always been the boss."

Padma shook her head in disbelief. "I can't imagine this place without you," she said. Then a thought tickled the back of her mind. "Wait, if you're retiring, then who'll be..." She trailed off, catching herself.

Toby raised an eyebrow. "The new Director of Emergency Medicine?" he asked.

Padma flushed, embarrassed that she was even thinking about her own career when she should be focused on her friend.

"Ah, come on," he said, noticing her discomfort. "I'm shocked it's not the very first thing you asked me."

"I just—I mean—"

He held up his hand. "You're ambitious, that's a good thing. Don't ever let anyone tell you otherwise. What's more, you're an excellent doctor." He glanced around. "Probably the best we have. There's a very good chance it could be you." He smiled. "And while it's not my decision, my recommendation will carry a lot of weight."

Padma's heart fluttered in her chest at the possibility of a chance at the role. "Thank you," she said. "I mean it."

"But not a word, remember?" Toby said. Then he held up his Diet Coke. "Now get back to work and let me enjoy my aspartame in peace."

After the freneticism of the morning, the afternoon dragged. Padma caught up on her patient charts, trying to keep her mind off Toby's retirement and what it could mean for her own career. In between patients, she texted Dana.

Walk tomorrow night?

The only exercise she didn't truly hate were her evening walks with Dana, which they tried to do at least a handful of times a week, panting and gossiping their way through the neighborhood streets.

Definitely

It's our first therapy session tomorrow so I'll need to debrief.

How are you feeling about it?

Weirdly, I'm looking forward to it. Like, nothing major is really wrong, we're just disconnected lately. I think it will be nice to have some help getting back on track.

Proud of you for asking for what you want

She and Dana were opposites in that way. Whereas Padma always had an opinion, Dana had always been more go-with-the-flow. Which was maybe why they worked so well as friends.

Thanks for encouraging me to 🩶

Right as her shift was about to end Padma was called in to stitch up the finger of a harried young mother who'd sliced it open while making dinner for her kids. Refusing to rush it, Padma executed the stitches with her usual meticulousness, which meant she was then late leaving the hospital. Getting into her car, a wave of fatigue came over her. Her stomach rumbled again and she realized she hadn't eaten since the potato chips. She sighed and glanced at the clock. She could still make it to her AA meeting. But how nice it would be to head straight home instead, to take a hot shower and then sit at the kitchen counter with Lars while he cooked dinner.

She shook the fantasy out of her head and put her car in gear.

Fifteen minutes later she slid into a folding chair at the back of a windowless room in a church basement. It smelled of coffee and must. She nodded at some of the other regulars and waited until her turn came.

"Hi," she said to the room. "My name is Padma and I'm an alcoholic."

THREE

DANA

Four days before

Dana knocked sharply on Ian's bedroom door. "Ian, are you up?" Silence. "Come on, get moving—your sister needs to leave in fifteen minutes." She cracked the door and was greeted by the musty smell of his room, mingled with a hint of what might be marijuana. Not knowing for sure made her feel old.

Ian lay sprawled on his back, his arm over his face, the same pose he'd slept in since he was a little boy. She watched his chest rise and fall, noting how his shoulders had broadened in the last year. With his wavy hair and square jaw there was no denying that he was an exceptionally handsome kid.

In sleep, Ian's face was peaceful, and Dana had to resist the urge to kiss him good morning, the way she'd done when he was small. She couldn't remember the last time he'd welcomed her touch. Having children was strange that way; one day, you craved a break from their constant grabbing and squeezing, and the next, you felt a physical ache at being in the same room with them, unable to hug and kiss them whenever you wanted.

"Mom, body autonomy," Izzy often complained whenever

Dana smoothed her hair one too many times. Yes, but not with *me*, Dana always wanted to reply.

"Honey," Dana said, shaking Ian's shoulder gently. "You need to get up. You're going to be late." He stirred, smacking his lips as she turned on the lamp. Ian pulled the covers over his head.

Eric poked his head into the room, his sweaty T-shirt clinging to him after his workout. "Ian, you awake?" he asked sharply. "You have fifteen minutes to get downstairs and into the car. If you make your sister late again, I swear—"

"You'll what?" Ian asked, sitting up, his chest smooth with only a few light brown hairs. His eyes narrowed at his father in challenge.

Eric let out a growl of frustration and turned away down the stairs. "Just get a move on," he called over his shoulder.

Dana gave her son a sympathetic smile. "Maybe take a quick shower," she suggested. "It's not exactly... fresh in here."

Ian smirked. "I'm sure Haven and Hearth has some artisanal air freshener or a hundred-dollar soy candle made by endangered monks that could fix that."

"Honey, please," Dana said. She didn't have the energy to argue with Ian about how the overpriced candles she sold were a crucial part of their livelihood. Or were meant to be. "Just get moving so your father doesn't blow his stack."

Downstairs, Izzy was packing her cross-country bag. "Mom, I don't have any clean compression socks," she said, her neat ponytail bouncing. Whereas Ian's hair was wavy, Izzy's was shiny and straight, and she'd gotten her mother's cool blue eyes. Her skin was lighter than his olive tone and a smattering of freckles stood out on her nose.

"Did you check the laundry room?" Dana suggested, pouring herself a second—or was it third?—cup of coffee. She'd been up since five a.m., the worries about her store circling in her head like a small tornado.

Izzy wrinkled her nose. "Yes, but it's all dirty. I need more than two pairs."

"Iz," Dana said, "those socks are forty dollars a pair from Lululemon."

"Good morning, sweetheart," Eric said as he entered the kitchen. He ruffled Izzy's hair, something she never would have let Dana get away with.

"Ew, Dad, you're so sweaty," Izzy said, though she grinned.

"That's what I'm paying my trainer for," Eric said, heading for the refrigerator. He tossed a sidelong glance at Dana. "You should try it, hon. There's nothing like starting the day on an endorphin high."

"Mm," Dana said, pressing her lips together. She'd tried jogging with him before, hoping to lose the fifteen pounds she'd gained during the pandemic. But each time, Eric would speed ahead, leaving her behind.

"Where's Ian?" Izzy huffed. "I can*not* be late. If he's not down here in five minutes, I'm leaving."

"I can drop him at school if you need to leave," Dana said.

Eric looked up from where he was scooping protein powder into the blender. "No, you can*not*," he said. "Ian needs to learn some discipline. You can't be rearranging your schedule to reward his laziness."

Dana opened her mouth to reply, but was saved by Ian sauntering in, hair damp and tousled, wearing a faded Stüssy T-shirt.

Izzy gave him a once-over and raised an eyebrow. "*Oh*, now I see what took so long. You really nailed the 'I woke up like this' look."

Ian grinned. "Yeah, my contouring's flawless, right?" He sucked in his cheeks and framed his face with his hands.

Izzy rolled her eyes. "Look out, Kardashians." She slung her backpack over one shoulder and hoisted her duffle onto the other. "OK, let's go already."

"What about breakfast?" Dana protested.

"Take one of my protein bars," Eric offered. "They only have three grams of carbs."

The kids exchanged a look. "Yeah, no, thanks," Izzy said.

"They taste like armpit," Ian added, grabbing his bag. He glanced at Izzy. "Starbucks?"

"Definitely."

After the kids left, Eric turned on the blender, its whirring filling the kitchen while Dana sipped her coffee with a growing sense of dread. Tonight was their couples therapy appointment —a suggestion Dana had made months ago, claiming they needed a space to reconnect. Which they did—but beneath that, Dana also needed a place to finally reveal to Eric the financial mess she'd made of her business. She'd thought about telling him countless times, but each time she lost her nerve. She hoped a therapist could help her get the words out, and guide them in making a plan to fix it.

Eric poured his concoction into a glass and headed for the stairs. "I'm going to hit the shower," he said. "Have a good day."

"See you at four," Dana reminded him. "Our appointment, remember?"

He froze, his back to her, then looked back and nodded. "Yup. See you then."

Dana was the first to arrive at the therapist's office that afternoon. In the waiting area she flipped through an old copy of *Time* magazine while her mind raced, outlining the flash sale she was planning at Haven and Hearth later that week. She'd spent the day in the store, trying to make a plan. She desperately needed to move some inventory and bring in some cash.

"Ahem."

She looked up, startled, to see Eric standing next to her, his face tight. The therapist entered the waiting room at that moment and introduced herself. Then she ushered them into her office as she adjusted her dark-rimmed glasses. The room, though comfortable, was bland, with neutral-toned furniture and an Impressionist print hanging over the desk.

"So," Regina began after exchanging greetings and explaining the confidentiality of the sessions, "why don't we start with why you're here?" She adjusted her glasses again as she looked at Dana.

Dana wiped her palms on her pants, shifting in her seat. "I guess I feel like we've drifted apart," she admitted with an awkward laugh. "Cliché, right?"

The therapist offered a small, encouraging smile. "It's not a cliché if it's your experience. Eric, does this resonate with you?"

Eric's face looked clammy, as if he might be sick. Dana felt a rush of warmth toward him. He'd never been great at talking about emotions, and he hadn't been enthusiastic about therapy, but he was here because she wanted to be.

"Eric?" Regina prodded.

Eric looked at Dana with a desperate, apologetic gaze before turning back to the therapist with a blank expression. "I'm here," he said quietly, "because I want a separation."

Dana's heart jolted like a bumper car had hit her head on. She gripped the arms of the chair, digging her fingernails into the soft leather. She wanted to speak—to laugh, really, because surely Eric must be joking—but all the breath had rushed from her lungs.

"I'm sorry," he said, his voice so low she could barely hear him. His eyes flickered to her, then down to his lap. "I know it seems sudden, but I've been thinking about it for a while."

A high-pitched ringing started in Dana's head, her thoughts ricocheting wildly. A *separation*? When had Eric been contemplating this? Was it while he was sweating through burpees with his trainer? Or while he meticulously measured out protein powder, spirulina, and the supplements now crowding their counter? Perhaps it was during his morning cold plunge in the portable tank he'd installed in the backyard. Or maybe—

Dana's thoughts screeched to a halt, and she leaned forward in her chair. "Are you cheating on me?" she demanded. Despite Eric's year-long life overhaul, their sex life had remained unchanged. If anything, it had improved. Though privately she rolled her eyes at his wheatgrass shots and exercise regimen, she had to admit he seemed reinvigorated—not to mention hot, with his newly flat stomach and muscled back. Their sex had grown more spirited and frequent, a stark contrast to the emotional distance now between them.

Eric's head jerked up from staring at his lap. "What? No! It's not like that."

Dana crossed her arms and blinked back the shocked tears that had appeared in her eyes. "Then what?"

"I just—" Eric hesitated, glancing at the therapist, who looked surprised but nodded encouragingly. "In the last year, I've been focusing on optimizing my life. I want to be at three-hundred-sixty-degree peak performance."

"Three-hundred-sixty-degree..." the therapist said, looking confused.

"To achieve optimization in all areas of life," Eric clarified. "Health, work, relationships, et cetera." He shot a disappointed glance at Dana. "I've been trying to get you to also take an interest in, well, bettering yourself, like I have."

"You think I need to be better?" Dana asked flatly.

Eric waved his arms defensively. "We're middle-aged, Dana. Don't you want to reach your peak potential and live your fullest life? I want to hike the Inca Trail, kite surf in Australia, maybe do a silent retreat in India, you know? But I feel like you're not interested in any of that."

"You want a divorce because I'm not interested in hiking or kite surfing?" Dana stifled an incredulous laugh. This was so ridiculous; it couldn't actually be happening. She glanced at the therapist, who watched them with the intensity of a referee at a tennis match.

Eric jutted out his chin. "You're just... drifting, Dana. Content with the status quo. I want you to crave more—for yourself, for us." He straightened in his chair. "I've tried to share my personal development journey with you, but you just dismiss it."

He was right: He had made an effort. He'd sent her podcasts on intermittent fasting by a Stanford neurobiologist and gifted her books with aggressive, off-putting titles, like *Be Obsessed or Be Average* and *Tools of Titans*. She let them gather dust on her nightstand, not realizing this was a deal breaker.

She crossed her arms, defensive. "Maybe I'm just fine as-is," she said. "Maybe I already love my life, so I don't need to hack my way to happiness. Did you ever think of that?" It was mostly true. She did love their cozy house, having Padma next door, cheering at Izzy's cross-country meets, their monthly date nights at their favorite Thai restaurant, and how Haven and Hearth had become a community cornerstone where everyone knew her. This last thought sent a shudder through her—what would people think if they found out she'd run her mother's business into the ground? She pursed her lips, resolute. She could never let that happen.

"Eric, what do you think about Dana's claim that she likes her life as it is? Is that something you think you could accept?" asked the therapist.

He hesitated, then lifted his eyes to meet Dana's. His voice was gravelly and sad. "No, I don't think I could."

FOUR
PADMA

Four days before

Padma walked in the back door, bypassing the cubbies and hooks Lars had installed for their shoes, bags, and keys. Instead, she dropped her keys on the kitchen counter and draped her jacket over a chair.

Lars, preparing dinner, still in his work pants and button-down shirt, glanced at the jacket. "Please tell me you're not just leaving that there."

She shrugged, grinning. "Yeah, probably. But if that's my worst trait in our marriage, I'd say you've gotten off pretty easy." She grabbed a cherry tomato from the salad he was assembling and popped it in her mouth.

He groaned. "Did you at least wash your hands?"

"I work in a hospital; all I do is wash my hands." She tipped her face up toward his and he planted a begrudging kiss on her lips.

"Save any lives today?" he asked, adding freshly chopped herbs to the bowl. Lars's hours at his architectural firm were much more regular than her emergency room shifts, so he made dinner most nights. On the nights Padma "cooked," they usually had takeout.

"It was a pretty standard day," she replied. "Nothing *General Hospital*-esque." She raised an eyebrow at Lars. He'd developed a love of the famously medically inaccurate soap opera when he was a Swedish exchange student in high school, and she never tired of teasing him about it. "Oh, except get this—Toby's retiring!" She pressed her palms on the counter, bouncing with excitement.

Lars wiped his hands on the towel over his shoulder and shook his head. "No way," he said. "Fake news. He'll never stop working. I bet he doesn't even own real clothes, only scrubs and that awful Hawaiian shirt he wears to the summer barbecue every year."

Padma laughed. "Seriously, he's done at the end of January." She paused. "Which means there'll be an opening for the Director of Emergency Medicine." Her stomach fluttered at the possibility. Though she loved her work, lately she'd felt restless, ready for more, to keep challenging herself.

Lars looked up from tossing the salad. "Do I even need to ask if you're going for it?"

"I'm the most qualified," Padma said. "Other than Gary." She scrunched her face. "But no one likes him. At least I bring cookies every week."

"Cookies that I bake," Lars pointed out.

"Shh!" Padma said, putting a finger to her lips. "Let them think I can do it all."

Lars laughed but then grew serious. "But can you handle it? The Director job sounds intense, and you're already pretty..." He hesitated.

"Good at my job?" Padma suggested. "Dedicated to excellent patient care? A rising star in my field?"

"I was going to say utterly consumed by work." Lars gave a wry smile.

Padma tilted her head. Lars was right; she'd never mastered work-life balance, which made her even more grateful for him. He was the steadying force that kept their family running smoothly for her to plug back into after three straight days of twelve-hour shifts. The one who kept their calendar and made sure they showed up for Maeve's orchestra concerts and had regular doctor and dentist appointments. The one who planned their family vacations, which she always enjoyed even if she grumbled about taking the time off. The one who made everything she did possible.

"I'm sorry," she said, feeling a flash of guilt. "You're right; I should work less, not more." Except, if she was honest, she didn't even know what she'd do with the extra time if she worked less. Spend more time with her family? Sure—but Lars was wrapped up in his own career, and at sixteen, Maeve had no interest in spending *more* time with her mother. And why bother taking up a hobby when all Padma really wanted was to be at the hospital?

Lars smiled and covered her hand with his. "That's not what I meant. I knew who you were when I married you. Sure, it would be nice if you knew where we keep the spare laundry detergent or didn't forget our anniversary—"

"I forgot *once!*" Padma protested.

Lars's grin widened. "And now I get to remind you of that for the rest of our lives." He paused. "What I'm saying is, if this is what you really want, then go for it. But you don't have to prove yourself to us—or anyone."

Padma felt a familiar prick of guilt deep in her chest and bit the inside of her cheek. After nearly twenty years of marriage, it often felt like he knew her better than she knew herself. "Of course it's what I want," she insisted. She glanced at her scrubs. "I'm going to wash the hospital off."

He nodded, squeezing her hand. "Dinner's in fifteen minutes."

After her shower, Padma came downstairs to find Maeve setting the table. "Hi, pumpkin," she said, smoothing her daughter's long, dark hair. Maeve's silvery-gray eyes shimmered in the light. At seventeen she was already taller than Padma and had inherited Lars's lanky build and long legs, reminding Padma of a newborn colt, though Maeve carried herself with a grace she had definitely *not* inherited from her mother. Lately, every time Maeve entered the room, Padma was stunned to see that her little girl was now nearly a woman.

"Hey, Mom," Maeve said. "How was work?"

"The usual," Padma replied with a dismissive wave. She avoided discussing the illness and death she encountered daily with Maeve. Once home, she preferred not to dwell on it. Padma had always been good at compartmentalizing—so good it had once almost ended her career. "How was your day?" she asked.

Maeve shrugged. "The usual."

"No fair," Lars interjected, placing a piece of honey-glazed salmon on Maeve's plate. "We need details."

"You never make Mom give details," Maeve shot back, raising an eyebrow at Padma.

"That's because Mom's job involves too many bodily fluids," Lars said, shuddering. He went weak-kneed at the sight of blood. He passed Maeve the salad bowl. "Did you hear anything about the orchestra?"

Maeve's face lit up, though she quickly tried to downplay her excitement. "I made first violin again," she said, tucking her hair behind her ear. "But it's no big deal."

"No big deal?" Lars asked, raising an eyebrow. He glanced at Padma. "Did she just brush off becoming first violin for the third year running, after all those hours of lessons and practice?"

Padma shook her head with a smile. "Not on my watch." She called out, "Alexa, play 'We Are the Champions' by Queen." As the music started, she and Lars swayed in their chairs and began to sing along.

Maeve sank lower in her seat. "Oh my God, you guys are so embarrassing."

"Sing it!" Lars urged as they hit the chorus, grabbing a serving spoon like a microphone and thrusting it toward Maeve while belting off-key, *"You are the champion!"*

"Seriously, Dad, stop," Maeve groaned, though she was smiling.

As the song ended, Padma turned down the volume and asked cheerfully, "Any other accomplishments you want to downplay?"

"After that? Definitely not," Maeve replied with a playful grimace. Maeve's face brightened. "Hey, for Homecoming this weekend, can I stay out later? Like maybe until one?"

"Of course," Padma said, secretly thrilled Maeve was even asking. Technically, her weekend curfew was midnight, but they'd never had to enforce it. Maeve was usually home and in bed long before Padma, a self-proclaimed night owl, turned in.

"Is there a party?" Lars asked, his tone a little too casual. Padma recognized the setup for one of his infamous *"Dad talks,"* as she and Maeve privately called them. Maeve shot her a look and Padma smothered a smile.

"Dad, you know I don't go to parties," Maeve said, rolling her eyes.

Lars nodded, maybe a little too hard. "Cool, cool. But if you did—hypothetically—you know you can always call us for a ride, right? No matter the time. No questions asked."

Maeve sighed and glanced at Padma for backup. "Dad, I don't drink."

"Right, but *hypothetically*, if you did—"

"I won't." Maeve's voice was firm. She tilted her head. "OK, new topic. Prairie dresses: cute, body-inclusive fashion trend or way too *Handmaid's Tale?*"

"Way too *Handmaid's Tale*," Padma said immediately.

Padma glanced at Lars, who seemed to deflate a little, his attempt at guidance dismissed. She reached over to pat his hand, her silent way of saying *I love that you try.*

Later, as Padma loaded the dishwasher, Lars leaned against the counter.

"Don't you think we should talk to her more about... drinking, drugs, sex?" he asked, the grooves between his eyebrows deepening—his "thinking bumps," Maeve had called them when she was little.

Padma rinsed a plate, shaking her head. "I really don't think we need to worry about that with Maeve."

Secretly *this* was what actually concerned Padma—that Maeve was so good. Padma sometimes worried her daughter was too focused on following the rules to figure out who she really was.

"I just want her to know we're here if she needs us." Lars sighed.

Padma turned off the water, wiped her hands, and leaned over to cup his face. Her heart swelled with love for him. "Oh, honey," she said softly, "she knows."

After Lars went upstairs, Padma was wiping down the counters when she received Dana's text:

Can I come over?

Sure

They usually didn't head out for the walk for at least another hour. A minute later there was a knock on the door. When Padma opened it, Dana's face was red and her eyes swollen. "Oh my God, are you OK?" Padma asked, trying to pull her inside.

Dana shook her head and crossed her arms. "Can we stay on the porch? I don't want Maeve to see me and tell Izzy. She doesn't know yet."

"Know what?" Padma asked, following Dana outside to the covered porch where they sank onto the overstuffed couch.

"That Eric and I are separating."

Padma's breath caught in her throat. "What? Since when?"

"About three hours ago." Dana's lower lip quivered. "He told me in our therapy session."

"Wait, in your first session you decided to split up?" Padma frowned. "Are you sure you picked the right therapist?"

Dana made a sound somewhere between a laugh and a sob. "It was clear he'd already made up his mind and was just waiting to tell me, just like I was waiting to tell him—" She stopped abruptly and pressed her lips together.

"To tell him what?"

Dana shook her head. "Nothing. Just, oh my God." She let out a soft wail and buried her face in her hands.

Padma moved closer and rubbed circles on Dana's back. "Oh, honey," she said. "I'm so sorry. Is it OK if I kill Eric in the most painful way I can think of? And maybe your therapist, too?"

Dana laughed through her tears. "How is this happening on top of everything else?" she moaned. "What did I do to deserve this?"

"Wait, what's everything else?" Padma asked, puzzled. She rubbed her bare arms in disbelief.

Dana sat up, wiping her eyes. "Nothing, just—work is crazy right now with the holidays coming up, and I'm so unprepared. Also, Ian's failing History and might be smoking pot in his room." Her face flushed and her voice dropped to a whisper. "What are people going to think when they find out?"

"Which people?" Padma asked.

"I don't know, everyone." Dana waved her hand. "My customers, other parents, the neighborhood—everyone."

Padma squeezed Dana's hand. "Listen carefully," she said. "Everyone can go screw themselves because this is none of their business."

Dana leaned back, resting her head on the couch. "I wish I was more like you. You've never cared what anyone thinks."

"Which has gotten me into trouble more than once," Padma reminded her.

Dana's eyes grew distant. "Eric said he wants to fulfill his potential but can't do that with me because I'm not interested in growing, that I'm just... drifting."

Padma's nostrils flared. "What the hell?" She wanted to storm across the lawn and strangle Eric on the spot. She'd watched his transformation over the past year from a slightly nerdy science teacher into a gym-obsessed, carb-avoiding Tony Robbins superfan. She hadn't said anything to Dana because she mostly liked Eric. He was smart and funny, and he always returned their pressure washer when he borrowed it. But breaking Dana's heart? That crossed the line.

"Maybe he's right," Dana said, running her hand through her messy hair. "Maybe I'm not ambitious enough, not living my best life."

Padma shook her head vehemently. "Stop it! Living your best life is a cliché for privileged idiots like Gwyneth Paltrow."

Dana glanced away, guilt on her face. "I bought her female Viagra supplement a few months ago."

Padma's eyes grew large. "You did not! That woman is a menace to science!" She paused. "Um, did it work?"

Dana nodded, tears welling up again. "It actually did. That's what I don't understand. We have good sex, and maybe we're not super connected all the time, but who is? Life's busy, the kids' schedules are insane..." She swallowed hard. "Padma," she said, eyes wide with fear. "I don't know what to do. How will I get through this?"

Padma leaned in, gripping Dana's arms. "*We'll* get through this," she said. "I'm here for you, whatever you need. That will *never* change."

FIVE

IAN

One day before

Ian stared at the laptop screen, struggling to write an essay for US History. Thanks to his mom's lobbying, his teacher had reluctantly allowed an extra credit assignment to help improve his failing grade. He tried to concentrate on the few words he'd written, but they blurred before his eyes. The digital clock on his nightstand showed he'd been working for twenty minutes since getting home from school. It was time to supercharge things.

Glancing over his shoulder, Ian walked to his closet and pulled down a shoebox from the top shelf—high enough that his five-foot-two mom would never notice. The feel of the shoebox in his hands was enough to send his synapses firing in anticipation of the pleasure that was to come. Lifting the lid, he took out an orange pill bottle with someone else's name on it. He'd only take half a pill, he promised himself. Just enough to get him through a draft of this essay.

But upon picking up the bottle he didn't hear the soothing, telltale rattle from inside. Opening it, his stomach sank. Empty.

Shit. He ran his hands through his hair. Had he really gone through this last batch so quickly?

Placing the bottle back in the box, he instead picked up a plastic baggie of weed gummies. He hesitated for a moment, then popped a whole one in his mouth. His friend Jenner had warned him they were potent, but whatever, Jenner was a lightweight.

Emerging from his room, Ian heard voices coming from his sister's bedroom. Poking his head in, he saw Izzy and her best friend Maeve working on a project.

"Hey," he said. Two matching red aprons lay on the floor, to which Izzy and Maeve were hot gluing empty spice containers. "Um, what's going on?"

"It's for Halloween," Izzy said without looking up, aiming the glue gun at a cinnamon container.

"We're going as the Spice Girls," Maeve explained. Her eyes met Ian's, then her cheeks reddened. A strand of her wavy hair had slipped from her ponytail, and she quickly tucked it behind her ear, her eyes darting away.

"Halloween is still almost two weeks away," Ian pointed out, slouching against the doorframe. "Also, we're too old to dress up." His gaze drifted to the magnetic board on Izzy's wall, cluttered with photos and mementos of her achievements. In the bottom right corner, beneath a blue ribbon from last year's science fair, was a photo of them as kids—dressed as Thing One and Thing Two, candy spilling from their buckets. When they were little, he and Izzy had always worn joint costumes, which he'd loved. Really, he'd loved doing anything with Izzy. He knew he could always count on her to have a plan, while all he had to do was tag along and enjoy himself. But after being teased mercilessly in sixth grade for their Mario and Luigi costumes, he'd sworn off Halloween.

"Just because you like doing everything last minute doesn't mean I have to," Izzy said, fluttering her eyelashes at him.

He jammed his hands into his cargo shorts pockets. Whatever. Just because she was perfect—honor roll, varsity cross-country, class VP—didn't mean everyone should expect him to be. Except they did. "Any relation to Isabelle Blair?" teachers would ask when they saw his name, clearly hoping for a mirror image of his overachieving sister. Until they realized he was nothing like her.

"Can you spot me twenty bucks?" Ian asked, pushing aside any thoughts of asking Izzy for help with his essay. He knew she didn't mean anything by her teasing—Izzy loved to poke fun but was never cruel. Still, he wasn't about to prove her point, especially not in front of Maeve.

"What for?" Izzy asked, handing the glue gun to Maeve and settling back on her heels.

"I want to hit up McDonald's." Ian shrugged, already anticipating the munchies in about twenty minutes.

Izzy raised a brow, eyes wide with faux innocence. "I don't think they have a weed drive-thru."

Ian laughed. "Yeah, well, if they did, they definitely wouldn't serve *you*." He gave her a slow once-over and smirked. "You basically look like a narc posing as a high schooler." He glanced at Maeve, who seemed to be holding back a giggle.

"Hey!" Izzy yelped. In a flash, she scrambled to her feet and lunged at him, wrapping her arms around his neck and jumping onto his back. "I do *not*!"

"Can't—breathe—" Ian wheezed, staggering backward, laughing too hard to shake her off.

"Say I don't look like a narc!" Izzy squeezed tighter, her legs locked around his waist as she lightly pounded his back with her fists. Their connection had always been intense, spilling over into roughhousing more often than not.

"You started wrestling in the womb," their mom liked to say. "I could feel it."

Maeve shrieked and scrambled out of the way as Ian lurched toward Izzy's bed, trying to shake her loose.

"Fine!" he gasped as she clung to him. "You don't look like a narc!"

Izzy loosened her grip, and Ian used the moment to tip her backward onto the bed, rubbing the spot on his neck where her hands had clung.

Maeve started to reach toward him, then hesitated and dropped her hand. "Are you OK?" she asked.

"Fine," he said, brushing it off, though his neck did sting. "My sister's too weak to do any real damage."

Izzy shot upright and swung a punch at his arm, but Ian ducked out of reach, catching the glint of mischief in her eyes.

Maeve glanced between them, wide-eyed. "You guys are so weird," she said.

Ian tilted his head. "Yeah, I guess as an only child you never had anyone to wrestle with," he said, the thought suddenly making him sad. As much as Izzy drove him crazy, sometimes it felt like they shared a brain, able to hold whole conversations with just a look across the dinner table.

Maeve laughed. "Nope. But I'm not really the wrestling type."

Ian gave a small laugh, and Maeve's cheeks flushed again. Then he flopped onto Izzy's bed beside her. "So, can I have the money or what?"

Izzy sighed. "Fine." She slid off the bed and rummaged in her top dresser drawer, drawing out a crisp bill. "Here."

After picking up a Big Mac and fries, Ian sat in the parking lot and pulled out his phone. His high had kicked in, but he worked best this way, loose and immune to danger. He typed something into his search bar, then after scrolling for a bit programmed an address into his GPS and drove north to a neighborhood of manicured lawns and winding driveways leading to sprawling houses tucked behind tall, stately trees.

Once he arrived at the address, he parked on the street and swapped his faded HUF T-shirt with a hole in the shoulder for a light pink polo shirt, and his baggy shorts for fitted golf ones. Adjusting the rearview mirror, he attempted to tame his wavy hair and forced a bright smile.

On the lawn of the house, a navy blue and white sign with a luxury realty company's logo announced an open house that evening. Ian tucked in his shirt and walked in without knocking, adopting what he hoped was a look of pleasant disinterest.

"Can I help you?" A willowy blonde in a white pantsuit approached, blinking her long, fake eyelashes at him skeptically.

"Hi, ma'am," Ian said, meeting her gaze. "I'm supposed to meet my mom here to pick up my baseball gear—I forgot it this morning and have practice later." He gave a sheepish smile.

"Your mom's coming to the open house?" the realtor confirmed, eyeing him.

"Yes, ma'am." Ian nodded. "We live a few streets over, but she's always looking for something new." He pulled out his phone and pretended to check it. "She should be here in about ten minutes. Can I wait here for her?"

The realtor's expression softened. "Of course."

As the door opened, a couple entered, followed quickly by two others. Ian greeted them all with a smile and, once they had drifted away with the realtor, he made his move. Checking over his shoulder, he headed upstairs.

The first bedroom he found had a pink frilly bedspread and a Peppa Pig stuffed animal, so he skipped the adjoining bathroom. Further down the hall, he came to a guest bathroom, where he quickly checked the drawers and medicine cabinet, finding only mouthwash and aspirin.

At the end of the wall lay the master bedroom. With voices still distant downstairs, Ian slipped inside and found the ensuite bathroom. He opened the medicine cabinet and saw a row of orange pill bottles. Most were useless—Viagra, prescription-strength antacids—but then he spotted a bottle of Adderall. He couldn't believe he'd gotten so lucky—often he had to hit three or even four open houses before he found something good. He quickly pocketed the bottle, just as he heard voices in the hall.

"The guest bathroom was recently redone and includes a rain shower head and heated floors..."

Ian's heart raced. He stole back into the master bedroom, peeking through the door crack to see the realtor and three couples heading into a room down the hall. Then he hurried down the hall and stairs as quietly as possible, and headed out the front door, his heart pounding.

Back in his car, Ian immediately slipped the bottle from his pocket.

He had his own prescription, of course—because didn't everyone his age have ADHD now? It was practically a rite of passage, the diagnosis handed out like participation trophies in middle school. But he couldn't double up on the pills the way he'd gotten used to, not without burning through the supply too fast and setting off alarms with his parents.

He shook two of the round, white pills into his hand, and suppressed the twinge of shame in his chest. He was simply doing what he had to do to get by—just like everyone else. Tipping his head back, he swallowed the pills with a sip of his Coke, then eased the car into gear and headed home.

SIX

DANA

That day

Dana loaded the coffee grinder with beans and pressed the button with more force than usual. Eric was upstairs meditating, and she hoped the grinder's noise had shattered any chance of his achieving enlightenment today.

For the third morning in a row, she'd woken up thinking it was just another day, only to be jolted back to reality seconds later as it all rushed back: the conversation in the therapist's office, her emotional breakdown on Padma's porch, and Eric moving his two hundred dollar "restorative" sunrise-simulating alarm clock to the guest bedroom.

With one hand on the coffee grinder, Dana used the other to press a spoon she'd chilled in the freezer against her puffy, red eyes. The previous day, SueEllen had noticed her bloodshot eyes and swollen face when she walked into Haven and Hearth.

"Just a weird allergic reaction," Dana had said, then retreated to the small office in the back, letting SueEllen handle things up front, partly because she looked like hell and partly to avoid another conversation about SueEllen's missing paycheck.

Eric cleared his throat, making Dana jump. The spoon slipped from her fingers and clattered onto the counter.

"I'm pretty sure the beans are ready," he said, nodding toward the still-whirring grinder.

Dana released the button, and silence settled like a heavy curtain between them. Eric stepped closer. He was already dressed for work in jeans and a navy polo shirt that stretched enticingly across his chest. For the first time, Dana noticed that his thick hair was now more gray than brown. She self-consciously touched her own bedhead, recalling that her roots needed attention. She wondered if Eric would start dyeing his hair or dating a younger version of her once they separated. She clutched the top of her fuzzy lavender bathrobe, wishing she had changed into something more presentable before coming downstairs.

"I think we should clear the air," he said, rubbing the back of his neck. "I don't want us carrying all this negativity around," he continued. "I think we should talk."

Dana had to keep herself from lobbing the heavy coffee grinder at his head.

"Talk?" She gave a short, mirthless laugh. "Funny, that's usually the point of couples therapy—to talk. But you'd already decided you were done with this." She gestured between them. "So it doesn't seem like there's much left to discuss."

He sighed, tilting his head back before looking at her. "I'm sorry, OK? I didn't mean for it to happen like this."

"Why didn't you say anything earlier?" Dana demanded, her chin trembling despite her effort to stay composed. She would *not* cry in front of him.

His shoulders heaved in a frustrated sigh. "Honey, I tried to include you in my emotional journey so many times. You just shut me down."

Dana flinched at the term of endearment. "Your *journey*?" she said, gripping the coffee grinder until her knuckles turned white. "Excuse me if I haven't had time to join you on an *emotional journey*. I've been too busy managing a business—and our family."

"That's your problem, Dana," he said, shaking his head, his expression one of self-righteous pity. "You're always busy, rushing from one task to the next, checking things off your list. You're not separating the urgent from the important, making time to go after your dreams."

"Ah yes, my dreams," Dana said icily. "I'm sure they'll all come true once I've separated—what was it?—the urgent from the important. Wait... what were they again?"

"Oh, come on," Eric said with impatience. "Running your mom's business was the last thing you wanted back in the day."

"Things change," Dana snapped, refusing to admit what they both knew: that taking over Haven and Hearth had never been her dream. Even as a child, she'd recognized she lacked her mother's sharp business instincts. She'd never cared about running a lemonade stand or selling Girl Scout cookies. And while her brother carefully saved his allowance, Dana's always disappeared—spent on candy or drugstore lip gloss she inevitably misplaced within days.

"What do we tell the kids?" she asked, pulling herself away from the swirl of painful emotions and switching into action mode. "They're going to notice that you're sleeping in the guest room."

Eric shifted on his feet, guilt washing over his face. "The kids, right." He looked away briefly and ran a hand through his hair. "Let's, um, give it a couple of days so we can, you know, process things. Then we'll figure out what to tell them."

"Process things... right," Dana said with a curt nod. "I'll add that to my to-do list." *Right between saving my business and keeping my son from failing high school.*

"Dana, please—" Eric began, but she was already walking

past him, leaving the coffee grinder behind. She'd stop at Star-bucks; one more Frappuccino wouldn't bankrupt her.

She called Padma from the car, who answered on the first ring, saying, "I was just about to call you. I want to ask how you are, but that feels... obvious."

Dana laughed as she glanced at her house disappearing in the rearview mirror. She remembered the day she and Eric had signed the closing papers for it. She'd been six months pregnant with Ian and Izzy, her belly so round that most people assumed she would go into labor any minute. After they got the keys, they wandered through the empty rooms, debating paint versus wallpaper for the nursery and planning where to put the Christmas tree for when they moved in the following month. Already Dana was working with her mother at the shop—temporarily, she told herself, until she figured out what she really wanted to do—and she began mentally positioning their furniture in the living room.

"I think we'll need a bigger rug," she'd said, turning to find Eric smiling at her in that way that always sent tingles through her body. They'd had sex right there, up against the wall, maneuvering around her belly.

Dana choked back a sob at the memory, then swallowed and wiped her eyes. "Eric wants to take some time to 'process things' before we tell the kids," she said to Padma, making air quotes with her fingers, knowing Padma would catch it through the call.

"Wait, what's to process?" Padma demanded. "He's the one who—"

"That's what I said," Dana said, her voice cracking. At least with Padma she didn't have to pretend. They'd been friends for over a decade, ever since Padma and Lars moved in next door and Izzy had made a beeline for Maeve playing in the front yard. In those ten years they'd weathered plenty together, including Padma's treatment for breast cancer, Dana's turbulent relationship with her mother, and the summer Ian had gotten kicked out of camp for selling counterfeit marijuana that was actually dried moss.

"Oh, sweetheart," Padma said. "I'm so sorry. It's all so cliché —Eric, obviously, not you."

Dana sniffled in agreement. "I just need to get through today. Can I come over later?"

"Of course," Padma replied quickly. "Whatever you need. I'll be home from the hospital around eight."

"See you then," Dana said, feeling relief that she at least had that to look forward to. "Love you."

"Love you more."

The store was still dark and empty when Dana arrived; SueEllen wouldn't be there for another hour. Dana decided to use the quiet time to tackle the growing stack of unopened mail. But after sifting through a few envelopes filled with past-due rent notices and inventory bills, she shoved the rest into a drawer and sat back in her chair, feeling queasy. Haven and Hearth had been open for nearly thirty years. Dana's mother, Cora, had started the shop and its associated interior design business as a way to channel her boundless energy—and, Dana suspected, to spend less time with her children. Over time she'd built her hobby into a thriving business, eventually outearning Dana's father. Now Dana might be at risk of losing it all.

"Hello? Dana?" SueEllen's voice called from the front of the shop with her gentle Southern drawl, jolting Dana from her thoughts.

SueEllen thrived as a salesperson because she was the epitome of Haven and Hearth's clientele: older women who booked weekly hair appointments before their bridge games and favored coastal chic décor. The trouble was, even those women —their most loyal customers—had begun turning to Wayfair and other online retailers, lured by lower prices and faster shipping.

"Back here," Dana replied. SueEllen appeared in the doorway, wearing ballet flats and a green and blue paisley Lilly Pulitzer shift dress.

"Hi there," she greeted. "How're you doing? Did your allergies clear up?"

Dana rubbed her still-puffy eyes. "Getting there," she said. "Hey, how was foot traffic after you put up the sale signs yesterday?"

SueEllen sighed and smoothed her dress. "Honestly, I didn't notice much of a change. Maybe we should consider some advertising?"

"Mm." Dana nodded. "Good idea." She didn't have extra cash for advertising right now.

"Also"—SueEllen shifted nervously—"how's that hiccup with payroll going? Any progress?"

Dana's stomach dropped. "I'm working to get it ironed out as soon as possible," she said, forcing a smile.

SueEllen cleared her throat. "I didn't get last week's paycheck, either."

Dana swallowed. "I'm so sorry, SueEllen. I'll call them again today. Thank you for letting me know."

"Of course," SueEllen said graciously, sending a stab of guilt through Dana. "I'm sure you'll sort it out."

Just then, Dana's phone rang. "I'm sorry," Dana said, pointing. "I have to take this." She picked up her phone. "Hello?"

"Hi, Mrs. Blair," came a young woman's voice, high and frightened. "It's Alexa, Izzy's cross-country coach? There's been an accident. Can you meet us at the hospital?"

SEVEN

PADMA

That day

Padma sank onto the wheeled stool beside an elderly man hooked up to a beeping heart monitor. "Sir, I'm pleased to tell you your heart is fine," she said, her tone brisk yet reassuring. "After a thorough examination and tests, the chest pain you're experiencing is due to indigestion, not a heart issue. I'll prescribe an antacid to help."

He blinked in confusion. "I'm sorry, dear, I don't hear so well anymore," he replied, his brow furrowing.

Padma leaned closer. "It's just gas, nothing serious!" she said loudly. Jasmine, her favorite nurse, stifled a smile from the other side of the bed. "I'm finishing your discharge papers, and you'll be all set to go." She stepped back and flashed a thumbs-up, earning a grateful smile in return.

Opening the curtain that separated her from the bustling emergency department, Padma stepped into the crowded hallway filled with beeping machines and hurried footsteps. Her phone buzzed in her pocket, and she glanced at it before checking her next chart.

> Izzy had an accident during practice. She's headed to the ER. I'm on my way.

Padma pressed against the wall as a stretcher rushed past, nurses on either side, and dialed Dana.

"Hey." Dana answered immediately, her voice laced with worry. "I'm in the car."

"What happened?" Padma asked, her pulse quickening.

"I'm not sure. Her coach mentioned a fall—maybe she did something to her leg? She's in an ambulance. Are you at work?"

Code Gray, third floor east, crackled the intercom.

"Yes," Padma replied, raising her voice over the noise. "I'll meet you here."

"Thank you," Dana breathed.

Padma left word at the intake desk to call her as soon as Isabelle Blair was admitted. She had just finished the discharge papers for the man with gas instead of heart problems when her phone buzzed with a notification.

Isabelle Blair in room 14.

Standing quickly, Padma turned on her heel and hurried down the hall. Pulling back the curtain, she found Izzy sprawled on the bed, clutching her leg, her face twisted in pain.

"Hi, honey," Padma said with a reassuring smile. She stepped closer, placing a hand on Izzy's shoulder and smoothing her hair, just as she would have for Maeve. The nurse gave her a strange look. "She's a family friend," Padma explained.

Really, Izzy felt like a second daughter. She had learned to ride a bike in Padma's driveway, slept over countless times, and even gotten her first period there—Padma had immediately called Dana to come over, and then gone to pick up an ice cream cake for the four of them to celebrate, thoroughly embarrassing both Izzy and Maeve.

"Hi," Izzy managed, grimacing in pain.

Padma shifted into doctor mode. "What's the situation?" she asked.

"I haven't had time to do a full intake or medical history," the nurse said, "but she has leg pain and can't walk on her own." She turned to the other woman in the room for confirmation, an athletic looking twenty-something brunette dressed in running tights and a fitted Nike jacket.

"I'm her coach, Alexa. I came in the ambulance with her," the woman said, her face even paler than Izzy's. "One minute she was sprinting, and the next she was on the ground, like, writhing in pain."

Izzy groaned. "The ambulance was so embarrassing. I'm *fine*, just my leg really hurts." She shifted on the bed and winced.

"Can you bend it?" Padma asked. "What happens if I press here?"

Izzy let out a cry of pain.

"Izzy?" Dana's voice called from outside the curtain.

"In here," Padma called.

"Oh, thank God," Dana said, pushing the curtain aside and rushing in.

"Owww," Izzy cried as Dana embraced her, pulling back to inspect for injuries.

"What's wrong?" Dana looked from Padma to Alexa, panic etched on her face.

"Mom, I'm fine," Izzy insisted.

Alexa stood, wiping her hands on her running tights. "Izzy, I'll let your mom take over, but I'll be in the waiting room, OK?"

"I'm going to order a scan and some X-rays right away," Padma said. "You're finished up with the antibiotics from your sinus infection, right?" Dana ran all of both Ian and Izzy's medical issues by Padma, so she knew Izzy had been on a course of amoxicillin.

Izzy nodded.

"OK, I'm noting no other medications or prior issues." Padma made a checkmark on the paper she always carried with her to help her track her progress with patients. Then she reached over to squeeze Dana's shoulder. "Let me go order the X-rays, and I'll see if I can give her something for the pain."

"Should I have Eric come?" Dana asked. "He's asking if he should leave work."

Padma looked around and lowered her voice. "I'll try to rush the X-rays through," she said. "So maybe just keep him posted for now—I'm hopeful I can have you out of here in not too long."

Dana nodded gratefully as Padma stepped back out into the hall.

Padma's hunch was that Izzy was just fine and had simply overtrained—after all, Izzy never did anything halfway. Not for the first time, she gave thanks that Maeve didn't share Izzy's relentless drive to excel in all areas of her life. Sure, she was a good student and a talented violinist, but she preferred to sleep in instead of run six miles before breakfast, and to spend the summers babysitting instead of running between a Tetris-like schedule of camps designed to build her college resume.

While waiting for Izzy's X-ray results, Padma treated a woman with an allergic reaction and a man with severe food poisoning. After administering IV fluids and prescribing anti-nausea medication for the man, she returned to her computer to a notification that Izzy's X-ray results were ready.

"Hey," came a voice just as Padma pulled up the results on her screen.

She looked up to see Toby approaching with a can of Diet Coke in his hand. "Hey yourself," she replied.

"How's everything going?" he asked.

"Pretty quiet day, actually."

"Shh," he warned, looking around for wood to knock. "You'll curse us."

Padma shook her head. "You're so superstitious." For a fleeting moment, she imagined what it would feel like to have Toby's job—to be the one other doctors turned to for guidance. The thought sent a thrill through her. Finally, all her hard work would mean something. She pictured the stack of medical journals on her nightstand—the ones Lars jokingly called her "Ambien reading" but that she genuinely enjoyed.

"Anything interesting?" Toby asked, glancing at Izzy's X-ray.

Leaning closer to the screen, she considered. At first glance, everything appeared normal. "I don't think so. My best friend's daughter came in with leg pain after cross-country practice. It looks like a classic overuse injury, nothing more."

Toby raised his eyebrows. Padma knew there was an unwritten rule against examining friends or family, but she hadn't wanted to trust anyone else with Izzy.

"It's fine," she assured him. "Very routine. I'm about to discharge her."

"You do you," Toby said, draining his soda and crushing the can.

"Paging Dr. Paulsen to room six. Dr. Paulsen to room six," crackled the intercom.

"Duty calls," Padma said, waving goodbye to Toby.

It was another forty-five minutes before Padma was able to return to see Izzy and Dana. By then Izzy's pain medication had kicked in, the color returning to her cheeks.

"How are you feeling, honey?" Padma asked, and Izzy smiled.

"Better, I think," she replied.

"Let's see if you can put weight on it," Padma said, helping her stand. With one arm around Padma's shoulder, Izzy took a tentative step.

"Ow," she moaned, sitting back down.

Padma nodded. "It'll be tender for a bit." She turned to Dana. "But there's nothing to worry about. Nothing's broken or sprained; you've just overdone it. We call it an 'overuse injury of the leg.'"

Dana nodded, relief washing over her face. "So she just... rests?"

"Yup," Padma replied, giving Izzy a pointed look. "Actual rest, Isabelle Blair. No practice or training for at least a couple of weeks until you can put weight on it without pain. We'll get you some crutches to take home."

"Crutches?" Izzy wailed. "But I have a meet next weekend!"

"No, you don't," Dana said firmly.

"But Mom—"

"Listen to your mother," Padma interjected. "And to me—your doctor." She raised an eyebrow. "You'll only make it worse if you keep training."

Izzy crossed her arms, sulking. "Fine," she grumbled.

"Thank you so much," Dana said, standing to hug Padma.

"Anytime," Padma said, squeezing her back. "I'm just glad it wasn't something more serious."

EIGHT

DANA

That day

Dana held Izzy's crutches as her daughter leaned on her and hopped on one foot up their front steps. As they stepped inside, the smell of pizza wafted over them, making Dana's stomach growl. The few bites of salad she'd eaten for lunch hours ago felt like a distant memory. They had spent nearly three hours at the hospital, waiting on paperwork and X-rays. Dana knew it would have taken even longer if Padma hadn't been there to expedite Izzy's discharge. She silently thanked her best friend; she would trust Padma with Izzy's life—but at least today, she hadn't needed to.

"Hello?" Dana called, tightening her grip around Izzy's waist as they moved through the formal dining room into the living area. Izzy grabbed the crutches and pushed her away.

"I'm *fine*," she snapped.

Eric rushed in, flipping on the lights. "Izzy, sweetheart, how are you? What happened? Crutches?" He wrapped an arm around her shoulder and shot a questioning glance at Dana, who had texted him from the hospital but hadn't given the full story.

Izzy shrugged off his touch. "I *said*, I'm fine!" she retorted, stomping clumsily out of the room on her crutches.

Eric turned to Dana, who sighed. "Apparently she really is fine. Padma said it's just overtraining, and she needs to stay off her leg for a couple of weeks."

Eric wrinkled his nose in disappointment. "A couple of weeks? That's going to kill her chance at cross-country regionals this season." He stroked the stubble on his chin. "I'll look into physical therapists—she can start right away, keep the muscles strong, at least."

Dana tried to keep the frustration out of her tone. "Maybe it wouldn't be the worst thing in the world for her to have a break," she pointed out. "She pushes herself so hard all the time."

"She's not going to want a break," Eric replied. "I know Izzy, and sitting around doing nothing will drive her crazy."

Like you, Dana wanted to say. Eric and Izzy shared the same relentless energy and ambition, always in motion, always striving. Dana, on the other hand, was perfectly content doing nothing. She sometimes fantasized about having a week—or even an hour—completely to herself, where she could just lie on the couch, alternating between napping and watching bad TV. Maybe that was why she had more patience for Ian's apathy, even when it drove Eric crazy. Sure, Ian could use more direction, but life was exhausting. The poor kid probably just needed a break. Dana could understand that.

"The important thing is that Padma said it's nothing serious," Dana said, and Eric's face softened.

"That's great," he said, and Dana felt her heart thaw at the genuine concern in his eyes. Despite everything between them, Eric was a good father—far more involved than her own had been. He'd left most of the parenting to Dana's mother, aside from teaching her to drive and slipping her the occasional twenty-dollar bill when she visited from college. Eric, on the other hand, went to every one of Izzy's cross-country meets, and when the kids were little, he'd been the one more likely to get up with them in the night.

She and Eric stood awkwardly for a moment before he cleared his throat and nodded toward the kitchen. "I, um, ordered pizza."

"Thanks." Dana kicked off her clogs and followed him into the kitchen, where Izzy had slumped into a chair, her crutches abandoned on the floor.

"Can someone get me a plate?" She scowled at the crutches. "I don't know how to do anything with those things."

"You'll get used to them," Dana said, sliding a slice of pineapple and Canadian bacon pizza—Izzy's favorite—onto a plate for her.

"That's what I'm afraid of," Izzy muttered.

Just then, Ian thundered down the stairs and skidded into the room, relief on his face. "You're back!" he said, then straightened his shoulders and forced his expression toward nonchalance. "I mean, what took so long? What happened?"

"*Those* happened," Izzy said with a hostile nod toward her crutches.

"Why didn't you text me?" Ian frowned, sliding into the chair next to her. "I didn't know if something really bad had happened." He eyed her pizza. "Also, pineapple on pizza is foul."

Izzy kicked him under the table with her good leg.

"Ow," he protested.

"Something bad did happen," Izzy said, slumping in her chair. "I can't train for a whole week."

"Two weeks," Dana interjected.

Ian rolled his eyes. "No, I meant something really bad."

Izzy tilted her head, studying him. Her expression softened.

"You would've known if it was really bad. Remember the hot tub?"

A shiver ran through Dana at the memory. The twins had been three, on a family vacation in Florida. Ian woke early from his nap, and Dana, exhausted, dozed on the couch while he watched TV with a snack. She jolted awake to Ian screaming Izzy's name and pointing at the locked back door leading to the yard.

"No, sweetie, Izzy's still napping," Dana tried to reassure him, but his cries were relentless. Finally, she opened the back door to show him no one was there, only to find Izzy had slipped out the window of the ground-floor bedroom and was flailing in the hot tub, her toe stuck in the drain, her little nose barely above the water. Somehow, Ian had known.

Ian nodded, considering this. "Yeah, you're right. I'd know." He reached for a slice of sausage and pepperoni pizza.

Dana and Eric fixed their plates—cheese for her, veggie lovers for him. She held back a sigh; no one in the family could agree on pizza toppings, no wonder things felt so disjointed lately.

"You two used to fight like cats and dogs," Eric said, shaking his head at Ian and Izzy. "And then, like clockwork, you'd team up to gang up on us."

Izzy's face lit up with her first real smile in hours. "Remember Ratatouille?"

Ian snickered.

Dana groaned. "Please, don't remind me."

That was all the invitation they needed. Ian and Izzy launched into a gleeful retelling of how they'd pooled their allowance at nine to buy a motion-activated rubber rat, delighting in all the places they'd hidden it for Dana to find.

"Remember when we stuck it in her purse at that wedding?" Ian grinned.

"Your cousin Emily did *not* appreciate that," Eric said in mock disapproval.

Izzy giggled, her light, easy laughter sending warmth curling through Dana's chest. It had been so long since the four of them had sat and chatted together like this.

Across the table, Eric caught her eye and smiled. For a moment, something familiar flickered between them, and Dana felt a sharp pang in her chest. She quickly looked back down at her plate.

Once they finished, Dana helped Izzy up the stairs to the bathroom the twins shared. "Do you need help?" she asked, hovering as Izzy leaned her crutches against the wall.

"Mom," Izzy interjected, rolling her eyes. "Please leave now."

"OK," Dana relented. "Just call me if you need anything."

"I won't," Izzy promised.

Dana headed into her bedroom to change into sweatpants, then sank onto their king bed, feeling a pang as she took in the smooth, undisturbed side that belonged to Eric. She glanced at her phone. It would be another hour until Padma got home. But suddenly she didn't feel so acutely in need of comforting. Maybe she would be all right, after all.

She lay back on her pillow, the day catching up with her. She'd just close her eyes for a minute, then she'd go clean up the kitchen and start researching other banks she could approach for a loan. There had to be a solution.

She startled awake to find Eric in the room. "Sorry," he said as he rummaged through his nightstand. "I left my heart rate monitor in here somewhere. I have my trainer in the morning."

Dana's mouth was dry and as she sat up she saw forty-five minutes had passed. Tilting her head, she realized she could still hear the shower running in the twins' bathroom. Good grief, did the girl think their hot water was endless?

Pushing herself up off the bed she stepped into the hall and knocked on the bathroom door. "Izzy!" she called. "Are you about done in there?" After a minute she knocked again, louder. "Izzy! Seriously, honey, you need to wrap it up."

Frustrated, Dana cracked the door open. "Isabelle!" she called sharply, peering into the room. Then her heart stopped, suspended in her chest as she processed what she saw: Izzy, crumpled on the shower floor, the water beating down on her slackened face.

"Izzy!" Dana cried, hurtling forward. She yanked open the glass shower door. She shook her daughter, as the water rained down on both of them. "Izzy, talk to me!"

But there was no response from her daughter.

NINE

PADMA

That day

Padma wrapped up her paperwork for the day, transferring a middle-aged man in gastric distress to the ICU for a kidney stone. Overall, it had been a good shift—busy enough to keep her engaged without feeling overwhelmed. She thrived on the adrenaline rush of juggling patients, keeping their cases straight, and thinking on her feet. The mix of cases had been ideal: straightforward issues like cuts needing stitches and broken bones, alongside trickier challenges, like diagnosing a woman with jaw pain as having a stroke. After nearly two decades as a doctor, Padma appreciated moments that tested her medical expertise rather than just requiring what she saw as advanced first aid.

Most importantly, there had been no fatalities. She'd pronounced her fair share of deaths, and each one felt like a punch to the gut. But in the ER, there was no time to process the aftermath of loss. There was only the opportunity to potentially save the next patient that awaited you.

Early in their relationship, Lars would ask about her worst

cases and whether anyone had died that day. He was troubled by what he called her "blasé" attitude toward tragedy. But to Padma, it wasn't indifference; it was survival. She didn't want to wade back into that territory later, not when she returned home to Lars and Maeve and needed to focus what was left of her emotional energy on them. Being a doctor demanded compartmentalization, and while Lars worried it wasn't healthy, for Padma it was a form of self-care.

Padma glanced at her watch and pulled the stethoscope from around her neck. Seven forty-five—she was only leaving fifteen minutes late, not bad. Her stomach growled as she wondered what Lars had made for dinner. He and Maeve would have eaten already, but he always left her a foil-covered plate on the counter. She remembered seeing eggplant parmesan on the menu he'd written on the whiteboard by the pantry, along with Maeve's activities, her shifts, and their weekend plans. "Heading out?"

Padma turned at the sound of Toby's voice and saw him leaning over the nurses' station, grabbing a brownie from a plate.

"Amazingly, yes," she said, shaking her head. "Hey, save some for the rest of us!"

Toby grinned sheepishly. "I can't resist Jasmine's brownies." He glanced at the nurse. "I swear, this is the last one."

She smiled. "It's fine, Dr. Lazzari. I always make extra when you're on shift."

"See?" Toby said, glancing at Padma. "OK, just one more, I swear," he said, reaching for a second.

"You enjoy," Jasmine said, then turned to Padma. "By the way, that girl you had routed to you earlier? She's back—just a few minutes ago."

Padma frowned. Izzy? It couldn't be. "Isabelle Blair?" she asked. "Seventeen? Long brown hair? Leg injury?"

Jasmine nodded but hesitated. "It didn't look like a leg injury. She came in on a stretcher. They were doing CPR."

Fear shot through Padma. "Where is she?"

"I didn't see where they took her," Jasmine replied, but Padma was already running.

She reached the exam rooms and began yanking back curtains, thrusting her head inside. "Dana?" she called. "Dana, are you here?" Each room revealed startled patients or annoyed glances from other doctors.

Finally, she pulled back a curtain to see a crowd of doctors and nurses bent over a hospital bed, shouting about blood pressure and resuscitation. In the corner, pressed against the wall, stood Dana, her face pale, her eyes wide with fear.

"What's happening?" Padma demanded. When no one responded, she raised her voice. "Someone tell me what's going on!"

A doctor turned toward her, exasperation plain on his face. "What are you doing here? This is *my* patient."

Padma's hands curled into fists. She and Gary Ackerman had never gotten along; she found him territorial and arrogant. "She was my patient earlier today," Padma said sharply. "An overuse injury to her leg. I discharged her."

Gary's thin eyebrows drew together, his lips pursing. "Well, you clearly missed something."

"Doctor, her oxygen levels are dropping!" a nurse called.

Padma rushed to Dana, grasping her friend's hand. "What happened?" she asked urgently.

"I don't know," Dana stammered, her voice trembling. "She was fine at dinner, then she went to shower. I found her collapsed in there." A strangled sob escaped her. "I don't know how long she was like that."

Padma craned her neck to look at Izzy, who lay pale and motionless on the bed, her lips tinged blue, her eyes rolled back. On the monitor, her blood pressure flashed dangerously low, the warning beeps growing more frantic. Padma's chest tightened as her thoughts spiraled. She tried to summon Izzy's chart in her mind, replaying every detail, every decision. What had she overlooked? Her throat constricted with anguish as a single question gripped her: *What did I miss?*

Dana squeezed Padma's hand harder. "Please," Dana pleaded. "Can you do something?"

Padma stepped forward. "Gary, have you—"

"Butt out, Padma," he snapped. "If you want to help, get the mom out of here." He jerked his head toward Dana.

Swallowing her retort, Padma took Dana's arm, gently steering her toward the hallway.

"No," Dana said sharply, shrugging her off. "I'm staying with Izzy."

"Ma'am," a nurse interjected, blocking Dana from moving closer to the bed, "you have to go."

"We'll wait right outside," Padma said firmly, guiding Dana through the curtain and down the hall, away from the escalating chaos.

In the hallway, Dana leaned against the wall, her hand pressed against it as though reaching for Izzy. "Was Izzy complaining of any pain?" Padma asked.

Dana shook her head. "Just about her crutches."

"You said she had dinner—did she eat?"

"Pizza," Dana said faintly, her voice hollow.

"Could this be an allergic reaction? Did she experience any swelling or disorientation after taking the pain medication?" Padma's mind raced. Izzy had seemed fine when she discharged her earlier. Was Gary right? Had she missed something?

"I don't know," Dana blurted, her voice sharp and high. "*You're* the doctor."

Padma stepped back, stung, but then drew a deep breath. Dana was terrified—that was all. They never spoke to each other harshly. Even during chaotic moments—like staying up past midnight baking hundreds of cookies for the fifth-grade graduation after Padma forgot to order them from the bakery, or enduring a torrential downpour in a leaky tent on a camping trip with the kids—they had always found ways to laugh. But no one was laughing now.

Padma watched Dana stare helplessly down the hallway toward Izzy's room. A wave of despair hit her. How unbearable it must be to know your child was in trouble and feel powerless to help. But Padma, at least, could help. Squaring her shoulders, she said, "I'm going back to check on Izzy."

Dana nodded, her face tense, and Padma turned—only to see Gary striding toward them. His expression, a mask of practiced neutrality that Padma knew well, made her heart sink.

His jaw tightened as he approached. "I need to speak to the patient's mother," he said, dismissing Padma with a curt nod.

"She can stay," Dana said firmly, grabbing Padma's arm.

Padma linked arms with Dana, and together they faced Gary.

His gaze flickered between them before he cleared his throat. "I'm afraid I don't have good news."

TEN

DANA

That day

The relentless beeping set Dana's teeth on edge. She scanned the machines surrounding Izzy, trying to locate the source. A tangled mess of wires sprouted from her daughter's body, connecting to an array of monitors displaying blinking numbers and fluctuating graphs. It felt like she'd stepped into NASA's control room—except these machines weren't launching rockets; they were fighting to keep her daughter alive.

"A coma?" she'd gasped when the doctor explained Izzy's condition. Her knees buckled, and Padma caught her, guiding her into a chair. After that, the doctor's words blurred. His lips moved, but Dana heard nothing. She felt detached, like a spectator watching the scene unfold on television. The surreal sensation only deepened as she registered the doctor's square jaw and sandy hair, graying at the temples. Surely she must have stumbled onto the film set of a hospital drama. This wasn't actually happening.

The doctor continued speaking as if he hadn't noticed her collapse. His voice came in and out like waves, and when he finally walked away, Dana remained frozen in the faded hospital chair, its orange upholstery worn to a dull peach. She was still sitting there, dazed, when Eric and Ian rushed toward her.

"Where is she?" Eric demanded, his voice tight with urgency. Dana opened her mouth to respond, but her tongue felt thick and uncooperative. She turned to Padma for help.

Padma squeezed Dana's shoulder and recounted everything the doctor had said. This time Dana listened, the words cutting through her fog: *shallow coma, stable, ventilator, brain activity, good news*. Each term settled in her mind like a stone sinking to the bottom of a pond.

"A coma?" Ian exclaimed, his voice cracking. "She was eating pizza an hour ago!"

"Where is she?" Eric pressed, his voice panicked.

"They moved her to the ICU," Padma said gravely. "She's stable. You can see her now." She helped Dana to her feet, her touch steady and grounding.

That had been four hours ago—maybe five? Time became fuzzy as Dana sat by Izzy's hospital bed, the beeping machines a relentless reminder of her daughter's still, unconscious form. The sound echoed in the cold room, which smelled faintly of rubbing alcohol and overcooked broccoli.

Eric had wrapped his arm around her when they first entered the room, and she'd leaned into him, grateful for his steadiness. Now they sat on opposite sides of Izzy's bed, each holding one of her hands.

"She just looks like she's sleeping," Eric said softly, his voice thick with tears as he stared at Izzy.

But Dana could see the difference. She'd spent countless hours watching Izzy sleep—from those early days when she lay on the floor beside the crib, waiting for the rhythmic rise and fall of her daughter's tiny chest before carefully crawling out of the room, to just last week when, unable to sleep as she worried about her business, she'd tiptoed into both Ian and Izzy's rooms at three a.m., seeking comfort in the gentle motion of their breathing. She imagined what Izzy might say if she woke to find her mother hovering: "Geez, Mom, creepy much?" But one day when she had children of her own, she'd understand.

If she had children of her own.

Dana swallowed the thought. Now was the time to stay positive. There was good news, according to the doctor. Nothing was wrong with Izzy's brain, for one. The TV-handsome doctor had repeated this several times, his expression resembling that of a game show host offering a consolation prize. Despite Izzy being deprived of oxygen for who knew how long after collapsing in the shower, her brain activity appeared normal, and she was responding appropriately to stimuli.

She just wouldn't wake up. The official cause, confirmed by the CT scan, was a pulmonary embolism—a blood clot that had likely caused her leg pain before traveling through her arteries to her lungs, cutting off oxygen to her brain. Dana had committed the diagnosis to memory, staring at the Google definition on her phone as she sat by Izzy's bed, yet it still didn't make sense to her.

It was after visiting hours now, and Padma had taken Ian home for much-needed sleep, despite his protests. One of the machines beeped loudly, and Dana jumped up from her chair, dropping Izzy's hand.

"What are you doing?" Eric asked. They had spoken very little as they kept their vigil, each scanning Izzy's body for movement, willing her to open her eyes and sit up, startled to find herself in a hospital room.

"I can't listen to that noise anymore," Dana snapped as she approached the machines.

"Whoa!" Eric said, springing up and moving to her side of the bed. He planted himself in her path. "I don't think we should touch any of those."

"I said I can't listen to it anymore!" Dana shouted, her vision marred by tears as she tried to push past him. He caught her by the arms, and she stumbled against his chest. For a moment, she resisted, her whole body feeling like one giant raw nerve. But eventually, she surrendered, slumping against him as waves of silent sobs overtook her.

They stood there, her body crumpled against his, the beeping echoing in the background for what felt like ten seconds or ten minutes. When she finally pulled away, the back of her neck was damp from Eric's tears.

"I'm so sorry," he said, his voice cracking. He lifted the hem of his T-shirt to wipe his eyes, revealing his toned abs, and a wave of sadness swept over Dana. She missed his old, soft stomach—the one she used to rest her head on while they watched TV together.

"Sorry for what?" she asked, her tone sharper than intended.

"For what I said in the therapist's office about separating. That wasn't the right time or place."

Dana stiffened. "*That's* what you're thinking about right now?" But she was thinking about it, too. As she looked at Izzy's slack face and the breathing tube in her throat, all Dana knew was that she wasn't sure how to get through this without Eric.

His cheeks flushed at her sharpness. "I just think... we should press pause. Before we tell the kids, or I move out... this is what matters right now." He gestured toward Izzy.

His words caused a small explosion inside her, and everything shifted. The idea of Eric moving out hadn't even crossed her mind—though clearly, it had crossed his. Because obviously, it wasn't a separation if he was just sleeping in the guest room.

Dana shook her head. "I can't even think about that right now." The machine beeped again, and a sudden realization struck her. "What if she can hear us?" she whispered, nodding toward Izzy.

Eric's eyes widened. "Shit," he murmured, glancing at the bed. "Right."

"Knock, knock," came a soft voice, and Dana turned to see Padma in the doorway, her face drawn and weary. She'd traded her scrubs for jeans and a bulky rust-colored sweater. "I offered to stay with Ian, when I took him home," she said, stepping inside. "But he just wanted to go to bed." Her eyes flicked toward Izzy. "How is she?" She shook her head quickly. "Never mind, stupid question." Padma shifted, biting her lip. "Sorry, I'm not sure whether to be a friend or a doctor right now," she admitted.

There was a moment of thick silence.

"Why did this happen?" Dana asked, her tone plaintive. "You said she was fine." She gazed at Padma, feeling an unfamiliar tension settle in her shoulders.

Padma shook her head slowly, anguish plain on her face. "I keep asking myself the same thing," she said. "I've gone over her chart, and I just don't get it." Her eyes flicked toward the bed, where Izzy's chest rose and fell in rhythm with the hiss of the ventilator. "There's no reason for someone young and healthy like Izzy to have a pulmonary embolism," she murmured.

Dana resisted the urge to sink to the floor and sob. Nothing made sense anymore—not her financial troubles, Eric wanting to leave, and, least of all, her daughter lying unresponsive in a hospital bed.

"You have to fix this," she said, her voice raw and desperate. "You have to save Izzy."

Padma met her gaze, and Dana thought she caught a flicker of guilt in her friend's eyes. "We'll go over her charts again," Padma said determinedly. "We must have missed something."

"You mean *you* must have missed something. You were the one who saw her first," Eric cut in sharply.

"I'm just trying to help," Padma said, hurt washing over her face.

"I'm sorry," Dana said quickly to Padma. "He's upset. We're all upset." But even as she said it, a speck of doubt crept into her mind before being buried under an avalanche of other emotions.

Her daughter was in a coma—her beautiful, perfect daughter. Dana longed to crawl into the bed beside Izzy, to close her eyes and wake up from this nightmare. Instead, she sank into the chair and gripped Izzy's hand tightly. "The machine won't stop beeping," she said dully.

Padma stepped over, studied the setup, and turned a knob. "I've reduced the volume," she said. "But the doctors will still get an alert if anything happens." She hesitated, looking like she wanted to say more, then pressed her lips together. "I'll give you both some space."

Dana nodded. "That's probably a good idea."

ELEVEN

IAN

Three days after

Before the night Izzy went to the ER, Ian had been to the hospital plenty of times. He'd broken his arm falling off the monkey bars when he was nine, and then his collarbone two years ago when he'd failed to land a jump at the skate park. Then there was the time he'd gotten mono at sleepaway camp. He'd stayed in the infirmary for two days before the nurse was convinced he wasn't faking it—Ian made no secret of his hatred of camp—and called his mom, who'd had to take him to be treated for dehydration. After that Ian had gotten his wish and never had to go back to camp.

Each of those times he'd never noticed how the hospital smelled. But now, sitting in Izzy's room, he couldn't ignore it. The place smelled of Band-Aids and the faint scent of soup left simmering too long. His mom kept complaining about how sickening the soup smell was, but Ian found it oddly comforting. Like, you're probably in good hands if you're in a place where someone's making you soup. No one had made Ian soup in a long time.

Ian had been at the hospital since early that morning, slouched in a stiff metal chair in the corner that made his back ache. He'd gotten up to use the bathroom once, and both his parents had jumped, like they'd forgotten he existed. The whole thing felt surreal, like time was both racing ahead and stuck on pause. It reminded him of the Kurt Vonnegut novel he was reading for English—the only class he didn't totally hate, mostly because Mr. Riley had this weird talent for making old books feel like they actually had something to do with being seventeen. When he'd told them *The Scarlet Letter* was basically about slut shaming, half the class had gasped and the other half had snickered.

Also, it was possible Ian's warped sense of time might have something to do with the little white pill he'd popped earlier. When he'd checked his parents' medicine cabinet yesterday, he'd found his mom had refilled her Ativan prescription, so he'd skimmed a few, to help him cope with the stress of everything going on with Izzy. The pill had smoothed the edges of the morning, making everything feel hazy and almost pleasant, which was pretty messed up given the reason they were there at the hospital. But that was the whole reason he took the pills. They kept him immune from the storm of everyday stresses, all stemming—according to his dad—from his long list of shortcomings.

At some point during the day, his dad convinced his mom to go get a cup of coffee, leaving Ian alone with Izzy. With his parents gone, Ian moved to the padded chair by Izzy's bed. He almost asked her what she thought of the soup smell, before remembering she couldn't answer. She could only lie there, eyes closed, a machine breathing for her.

After a brief hesitation, he reached for her hand, lifting it gingerly at first, as if she might wake up and wonder why the hell they were holding hands like kids again. But somehow, he felt like his touch might help—that maybe, just maybe, she could sense him there with her.

When she didn't stir, he wrapped his fingers more tightly around hers. Her hand felt heavy, like dead weight, and so much smaller than his. It was hard to believe they'd ever been the same size. Izzy had even weighed an ounce more than him at birth, but now he towered over her.

Ian knew he was lucky to be tall—especially with a mom who was five foot two and a dad barely five nine. Lucky in so many ways, his mom often reminded him, usually while begging him to bring up his grades or join a school club. Because with luck, apparently, comes the responsibility to make something of yourself.

Ian cleared his throat, the sound startlingly loud in the quiet of the room. "I can't remember the last time we were in the same room this long without fighting," he said. "Turns out you're less of a pain in the ass when you're in a coma."

A noise behind him made him jump. He turned to see a nurse standing in the doorway, smiling.

"Sorry," she said. "I didn't mean to interrupt." She had a warm expression and a cascade of tiny braids pulled back into a thick ponytail.

"No problem," Ian muttered, his face flushing as he dropped Izzy's hand and gave a casual shrug.

"Keep talking to her," the nurse said, moving toward the machines to check the readings. "Chances are, she can hear you."

Ian sat up straighter. "Really?"

"For real." She nodded, wrapping a blood pressure cuff around Izzy's arm. "Lots of coma patients still have residual auditory awareness."

"Um, what does that mean?" Ian asked, hoping he didn't sound as dumb as he felt.

"Just that they retain the ability to hear and process sounds, especially voices that are familiar to them, even if they can't respond."

"Wow," Ian murmured, watching Izzy's eyes flicker behind her closed lids. He cleared his throat. "Will she, um, wake up?" His voice cracked on the word "wake," and the lump in his throat took him by surprise. He'd hadn't followed all the medical terms when the doctors had briefed his parents earlier.

The nurse, removing the blood pressure cuff, gave him a sympathetic look. "I hope so," she said softly. "Are you her brother?"

Ian nodded. "Her twin."

"I'm Tonya," the nurse said, extending her hand.

"Ian." He swallowed hard and waved awkwardly.

Tonya glanced at Izzy, as if she had more to say, but then pressed her lips together and nodded. "See you later, Ian."

Once Ian was alone with Izzy again, he scooted his chair closer to the bed. "So," he began, leaning forward with his elbows on his knees, "I guess I'm supposed to talk to you." He cleared his throat, searching for something to say.

These days, he and Izzy didn't talk much, aside from teasing each other or swapping gossip about who crashed their new car or had gotten dumped over the weekend—stuff Ian didn't even really care about. He was so out of the loop with high school drama he might as well have been in outer space. Still, he liked hearing Izzy talk, liked being around her. Though he'd never admit it, those morning drives to school with her were the best part of his day—the only time he felt like he could just be himself without letting anyone down.

"I still haven't finished my History essay," Ian said. "Maybe I'll get an extension with the whole sister-in-a-coma thing." He sighed, shaking his head. "I was going to ask you for help. Wish I had, because I have no idea how I'm going to finish it on my own."

He let out a frustrated breath. "Not that it matters. If it's not

History, I'll probably just fail something else. That's kind of my thing, right?" He gave a wry smile, as if Izzy could see him. "Just ask Dad."

He'd recently overheard his parents arguing about how to "handle" him. His mom wanted to give Ian space to "figure things out" which only seemed to infuriate his dad.

"Seriously, Dana?" he'd snapped. "Ian's not a self-starter like Izzy. He needs real consequences, or he'll end up a high school dropout living in our basement."

"He's just a late bloomer," his mom had replied.

"You're missing the point!" his dad had said, his voice growing louder. After that, Ian had closed his bedroom door and put on his headphones to drown them out.

"Anyway," Ian continued, scooting closer to Izzy's bed until his knees touched it. "At least I've made you look good with all my fuckups." He paused, knowing Izzy would have rolled her eyes at that, but also laughed.

Someone cleared their throat behind him, and Ian spun around to see Maeve standing in the doorway.

"Hey," she said with a small smile.

Ian felt his ears redden and brushed his hair forward to hide them. "The nurse said I'm supposed to talk to her," he muttered, nodding toward Izzy. "Like maybe she can hear us."

Maeve stepped closer. "Does it seem like she can?"

She was wearing an off-white turtleneck sweater over gray sweatpants and those same white Nikes all the girls had. *So basic*, Ian thought. He shrugged. "No idea."

Maeve glanced at the chair next to him. "Mind if I sit?"

"Uh, yeah, whatever." Begrudgingly, he scooted his chair an inch to the right. He didn't want her there. Sure, Izzy was Maeve's best friend, but she was his twin. This was his jurisdiction, and Maeve felt like an intruder.

As they sat in silence, Ian stole a glance at Maeve. She had a snub nose dotted with freckles and thick, wavy hair the color of their mahogany dining table at home—the one they never used. Her eyes were striking, almost too big for her face, a silvery gray he'd never noticed before. They were rimmed with red, like she'd been crying.

She caught him staring, and he quickly looked back at Izzy.

"I just can't believe this is happening," Maeve whispered.

The tremor in her voice softened his irritation. Maeve and Izzy had been best friends as long as Ian could remember. At first, he'd resented it—it had always been just him and Izzy, and suddenly Maeve was always there, and Izzy chose playing Barbies with her over making mud pies with him. But then Ian met Ben down the street, and they were inseparable until Ben moved away at the start of high school. After that, Ian was alone again. By then, Izzy was too busy being the best at everything to notice he'd started drifting. That's when his troubles had really started.

"Do they think she'll..." Maeve's voice faded, her eyes filling with tears.

"They don't know," Ian muttered, fighting back his own. Their chairs were pressed close together by the bed, and she smelled faintly of grapefruit and sugar. He leaned the slightest bit toward her, his shoulder bumping hers—a small, wordless gesture of comfort. It was all he had to give.

"Maeve," his mother's voice sounded behind them, and Ian quickly shifted away as his parents entered the room. "I didn't know you were here."

Maeve jumped to her feet, nervously knitting her fingers together. "My mom brought me."

"Your mom? Is she working?"

Ian glanced at his mother and caught the slight hardening of her expression as she walked toward the bed, positioning herself between Izzy and Maeve as she stroked Izzy's hair. His dad entered the room quietly behind her.

"No," Maeve said, shaking her head. "But I think she went to talk to someone about a chart?"

Maeve's mom knocked softly on the open doorway. Her hair was pulled back in a thick braid and she wore black leggings and an oversized dark green sweater. There was a softness to her that Ian's mom didn't have, and he liked the way her forehead and the corners of her eyes crinkled at the corners when she smiled. His mom's face, on the other hand, was smooth but had a hardness to it, sometimes seeming so brittle it might crack.

"Hi," Dr. Paulsen said gently. "I wanted to check on you. And Izzy." Her gaze shifted between Ian's mom and his sister.

"I have no idea how she's doing," Ian's mom said, desperation in her voice. "No one will tell us anything."

"They're still running tests," Dr. Paulsen said in a measured voice.

"It's been hours," his mom said, looking like she might burst into tears. "And no one can tell us what happened."

"You'd tell us if you knew something, yes?" Eric said. It sounded more like an order than a question.

Maeve's mom tensed, but she nodded. "I just checked with Toby, my boss. No one has answers yet." She glanced at Ian's mom. "But of course I'd tell you."

"It doesn't make any sense," his mom muttered, repeating the words she'd been saying all morning. Her voice cracked. She closed her eyes, her shoulders trembling.

"Honey," his dad said softly, moving toward her to put his arms around her.

"No," she said, pushing him away, tears streaming down her face now.

"Dana," Dr. Paulsen said, stepping forward, her voice full of concern.

"No," his mom said again, more sharply, holding up her hands. "Just leave me alone. You don't understand. This is my daughter." She pointed at Izzy. "My daughter!" Her voice broke into a high-pitched wail as she collapsed to the floor, clutching Izzy's hand. A surge of fear ran through Ian. What was happening to his mother?

He glanced at Maeve, who looked just as scared.

"Come on, kids," Maeve's mom said firmly, placing a hand on each of their shoulders and guiding them toward the door. "Let's give them some space."

TWELVE

DANA

Six days after

After almost a week at Izzy's bedside, Dana had learned the rhythm of the hospital. She liked the early mornings best, before the hallway filled with harried doctors and coded announcements over the intercom. She'd been sleeping on a cot in the corner of Izzy's room, and though it left her with a stiff back, she savored the quiet before the nurses came in to check Izzy's vitals. In those moments, as the sun peeked through the flimsy hospital blinds, it felt like it was just her, Izzy, and the hope that today might be the day her daughter woke up and this nightmare would end.

This morning, though, Dana woke to darkness. It took her a moment to remember she was in her own bed. After nearly a week of waking every three hours for nurses checking vitals or rotating Izzy to prevent bedsores, Eric had finally persuaded her to let him take a turn at the hospital so she could get some real sleep at home.

In the pitch black, courtesy of their expensive blackout curtains, Dana fumbled for her phone on the nightstand.

Nearly seven-thirty. She ignored another missed call from her mother and flung off the covers. The last thing she needed was Cora's frantic worrying about Izzy adding to her own. Besides, just seeing her mother's name on her phone filled Dana with guilt. Sooner or later, she'd have to confess Haven and Hearth's financial troubles, and the thought made her stomach churn.

Dana stumbled toward the bathroom, knowing she had to hurry or risk missing the doctors' morning rounds. Since Izzy's pulmonary embolism diagnosis, no new information had been offered. Eric was useless during the brief meetings with the doctors, wasting precious time with questions about obscure clinical trials or homeopathic remedies he'd seen on Reddit. That left Dana to press for answers and push for more tests— anything that might help her daughter.

She kept a mental checklist of actionable steps—things that might actually help, unlike Eric's tangents. Despite her growing frustration with the slow test results and uncertainty surrounding Izzy's diagnosis, Dana trusted Padma, who had assured her that everything possible was being done. Trusted her, except for the tiny seed of doubt Eric had planted, which in her darker moments she was struggling to ignore.

After splashing water on her face and brushing her teeth, Dana quickly dressed in jeans and an old T-shirt declaring "Eat, Beach, Sleep, Repeat." The irony made her want to cry, but after a week of hospital living, it was the only clean shirt she had.

The hospital was always cold, so she searched for her favorite sweatshirt, the one displaying Van Gogh's *Starry Night* —a souvenir from a family trip to the Museum of Modern Art in New York two years ago. Then she remembered Izzy wearing it.

Opening the door to Izzy's room, Dana hesitated. She had avoided this space all week, coming home only long enough to shower before rushing back to the hospital. Now it felt frozen in time, painfully preserved, like a scene from Pompeii. The scent of vanilla jasmine body spray still lingered, mixing with the odor of dirty running clothes spilling from the hamper. On the floor lay the red overalls Izzy had glued spice containers to for her Halloween costume. A twist of pain gripped Dana's chest, wondering if Izzy would even get a chance to wear her costume next week.

Her eyes drifted to the desk, where textbooks were stacked, and the lamp glowed softly. Dana crossed the room and switched it off.

Izzy's Chemistry textbook lay open, next to a notebook filled with neatly written formulas. Beside it was her phone. Frowning, Dana picked it up, and the screen lit up with notifications—136 texts and missed calls, mostly from names she recognized as Izzy's friends and classmates.

Pocketing the phone, Dana moved to the dresser, still searching for her sweatshirt. The top drawer jammed as she tried to open it, and when she finally succeeded, she found the culprit: a photo album. It was the one Maeve had gifted Izzy for her sixteenth birthday, filled with snapshots of the two girls over the years.

Flipping through the pages, Dana watched them transform from gap-toothed kids to young women dressed for Homecoming in party dresses and Converse sneakers. The weight of the memories pressed down on her, and she slammed the album shut, shoving it back into the drawer.

As she did, something caught on the edge. Reaching in to investigate, her fingers closed around a pale pink plastic case—birth control pills.

Dana inhaled sharply, dropping the case onto the dresser and jerking her hand back as if it were a cockroach. Slowly, she picked it up again and flipped it open. The last pill had been taken last Friday—the day Izzy collapsed. Snapping the case shut, she stuffed it into her pocket along with Izzy's phone and hurried out of the room.

. . .

Dana reached Izzy's room just as Dr. Roberts was about to leave. "Wait!" she called, blocking his path down the hallway. "I'm sorry, I overslept. Can you give me an update?"

Dr. Roberts, who seemed to be Izzy's primary physician, had a round face, a receding hairline, and the tiniest teeth Dana had ever seen on an adult. His brow was perpetually furrowed, giving him the appearance of an overgrown baby attempting a bowel movement.

He waved his hand toward the room. "Not to worry, Mrs. Blair. I've briefed your husband. Unfortunately, there are no new developments."

Dana planted her hands on her hips. "What about a lumbar puncture to rule out meningitis or encephalitis? Did you order that?"

The crease in Dr. Roberts's brow deepened. "As I explained before, Mrs. Blair, we really don't think there's any chance that this was caused by meningitis."

"But don't you want to rule it out completely?" Dana pressed.

He cleared his throat, his voice sympathetic. "I know you're searching for answers, Mrs. Blair, and we are, too. It's extremely rare for someone as young and healthy as your daughter to experience a pulmonary embolism. But sometimes, these things just... happen."

Anger flared in Dana. This was the best hospital in Atlanta, and Padma had assured her that Dr. Roberts was an excellent doctor. So why didn't anyone have answers? Frustrated, she jammed her fist into the sides of her legs and felt the plastic shell in her pocket.

Pulling it out, she held it toward Dr. Roberts. "I found these this morning," she said, her voice shaky. She hadn't had time to consider what the pills meant for Izzy, and she had the odd sensation that she was tattling on her own daughter—though clearly Dana was the one Izzy had been hiding the pills from.

Dr. Roberts raised an eyebrow as he took the pills. "Oral contraceptives? But these weren't listed in her chart."

A flush crept across Dana's face. "I didn't know about them."

He frowned. "But they should have taken a full medical history from her when she came to the ER the first time."

Dana flashed back to sitting in the exam room with Izzy, watching her writhe in pain while Padma smoothed her hair. "Padma," she said.

"I'm sorry?"

"Dr. Paulsen. A family friend. She saw Izzy when she came in initially."

"Ah, yes." Dr. Roberts nodded, pursing his lips as he shook the pills in his hand. "Well, this changes things."

"How do you mean?" Dana asked. Her mind raced. She didn't remember Padma asking about Izzy's medications, but the whole thing had been a blur.

Eric stepped into the hallway and Dana tensed as he placed a hand on her back in greeting.

"Birth control pills, especially combination pills like these that contain both estrogen and progestin," Dr. Roberts said, holding up the pills, "can increase the risk of blood clots. Estrogen can make the blood more prone to clotting. To be clear, birth control pills don't cause blood clots in everyone, but given that Izzy was otherwise very healthy, I'd say the pills were a factor in the blood clot that traveled to her lungs."

Dana struggled to process what he was saying, feeling as if all the air had been sucked from her lungs. She pressed a hand against the wall to steady herself.

"I'm sorry," Eric interjected, rubbing the stubble that had grown on his chin over the past week. "Why are we talking about birth control?"

He turned to Dana, and a wave of shame washed over her, as if she were the one sneaking pills. How had she not known this about her daughter? When had Izzy started keeping secrets? While they didn't have the cozy mom-daughter relationship of shows like *Gilmore Girls*, Dana had believed they were close. She knew all of Izzy's friends, and just a few weeks ago, when they'd come over to get ready for Homecoming, Dana had brought sparkling grape juice and a cheese plate to Izzy's room, earning a grateful smile. She'd loved that the girls were going to the dance together and had felt relieved Izzy seemed focused on school and extracurriculars instead of boys—or so she had thought.

"Izzy was apparently on the pill," Dana said, a pit of guilt forming in her stomach. What kind of mother didn't know this about her daughter? This was the sort of secret she might have expected from Ian—God only knew what he got up to—but not from Izzy.

"What?" Eric exclaimed, his voice rising in disbelief. "Why? Did you know?"

Dana glanced over his shoulder into the room, where Ian sat quietly in the corner. Lowering her voice, she signaled for him to do the same. "I just found them this morning."

Dr. Roberts shifted uncomfortably. "I'll check back with you two this afternoon, once I've had the chance to fully consider this new information."

He hurried away, leaving Dana leaning against the wall as Eric stared at her, his expression accusatory.

"Is she having sex?" he asked bluntly.

"I don't know," Dana replied defensively. "This is all news to me, OK?"

Remembering, she pulled Izzy's phone from her pocket. She had the passcode and had always told both kids she might check their phones, though she couldn't recall the last time she'd actually looked at Izzy's—her daughter had never been in trouble.

Now, she opened the phone and began scrolling through the text messages. Most were from Izzy's friends, expressing concern and asking for updates, as if Izzy could somehow reply in her unconscious state. Mixed in were several messages from someone named Taylor, a name Dana didn't recognize, starting last Thursday—the day Izzy ended up in the hospital.

> Hey, u ok? heard you left practice in an ambulance??

Izzy had responded.

> Oof, embarrassing. I'm fine, just on stupid crutches and can't train for a while.

> Sucks. But running is dumb anyway. See you tomorrow? Same place?

Izzy had liked Taylor's last message. Then, on Friday, Taylor had texted again.

> Hey, missed your face at school. There's a crazy rumor you're in a coma?? Pls tell me it's not true and we're still on for later.

Dana scrolled back up to the top of the messages, hoping more would load, but that was it.

"What are you looking at?" Eric asked, craning his neck.

She shook her head. "I don't know, but I'm going to find out." Turning back into the hospital room, she held the phone out toward Ian. "Who's Taylor?" she asked, her voice sharp with urgency.

Ian looked up from where he'd been staring blankly at the floor beside Izzy's bed. He had been skipping school to sit by Izzy's side during the day. Dana wasn't sure if that spoke more to his devotion to Izzy or his reluctance to face school. Now, as she really looked at him, guilt pricked her. His eyes were bloodshot, his hair matted from sleep, and she was fairly certain he'd been wearing that same Jackson Hole T-shirt for days. Clearly, he was struggling, but Dana barely had the emotional bandwidth to handle her own feelings, let alone Ian's.

"Taylor?" he repeated, squinting at the screen as she handed him the phone. He shrugged after a moment. "I don't know. I mean, there's a couple of Taylors at school, but Izzy's not friends with them."

"Hey there." Dana whirled around to find Padma in the doorway, her scrubs fresh and her hair neatly twisted into her trademark thick braid.

"I'm just starting my shift but wanted to swing by," Padma said, an unusual tension hanging in the air between them, like static before a storm. "Did Dr. Roberts already do rounds?"

Dana's gaze flickered to Ian, then she brushed past Padma into the hallway, gesturing for her to follow. "Izzy was on birth control," she hissed, ensuring they were out of earshot.

Padma's eyes widened. "But you said—"

"Dr. Roberts thinks that's what caused this." Dana pointed toward the hospital room, her finger shaking with anger. "You never asked about her medications."

"What's going on?" Eric appeared behind Dana.

Padma blinked, tugging at her braid, her face frozen in something that looked like fear.

"The first time Izzy came in," Dana explained to Eric, "Padma didn't ask about her medications." She turned back to her friend. "You're supposed to ask—Dr. Roberts said so. What if the clot was already there then? If you'd known—if you'd asked, then maybe..." Her words tumbled out, faster than she could control. Was this Padma's fault? The more she spoke, the more it felt that way.

Padma's face went pale. "But I know Izzy, and I knew she wasn't—"

"You're supposed to ask!" Dana said, her increasing volume drawing a concerned look from a passing nurse.

Padma shrank back, her eyes pleading. "Dana, calm down—"

"Don't tell her to calm down," Eric snapped, stepping toward Padma.

Dana turned to her friend, whose eyes were filled with hurt. "Don't you understand?" she said, her voice breaking. "Maybe none of this would have happened."

THIRTEEN
PADMA

Six days after

Padma sat in her car in the hospital parking garage and leaned her head back against her seat. She'd just finished an unusually punishing shift, where they'd been short-staffed and she'd nearly peed her pants after holding it so long, trying to squeeze in one more consult, order one more test, dash out notes on one more chart, before she finally gave up and sprinted to the restroom.

"Must be a full moon or something," Toby had said, who'd jumped in to help Padma and the other doctor on shift after the third ambulance had arrived in the span of twenty minutes.

She was exhausted, hungry, and dehydrated, yet sitting there in her car, she thought about going back inside and clocking in. Because if she was working, then at least she wasn't thinking about the anger and devastation on Dana's face as she'd told Padma about Izzy's birth control pills.

Her mind raced. Was Izzy's coma her fault? Normally when it came to her patients Padma did everything by the book, triple-checking medication requests and reviewing test results multiple times. She'd learned the hard way.

Her mind catapulted back to her third year of med school. She'd been treating Julia Kim, mother of three, for atrial fibrillation. Her supervising doctor had caught the dosing error just in time to pump Julia's stomach, sparing her from the worst. But Padma shuddered, remembering how he'd berated her in front of the other med students.

"You gave her enough anticoagulant to take down an elephant!" he'd yelled, his face purple with rage. "What the hell is wrong with you?"

Half a bottle of vodka to help her sleep, that's what had been wrong—as everyone in her program soon learned.

Padma realized she was trembling and gripped the steering wheel tightly, willing her hands to steady. Her mind flashed back to her recent conversation with Toby, when she'd told him about Izzy. He had expressed his sympathy but had been otherwise unfazed. It was a hospital. Terrible things happened every day.

But Toby didn't know about Julia Kim. No one other than Lars and Dana did. It had happened so long ago that Padma hadn't disclosed it when Midtown Hospital hired her. It was buried in the past, she reminded herself. But now, what if she'd made another mistake—this one even more devastating?

She exhaled shakily. There was no one more qualified than her to become the next Director of Emergency Medicine, and while one error might not derail her career—everyone made mistakes—two certainly could.

Pushing the thoughts away, she drove home.

Once there, Lars took one look at her and set down the wooden spoon he was using to sauté peppers. "What happened?" he asked. "Did your mom fall again?" Padma's parents lived an hour outside Atlanta and in the past year her mother had fallen twice, once breaking her wrist and the other badly bruising her hip.

Padma shook her head. "It's Izzy," she said with a shaky voice, then proceeded to relay her conversation with Dana to Lars.

Lars's face tightened as he walked over to her. "I don't care what Dana says, it wasn't your fault."

Padma tried to smile. "You don't know that," she said quietly. "Everyone makes mistakes. Especially me."

He shook his head, vehemently. "That was decades ago. And it was different. You were..." He trailed off, looking down.

"Drunk?" she finished, trying to force a smile.

Lars wrapped his arm around her shoulder. "Yes, you made a mistake. But, honey, you've got to forgive yourself. You've done so much good since then. It has to balance out at some point."

Padma bit her lip, looking out the window at their small backyard, which was crowded with Lars's vegetable garden and Maeve's old treehouse. "I don't think Mrs. Kim's family would agree," she said, her voice catching.

She closed her eyes, remembering twenty-six years ago, sitting across from the Assistant Dean of the medical school. She had stared at the liver spot on his forehead, avoiding his eyes as he terminated her from the program.

"I suggest you get yourself together," he had said pointedly as she stood to leave his office.

Lars drew her close and she inhaled his comforting scent of pine needles and warm bread. "It's going to be all right," he promised.

For a fleeting moment, Padma nearly gave in to his embrace, tempted to let the fears swirling in her mind spill out, to let her vulnerability show. But she knew that once uncorked, it would be difficult to contain emotions again. She couldn't afford to fall apart right now, not when her dream job was on the line. So instead, she stepped back, forcing a shaky smile onto her face. "I hope you're right."

FOURTEEN

MAEVE

Eight days after

Typically, Saturday mornings meant Maeve and Izzy grabbing donuts and iced coffees before settling in for homework at one of their houses. But today, after getting dressed, Maeve sat at her desk, unable to focus. Her mind kept wandering. She reached for her phone to text Izzy, then remembered. For the millionth time, she scrolled through their recent texts, which they exchanged constantly despite sharing half their classes and the same lunch period.

omg I totally bombed that Bio test

you always say that

No for real this time.

You always say that too

Then later that day there was another exchange.

he wants to meet tomorrow after school. I think
I might explode with happiness

don't you have practice?

yeah but I'd much rather be with him

you don't think it's weird he doesn't want anyone else to know?

we're just taking it slow

being naked together is taking it slow?

No like the social part lol. I don't want to make it weird.

just be careful. I don't want you to get hurt.

love you

love you more

Maeve set her phone down. *Focus*, she told herself. But after ten minutes of rereading the same paragraph in her textbook, she gave up and headed downstairs.

Making a Starbucks run

She texted her parents as she closed the front door behind her. Just as she reached the driveway, she heard the Blairs' front door open and turned to see Ian coming down the steps in baggy sweatpants and a black hoodie.

"Oh," he said, nodding. "Hey."

Maeve froze. "Hey," she forced out, her voice nearly drowned by the hammering of her heart. "Good morning. How are you?" As soon as the words escaped, she fought back a full body cringe. Why did she have to sound so proper? She might as well have curtsied.

Ian scratched his ear, unfazed by her silent humiliation.

"Uh, yeah, good. Well, not good, obviously, with everything, but you know." His eyes met hers.

"I do know," Maeve said quietly, breaking eye contact to glance down at his feet. Looking directly at Ian felt as dangerous as staring into the sun; she feared being blinded by her feelings if she lingered too long on his beautiful face. Instead, she focused on pieces of him—the side of his head, the slope of his shoulder, his scuffed Vans as he walked toward her.

"Headed out?" he asked once he was standing in front of her.

Maeve nodded, her gaze drifting to his warm, hazel eyes, noting the golden fleck near the iris of his left eye. Standing this close, she had to stop herself from reaching out to touch him.

She'd loved Ian for years. By eleven, she was almost as excited to see him at Izzy's sleepovers as she was to see her best friend. Not that he'd ever think of her that way—she was sure he only saw her as Izzy's best friend, the little girl who once wet the bed at his house and cried during *The Lion King* because it was too scary. Even if he did notice her—which seemed impossible, given he was gorgeous and had half the girls at school crushing on him—he was Izzy's twin. Maeve could never do that to her.

"Starbucks?" Maeve blurted, and Ian looked at her with confusion. "Do you want to go? I mean, right now. I'm going. You could come." *Oh my God, Maeve*, she thought, heat rushing to her face. *Talk like a normal person much?*

But Ian just shrugged. "Yeah, sure." He glanced back at his house before heading for her car. "Pretty sure no one will miss me."

As she drove, Maeve tried to focus on the road and not the fact that Ian was next to her in the passenger seat. She hoped her car smelled OK. She hoped *she* smelled OK. They were quiet for a few minutes, and she wracked her brain for something interesting to say.

"This is weird," Ian said, gesturing to the two of them, and Maeve's heart sank. "Like, I'm usually in the backseat," he added.

"Oh, yeah." Maeve laughed with relief as understanding set in. When the three of them rode to school together, Izzy usually drove, with Maeve riding shotgun and Ian in the back, either zoned out or with his eyes closed. She could never tell if he was high or asleep. "It is kind of weird," she agreed, then confessed, "I don't like to drive."

"I know."

She eyed him curiously. "You do?"

"Yeah, remember we were waiting outside for Izzy, talking about driverless cars? You said you couldn't wait for them because you hate driving."

"You remember that?" Maeve asked, her heart fluttering. The conversation had happened over a year ago, and she only remembered it because it had been one of their longest talks alone. She'd been disappointed when Izzy had finally come out to head to school.

Ian looked over at her. "Of course I remember. I'm not stupid." He turned away, and muttered, "Even though everyone thinks I am."

"I don't think you're stupid," she said, honestly, then blushed when he looked back at her. "You just don't want to, like, work hard."

Ian laughed. "So I'm just lazy? God, you sound like my dad."

"No!" She backtracked, her cheeks reddening further. "What I meant was, you like to have fun."

He snorted. "Yeah, I get it. So I like to party, big deal."

"I didn't mean it like that," she insisted, though she couldn't deny his reputation at school. She tried again. "Having fun is a good thing," she said, then sighed. "I never have fun."

Ian turned to her, his grin making her heart stutter. "You

should," he said, but then his smile faded, and his shoulders slumped. "And I should work harder."

"So we both have something to work on," Maeve said brightly.

He tilted his head, considered for a moment, then shrugged. "Yeah, I guess we do."

They drove in silence for a couple of minutes until Maeve pulled into the Starbucks parking lot. Inside, Ian realized he didn't have his wallet, so she paid for his venti Strawberry Crème Frappuccino.

"That's basically a milkshake, not coffee," she teased.

"Yeah, but it's a *fancy* milkshake," he shot back with a lopsided grin that stole Maeve's breath.

Back in the car, he drummed his fingers on the armrest and cleared his throat. "So, um, can I ask you something?"

Maeve's heart leapt. "Of course," she said, trying to sound calm and nonchalant.

He shifted in his seat, fiddling with his seatbelt, then took a long sip of his drink. "Did you know Izzy was on the pill?" he asked finally. "Is she..." He trailed off, blushing.

Maeve's stomach dropped. No one was supposed to know about that. That's why Izzy had gone to Planned Parenthood instead of their family doctor. Confusion bubbled up in her chest. "How do you know about that?" she asked, twisting a strand of hair around her finger.

Ian fiddled with his straw. "It's amazing what people will talk about in front of you when they think you're too stupid or zoned out to understand." His eyes narrowed as he studied her. "So why was my sister on the pill?"

Maeve bit her lip. "Can you keep a secret?"

FIFTEEN

DANA

Seventeen days after

Dana stood by Izzy's bed, gently brushing her daughter's hair. She had just lifted the flimsy hospital blinds to let in the early morning sun, making the room feel quiet and almost sacred before the hospital's frenetic pace began. In the calm of the room, Dana felt a rare moment of peace from her own racing thoughts.

Brushing Izzy's hair had always been a battle when she was younger. Dana could still picture herself chasing four-year-old Izzy, brush in hand, threatening to cut it all off while Izzy screamed. Not her finest parenting moment. Now, she smoothed the brush through her silent daughter's hair, which seemed thinner after two and a half weeks in the hospital. The nurses assured her that hair and nails still grow normally in a coma, but the change unsettled her.

Once she finished, Dana moistened a washcloth with warm water and began washing Izzy's face, then applied the serums and moisturizers she'd brought from home. Izzy had been devoted to her skincare routine, and Dana hoped that wherever her brain was, it could sense this small act of normalcy. Like somehow maybe her Drunk Elephant vitamin C serum could keep her connected to her real, pre-coma self—and remind her to come back to them.

The ring of Dana's phone pierced the calm. Seeing her mother's number, her shoulders tightened. Cora had called twice the day before, leaving long voicemails asking when she could visit Izzy. Dana knew she couldn't put her off much longer—she would just keep calling.

"Hi, Mom," she said, answering.

"Dana, darling, how is my beautiful granddaughter?"

Dana pressed a knuckle to her forehead, trying to ward off the headache forming there. If only she knew how to answer. Izzy had been in a coma for two and a half weeks now, with no medical breakthroughs or treatments to offer hope.

"She's the same," Dana said quietly.

Cora made a worried sound. "When can I see her?"

Dana held back a sigh. She knew her mother meant well—she adored Izzy. But Cora no longer drove, and Dana couldn't take the time to fetch her from the assisted living facility. She needed to be with Izzy. She'd already sacrificed being at the shop, leaving it to SueEllen to keep things running. And she definitely didn't have the emotional bandwidth to handle her mother's grief on top of her own. The weight of Cora's worry was suffocating enough over the phone; in person, it would crush her.

"It's immediate family only for visits right now, Mom," Dana said.

Cora clucked her tongue. "But I—"

"Mom, the doctor's here, I have to go. I'll call you back soon." Guilt surged through Dana as she ended the call. Hearing her mother's voice had already resurfaced all her financial anxieties—seeing her in person would only magnify them, along with the guilt of keeping it all from Cora. Right now, Dana just couldn't handle it.

"Good morning, ladies."

Dana looked up as Tonya, the nurse with the braids, entered the room. Tonya was one of the good ones. She treated Izzy like an actual person, chatting as she stretched her legs or rotated her to avoid bedsores. Some of the others might as well have been tending to a lump of clay.

"Good morning," Dana replied.

Tonya handed her a disposable toothbrush, already knowing Dana preferred to handle as much of Izzy's hygiene as they'd allow, then began recording Izzy's blood pressure and temperature.

"She has such good skin," Tonya observed, removing the blood pressure cuff from Izzy's pale, thin arm. She nodded toward the small display of skincare products on the side table. "I need to get me some of whatever she's using."

Dana smiled faintly. "You and me both."

"I'll leave you a shampoo cap," Tonya said. "I know you like to wash her hair every couple of days."

"Thanks." Dana nodded. Over the past two and a half weeks, she'd received a crash course in caring for coma patients, and nothing had impressed her more than the pre-moistened shower caps Tonya used. With a simple massage, they cleansed Izzy's hair without needing to rinse. "I need some of those!" Dana had exclaimed the first time. "It's so fast!"

Tonya had laughed. "Best invention ever." Somehow, Dana could relax around Tonya when it was just the two of them, able to set aside her anguish for a few minutes. Around the other nurses and doctors, she worried that if she didn't appear constantly grief-stricken, they might not try as hard to help Izzy —as though her sadness and devastation were a currency for better care.

"How's Ian?" Tonya asked now as Dana squeezed toothpaste onto the toothbrush. "I haven't seen him in a while."

"Back at school," Dana sighed. "And not happy about it." Her throat tightened, remembering Ian's anger when she and Eric insisted he return earlier that week.

"But I should be with her," he'd said flatly.

"Buddy," Eric replied in his trademark soothing tone, "it's been over two weeks. We don't know how much longer—" His voice faltered as he drew a shaky breath. "How much longer it's going to be."

"You can't miss any more school," Dana interjected, and the force of Ian's glare nearly knocked her off balance.

"She needs me there," Ian said, turning to Eric, his voice desperate. "You can't do this."

"She's getting excellent care," Eric began, but Ian slammed his fist onto the counter, startling them both.

"Oh my God," Dana exclaimed, blinking rapidly as Ian winced, cradling his hand. "Sweetheart, what were you thinking? Let me get you an ice pack. God, I hope you didn't break anything." But before she could move toward the freezer, Ian turned and stormed upstairs, slamming his bedroom door.

Dana finished brushing Izzy's teeth and wiped a dot of toothpaste from her chin with her thumb.

"They seem really close," Tonya said, bundling the blood pressure cuff and stowing it neatly in her cart.

Dana thought of Ian as a toddler, always trailing after Izzy. She'd been steadier on her feet, while Ian wobbled three steps behind, calling, "Iz! Iz!" in his sweet baby voice.

"They are," Dana replied. "I think. He... struggles. With a lot of things. Izzy kept—keeps him grounded." She caught herself, refusing to slip into the past tense.

"Well, I hope I'll see him around soon," Tonya said, pressing her lips together like she wanted to say more. Then she nodded, smiled, and rolled her cart away.

Alone by Izzy's bed, Dana opened her laptop. She felt guilty thinking about work, but time was slipping away—time she didn't have. She hadn't been to the shop in over two weeks since Izzy was hospitalized, and she'd only spoken to SueEllen a few times. Now, she had several urgent emails from her, plus two past-due bill notices from vendors threatening to send her account to a credit agency. She had to figure something out.

Her phone buzzed in her pocket with a text from Eric:

Don't forget about our meeting.

A bubble of nausea churned in Dana's stomach. In an hour, they were meeting with a medical malpractice lawyer—Eric's idea. He seemed so certain Padma had made a mistake, that Izzy's coma was her fault. Dana wanted to dismiss the idea outright, to call it absurd, but the small echo of doubt in the back of her mind refused to be silenced.

The thought of sitting across from a lawyer to "explore their options," as Eric had phrased it, made her feel sullied, like it would leave a stain on their friendship she could never wash clean. This was *Padma*. Other than Eric, Dana had been through more with Padma than with anyone else in her life. Padma had been her lifeline in moments when Eric couldn't— or wouldn't—be. The idea that Dana could even consider betraying that friendship made her lightheaded and nauseous.

Still, later that afternoon she found herself at the Midtown offices of Putman & Ricard. The conference room into which she and Eric were ushered was as cold and clinical as the hospital, with sterile glass walls and gleaming chrome and metal chairs. Dana shivered as she stepped inside, her arms wrapped tightly around herself. Eric placed a reassuring hand on her back, guiding her to one of the high-backed chairs around the imposing table.

Ben Ricard, the lawyer Eric had insisted they meet, stood as they entered, offering a warm smile that seemed at odds with the chilly room. He wore a navy suit tailored close to his lanky body and looked to be around Dana's age—mid-forties—with closely cropped blond hair and a kind smile that softened his angular face.

"Dana, Eric," Ben said, extending a hand to each of them. "Thank you for coming. Please, have a seat."

Dana hesitated but finally sank into the chair Eric pulled out for her. She shot him a glance that conveyed her unease. This meeting was his idea, after all. She'd only agreed to it in order to put the matter to rest once and for all. There was no way she was suing her best friend.

"I'm sorry about what you're going through," Ben began as he sat across from them. "I've worked with families in situations like yours before, and I know how overwhelming it can feel."

Dana's hands clenched in her lap. Overwhelming didn't even begin to cover it. Nearly three weeks of sitting beside Izzy's motionless body, watching the machines breathe for her, had pushed her beyond exhaustion into a kind of numb despair.

"Why don't you start by telling me what happened?" Ben prompted gently.

Eric nodded encouragingly, but Dana shook her head. "I... I don't know where to start," she admitted, her voice trembling.

Ben leaned forward, resting his elbows on the table. "Take your time. There's no rush."

Something in his tone broke through her defenses. The story spilled out of her in halting sentences as she relived the first trip to the emergency room, then Izzy's collapse in the shower and the ambulance that had ferried them back to the hospital.

By the time she reached the moment the doctor had come out to tell them Izzy was in a coma, Dana's voice cracked. Tears streamed down her face, and she buried her head in her hands, unable to finish. Eric jumped in, explaining the discovery of

Izzy's birth control pills and the revelation that they weren't noted in Izzy's medical history.

When Eric finished, Ben sat back. "Given what you've told me about the breach in medical protocol, I think you have a case," he said in a firm, steady voice. "There are no guarantees in medical malpractice suits, of course, but I'd love to help you get some accountability for what happened to your daughter."

Dana looked away, her gaze unfocused. Accountability—as in Padma. Was she really responsible for this? Had her best friend actually caused her daughter's coma? Her throat tightened in anger. She'd trusted Padma—and look what had happened. Still, even being here in this conference room felt like a betrayal of their friendship.

"She's my best friend," she blurted.

Ben looked confused.

"The doctor," Dana explained. "The one who didn't take the full medical history. We've been friends for years."

"Honey, this isn't personal—" Eric began.

"Suing someone isn't personal?" Dana interjected.

"Mrs. Blair," Ben added, his tone gentle but practical, "I'm so sorry to learn of this... complication. But I feel compelled to point out that a malpractice suit isn't just about accountability. It can help with the financial burden. You and your husband are about to face some significant medical bills—possibly for quite a long time. The goal of a suit like this is to ensure your family's financial well-being is protected."

Dana's chest tightened. The expense of Izzy's situation hadn't even occurred to her. She was barely keeping Haven and Hearth open; there was no way she could bear any more debt. Her mind raced and she felt something inside her waver.

As they wrapped up the meeting, Ben shook her hand firmly, his gaze meeting hers. "Whatever you decide, I'm here for you. You don't have to go through this alone."

Dana and Eric left the office in silence. As they walked to

the car, Dana's thoughts swirled, leaving her lightheaded. She reached for Eric's hand, needing something solid to anchor her.

"I don't think I can do this," she admitted, her voice barely above a whisper.

Eric's face twisted, pained but resolute. "Look, I know she's your friend—"

"*Best* friend," Dana corrected, dropping his hand.

Eric pressed his lips together in a grim line. "Fine. Best friend. But Izzy is our *daughter*, Dana. It's our job to protect her. Simple as that."

A surge of guilt and rage flared in Dana's chest, burning hot and fast. How dare he? She knew better than anyone what it meant to protect their children, to sacrifice for them. Just because she'd been preoccupied by the financial strain of keeping the shop afloat, just because she hadn't been as present as she should have been with Ian and Izzy, didn't mean he had the right to question her love or her instincts as a mother.

"Of course I know that," she snapped. But if it was as simple as he claimed, why did it feel like her chest was being torn apart? Why did protecting Izzy have to come at the cost of betraying Padma, the person who had stood beside her through every moment that Eric hadn't. The thought carved a hollow ache in her, one that no justification could fill.

They continued walking toward the car in silence. When they reached it, Dana swallowed, hard and painful, like her throat was suddenly filled with gravel. "Do you really think this is the right thing to do?" she asked, her voice low and scratchy.

Eric turned to face her, his face grim and pleading. "All I'm asking is that you don't rule it out," he said.

Dana gave a small, reluctant nod and climbed into the car. As Eric started the engine and drove back to the hospital, she leaned her forehead against the cool glass of the window and watched the city blurring past.

SIXTEEN

IAN

Twenty-one days after

The moment Ian stepped into the hospital after school, he felt his jaw unclench and the tightness in his chest ease. It wasn't that he liked the fluorescent lighting or the smell of bleach—it was that Izzy was here.

Ian hated being at school without her, despite the fact that normally they barely saw each other during the day. Izzy was in all the AP classes, and while they had the same lunch period, Izzy ate in the cafeteria with Maeve and her other high-achieving friends, while Ian and his friends grabbed food from the vending machines and hung out in the parking lot trying out skateboard tricks. Lately lunch was also about how far into the day Ian was able to get before he needed another pill, either a benzo if he was feeling too high strung from the Adderall he'd started the day with, or another round of Addy to keep him focused for the afternoon.

Still, knowing Izzy was in the same building made him feel settled, somehow, like all of him was present. He hated the days she had to leave school early for cross-country meets. Those days, he felt off balance, as if he'd left the house forgetting something important but couldn't quite remember what.

Now, as he moved through the hospital lobby, Ian waved to the receptionist and fist-bumped the security guard—both familiar faces after three weeks of near-daily visits. Taking the elevator to the ICU floor, he knew his parents would already be there—they barely left.

Pausing outside Izzy's room, Ian took a deep breath to steel himself. Being near her brought a sense of relief, but seeing her pale and motionless still felt like a punch to the gut.

When he stepped inside, his parents were on opposite sides of Izzy's bed, as far apart as the small room allowed.

"Hey, sweetheart," his mom said, offering a tired smile. "How was school?"

"How was your History test?" his dad asked before he could reply.

"Uh, fine, I think." Ian shrugged. Not fine, if he were honest. Without Izzy to help him cram, he'd probably bombed it. Maybe his teacher would take pity on him.

He was definitely getting special treatment at school because of Izzy—constant comments about how sorry everyone was, how great Izzy was, how unbelievable it was that this had happened to *her*, as if someone else deserved to be in a coma more than she did. Someone like him.

The worst were the girls who started by saying how hard it must be for him, only to end up crying about how upset *they* were. Some even hugged him, which was super awkward. More than once, during these encounters, he'd caught Maeve's eye across the hallway, and they'd shared a private eyeroll.

"Honey," his dad said, moving to stand behind his mom's chair, "why don't you go home and grab a nap or a hot bath? Ian and I can hold down the fort."

Ian watched his mom tense as his dad approached, then bite her lip and glance toward Izzy.

"She'll be fine," his dad said softly.

After a pause, his mom nodded and rose. "I'll be back in an hour, tops," she said, looking past his dad at Ian.

Once his mom left, Ian sat beside his dad near Izzy's bed.

His dad reached over and ruffled his hair, like he used to when Ian was little. "So, what's new?" he asked.

Ian leaned into the his dad realizing how much he missed being touched. Over the past couple of years, he'd stopped accepting hugs from his parents, and eventually, they'd stopped offering. But now he missed it. Sometimes he picked fights with Izzy just to get her to tackle him or pull his hair. He missed the nights when, despite having separate rooms, they'd sleep back-to-back in one bed.

"Same old," he said, not even knowing where to begin.

His dad leaned sideways until their shoulders touched. "I know it must be hard being back at school while Izzy's... here," he said.

"Yeah, it's not great," Ian muttered. He hoped this wasn't about to turn into a heart-to-heart. Over the past year, his dad had started talking like a life coach, throwing around phrases like "growth mindset" and "limiting beliefs." It was like his dad had suddenly realized how much more energy they'd always devoted to Izzy and was trying to make up for it—but it was way too late. Ian had already gotten used to blending into the background and staying under the radar. Most of the time, he preferred it that way.

Ian braced himself for a talk about self-awareness and resilience, but his dad stayed quiet, still leaning his shoulder against Ian's.

"I think I'll grab a cup of coffee," his dad said after a few minutes. "Can I get you anything?"

Ian shook his head. Once his dad left, he turned to Izzy, realizing it was the first time they'd been alone together in the last two weeks without the ever-present hovering of at least one of his parents. "OK, seriously, Izzy—Taylor Andrews?" he said, his voice full of disbelief. Maeve had told him Izzy had been hooking up with Taylor, their school's star football player and resident dumb jock, for months, and he still couldn't wrap his head around it.

Izzy's ventilator hissed gently in response.

"The guy's a total douche," Ian continued. "Like if you were casting a toxic high school jock in a teen movie, it'd be him."

He angled his chair to get a better look at Izzy's face, her slack features like someone had pressed pause on her and forgotten to hit play again. "And if he likes you, he should ask you out on an actual date. Like, in public. Why do girls let guys get away with that shit?"

He paused, thinking of the girls he'd ghosted after sneaking out of basements or cars before their parents got home. He always felt a flicker of guilt after, but it hadn't stopped him from doing it again—just like with the pills. He shook his head.

"Yeah, I know what you'd say." His voice softened. "But you've got so much more going for you than Emerson or Kylie." A crooked grin tugged at his mouth. "Fine, OK, also Zanaiya and Hannah. But seriously, Iz, Taylor Andrews? Have some self-worth. Be with someone who's proud to be with you."

He shook his head. He didn't understand why girls let themselves be treated like crap—and yeah, he knew he probably shouldn't take advantage of that, but they made it so easy. They'd look at him like he was the answer to a question they hadn't even asked, and for a little while, it felt like maybe he was. Hooking up was like the pills—it took him out of his head, let him forget he was a loser who didn't have his life figured out when everyone else seemed to.

He sighed, closing his eyes and picturing how Izzy would react to his lecture. "Yeah, I know," he said aloud. "I sound like Dad. I'll stop. You get it."

His eyes flew open at a noise behind him.

"Hey," Tonya greeted, waving as she stepped in, her hot pink scrubs bright against the sterile room, her braids piled in a topknot. "Sorry to interrupt. Sounded like some intense conversation. Relationship drama?"

Ian's cheeks burned. "Yeah, I just—I mean..." He trailed off.

"You don't have to explain," Tonya said with a grin. "I was a teenage girl once, too. It's the worst." She held up a blood pressure cuff. "I'll be quick. Just need to check her vitals."

Ian watched as Tonya moved efficiently around Izzy, adjusting machines and jotting notes.

"All done," she said after a moment. "You can get back to lecturing your sister."

"I'm not—it's just, of all the guys for her to like, you know?" Ian threw up his hands, exasperated.

Tonya smiled knowingly. "People have to make their own mistakes. Also, forgive me, but what makes *you* an expert on healthy relationships?" She raised an eyebrow. "I mean, *also* Zanaiya and Hannah?"

Ian groaned, his face reddening. Tonya's grin widened. "Relax, I'm teasing. It's good you're keeping it real with her." She glanced around. "It's been a little, um, tense around here lately."

Ian gave a wry smile. "Yeah, well, that's kind of my mom's MO—tense."

Tonya's expression softened. "I get the feeling she's carrying a lot, even beyond this." She gestured toward Izzy. "Maybe cut her a little slack."

Ian shrugged. "Yeah, OK, whatever."

Tonya waved as she left. "See you later."

"See you," Ian muttered, slumping back into his chair.

He scooted his chair closer to the bed and sat in silence. Izzy's chest rose and fell in steady rhythm, and a vise tightened around Ian's heart. "The only thing Mom has going on," he said bitterly, "is wishing it was me in that bed instead of you." He reached out and clasped his sister's limp hand. "I wish it was me, too, Iz. You know I'd trade places in a heartbeat."

His voice cracked. "You'd kill me if you knew half the crap I've pulled," he muttered. But her silence didn't make it any easier to confess. It only reminded him of everything he should have said when she could still hear him. Brushing at his cheek, he realized it was wet with tears. "You've gotta pull through this," he pleaded. "You can't leave me. Please. I'll do anything. I'll study more, cut back on the pills, join Student Council, feed orphans—whatever it takes. Just wake up, Izzy. Please wake up."

Tears spilled over as he clutched her hand, but beyond the sadness, a strange bloom of hope stirred in his chest. What would it feel like not to see disappointed gazes from his teachers or hear the frustrated sighs of his father? Being good had always been Izzy's thing, but maybe he could pull it off, too—at least for a little while.

He wiped his face and leaned forward, resting his head and chest on the bed. He was so tired. He stayed like that for minutes until the thought of his dad or Tonya walking in made him straighten. Releasing Izzy's hand, he rubbed his face.

His phone buzzed in his pocket. Jenner had texted.

Hey man, party at Sadie's tonight, you in?

Ian hesitated. Sadie Kemp's parties, packed with wannabe TikTok influencers and the school's star jocks, weren't his scene.

Max gonna be there?

Ian's pill stash was running low again and Max, Sadie's college-age brother, was usually a good source of replenishment.

yeah I think so.

Ian slipped his phone back into his pocket, feeling the pleasant rush he always got at the possibility of scoring.

"One last time," he murmured to Izzy. "Then I'll be good, I promise."

SEVENTEEN

DANA

Twenty-one days after

Dana paced the hallway outside Izzy's hospital room, gripping her phone tightly. "Mom, we've been over this," she said. "The doctors here are already consulting specialists—"

"But don't you want to exhaust every option?" her mother interrupted. "This is your daughter we're talking about."

Dana pinched the bridge of her nose, willing herself not to snap. "Yes, and I've spent every minute at her bedside. I know what's best for her."

"I'm sure you do, honey," Cora said, her dismissive tone making Dana's stomach twist with resentment. "But the doctors here already missed something critical once, didn't they? You can't just trust them blindly. It's your responsibility to make sure Izzy gets the absolute best."

Dana's jaw tightened. "I am making sure. I'm doing everything I can."

"I'm just saying," Cora pressed, "I can help. Make some calls—"

"Mom, no," Dana snapped, her voice rising. "I don't need you to take over."

There was a pause, heavy and pointed, before Cora shifted gears. "I had a message from SueEllen earlier," she said briskly. "Something about a payroll glitch at the shop? She didn't want to bother you, so she reached out."

Dana's chest tightened, her mind racing to the pile of bills she hadn't touched in weeks. She hesitated, wondering if she should finally come clean. She shuddered in humiliation, imagining the judgment from her mother. "It's ‚fine," she said quickly, forcing calm into her voice. "Nothing serious."

"Well, you know I'm happy to help—"

"I said I'll handle it," Dana repeated, her words sharper than she intended. Getting honest with her mother about Haven and Hearth's financial jeopardy would have to wait; she couldn't stomach it right now.

Another pause. "All right, if you insist."

After ending the call, Dana sank into the stiff vinyl chair by Izzy's bed, her body heavy with the weight of her mother's words. She reached for Izzy's arm, her fingers brushing the soft, unresponsive skin, as though the motion might ground her— might remind her of the only thing that truly mattered right now. But even as she sat there, her thoughts frayed, unraveling into worries about the shop—the mounting bills and SueEllen's increasingly concerned texts.

Her phone buzzed again, the vibration sharp and insistent against the silence of the room. Her first instinct was to ignore it, to let the world fall away for a moment. But glancing down, she saw Ben Ricard's name on the screen.

"Hello, Mrs. Blair," he said. "Is now a good time to talk for a minute?"

Dana glanced at Izzy, at the slow rise and fall of her chest. "It's fine," she said, smoothing a hand over her daughter's arm. In truth, she had no idea what *fine* felt like anymore.

"Good," he said. "I just wanted to see if you'd given any more thought to our meeting. I thought perhaps it could be helpful for me to walk through the process—should you decide to move forward."

"Sure," Dana said, nodding as she continued to stroke Izzy's arm with one hand and held the phone to her ear with the other. She tried to focus on what Ben was saying, but his words came rapid-fire, filled with legal jargon—*discovery phase, breach of duty, deposition.* A tight knot formed in her chest.

"Look, I know this is a lot to process," Ben said, sensing her hesitation. "But the fact remains: A mistake was made. Right now, we don't know how it will impact Izzy's life—and yours— in the long term, but you deserve to be able to plan for every possible contingency." His voice was smooth and reassuring. "Izzy's current care is going to be expensive, and I know you don't want to think about it, but imagine the worst-case scenario: your daughter needing long-term care, even after you and your husband are gone. Who's going to provide for that?"

Dana sucked in a breath and gripped Izzy's arm as though she could tether them together for eternity. Ben had made this same argument when she and Eric had initially met with him, but somehow sitting there listening to the steady hiss of Izzy's ventilator, it landed differently. What if he was right—what if Izzy never woke up? The thought wrapped itself around Dana like a vice, squeezing the air from her lungs as her mind betrayed her with images of years ticking by: Izzy here in this sterile room, her chest rising and falling with the rhythm of a machine, while the world outside spun forward. She pictured Izzy growing older, the soft curves of her youth giving way to a body time would sculpt without her consent, a future spent tethered to a bed instead of chasing the dreams Dana had for her—college, a career, marriage, children of her own. The milestones that once felt inevitable now dangled just out of reach, like stars she couldn't touch no matter how far she stretched.

A slow, deep crack began to splinter through Dana's heart, widening with each dreadful scenario she conjured. What kind of life was this, really? Could it even be called living?

And yet—the alternative loomed like a shadow at the edge of her thoughts, too monstrous to fully face. A world without Izzy. A life without her daughter's brilliant smile, her stubborn fire, her quiet moments of kindness that always seemed to catch Dana off guard. The mere thought of it made Dana's chest seize, as if her ribs were caving in. She clutched at her stomach, as if she could physically hold herself together, and shook her head to dispel the horrific image.

She forced herself to refocus on the conversation with Ben, the only thing she could control in the moment.

"How would being... provided for work, exactly?" she asked, trying to push away her guilt at asking the question.

"An insurance payout—which I believe is likely in this scenario—will help with all of that."

"The insurance company would pay, not Padma?" Dana asked. Her mind swirled, envisioning the medical bills that were surely headed their way, not to mention all of Haven and Hearth's overdue bills.

"Correct. Essentially there's no financial risk for the doctor," Ben confirmed. "Their life continues as normal. Though of course we hope they're more careful with how they practice medicine going forward." He paused. "Mrs. Blair, I understand that this may feel complicated due to your prior relationship with Dr. Paulsen. But I believe doctors, in whom we place our trust, should be held accountable when they make mistakes that endanger others. In the end, knowing there are consequences for their actions is often part of what makes someone a better, more conscientious doctor."

Dana thought of Padma. Dana had never had any reason to believe her friend wasn't a good doctor. She knew about the nearly tragic incident from Padma's past, of course, but that was different... wasn't it?

"No one will blame you for taking action, Mrs. Blair," Ben said. "All they'll see is a mother trying to protect her daughter. It's not personal."

Looking down at Izzy, Dana pressed her trembling lips together. She would do anything for her daughter. "OK," she said to Ben. "Let's move forward."

She hung up feeling lightheaded, her heart racing.

Eric entered just then, carrying two cups of coffee. "Who was that?" he asked, handing one to her.

"Ben," Dana replied, accepting the familiar light brown hospital cafeteria cup. She tugged at a strand of her hair, her gaze fixed on the floor near Eric's feet. "I, um, decided we should move forward with it. At least for now." The words felt heavy as she spoke them, unleashing a flood of guilt. Realizing she was still gripping her phone, she had the sudden, overwhelming urge to call Ben back and undo it all.

"The lawsuit?" Eric sank into the chair beside her, his expression shifting to shock. He sat back, clearly processing. "I never thought you'd do it."

The way he said it stung. "What's that supposed to mean?" she asked, frowning.

"Just that you're not usually... decisive," he said carefully. "You tend to let things happen to you, not the other way around. That's what I've been trying to tell you—" He cut himself off and shook his head. "Never mind. The important thing is, you did it. You made something happen."

"But do you think it's the right thing?" she asked, unable to ignore the anguished uncertainty she still felt.

"I do," he said without hesitation. "It's complicated, obviously, but Ben has a point. We need to think about Izzy's future —and ours."

He set his coffee aside and reached for her hand. She stiffened but didn't pull away. "Doesn't it feel good to take action?" he asked, his voice low and steady. "To make something happen?"

He leaned closer, and before she could process it, his lips brushed hers. Startled, she pulled back and met his questioning gaze. For a moment, she hesitated. Then something inside her loosened, and she leaned into the kiss, letting her body answer what her mind couldn't.

His lips grew urgent, and the rush of heat between her legs felt like her body betraying her. How could she still want him, after everything?

"Wait," she breathed, pulling away. Eric's face fell.

I shouldn't do this, she thought, but the heat within her continued to build.

"Just, not here," she said, glancing toward Izzy, just feet away.

Without a word, they stood and made their way to the small bathroom, Eric's hands already roaming her body, grabbing and tugging. Dana hesitated, then pushed the door shut with her foot. She yanked up his shirt, fumbling with his zipper, feeling how ready he already was. Eric paused, looking around the bathroom with its safety bars and shower stool. "Here?" he asked. She nodded, breathing hard.

Their eyes locked, then his mouth found her collarbone as he pushed her sweater up and slid his hand into her bra. They didn't even fully undress, yanking fabric aside and bracing themselves between the wall and sink. Dana bit her thumb to smother her moans. She came before he did, then again as Eric let out a low groan and slumped against her. Together, they slid to the floor, breathless. Dana's body hummed with pleasure, but her mind raced. What had come over them? What did this mean? Did Eric still want to split up, or was this just sex?

A beep from one of Izzy's machines outside jolted her back to reality. She shot to her feet, pulling up her jeans and smoothing her hair. "What are we doing? Someone might come in," she whispered, gesturing for Eric to get up, too.

"And?" he teased, flashing a lopsided grin.

Dana raised an eyebrow, unable to hide her smile. "I'm pretty sure this isn't allowed."

Eric leaned in to kiss her again just as her phone buzzed on the bathroom floor, where it had fallen from her pocket. She reached for it, and, reluctantly, Eric stepped back. Glancing at the screen, she saw the number for Haven and Hearth. "It's SueEllen," she said apologetically. "She's been trying to reach me."

"Hello, Dana," SueEllen began, her tone unusually formal.

"SueEllen, hi!" Dana replied, forcing brightness into her voice. "I'm so sorry I haven't returned your calls. Things have been hectic at the hospital."

"I emailed, too. And texted," SueEllen said flatly.

"Give me two seconds," Dana said, covering the phone. She slipped past Izzy's bed and into the hallway. "OK, I'm here," she said once she was far enough away.

"Dana," SueEllen said, her voice softening, "your mama and I go way back, and you know I love you like a daughter. But, sweetheart, I haven't been paid in over a month."

Dana's stomach twisted, heat rising in her cheeks. She walked further down the corridor. "I'm so sorry," she said, her mind racing. Could she pull from the joint account without Eric noticing? "I'll call the payroll company today. They must not have fixed the glitch—"

"There's no glitch, Dana," SueEllen interrupted, exasperation lacing her tone. "I'm no dummy. I've seen how slow business is." Her voice softened again. "I'm sorry, honey. I know things have been hard, but I've got bills to pay, too."

"Of course," Dana said quickly, fighting the crack in her voice. "I'll fix this, I promise. Can you give me a week?"

SueEllen hesitated, then sighed. "Fine."

After the call, Dana leaned against the wall, shoulders slumping under the weight of it all. She wiped away tears, wondering if she'd ever make it through a day without crying.

"You OK?" a passing nurse asked, offering a sympathetic smile.

Dana straightened, forcing a nod. "I'm fine," she said, her voice steady. Because what other choice did she have?

EIGHTEEN
PADMA

Twenty-two days after

Padma sat on their tiny back deck, cradling her coffee mug against the chilly November morning. Halloween had come and gone over a week ago, and she'd barely noticed. Normally, it was her favorite holiday. As a child, her immigrant parents had embraced the uniquely American tradition with enthusiasm, determined to assimilate. Her typically frugal father, who begrudged even the smallest Christmas tree each year ("Why pay for something that grows everywhere?" he'd grumble), transformed on Halloween, splurging on plastic skeletons, witches, and even rigging an outdoor speaker to play "Monster Mash" on repeat for trick-or-treaters.

Usually, Padma and Lars celebrated Halloween at Dana and Eric's, enjoying cocktails—seltzer for Padma—and burgers on the grill. The tradition started years ago, with the two families taking the kids trick-or-treating before gathering for dinner as the little ones rode their sugar highs. Over time, it evolved into just the four of them sitting on the Blairs' front porch, sharing laughs and handing out candy to the neighborhood kids.

Now, Padma winced at the memory of Dana's sharp tone when she'd confronted her about Izzy's birth control pills. In the two and a half weeks since, Dana had grown distant, responding to texts with one-word replies and offering Padma a cold reception during visits to Izzy's room. The curt behavior stung, but Padma chalked it up to stress. She was used to bearing the brunt of anger from patients' families desperate for someone to blame. Still, she missed her friend—and couldn't shake the nagging guilt that she might be responsible for Izzy's condition.

"Hey." Lars slid open the glass door and stepped onto the porch. "There you are. It's early for a Saturday. You never sit out here." He wore navy sweatpants and a gray Henley, rubbing sleep from his eyes behind his dark-rimmed glasses.

"Couldn't sleep." Padma gave a tired smile. He was right— she usually took her coffee to the front porch, which was larger, screened in, and furnished more comfortably. But the back deck, with its weathered table and wobbly chairs, at least offered the chance to avoid Dana's comings and goings from the hospital. Padma still visited Izzy daily—out of love for both Izzy and Dana, but also as penance for the mistake she feared she'd made. Beyond that, she was trying to give Dana space while still quietly letting her know she was there.

"Top you up?" Lars asked, eyeing her half-empty mug. She handed it over with a nod of thanks. As he disappeared inside, she turned back to the printouts scattered across the table.

When he returned, she didn't need to taste it to know he'd made it just right: a splash of half and half and a drizzle of simple syrup.

With a sigh, she gestured to the pages. "Izzy's chart. I keep rereading it, hoping I missed something—some other explanation for what happened."

Lars frowned. "I told you, it's not your fault. You have nothing to prove. Stop torturing yourself."

"Mom?"

Padma turned to see Maeve peeking through the sliding door. She beckoned her over. "Good morning, honey. Come on out."

Maeve shivered as she stepped outside in bare feet and cotton pajama pants. "It's freezing. Why are you even out here?"

Lars raised an eyebrow. "I was wondering the same thing."

"Oh please, I grew up in Georgia," Padma said, trying to sound lighthearted. "If anyone's supposed to have thin skin, it's me, not Mr. Polar Plunge." Lars had spent his childhood in a small Swedish town, where frozen lakes and towering snowbanks were normal.

"What do you need, sweetheart?" Lars asked, tossing a playful glance at Padma.

"I was wondering if you're going to the hospital this morning," Maeve said, looking at Padma. With her lopsided bun and sleepy eyes, she looked younger than seventeen. Her long, lithe frame was just starting to fill out with curves—a late bloomer like Lars's side of the family, unlike Padma, who'd been a C cup by age twelve.

"A little later, yes," Padma replied. "Did you want to come?"

Lars frowned. "But you just got home a few hours ago. Maybe take today to relax. And to give Dana some space."

Maeve glanced between them. "Why does she need space?"

Padma stood and draped an arm over Maeve's shoulder, rubbing her goosebumps. "No reason," she said, shooting Lars a look. Maeve didn't need to be drawn into this. Besides, Padma and Dana would work it out—they'd been friends too long not to. "We'll go in a couple of hours, once visiting hours start."

Maeve nodded, yawning. "OK. I'm going back to bed."

"Good idea," Lars said. Once Maeve disappeared inside, he

rose and kissed Padma's arm, then tugged her toward the door. "Come on," he said. "We're going back to bed, too."

A little while later, Padma lay with her head on Lars's bare chest, listening to his heartbeat as she caught her breath, the sheet pulled up to cover her nakedness. At fifty-two, she was fleshier around her hips and bottom than when she and Lars first met, but he didn't seem to mind.

"We should do this more often," he said, stroking her hair.

"We should," she agreed, a smile spreading across her lips. As her body relaxed against his, she felt her eyelids grow heavy despite the three cups of coffee she'd had earlier.

"You know," he said, moving his hand to cup her breast, "if you get Toby's job, you'll have less time for things like this, not more."

She stiffened, halting his hand with her own. "Please don't try to talk me out of it—not like this." She gestured to their nakedness. "Can I at least enjoy my afterglow?"

He sighed, propping himself up on one elbow to look at her. "I just worry about you. Don't you think your job is stressful enough? And now with the whole Izzy thing... how are you, really?"

Padma rolled away in frustration. She knew exactly where this was headed.

"I'm fine," she said, forcing herself out of the warmth of the bed and starting to dress. "Still sober, going to my meetings, not thinking about drinking—because that's what you're really asking, right?" She put her hands on her hips and regarded him.

Lars bit his lip, guilt etched on his face. But could she really blame him? Outside of Dana, he was the only person to whom she had confided her story. Even her parents didn't know why she had abruptly withdrawn from medical school in her third year, opting instead to work as an office manager for a chain of dry cleaners—as far from medicine as she could get. He knew about her nightly ritual of escaping her anxiety at the bottom of a bottle of vodka and how, trembling from withdrawal after trying to quit cold turkey, she had stumbled into an AA meeting. Then another, and another, until finally, a year sober, she found a sponsor who was a doctor and had encouraged her to give medical school another try. Lars had caught her on the upswing, her life back in order, her sobriety and career firmly established.

"Hey," he said, grasping her hand. "I'm on your side, sweetie."

Padma fought the urge to pull away. She should talk to him. She knew what happened when she kept things bottled up. She bit her lip, could taste her anxiety and fear on the tip of her tongue. It would be so easy to let it all out. Instead, she sucked it all back in.

"You're thinking about last year," she muttered darkly. A shadow crossed his face. "I knew it," she said, shame and anger flooding her. She looked away. "I slipped, OK? But I caught it, and I'm fine."

She closed her eyes, the memory rushing back. After oral surgery for an abscessed tooth, she'd been prescribed Vicodin. With twenty-five years of sobriety under her belt, she told herself she could handle it—pills had never been her problem, anyway, only booze. She'd opted not to mention the prescription to Jamie, her sponsor, which should've been her first clue it wasn't a good idea. Two days in, she found herself white-knuckling through the pain to hoard pills and take more than the recommended dose at once. She was rewarded with the same pleasant numbness she used to find in a bottle of vodka. So she did it again. And again.

Lars had sensed something was wrong, but Padma had slipped back into old habits of lying and denying. She still remembered the hurt on his face the evening she'd finally been too high to cover it up. It was the only major fight they'd ever had, but it had been a doozy. Afterward, she came clean with

Jamie and doubled down on her meetings, but it was months before she felt Lars let his guard down again.

Lars sat up in bed and reached for her hand. "Please just don't push yourself too hard, OK? You know I'd never survive without you to cook for, clean for, do your laundry, buy Christmas and birthday presents for your parents—"

Padma cut him off with a groan, but felt herself softening. "OK, you've made your point." She gave a begrudging smile as he pulled her in for a kiss.

Lars left for a run while Padma showered, and then she went to wake Maeve so they could head to the hospital to see Izzy.

"Honey?" she called, knocking gently before peeking into the darkened bedroom. "I'm heading to the hospital in about fifteen minutes if you want to come with me."

On the wall, Maeve still had the same framed poster that Padma had hung in the nursery when she found out they were having a girl: "She Believed She Could So She Did." Over the years, Maeve had added framed photos she'd taken on their family trips—a red phone booth in London, a sunset over a Swedish lake, two monkeys fighting over a banana in Costa Rica. Maeve had a natural eye for framing beautiful shots, yet when Padma suggested a photography class, she'd declined. Unlike her mother, Maeve seemed able to enjoy something without turning it into an obsession.

Maeve lifted her head from the pillow and yawned. "OK, I'll be right down."

As Padma stepped out of Maeve's room, her phone rang. She pulled it from her pocket and saw Toby's name flashing on the screen.

"Hey, Toby," she answered. "Everything OK? Do you need me to cover a shift?" Padma was usually his first call if another doctor called in sick, and she almost always said yes.

"Uh, no, nothing like that." The hitch in his voice caused goosebumps to rise on her arms.

"Is it about Izzy?" she demanded. Toby had noticed Padma slipping away to the ICU whenever she had a spare moment, and he had privately expressed concern that she was obsessing over the case.

"Izzy's fine," he said quickly. "Well, not fine, obviously, but you know, the same." He offered a nervous chuckle.

Padma felt her jaw tighten. "Then what's going on?"

"The hospital received a certified letter yesterday," he replied. "From Dana Blair's attorney."

Padma froze at the top of the stairs outside Maeve's room. "Her attorney?"

"Informing us they intend to file a malpractice suit. Against you."

NINETEEN

MAEVE

Twenty-two days after

Maeve sat up in bed, straining to catch the conversation in the hallway.

"Suing me? For malpractice?" Her mother's stunned voice carried through the crack in the door.

Now wide awake, Maeve slipped out of bed and crept closer to her door. Through the gap, Maeve saw her mother pacing the hallway, raking a hand through her damp hair.

Her mom glanced at her watch, turned, and paced back toward Maeve's room. Heart racing, Maeve darted back from the door, pressing herself against the wall, but not before she saw the shock and anguish etched on her mother's face.

"On what grounds?" Padma's voice was quieter now. Then came a short, disbelieving laugh. "This is about the birth control pills not being listed in her medical history, isn't it?" She tipped her head back in despair, her voice dropping to a whisper. "I just can't believe Dana would do this."

Maeve's chest tightened. A lawsuit? Mrs. Blair? What was happening?

Her mom walked into her own room, leaving the door ajar. Maeve tiptoed into the hallway, straining to hear, but the conversation was too muffled. Then her mom's footsteps approached.

"What's going on?" Maeve asked, trying to keep the panic out of her voice.

Her mom jumped, placing a hand on her chest. "Oh, hey, honey," she said, forcing a smile, though her brow remained furrowed with worry. "Nothing. Everything's fine."

"Izzy's mom is suing you?" Maeve blurted.

Her mom froze, her expression that of a criminal caught in a police floodlight. Several seconds passed. "It's fine," she said finally. "It's a misunderstanding, and it's going to be fine."

"But why?" Maeve felt close to tears. Growing up, she loved baking cookies with Mrs. Blair and playing dress-up with her silk scarves and costume jewelry—things she never did at home since her own mother didn't bake, nor own extraneous scarves or necklaces. Mrs. Blair had always welcomed her warmly, telling her the Blairs' home was an extension of her own.

"It's a misunderstanding," her mom repeated, sharper this time. Maeve drew back, stung, and her mom sighed, her tone softening. "I'm sorry. This is just... between the grownups, OK?" She gave a tight smile that didn't reach her eyes and stroked Maeve's cheek. "There's something I need to do. I'll see you later, all right?"

"Are you going to the hospital?" Maeve called as her mom headed downstairs. "Can I come?"

"Another time, honey," her mom said over her shoulder, then she was gone.

Tears flooded Maeve's eyes. A seismic crack had gone through her world when Izzy ended up in the hospital, and now she felt it widening to the point where her whole existence as she knew it might vanish into the crevasse.

Ducking back into her room, she grabbed her phone. She needed to get out of the house, away from her thoughts.

Starbucks run?

I'll drive.

They left their houses at the same time. Ian was in gray sweatpants and a hoodie, his hair falling adorably into his eyes. Maeve glanced down and cringed—she was still in her pajamas: flannel pants and an oversized T-shirt with a hole in the armpit. Crossing her arms against the morning chill, she wished she'd at least grabbed a jacket.

"You want to run back inside and get a jacket or something?" Ian asked.

Maeve shook her head vehemently.

He shrugged and unzipped his hoodie, handing it to her. Pulling it on, she caught the scent of laundry detergent and the faint hint of marijuana smoke.

"You OK?" he asked, giving her a sidelong glance as they climbed into the car.

"Just drive before anyone sees us," she muttered, hugging herself.

He frowned but obeyed. When they were a few blocks away he looked over at her again. "So should I ask why you don't want anyone to see us?" he said.

"Not anyone—just our parents," she admitted.

"Um, OK." He looked puzzled.

Maeve blinked rapidly, trying to fight the tears rising in her eyes. "Your mom is suing my mom," she blurted.

"What?" Ian asked, his head snapping toward her. The car swerved slightly.

"Whoa, watch out!" Maeve lunged for the wheel, yanking it just in time to avoid a parked car. Ian slammed on the brakes, and they both jerked forward.

"Shit," Ian muttered, slumping back in his seat before sitting upright again. "What the fuck? Why?"

"For malpractice. Because of Izzy."

Ian coughed like a kernel of popcorn had caught in his throat. Immediately Maeve felt a rush of guilt and fear. Ian was Izzy's brother. If her mom had done something wrong… well, whose side would he be on?

She shook her head. "I shouldn't have said anything. I shouldn't even be here with you." She moved to get out of the car and he grabbed her arm and gave it a gentle squeeze.

"No, please don't," he said. "I want you to be here with me."

Her head spun from his touch and the swirl of emotions inside her.

"Tell me what you know," Ian urged, his hazel eyes locking on hers. "Please."

A car horn blared behind them, and they both jumped.

"Fine," Maeve sighed, her lips twitching into a small smile. "But can we at least get coffee first? I'm pretty sure you owe me a Frappuccino."

TWENTY

DANA

Twenty-two days after

Dana stood in the kitchen, staring at the coffee maker as it gurgled to life, willing it to brew faster. It had been her night to sleep at home while Eric took the cot in Izzy's hospital room, but despite the high-thread-count sheets and expensive mattress, she'd barely rested. She'd tossed and turned, flipping her pillow a hundred times in search of the cool side, her last conversation with Ben replaying relentlessly in her mind—especially her final words: *Let's move forward.*

That afternoon, he'd sent over a flurry of documents, which she'd signed with the press of a button before she could second-guess herself. But as she'd lain awake, she felt like she'd boarded a speeding train, hurtling toward an unknown destination she wasn't sure she wanted to reach.

Then there was the unexpected, and frankly amazing, sex with Eric. That had sent her thoughts spiraling even faster. Did it mean they were back on track? Or had it just been an emotional escape for them both in the middle of all the chaos?

As the coffee finally began streaming into the pot, she heard the front door open. Eric strode into the kitchen, looking rumpled and tired.

"Hey," he said.

Dana's heart quickened as he moved toward her. Was he going to kiss her hello, like in the old days? And did she even want him to?

He hesitated, then settled for an awkward side hug.

"Get some sleep?" he asked.

She rubbed her eyes. "Sort of. It's hard to turn off my brain."

Eric reached for the blender on the counter. "Try meditating before bed," he suggested. "And getting more sunlight and fresh air. Your circadian rhythms are probably all messed up from spending so much time inside."

Dana yanked the coffee pot off the holder and poured the barely brewed liquid into her mug. "When exactly am I supposed to find time to meditate and bask in the sunshine?" she asked, irritation creeping into her voice.

Eric held up his hands. "Just sharing what works for me."

Dana took a sip, wincing as the scalding liquid burned her tongue.

Eric eyed her. "You're probably also drinking too much caffeine."

She set the mug down with a loud thunk. "I should get to the hospital." She'd grab coffee on the way—somewhere she wouldn't have to hear Eric's unsolicited advice.

"Sure," he said. "Oh, hey—I signed and sent all those docs back to Ben yesterday. Did you do yours?"

Dana nodded, a bitter taste rising in her throat.

"His retainer fee is *steep*," Eric said. "But we can cover it from the shop's profits, right?"

A wave of nausea rolled through her.

"I'll figure it out," she said. There was no other option.

· · ·

Dana strode down the ICU corridor, her eyes skimming the newly hung red and green decorations that had replaced the jack-o'-lanterns and skeletons. It was only the first week of November, but the halls were already decked. Normally, she'd be planning her own decorating spree, hauling out boxes of ornaments and the artificial tree the day after Thanksgiving to rouse her family from their food coma.

Coma.

She swallowed hard, her stomach twisting. Would Izzy spend Christmas like this—unmoving, unresponsive? Did it even make sense to decorate this year? A pang cut through her as she thought of their annual tradition with Padma and Maeve: taking the girls to see *The Nutcracker* and having high tea downtown. Every year, she assumed the girls would outgrow it, but they never had.

Entering Izzy's room, Dana froze. By Izzy's bedside, with her back to the door, stood Padma.

Padma turned slowly, her face streaked with tears. Dana's breath hitched. Padma wasn't a crier. Even during chemo four years ago, her coping mechanisms had been gallows humor and pistachio gelato, not tears.

"Hi," Padma said, her voice unsteady. "I was hoping we could talk."

Dana's body tensed, every muscle coiling tight. Words flickered through her mind like paper caught in the wind, none of them landing. She could barely process Padma being here, let alone the surge of emotions rising within her.

"Dana," Padma began, stepping closer, "what you're doing—it's serious."

Resentment flared hot and fast in Dana's chest. "And this isn't?" She gestured sharply toward Izzy. "My daughter in a coma—that's not serious?"

"Of course it is." Padma ran a hand through her hair, her voice breaking. "But a lawsuit? Why didn't you talk to me first?"

Dana crossed her arms. "You made a mistake," she said defensively. "This is how the system works. It's not personal." Even as she repeated Ben's words, they felt hollow.

Padma's eyes widened in disbelief. "It's not personal?" she echoed. "Dana, this is my career—my reputation!"

Dana flung her arm toward Izzy, her voice rising. "And this is my daughter! Your career will be fine, but Izzy might not be. It's my job to protect her, to fight for her, and I failed at that." Her voice hitched as her gaze locked on Padma's. "And so did you."

Padma flinched, her face crumpling. "I made a mistake," she whispered. "I'm sorry. If I could go back, I would. It's all I think about, every second of every day. But, Dana, please..." Her voice faded to a whisper as she stepped closer. "I'm on the verge of getting the job I've worked my whole life for."

Guilt and anger churned inside Dana, roiling in her stomach. She closed her eyes as memories of Padma flashed through her mind: snippets of shared laughter, complaints, confessions.

"She cried over an A—can you imagine? I worry she's too hard on herself..."

"...won't have sex for a month, then bam! Twice a day for a week!"

"...so embarrassing, they asked us to leave—all because of the peanut butter sandwich!"

"...I don't want him to ask what he can help with; I just want him to know!"

"...what's her name, the loud breather from the PTO?"

"...just feel like a bad mom sometimes, you know?"

Opening her eyes, Dana's voice turned cold. "Maybe you don't deserve it."

Padma recoiled as if she'd been slapped. Then she bit her lip and pushed past Dana out of the room.

TWENTY-ONE

IAN

Twenty-four days after

Ian sat in the school parking lot on Monday morning, staring at the brown brick facade. It loomed over him like a judgment, and he gripped the steering wheel tighter. *You can do this*, he told himself. *You don't need it.*

Friday night at Sadie's party had been a blur—loud music, sticky floors, and clusters of kids crammed onto couches or spilling onto the lawn. Jenner had wanted them to play beer pong, but Ian only had one goal: finding Sadie's brother, Max.

Max, a Georgia Tech engineering student, always seemed to have the hookup. And getting pills from him felt less like a big deal somehow. Max had his life together, Ian reasoned. *If Max can handle it, I can, too*, he thought as he pocketed the stash. He'd left early, pissing off Jenner, who'd felt ditched, but Ian wanted to enjoy the three Addys he'd popped. They hit hard, silencing the noise in his head like a wave crashing over him. He'd stayed up for hours, laser-focused on his PlayStation before finally downing two of his mom's Ativan to get a few hours of sleep.

By Sunday, he'd used more pills to power through his home-work, then spent the night tossing and turning, unable to come down.

Now it was Monday, and Ian told himself it was time to get a grip. No more pills during the week. Party on the weekends only. No problem.

Except the longer he sat in his car, the louder the anxiety roared in his chest. His mounting problems at school. Izzy in the hospital. The perpetually disappointed look on his dad's face whenever Ian failed to meet his sky-high expectations. He needed a way to shut it all out.

His hands fumbled for the gym sock stashed in the glove box. He pulled out a pill from the toe and swallowed it. Just one, to take the edge off, he told himself, already hating the lie.

Inside, the hallway was its usual chaos. Fluorescent lights buzzed like hornets, and voices ricocheted off the cinder block walls. The cacophony scraped against his nerves, so he tugged his stocking cap low over his eyes, like blinders, and ducked his head. At his locker, he grabbed a textbook then slammed it shut, eager to escape the swirl of motion and noise. For once, he made it to class early.

The English classroom offered a quiet reprieve, and Ian exhaled as he slid into his chair, waiting for the pill to kick in.

"Ian, hi."

Ian looked up to see Mr. Riley, his English teacher, walk in. Younger than most of the other teachers, Mr. Riley had messy dark blond hair and wore rumpled dress shirts, usually with the sleeves rolled up.

Ian shifted in his seat. "Oh, hey."

"Good weekend?" Mr. Riley asked, heading to his desk.

Ian's cheeks flushed.

"Yeah, it was fine," he mumbled, though the image of himself in his room, ignoring Jenner's texts and staring glassy-eyed at his PlayStation, flashed in his mind. Some friend he was.

Mr. Riley shuffled through a stack of papers. "I'm handing back *The Glass Menagerie* essays today," he said, and Ian's stomach tightened. He'd actually enjoyed this one, writing about the tension between Tom's family's expectations and his longing for freedom. He'd even drawn a parallel to his own life, touching on the disconnect he felt with his own family and how they always compared him to Izzy.

At the time, being that honest had felt cathartic—maybe even bold. Now it just felt cringey. School was Izzy's domain. She was the straight-A golden twin, while he was the screwup who barely made it to class some weeks. Why had he even bothered trying?

"Yeah?" he said, feigning disinterest.

Mr. Riley pulled a stapled essay from the pile. "You surprised me," he said, and Ian's stomach sank further. So, it was really that bad. "I appreciated your honesty. I can tell you connected with Tom." He paused. "You're a good writer, Ian. I'm glad to see you putting in the effort."

The bell rang, and students began to stream into the room as Mr. Riley placed the essay on Ian's desk. "Keep it up," he added before walking away.

Ian looked down to see a red *B+* on the paper. His shoulders dropped, and a smile tugged at his lips.

By lunchtime, the pill Ian had taken that morning had worn off, leaving his mood sharp and brittle. "Watch it, will you?" he snapped when the girl at the locker next to his clipped his arm with her backpack.

The irritation clung to him as he and Jenner hit up the vending machines for lunch. When the machine swallowed his money and left his chips dangling in the coils, Ian pounded the glass so hard Jenner flinched. "Take it easy, man," Jenner said, holding out his Snickers bar like a peace offering.

"I just want my fucking chips," Ian snapped, his voice harsher than he intended. Embarrassment surged immediately. "Sorry, dude," he muttered, shaking his head.

After school, Ian headed straight for his car, yanking open the glove box. He deserved this, he told himself, popping two pills into his mouth. A B+ on his English essay was worth celebrating, wasn't it? He swallowed the pills dry, leaning back against the seat as his phone buzzed with a text from Jenner.

Gran Turismo marathon at my place?

Gotta go to the hospital

It wasn't exactly true. No one had asked him to go, but he needed to see his sister. Maybe being near her, breathing the same air, would rub off on him somehow—like her goodness was contagious, and he was desperate to catch it.

When the elevator doors opened onto Izzy's floor, Ian found himself hoping his parents wouldn't be there. He wanted to be alone with her, to talk—really talk. But when he opened the door to her room, he froze. It wasn't his parents inside, but Maeve, sitting in the chair by Izzy's bed, her back to him as she spoke softly.

"...and then I thought, you'd have had the perfect comeback," Maeve was saying. "But I always, like, freeze in those moments."

Ian cleared his throat, and Maeve turned sharply, her face flushing crimson.

"Oh," she stammered. "Hey."

"Hey," Ian said, grinning despite himself. Her embarrassment was kind of cute.

"Sorry," she said quickly. "I was just..." She gestured vaguely at Izzy.

"Talking to her?" Ian asked, stepping farther into the room. "Yeah, I do it, too."

Maeve relaxed a little, giving him a tentative smile. "You do?"

He nodded. "Yeah. The nurse said it's good for her to hear our voices. And honestly…" He glanced around to make sure no one else was there. "I kind of like it, you know? Makes her feel less… gone."

Maeve nodded, relief washing over her. "Yeah."

They paused in silence for a moment, the quiet almost comfortable. Ian took the chair next to hers. "So, um, how are you?" he asked, folding his hands in his lap.

Maeve shrugged. "OK, I guess. School's super weird without her." She paused. "Everything's super weird without her."

"Yeah," Ian said. "I know." He opened his mouth to say more, but before he could, his mom walked in.

Her gaze landed on Maeve, her expression shifting from surprised to something harder.

"Maeve," she said sharply. "What are you doing here?"

Maeve blinked, startled. "Oh, I—I was just—"

"You should go," Ian's mom interrupted, her voice cold. "Now."

TWENTY-TWO
PADMA

Twenty-five days after

Padma poured herself a cup of coffee. She knew she shouldn't have caffeine after her overnight shift when she was about to try to go to bed, but the rich, fragrant scent was too tempting. Besides, it always took her a couple of hours to wind down enough to sleep after working.

Her phone buzzed and she saw Toby calling.

"Hey," he said, clearing his throat. "How are you?"

Padma stiffened. Toby wasn't one for greetings or small talk. "What's going on?" she asked.

"Just checking on you," he said, his tone evasive. "I thought I'd see if you wanted me to, uh, cover your shifts this week. To, you know, give you some time."

Toby had never once before offered to cover a shift for her unless she'd asked him. "You mean because my best friend's suing me?" Padma asked flatly.

"Well—" Toby hesitated. "Yeah, basically. I thought work might not be top of mind."

"Work is always top of mind, Toby."

He sighed. "That's what I worry about. You sure you don't want to take a day or two to—"

"Are you suspending me?" she demanded.

"What? No!" he exclaimed. "We're definitely not at that point."

"Yet."

She could almost hear him smoothing his hand through his gelled hair in frustration. "I'm sure this will all blow over."

"That's what I'm counting on," Padma replied, her jaw set. She hesitated. "What about..."

"The promotion?" Toby asked. He knew her so well.

"Yes." Padma tugged on a piece of her hair. "I feel guilt even thinking about it right now, but..."

Toby sighed. "I get it. Look, one in three doctors will get sued at some point. It's not unusual. As far as I know, this hasn't even made its way up the chain to Lyle and the other bigwigs who'll be making the hiring decision. And it may not, especially if this all blows over or you can settle quickly."

Padma made a face, thinking of Lyle Blankenship, the hospital's COO. He made an appearance every year at the Emergency Department's holiday party and was known for his inflated ego and loud suit jackets.

"Settle?" Padma exclaimed. "So you think I did something wrong?" Never mind that she herself still wasn't sure if she had. Having Toby think she'd made a mistake was almost more than she could bear.

"Padma, I—"

Padma heard a noise on the stairs and turned to see Maeve descending, wearing a bulky sweatshirt over jeans, her heavy backpack slung on one shoulder. "I'll talk to you later at work," she interrupted Toby.

"Are you sure you want to come—"

"I'll see you there," she said firmly, then ended the call.

"Good morning, honey," she said, turning to her daughter.

"How did you sleep?" Only then did she notice her daughter's puffy, red eyes. "Hey, everything OK?"

Maeve let her backpack fall to the kitchen floor with a thud. "No," she said, crossing her arms. "Everything is not OK."

Lars bounded down the stairs behind Maeve, fresh from the shower and dressed for work. "Good morning—" he began, then caught Maeve's dark expression. He looked from her to Padma. "What's going on?"

"Ask Mom," Maeve retorted, arching one of her thick eyebrows. Lars shot Padma a questioning look. "She wouldn't even let me see Izzy," Maeve continued, her voice quaking as she wiped her eyes. "She made me leave." She looked back at Padma, her face stony. "And it's your fault."

"What's Mom's fault? Who wouldn't let you see Izzy?" Lars asked, his eyebrows knitted together in confusion.

Padma's heart sank. It was Tuesday, a full three days since Toby had called to tell her Dana was suing, and she still hadn't told Lars. She'd meant to, but things were so busy; she'd worked an extra shift and they'd barely seen each other that week... at least that's what she was telling herself. Plus, in the back of her mind there was the hope that Dana would come around and it might all just fizzle out.

"Um, so what I think Maeve's talking about..." Padma began slowly.

"She's getting sued for medical malpractice," Maeve interjected hotly. "By Mrs. Blair."

Lars's normally neutral, Scandinavian expression turned to disbelief. He looked at Padma. "What is she talking about?"

Padma looked down at her coffee, a wave of shame crashing over her. "It's true," she said quietly. "Dana's suing. Saying I'm responsible for Izzy's coma because I didn't take a full medical history, so we didn't know she was on hormonal birth control, which likely caused the pulmonary embolism."

"Oh my God," Lars said, crossing to her and placing his

hand on her arm. "Sweetheart, that's... insane. I'm so sorry. Did you find out at work last night? You should have called me."

Padma shook her head, a sick feeling in her stomach. "Saturday."

Lars's hand fell away, and he stepped back sharply, hurt flashing across his face. "As in last weekend? And you didn't say anything?"

Padma cleared her throat and looked at Maeve, then back to Lars. "Um, maybe we should..."

But Maeve stood, arms crossed, regarding her mother. "What did you do?" she demanded, her brow furrowed. "Is Izzy... is it your fault?"

Padma inhaled sharply and set her coffee mug down, fearing it might slip from her trembling hands. She looked to Lars, hoping for compassion, but his eyes only held questions, just like Maeve's. She swallowed. She'd put off telling him because she didn't want him to know she was capable of making such a mistake.

"I'm not sure," she said to Maeve, her chest constricting as she voiced her doubts for the first time.

Maeve's eyes widened. She began to speak, but Lars raised his hand.

"Maeve," he said gently. "Can you give us a minute?"

Maeve hesitated, then nodded. "I have to get to school, anyway."

"Have a good day, sweetheart," Padma said, swallowing the tears. "I love you." She wanted to embrace her daughter, but the few feet between them suddenly felt like a chasm.

After Maeve left, she and Lars stood in silence for a minute.

"How could you not tell me?" he said finally. The hurt on his face felt like a knife twisting in her chest.

"I wanted to," she whispered. She wished he would comfort her, but instead he retreated to the other side of the kitchen island, placing his palms on the counter. "I thought I could talk

Dana out of it—make her understand it wasn't my fault." She caught herself. "At least, I don't think it was." She swallowed the lump that had appeared in her throat. "I assumed I would have known if Izzy was on the pill—Dana and I talk about everything." Her voice quavered.

The hurt and anger on Lars's face softened slightly. He reached for her hand across the island. "I'm really mad at you," he said.

"Because I screwed up?" Padma asked, tears rushing into her eyes.

He sighed exasperatedly. "Jesus, honey, no. Because you didn't tell me."

She hung her head. "I didn't want you to be disappointed."

He shook his head. "I'm not your father. I don't expect you to be perfect."

Padma tried to laugh, picturing the way her father boasted to anyone who would listen about how his only daughter was a doctor at a prestigious Atlanta hospital, but it turned into a sob instead.

Her tears caught them both off guard. In their entire relationship, she'd only cried twice—once at their wedding and once when Maeve was born. Suddenly, Lars was at her side, arms around her. "Shh," he murmured into her hair as she leaned against his chest, shoulders convulsing. "It's going to be OK."

But Padma knew that was far from the truth.

Once she'd managed to slow her sobs, Padma explained to Lars what she knew about the lawsuit. There would be a discovery period to gather evidence, a deposition, and eventually a trial if Dana didn't back down.

"You need a lawyer," Lars said grimly. "A good one."

"Toby recommended someone," Padma replied. "He said she's excellent."

"Call her today," Lars instructed.

Padma nodded, relieved that Lars was now on the case. He was the detail person in their relationship, the one who kept track of deadlines and followed up.

"I'm late for work," he said, squeezing her hand. "We'll talk more later."

Padma stood on the front steps, watching Lars's car disappear as she sipped her cold coffee. It felt fitting—she was a doctor who made terrible mistakes that endangered her patients; cold coffee was the least of what she deserved.

From the corner of her eye, she saw the Blairs' garage door open. Her body went rigid as Dana's white Escalade inched into the driveway.

Before she could stop herself, Padma was down the steps and across her driveway into Dana's. The SUV jolted to a hard stop as she approached the car and knocked on the window.

Slowly, Dana rolled it down. Her damp hair was combed back as though she'd just showered, and she wore a denim button-up shirt over black jeans.

"Maeve should be able to see Izzy," Padma blurted. "They're best friends."

A guilty, pinched expression crossed Dana's face.

"Maeve shouldn't be there while we're..." She gestured between them. "That's what my lawyer said."

"They're children, Dana," Padma pleaded. "Please. I can understand if you don't want me there, but Izzy and Maeve are practically sisters."

Dana's jaw tightened. "But they're not sisters, are they?"

"I can't imagine it," Padma said, her voice rough. "I keep trying to put myself in your shoes, Dana, picturing what it must be like to sit with Izzy, day after day, feeling what you must be feeling." A dull ache bloomed in her chest as she briefly pictured Maeve in that hospital bed instead. The thought alone sent her heart racing and her breath catching, and she pushed the image away, unable to hold it. She wanted to connect with

Dana's pain—she owed her that much—but even the thought of it was too much to bear. Tightening her hands into fists, Padma's voice dropped. "I keep asking myself if I would have done what you're doing to me."

In the car, Dana stiffened. "You have to understand—" she began.

"I don't think I could ever do that to you," Padma said quietly. But even as the words left her mouth, she felt the weight of Dana's decision pressing down, and with it, the crushing anguish behind it.

Dana's lips pressed into a thin line. "Then I guess you're a better person than me."

Padma gave a sad, short laugh. "We both know that isn't true."

Dana looked away, but not before Padma saw tears well in her eyes. But when she looked back, they were gone, replaced by a chilly gaze. "I need to get to the hospital," she said.

Padma stepped back and the car window rolled up as Dana backed into the street. In the empty driveway, Padma shivered in the chilly air and headed inside, a yawning pit of despair in her chest. In the kitchen, she poured the rest of her cold coffee down the sink. She climbed onto the counter to reach the top shelf, where Lars kept a bottle of bourbon. He liked to mix himself the occasional Old Fashioned on weekends, which Padma had never minded. After her early sobriety, she found it didn't bother her to be around others drinking—it was like a switch had flipped in her head concerning alcohol, and she never had the craving for it that she heard other alcoholics describe in her meetings.

As she turned the bottle over in her hands, feeling its weight and rubbing her thumb over the label, for the first time in a long time, Padma wanted a drink.

TWENTY-THREE
MAEVE

Twenty-five days after

Maeve slammed her locker shut as the final warning bell before class rang. She stood frozen as the hallway emptied, willing her feet to move, but they felt like they were stuck in wet cement. The night before, she'd tossed and turned, haunted as she relived Mrs. Blair's face, ordering her out of Izzy's hospital room, feeling the same sting of hurt and embarrassment flood her body every time she closed her eyes.

Finally, around eleven, she gave up and texted Ian—and he'd surprised her by texting her back immediately. She'd sat bolt upright in bed, staring at her phone for the full three minutes it took him to call, afraid to blink and miss him.

"You OK?" he'd asked without a greeting, sending a giddy rush of warmth through her. "I'm so sorry about my mom. That was so messed up."

"Yeah," she agreed.

Then he'd told her funny stories, like the time he'd chipped his front tooth at ten trying to "surf" in his wagon on the driveway. Terrified of getting in trouble, he'd tried to talk with his lips covering his teeth until his mom caught him and took him to an after-hours dentist.

She knew he was trying to cheer her up and she soaked it up. It was the most attention he'd ever given her, and when they hung up, she felt a twinge of guilt for laughing so much while her best friend was in the hospital. Still, she fell asleep with a smile, clutching her phone to her heart.

Now, another school day without Izzy stretched before her. They always walked to class and sat together at lunch with their friends—who Maeve knew well enough but mostly saw as Izzy's friends.

Without her best friend to anchor her, Maeve felt like she was drifting, unsure of who she was. And now she couldn't even visit Izzy, she remembered bitterly. The thought weighed down her chest, making it hard to breathe.

"Hey."

Maeve whirled around to see Ian standing in the nearly empty hallway, his backpack slung over one shoulder, hands buried in his camo hoodie pockets. A bolt of heat shot through her body, and an uncontrolled grin spread across her face.

"Hey," she replied.

He grinned back and her legs went wobbly. "What are you doing right now?" he asked.

She leaned against the lockers to steady herself, trying to appear nonchalant. "I have AP Calculus first period," she said.

"And you're probably getting an A, right?" he said, stepping closer. She caught the fresh scent of his deodorant mixed with something musky and had to will her knees to keep from buckling.

"Uh, yeah." She flushed, suddenly embarrassed by her academic success. It probably didn't seem cool to him.

"So then you can miss one class, right?" Ian raised an eyebrow.

Maeve felt her eyes widen. "You mean like skipping

school?" she said, immediately wishing she could take it back. He probably thought she was such a loser. Glancing over his shoulder, Ian put a finger to his lips. She blushed further and lowered her voice. "It's eight in the morning, what would we even do?"

"I don't know," he said, then winked. "But I guarantee it'll be more fun than Calculus."

Minutes later, Maeve was buckling her seatbelt in the passenger seat of Ian and Izzy's Honda CRV. "I can't believe I'm doing this," she said, ducking as he navigated out of the school parking lot.

"You don't have to, like, hide," he said, laughing. "It's not like I'm smuggling you across the border or something."

Maeve covered her eyes, her heart thudding. "I've never done this," she explained. "How does it work?"

"What do you mean?" Ian signaled and turned onto the street.

"Do they call my parents?"

"Yeah, probably."

"Wait, what? Oh my God, I'm going to be in so much trouble."

"Your best friend's in a coma," Ian scoffed. "You can get away with basically anything right now."

Maeve considered this. "I don't know," she said. "I feel like that's wearing off. It's been almost a month now. At first, everyone was coming up to me all the time—people I didn't even know knew I existed. Teachers pulling me aside and stuff. But now it feels like people are avoiding me. Right away, everyone wants to talk to the girl whose best friend's in a coma, but when she's still in a coma three weeks later, no one knows what to say anymore."

"Oh my God, yes." Ian thumped the steering wheel in agreement. "That's exactly how it is. Except for Ms. Boswell," he said, referring to their guidance counselor. "I swear I get called to her office every other day for a 'check-in.'" He made air quotes.

Maeve laughed and glanced at his profile, her eyes lingering on his jawline. If only she could reach over and trace her finger along it. "She's only met with me once," she said. "She must be trying to reform you or something."

"Many have tried, few have succeeded." Ian looked over, offering a wry smile, and Maeve's heart did a tiny cartwheel.

She turned to look out the window to hide the stupid grin plastered on her face. "So where are we going?"

"You'll see."

Ian wound them back towards their neighborhood and for a minute Maeve wondered if he was headed back to one of their houses. She wondered if she should warn him that her mom was home—though probably asleep—after working the night shift. Guilt rose in Maeve's throat as she thought about their conversation earlier that morning, where Maeve had been the one to announce to her dad that Mrs. Blair was suing Mom. Still, she couldn't believe her mom hadn't told him before then. They were always so lovey dovey and seemingly close.

"Here we are," Ian said.

Maeve looked up and saw they were parked on a dead-end street, near a tired-looking auto body shop and an old warehouse now serving as a kickboxing gym. The street was deserted, and for a moment she wondered if this was where he brought the girls he hooked up with—of which she knew there'd been a few. High school gossip traveled fast. But then he was getting out of the car, beckoning to her to do the same.

"Is this when I find out you're a serial killer?" Maeve asked, glancing around the empty street.

Ian laughed and started walking toward a small gap in the wooden fence, where a brown plaque read *Upper Creek Nature Preserve*. "Come on," he said. "We're going for a walk."

Beyond the fence, the trees parted to reveal a shaded, well-trodden trail. Maeve shivered, rubbing the goosebumps on her bare arms, wishing she'd grabbed her sweatshirt from her locker.

"Here," Ian said, noticing. He pulled off his hoodie, his T-shirt riding up to reveal his flat stomach and the waistband of his boxer shorts peeking out from his cargo pants. Maeve's cheeks burned, and she looked away.

"Thanks," she murmured, taking the hoodie and inhaling deeply, the musky scent of it making her heart race.

"This way," he said, pointing left where the path forked.

"I had no idea this was here," Maeve marveled as they followed the well-maintained path past a small clearing with two picnic tables.

"Yeah, we used to come here with my parents for picnics. Izzy and I thought it was so boring." Ian kicked a large rock aside.

They walked further until she heard running water. Following Ian off the main path onto a rougher trail that led down a sharp embankment, Maeve's nerves tingled at their proximity.

"Whoa," she cried, losing her balance as a rock slipped from under her foot. Ian grabbed her hand before she fell, then held onto her as they descended to the creek's edge. Maeve felt like fireworks might explode from her hand where he held it.

He released her as they stepped onto a wide, flat rock by the water. "Welcome," he said with a wave, then plopped down.

Maeve lowered herself onto the warm rock, shielding her eyes as she peered into the clear, shallow water. "Wanna skinny dip?" Ian teased. She jerked her head around, her eyebrows shooting up. "I'm just kidding," he added quickly. "I'm sure it's freezing."

She forced a laugh, trying to shake the image of a naked Ian from her mind. "It's pretty," she replied.

"Yeah," he agreed. "I come here a lot."

They sat in silence for a moment before Ian shifted and dug

into his pocket, pulling out a Ziploc with a joint and a plastic lighter. He held it up in invitation. Maeve's cheeks flushed. "Oh, no, thanks, I don't—I mean, I've never..."

"Never?" Ian's eyes widened. "Like, not even a tiny puff?" She shook her head. "Jeez," he sighed, stuffing the bag back into his pocket. "You've been spending way too much time with my sister."

"No, sorry," Maeve said quickly. "I didn't mean—I don't mind if you do." God, he must think she was so lame.

"Nah, it's fine." He waved his hand. "I should probably cut back, anyway... on everything." A shadow flitted across his face so fast Maeve was left wondering if it had really been there at all.

She closed her eyes, savoring the sun warming her face and the sound of the burbling water. When she opened them, she found Ian studying her intently. "What?" she asked, tucking her hair behind her ear self-consciously.

"Why are you such good friends with my sister?" he asked.

She picked a piece of lint off his sweatshirt. "We just always have been." She shrugged.

"But why?" he persisted.

She tilted her head, considering. Maeve loved being friends with Izzy because Izzy's drive and goals gave Maeve's life structure, too. Whether striving for honor roll or planning to binge *Gossip Girl* over winter break, Izzy was always working toward something, and Maeve was happy to follow. Izzy was always so sure of herself and of what she wanted, while Maeve often felt like she was still waiting for the key that would unlock her own ambitions. In the meantime, participating in Izzy's life felt like the next best thing.

She didn't know how to explain this to Ian without seeming like a pathetic loser; to make him understand that her reliance on Izzy wasn't weakness, but felt like a safe way to navigate the chaos of high school until she figured out her own life direction.

"She's... fun," she said finally. Ian snorted, and Maeve frowned. "What?"

"I would not describe my sister as fun," he replied. "I mean, I love her and everything, but I feel like achievement junkie is more her brand."

"Well, yeah, that too," Maeve admitted. Ian laughed, and warmth spread through her chest. She liked making him laugh.

Then his expression sobered, and he picked up a small rock. "At least my parents got one good one," he said, flicking it toward the water where it skipped across the surface.

Maeve watched the ripples spread. "Oh, come on, you're not so bad," she said.

He gave a dismissive shrug. "Pretty sure my mom wishes I was the one in the coma."

"Of course she doesn't!" Maeve exclaimed, horrified.

He offered a sad, lopsided smile. "It's fine. And honestly, most of the time so do I." The sadness in his eyes deepened. "It shouldn't be Izzy."

He reached for another rock, and before Maeve could think, she placed her hand over his. "Hey," she said softly. "For the record, I would never want it to be you."

He stared at her hand for a split second, then flipped his over to lace his fingers through hers. "Thanks," he said.

They sat quietly for a moment, watching the water flow by. Maeve's phone buzzed in her pocket, but she ignored it, wishing time would stand still. Then it buzzed again—and again.

"Do you, uh, need to get that?" Ian asked.

Reluctantly, she pulled her hand from his to check her phone. Two missed calls from her mom and a text flashed on the screen:

WHERE ARE YOU?? CALL ME ASAP!!

Peering over her shoulder, Ian laughed. "Uh oh," he said. "Looks like you're busted."

TWENTY-FOUR

DANA

Twenty-eight days after

Dana sat in the parking lot outside Haven and Hearth, gripping the steering wheel to steady herself. She resisted the urge to check her reflection; she already knew what she'd see—red, swollen eyes and a face that had aged a decade in weeks. She didn't want to show up looking like this, but she had no choice. Somehow an entire month had passed since she'd set foot in her store. Time at Izzy's bedside had consumed her, but reality pressed in—life outside the hospital demanded her attention. Ian was spending too much time home alone, Haven and Hearth was barely holding on, and Eric had used up his leave and returned to work. It was time she did, too.

Walking inside, she was greeted by the scent of fresh pine and cinnamon. It was mid-November, and SueEllen had transformed the shop for the holidays—garlands, twinkling lights, a festive candle near the register. Normally, they decorated together. A flicker of gratitude softened Dana's heart. SueEllen had kept things running in her absence. Without her, the store wouldn't have survived.

Dana paused to straighten a row of candles, fighting the creeping panic of stepping back into the role of business owner. Her thoughts drifted to her mother, who had left multiple voicemails over the past few days, each filled with urgent suggestions about celebrity doctors and transferring Izzy to a prestigious hospital. Dana had deleted them all. Guilt stabbed at her, but she couldn't handle Cora's need to take control right now, nor did she want to have to keep lying about the financial state of her business.

"Foot traffic is good," Dana said after the two browsing customers left empty-handed.

SueEllen shook her head. "One of them took a picture of a vase to find it cheaper online."

Dana forced a smile, even as her heart sank. "Plenty of people in this neighborhood still shop local, especially around the holidays," she said, willing herself to believe it.

SueEllen gave a grim nod, then her face softened. "How's Izzy?"

If only I knew, Dana thought. She had spent countless hours staring at Izzy's face, wondering if somewhere beneath the coma, Izzy could hear her or feel her hand clasping hers. Sometimes, when no one was around, Dana would climb into the bed and hold her daughter. As a teenager, Izzy had stopped allowing that kind of intimate, familiar touch. Dana had longed to run her fingers through Izzy's hair, to stroke her cheek without protest. Now, the irony was unbearable: She could touch her daughter all she wanted, but Izzy wasn't truly there. What she would give for just one eyeroll, one dismissive teenage shrug.

"No changes," Dana replied, forcing a smile.

SueEllen nodded, then shifted on her feet. "Can we talk?" she asked.

"Of course," Dana replied, though her stomach dropped. She couldn't keep stalling. She'd already scraped together Ben's retainer by pulling funds meant for Haven and Hearth's payroll. Last night, she'd stared at her and Eric's joint account, wondering how much she could take before he noticed. He wasn't meticulous with their finances, but he wasn't oblivious either.

"I'm resigning at the end of the week." SueEllen blinked, looking down at her feet.

Panic surged through Dana. Thanksgiving was two weeks away, kicking off the season she was counting on—praying for—to inject cash into the shop before her loan repayment hit in January. "No, SueEllen, please," she said, her voice trembling despite her effort to steady it.

"I'm sorry," SueEllen said, regret in her eyes. "I know the timing is terrible, but I've missed four paychecks now. I can't afford to work for nothing."

Dana's pulse pounded. "I'm so sorry," she said, gripping the counter to keep herself steady. "I didn't realize it had been that long," she lied. "I'll write you a personal check today. Just... don't leave. Not now."

SueEllen's face softened, but her eyes filled with pity. "Dana, I wish I could help, but I have bills, too. And with the holidays coming up, I've already found another position."

Dana felt hollow, like someone had scooped her insides out. "But how will I—who will..." Tears welled in her eyes, her throat too tight to finish.

SueEllen stepped closer, her voice thick with emotion. "You'll figure something out. You and your mother are two of the most resourceful women I know. I'm so sorry I can't stay."

Dana swallowed hard, forcing herself to stand tall. "I understand," she said, her voice clipped.

SueEllen's face crumpled. "Thank you for everything, Dana," she said softly.

Dana nodded, then turned and walked quickly toward the office, the tears she'd been holding back spilling over as soon as the door clicked shut. She collapsed into her chair and buried her face in her hands. Without SueEllen, there was no one to keep the shop open while she was at the hospital with Izzy. But closing the store during the busiest time of year wasn't an option.

SueEllen's words echoed in her mind: *You and your mother are two of the most resourceful women I know.*

People always assumed Dana was like her mother—scrappy and unshakable. But now the truth would come out. When Haven and Hearth failed, everyone would see it, including Eric and her mother.

Her phone rang, and Dana's stomach clenched as she glanced at the screen. "Hello?" she said, already bracing herself.

"Dana, it's Rhett Randolph. I'm calling about the back rent."

Despite his syrupy Southern name and slow drawl, Haven and Hearth's landlord was not one for pleasantries.

"Oh gosh, did the transfer not go through?" Dana asked, infusing her voice with an artificially bright tone. "I've been having so much trouble with those—a new system at my bank. I'll call them today and get it sorted."

"Please do," Rhett said flatly. "Three months of arrears is unacceptable. I never had these issues with your mother—"

"I said I'll call them today," Dana interrupted sharply, her patience snapping. She winced as soon as the words left her mouth and inhaled deeply, willing herself to calm down. "I'm sorry, Rhett. My daughter's been in the hospital for the past few weeks, and..." Her voice faltered, splintering into silence as she trailed off. She pressed her lips together, as though sealing them shut could keep the raw noises of despair clawing at her throat from breaking free.

"I'm sorry to hear that," Rhett said, his tone softening. "Is it serious?"

Dana gritted her teeth. "She's in a coma," she said, the

words emerging brittle and unfamiliar, as if someone else had spoken them. For a fleeting moment, she barely recognized her own voice. But then the weight of the truth hit her, and the pain of her helplessness ignited, roaring to life and feeling hot on her lips, as though she'd taken a sip of scalding coffee.

At the other end of the line there was only the sound of the sharp intake of Rhett's breath.

"Oh, Dana," he finally said. "I'm so very sorry to hear it."

"Thank you." She put her knuckle to her lips and bit down on it. The heaviness of his sympathy felt like it might crush her.

"I'll keep you in my prayers," Rhett said. "We'll talk soon."

Dana spent the rest of the day going through the motions at the shop—covering the front while SueEllen went to lunch, but mostly hiding in the back, verifying inventory and responding to messages from vendors demanding payment. Her head throbbed as she packed up to leave, avoiding SueEllen, who was busy with a customer.

Back at the hospital, Eric sat beside Izzy's bed, grading a pile of student quizzes.

"Hey," he said, glancing up as she entered. "How was the shop?"

"Not great," she sighed, massaging her temples. "SueEllen's quitting."

"What?" Eric looked up. "Why?"

For a moment, Dana considered telling him everything. Her eyes flickered toward the bathroom, recalling how, just days ago, they had fallen over each other like teenagers. She blinked back tears. For that brief moment, they had felt like a team again. She'd thought it was a turning point. But since then, they'd reverted to treating each other like near strangers. *Can't you see how much I need you?* she wanted to scream. *I don't know what I'm doing, but I can't do it alone. Please don't leave me.*

She wished she could rewind time. But how far? To the day Izzy collapsed? The therapy session when Eric had asked for a separation? The moment her mother handed her the business? She wasn't sure when things had fully derailed, but she knew she'd do anything to fix it.

"It was just time for something new for her," she said instead.

A nurse in lavender scrubs entered without knocking, barely acknowledging them as she began taking Izzy's vitals. *This is what we've become*, Dana thought. *Part of the scenery.*

The nurse rolled Izzy roughly to one side to check for bed sores, her limp arm flopping off the bed.

"Stop!" Dana cried, rushing forward. "Not like that."

The nurse set her jaw. "Ma'am, I need to check for—"

"I know," Dana snapped. "But you don't have to shove her around."

The nurse crossed her arms. "I wasn't—"

"Afternoon, all," came a cheerful voice. Dana looked up to see Dr. Roberts stepping in. "Is there a problem?"

"No problem," the nurse said stiffly.

"She was being too rough," Dana said, gesturing towards the nurse.

"I'm just doing my job!"

"That's fine, Alicia," Dr. Roberts said with a knowing look. The nurse rolled her eyes, grabbed her cart, and left.

"How are we all doing today?" Dr. Roberts asked with a congenial smile.

"Well, as you may have noticed," Dana snapped, "my daughter is still in a coma."

"Dana," Eric warned, stepping forward. He nodded at the doctor. "We're fine, just a little tired."

"We are not fine!" Dana cried, clenching her fists. "It's been a month, and no one seems to be able to help her."

Dr. Roberts nodded somberly. "I understand your frustration, Mrs. Blair. We're doing everything we can, but our resources are finite. Isabelle has been here nearly a month, and while she's stable, she's not making discernible progress." He looked between them, his face serious. "Which is why we need to discuss moving her to a step-down unit."

"A what?" Eric frowned.

"Out of the ICU," the doctor clarified. "To a unit designed for long-term care of non-responsive patients."

"Long-term?" Dana repeated. "Like how long?"

Dr. Roberts adjusted his glasses. "She's stable, which is good. But the longer she remains comatose, the slimmer her chances of recovery. It no longer makes sense for her to stay in the ICU when her bed could go to someone in critical need."

The room tilted, and Dana sat back on Izzy's bed to steady herself. A loud whooshing filled her ears, like an airplane taking off. "Someone who needs it *more*?" she managed. The helplessness was crushing. When the twins were babies, she'd had a recurring nightmare of them being swept out to sea while she stood trapped on shore, unable to reach them. Now, every minute of every day felt like that.

"Honey?" Eric's voice was gentle, his hand on her arm.

"We'd like to arrange the transfer next week," Dr. Roberts continued. "The unit is on the fifth floor. She'll receive excellent care for as long as she needs."

As long as she needs.

Dana sank onto the bed beside Izzy, her body folding around her daughter. Izzy's body, once strong and muscular, felt slight and fragile in her embrace. Pressing her face into Izzy's hair, she let her tears flow, no longer caring who might see. She was utterly spent from the futile effort of holding herself together—for what? Izzy was gone, and there was no promise that she'd ever find her way back.

TWENTY-FIVE

IAN

Thirty-one days after

Ian led Maeve down the hallway, scanning nervously for his mother as if the hospital was a haunted house and she might pop out wielding a bloodied chainsaw.

"Wait here," he murmured, nodding toward the vending alcove a few doors down from Izzy's room. Maeve's silver eyes flashed with excitement.

"I don't know," she'd said earlier when he first suggested sneaking her in. "What if we get caught?" They'd been sitting on the rock by the creek, their shoulders brushing. She smelled like tangerines and vanilla, like the creamsicles Izzy used to get from the ice cream truck. Maeve always chose chocolate-vanilla twist with rainbow sprinkles. Ian wondered if she had random memories like that about him, too.

"It's not an actual rule," he pointed out. "It's just something my mom said."

Maeve considered, then bit her lip. "Yeah, OK," she'd agreed, a sly grin spreading. "Let's do it."

Now, as Ian approached Izzy's room, he checked his phone.

Three p.m. His dad would be here by now, meaning his mom might not be. He crossed his fingers and opened the door.

The room was empty except for Izzy, and for a moment, he thought they'd lucked out. Then a toilet flushed, and his dad emerged from the bathroom.

"Hey, buddy," his dad said, tucking in his shirt. "How was school?"

"Uh, OK." Ian nodded.

"Since you're here, I need to track down some paperwork," his dad said, frowning. "They're moving Izzy out of the ICU tomorrow."

A surge of hope shot through Ian and he looked toward his sister. "Is she better?"

His father's face seemed to cave in before he composed himself. "She's the same," he said. "But since she's been stable for a few weeks, they want to free up the ICU bed and move her to a long-term care unit."

Ian's hope faded like fireworks against a night sky. "Longer term? Like how long?"

"They don't know," his father said gently.

Ian turned away before his dad could see the tears in his eyes. "Go do what you need to do, I'm here," he said gruffly.

Next to him, he felt his dad hesitate, then leave.

"Damn it," Ian muttered, wiping his eyes as he walked to Izzy's bed. "What's wrong with you?"

Anger flared hot and bright in his chest. He fought the urge to shake her. She was so goddamn good at everything—spelling bee champion, cross-country star, the one who, against all odds, had convinced their parents to extend their curfew to midnight last year. There was nothing Izzy couldn't do.

Except, apparently, wake the fuck up.

Sucking in a sharp breath, he pulled out his phone to text Maeve.

Coast clear.

A minute later, Maeve slipped in, glancing over her shoulder before closing the door. As she approached the bed, her face froze in shock. "Oh my God, she's so pale," she whispered.

"Yeah." Ian swallowed, forcing back the lump in his throat. Izzy's naturally rosy complexion had faded to a ghostly white over the past weeks. "Not a lot of rays soaking up in here. Maybe we should order her a spray tan."

But Maeve wasn't listening. A smile stretched across her face even as tears welled in her eyes. Ian had to stop himself from reaching out to wipe them away. "I'm just so happy to see her," she said, glancing at him. "Is it weird if I, like, talk to her?"

"I do it all the time," he admitted. "She's a really good listener like this."

Maeve laughed softly and perched on the bed beside Izzy. "Hey," she said. "God, it's so good to see you."

Ian felt a pang of jealousy as Maeve's attention shifted from him to Izzy. But seeing how happy she looked, he smothered the feeling. "I'll be right outside," he said, and she flashed him a grateful smile as he left the room.

In the hallway, he checked his phone: two texts from Hannah, wondering if he wanted to hang out, one from Jenner about hitting the skate park, and one from Max, replying to Ian's earlier message asking when he could buy more pills. Ian still had some, but he was rationing them, which left him on edge. Lately, he needed two or three at a time to feel anything.

Got nothing right now

Check back next week.

Ian's whole body tensed. His teeth clenched as he started

the complicated mental math—how many pills left versus how many days until next week.

"Hey, Ian."

He looked up from his phone to see Tonya in blue scrubs patterned with tiny lightning bolts.

"Oh, hey," he said.

She glanced over her shoulder and lowered her voice. "I don't mean to pry, but I saw that girl go in there—the one your mom, um... kicked out." She shifted on her feet. "Sorry, we nurses hear everything."

"It's OK," Ian said defensively. "She's with me."

"Oh no, I'm fine with it," Tonya replied, holding up her hands. "But your mom just got here. She's at the nurses' station with your dad, signing some things." She gave a half-smile. "Just thought you should know."

"Shit," Ian muttered, running a hand through his hair. "Yeah, thanks."

He yanked open the door to Izzy's room. "We gotta go," he told Maeve, who was mid-sentence, gesturing as she spoke.

"Just a minute." She waved him off.

"Like, now," he insisted, grabbing her arm. "My mom's back."

Maeve's eyes widened, and she scrambled down from the bed. "Oh, crap."

Tonya stood nearby as they slipped out.

"Take the stairs," she murmured, nodding in the opposite direction of the nurses' station.

Ian nodded, grabbing Maeve's hand and pulling her into the stairwell. They thundered down the stairs, bursting into the ground-floor lobby, panting. Despite the close call, he couldn't stop grinning. Adrenaline pumped through him—it felt like he'd just saved a puppy from a burning building. Better than any high from an orange pill bottle. He glanced at Maeve, who was grinning, too. Making her happy felt good. Making anyone happy felt good.

They stood facing each other. "You, uh, need a ride home?" he asked.

She shook her head. "I've got my car."

Ian tried to hide his disappointment. He didn't know exactly what he was feeling, just that being around her made him feel like maybe, deep down, he wasn't such a piece of crap after all. She didn't look at him the way Hannah or the other girls did—flirting, hoping to hook up. With Maeve, it felt like she actually saw him.

Maeve bit her lip. "Walk me out?"

His heart gave a tiny leap of joy, a foreign sensation.

"Yeah, sure," he said.

At her car in the parking garage, Ian climbed into the passenger seat. "Safety inspection," he said, tugging the seatbelt and jiggling the steering wheel with mock seriousness. Then he remembered—it was Maeve, not some girl he needed to impress. He leaned back.

"They're moving Izzy out of the ICU tomorrow," he said. "Somewhere for long-term care." The words made his stomach turn.

"Like she might be in a coma a long time?" The fear in Maeve's voice matched the knot in his stomach. Without thinking, he reached out and took her hand.

"Yeah."

Her fingers were cold, and he wrapped his other hand around them, warming them. The parking garage was dark and quiet, like their own private cave. He realized he liked being with Maeve. Growing up, he'd never really seen her—just assumed she was another overachiever like Izzy. But now, he sensed she was figuring herself out, just like him. Except she seemed to be doing a better job.

"You're so good," he blurted.

"At what?" She wrinkled her forehead.

"No, I mean... you're a good person."

She made a face. "That makes me sound so boring. Like, is that how I'm going to be remembered in our yearbook? *Maeve Paulsen—she was nice.*"

"I said *good*, not *nice*. But for the record, you're also nice."

"Great." She rolled her eyes.

"Is that so bad?" Ian asked softly. "I wish I was good."

"You could be," Maeve replied, and he flinched at how she didn't even bother to disagree with him.

"Nah, Izzy cornered the market on good." He turned her hand over, tracing the lines on her palm. A strange warmth tingled through him. Touching her felt so natural.

"Who Izzy is doesn't determine who you 'can be," Maeve said, squeezing his fingers. "You can be whoever you want. It's a choice, not a default."

Ian held her gaze, wondering if she could see how lost he felt. He wanted to believe her—to believe things could be different. That *he* could be different.

Instead, he looked away. "So why Taylor?" he asked, changing the subject. "What does my sister see in him?"

Disappointment flickered across Maeve's face as she pulled her hand away, leaving his feeling cold and empty.

"What do you think?" she sighed. "The same thing Hannah sees in you. Girls apparently like guys who aren't nice to them."

Ian flushed. He wasn't stupid—he knew his reputation. But hearing it from Maeve stung.

"What about you?" he asked after a beat.

"What about me?" She kept her eyes forward.

"Do you like guys who aren't nice to you?"

She turned slightly, meeting his eyes. "I don't know," she said. "Jury's still out."

TWENTY-SIX

PADMA

Thirty-two days after

As Padma drove to work, a reminder popped up on her phone: *Call Jamie.* She'd been working with her AA sponsor since before Maeve was born—her longest relationship aside from Lars. Normally, she looked forward to their twice-weekly calls, a chance to vent about work drama or world politics while Jamie reminded her she couldn't control everything.

Today, though, her stomach tightened at the thought. There was too much to talk about.

"Hey, Padma." Jamie picked up on the first ring, his gruff voice filling the car. "How's it going?"

"I'm fine," she said, forcing a breezy tone. "Just heading to work."

"Uh-huh. And how's that going?"

Jamie had never been one for small talk, which was one of the reasons Padma had gravitated to him years ago. On the surface, they were an unlikely match—she, a second-generation Indian doctor; he, a gay Black man—but his mix of humor, humility, and tough love had drawn her in.

"Oh, you know, same old," she said, adjusting her rearview mirror. "How are you?"

"You didn't call to hear about me," Jamie replied flatly. "Last I checked, you were being sued by your best friend for putting her daughter into a coma. Also, you missed Monday's meeting."

"I did?" Padma feigned surprise. "What day is it?"

"Tuesday, but I assume you know that since you're headed to work," Jamie said dryly.

Padma slumped in her seat, chastened. "OK, fine. I'm sorry. I was just so tired." She'd left work that night, hesitated for a split second before heading home instead of St. Mark's. Lars was on an overnight trip, meaning no one would question why she was home early. She could eat popcorn with M&Ms for dinner, maybe convince Maeve to watch trashy reality TV instead of sipping bad coffee in a church basement.

"Addiction doesn't take a day off," Jamie said. "So we don't, either."

"I've been sober for twenty-six years," she snapped. "Missing one meeting isn't going to tank the ship."

"Sobriety is a journey, not a destination."

"That would look nice on a throw pillow," she mused.

He snorted. "I've got a million of 'em. Want another?"

She pulled up to a red light and closed her eyes briefly, picturing the bottle of bourbon in her hands a few days ago. She'd opened it, inhaling the antiseptic, oaky smell. It had made her stomach churn but still she'd had to stop herself from putting the bottle to her lips. She shuddered at how close she'd come. "I'll be there next week, I promise," she said.

At work, Padma pulled her hair into a tight braid and grabbed her charts. She was heading to see her first patient when Toby appeared.

"Hey, can we talk?" he asked. His white coat bore the stains of his breakfast—egg and cheese on a roll with extra Tabasco from the bagel shop in the lobby.

"Hello to you, too, Toby," she replied pointedly. "How are you, et cetera."

He shook his head. "Please, we've known each other too long for that."

Padma followed him into his office, aware of the three nurses nearby watching her. For a moment, she wondered if they knew. Toby was the only person outside her family who knew about the lawsuit, and she preferred to keep it that way. It wasn't like she had anything to hide. She just didn't want it to become a distraction.

"What's up?" she asked, surprised when he shut the door behind them.

He clicked his pen, hesitating. "Just wanted to check in," he said.

She eyed him. "And?"

He sighed, sinking into his leather chair, which creaked under his weight. "Everyone knows."

Padma froze. "About the lawsuit?"

He nodded. "I heard Jasmine and the other nurses talking this morning. And if Jasmine knows..."

"Then everyone knows." Stomach acid rose into her throat. She imagined walking back onto the floor, giving orders to Jasmine or consulting with other doctors, while they stared at her, knowing what had happened. She'd always been the go-to for gut checks or second opinions on patients—but what would they think of her now? Her heart clenched. "Lyle, too?" she asked.

Toby looked away, then back, nodding.

"I'm on your side," he said. "I want you to know that."

"But?"

He sighed. "It's not a sympathetic story—teenage girl in a coma, devastated parents. And the media is poking around."

Padma felt her heart skid off course. She gripped the back of the chair in front of her.

"Lyle doesn't know that part—yet," Toby continued. "I'm trying to shut them down with HIPAA, privacy laws, all that. But I can't stop the family from talking." He met her eyes, his face lined with sympathy. "I thought you should know."

Padma nodded, struggling to breathe. Toby stood and guided her into the chair. "Shit, Padma, I'm sorry," he said, running a hand through his hair. "It's the pits. But you'll get through it."

"I'm meeting with the lawyer today—Sharon," she offered. "Deposition prep."

Toby whistled. "That's fast. I figured the plaintiff would want more time in discovery."

Padma winced at the word *plaintiff*. It sounded so official.

He noticed and his face softened. "Let me know how it goes, OK? I'm here for you." He squeezed her shoulder. "I've got a meeting, but sit here if you need a minute."

She nodded, blinking back tears as he left. Glancing around the office, she tried to picture it as hers—her family photos on the desk instead of Toby's, her medical licenses on the wall. She eyed the messy stacks of paper. God knows she'd keep it neater than Toby did.

But just as she grasped the vision, it grew fuzzy and faded. Her dream job, once so close, now felt like it was slipping through her fingers. And she had no idea how to stop it—how to stop any of this.

Padma spent the rest of the day feeling the weight of her colleagues' gazes—real or imagined. Conversations stalled when she approached, and she found herself triple-checking every medication order, repeating questions to patients to cover her bases. The extra caution left her scrambling to keep up, skipping her usual break just to stay on track.

As she rushed between exam rooms, her thoughts pingponged around in her head. Would Dana really speak to the media? What did that even mean? Would reporters show up outside her house? Should she stop letting Maeve drive alone? Get a security system?

By the end of her shift, she was as drained as she'd been in med school, when everything was new and overwhelming. It was only four p.m., but all she wanted was to collapse into bed. Instead, she had a meeting with her lawyer.

Her lawyer.

The words made her stomach churn. That she even *needed* a lawyer felt surreal.

Yet here she was, driving to meet Sharon Callaway, preparing for a deposition that was now just two days away.

"A deposition is where the opposing attorney questions you about your treatment, medical decisions, and the facts of the case," Sharon had explained during their first call. "It's an interview—less formal than a courtroom, but your answers are recorded and can be used later in trial. It's nothing to worry about unless there's something you haven't told me. We'll prepare so you feel confident explaining the medical care you provided. I'll be with you the entire time to protect your interests and keep the questioning fair."

It sounded simple, but when Padma arrived, she saw a video camera set up in the conference room.

"It's for our practice session," Sharon said. Tall and broadshouldered, she wore her steel-gray hair in a sharp bob and red lipstick that somehow looked both commanding and effortless. "I'll ask you to watch it after, so you can see how you come across."

Padma felt sweat prickle on her back. "And how should I

come across?" she asked, wiping her palms on the jeans she'd changed into after work.

Sharon smiled, revealing a small gap between her front teeth that somehow looked stylish. "Like what you are—a compassionate, knowledgeable doctor."

Guilt tightened in Padma's chest. She'd built her career on precision, becoming a by-the-book physician after the Julia Kim incident. Perfection was her only acceptable standard. She knew this made her hard to work with and that many of the nurses weren't her biggest fans. But it also made her unimpeachable. And yet, the one time she'd glossed over something— just once—Izzy ended up in a coma. A chill ran through her. But medical malpractice? This wasn't like Julia Kim. She hadn't been drinking. She'd been careful. She'd done all the right things.

Almost.

Padma tugged at a strand of hair, her gaze flicking to Sharon's steady, encouraging expression. "Does the deposition cover anything... historical?" she asked, her throat tight.

"Generally, no," Sharon replied. "It focuses on the incident in question. I'm also working on securing a medical expert who will confirm you acted in good faith and followed standard procedures."

Padma pulled harder, a sharp sting at her scalp. "What if I didn't?" she murmured.

Sharon folded her hands, her tone turning firm. "Dr. Paulsen, I understand the guilt you're feeling. I see it all the time. But from everything I've reviewed, you did nothing wrong. The nurse should have recorded Izzy's medical history before you even saw her."

"Things move fast in the ER." Padma forced a tight smile.

"They do," Sharon agreed. "But you're not responsible for all of them." She gestured toward the camera. "Now, shall we begin?"

TWENTY-SEVEN
DANA

Thirty-two days after

Dana pulled open the blinds in Izzy's new room, letting in the soft morning light. The space was larger than the ICU's, warmer, less sterile. The armchair in the corner, which unfolded into a bed, had been far kinder to Dana's back last night than the ICU cot had.

Walking the hall earlier, she'd peeked into rooms adorned with throw pillows, potted plants, and bulletin boards cluttered with photos and get-well cards. Long-term patients. The thought sent a shiver down her spine. But unlike the ICU, the floor felt less urgent. The constant crackle of the intercom was replaced by the sounds of television and cheerful conversation spilling from many rooms. The nurses moved more slowly. Everyone smiled more.

In short, the entire floor seemed designed to encourage settling in and getting comfortable—which Dana was determined not to do.

"Good morning, sweetheart," she said to Izzy. "Rise and shine." She smoothed Izzy's hair and kissed her warm, soft skin.

She thought back to when the twins were babies, how she'd loved dozing beside them, stroking their velvety cheeks. Ian had been the easy one—breastfeeding easily, sleeping through the night early. Izzy had been demanding, her little face turning purple with fury if she had to wait too long to be fed or held.

That intensity never faded. As a toddler, Izzy thrived on structure, while Ian chafed under rules. She still remembered his tiny frown and the way he clung to her during school drop-offs, while Izzy ran inside, eager for praise and gold stars.

Dana picked up a brush from the nightstand and ran it through Izzy's hair, working out the snarls. It was a beautiful shade—rich brown with auburn strands. She absently touched her own hair, remembering the gray roots she'd spotted yesterday. She was overdue for a touchup, but the thought of sitting in a salon for two hours, pretending life was normal, felt impossible.

Glancing at her watch, she tensed. If she didn't leave now, she'd be late for her meeting with Ben. The last thing she wanted was to walk away from Izzy, but the demands of life outside the hospital refused to wait.

"I'll be back as soon as I can," she murmured, bending to kiss Izzy's forehead. The only response was the steady hiss of the ventilator.

Her phone rang as she headed for the elevator, and her and Eric's wedding picture flashed on the screen—both of them smiling, faces turned toward each other. A pang of regret hit her. She really needed to update that photo.

"Hi," she answered. "I only have a minute—I'm on my way to meet Ben."

"Oh, right," Eric said. "I'll be quick. I was just trying to place an order for my classroom, but the credit card won't go through. Can you look into it?"

She bit back a sigh. The problem with the credit card was

that it was maxed out. She'd have to shuffle money around again —or finally tell Eric the truth.

"I'll figure it out," she said, exhaustion settling over her.

"Cool, thanks," he said. There was a pause. "Well, um, have a good meeting. Bye."

"Bye."

The transactional nature of the conversation stung. Dana leaned against the wall by the elevator, closing her eyes and briefly wishing she could stay there forever.

Arriving at Ben's Midtown office, Dana immediately felt underdressed in black leggings and an oversized sweater. Her eyes swept over the leather furniture, mentally calculating its cost. No wonder he was so expensive.

A young, blonde receptionist led her to a sleek conference room with frosted windows and metal-and-glass furniture. Dana sank into an office chair, fumbling to adjust the height, feeling small until Ben arrived a minute later.

"Mrs. Blair," he greeted, shaking her hand, his white teeth gleaming. Tall and lanky in a slim-cut navy suit, he towered over her. His receding blond hair and angular features gave him the look of a young Kevin Bacon.

"Shall we?" he asked, dropping a folder on the table.

Dana nodded, appreciating his directness. She was grateful he hadn't asked how she was. Sympathy was exhausting, and no one wanted the truth: that she was angry and bitter most of the time, that while she desperately wanted Izzy to wake up, she feared Eric would leave her once she did, and that she worried she was failing her other, conscious child by spending all her time at Izzy's bedside—who might not even know she was there.

"So," Ben said, opening the thick folder, "my team has been doing some digging and so far we haven't come up with much."

"What do you mean?" Dana asked, trying to sit taller.

Ben tapped a printout with his index finger. "Meaning that much of what happened that day in the exam room is open to interpretation—who should have done what, et cetera. So, we've been looking into Dr. Paulsen's work history, to see if there is anything there."

Dana felt a twinge at hearing him refer to Padma so formally. It stirred the same old doubts lurking in the back of her mind, questioning whether she was truly doing the right thing in pursuing a lawsuit. She wished Eric were here to reassure her, but he had to be at work—one of them needed to keep a steady income.

"Her work history?" she asked, frowning. "I thought the deposition was limited to the, um, incident." She tried not to cringe at the cold, clinical term for what had happened to her daughter.

"True," Ben said, nodding. "But if there's anything in Dr. Paulsen's background—a pattern of negligence, for example— we might be able to introduce it. And once it's on the record, it has to be considered." He tapped the folder. "So far, all I see is that she works a lot—maybe excessively—which we could argue led to fatigue and impaired judgment. But there are no past incidents or disciplinary actions."

"Padma loves her job," Dana murmured.

Ben frowned. "If this goes to trial, we need the jury not just on your side, but against Dr. Paulsen." Dana felt another twinge of doubt but pushed it down. "They'll sympathize with Izzy's condition, but we need clear evidence of repeated negligence, not just a single mistake. And with the deposition on Thursday, we're running out of time."

Dana gripped the chair's arms as nausea churned at the words "trial" and "jury."

Ben leaned forward. "I understand you and Dr. Paulsen have known each other a long time. Can you think of anything

—anything she's told you—that might suggest a pattern of negligence?"

A cold sweat prickled Dana's neck. Ben's eyes flickered with interest before settling into a sympathetic smile. "Remember, Mrs. Blair, this is for Izzy."

The room spun slightly. Dana sat in silence as Ben watched her, waiting. Finally, she swallowed hard and said, "There is one thing…"

TWENTY-EIGHT
PADMA

Thirty-four days after

Padma sat stiffly in the stark conference room, where the furniture seemed designed for discomfort. She clasped her hands in her lap, her white button-up and gray blazer suddenly stifling. The fluorescent lights buzzed overhead, casting harsh shadows. Across from her, Ben Ricard, Dana's attorney, watched with cold blue eyes, the voice recorder between them humming softly. Sharon sat beside her, offering a reassuring presence, but it did little to ease the tightness in Padma's chest.

So far, the deposition had been straightforward—questions about her education and work history, all easily answered with a yes or no. But now, as Mr. Ricard turned to his next set of questions, Padma felt the energy in the room shift.

"Dr. Paulsen," Ben said, leaning forward, elbows on the table. "Can you walk us through the afternoon of October sixteenth?"

Padma glanced at Sharon, who gave an encouraging nod.

"I was at work," she said.

"Where you treated Isabelle Blair, the plaintiff's daughter?" prompted Ben.

Padma's stomach twisted at hearing Dana referred to as "the plaintiff." It all felt surreal—the lawyers, the sterile room, Lars pacing outside, waiting while her career hung in the balance. "Yes," she confirmed. "Izzy—Isabelle—came in from cross-country practice complaining of leg pain."

"And you specifically requested to treat her, correct?"

Padma nodded. "She's a family friend." She swallowed at the flimsy, two-dimensional description of her relationship with Dana and Izzy.

"Can you walk me through your medical assessment?" Ben said, his smile not reaching his eyes.

Padma had rehearsed this response with Sharon so many times it felt scripted. She recited it mechanically, hearing her own voice as if from a distance.

"...no past health issues... stable vitals... overuse injury of the leg..."

Ben's eyes gleamed, like a predator locking onto prey in the nature documentaries Padma used to watch with Maeve. "Did you take a full medical history?"

Padma swallowed. "I was already aware of certain details due to my close relationship with the family."

"Did you ask about current medications?"

"No. Because I knew Izzy and her mother, I assumed—"

"So you didn't ask if she was on hormonal birth control?"

"No." Padma wiped her sweaty palms on her thighs beneath the table.

"And later it was determined that hormonal birth control likely caused the pulmonary embolism that put Isabelle in a coma."

"Yes." Her suit jacket felt two sizes too small and suddenly suffocating.

"So we can conclude that because you failed to take a full

medical history, Isabelle ended up in a coma." Ben raised an eyebrow.

"Objection," Sharon cut in. "This is a deposition, not a courtroom. Counsel, you're making conclusions."

"Fine, fine." Ben held up a hand, leaning back. He scanned his notes before looking up. "Let's discuss the incident involving Julia Kim during your time as a third-year medical student at UNC."

His mouth moved, but all Padma heard was a high-pitched ringing. Panic locked her body in place, as if a bomb had just gone off. Next to her, Sharon stiffened, snapping her head toward Padma.

"Objection!" Sharon exclaimed. "Deposition testimony is limited to the incident at hand."

"That was an accident," Padma blurted. "I—I was under extreme stress. And the supervising doctor caught the dosing error before—"

"Stop talking," Sharon hissed.

"You'd been drinking, yes?" Ben pressed. "And you were dismissed from medical school because of it?"

"Objection!" Sharon shot up from her seat, seething. "This is inadmissible!"

"Yes, but I don't drink anymore," Padma said defensively. "I've been sober for—"

"I said shut up *now*," Sharon spat at Padma, glaring at Ben, who looked smug, like he'd just sunk the winning shot in overtime. "I'm calling a recess."

In the hallway, Sharon looked ready to explode. "What the hell was that?" she demanded. "You better tell me what happened because now that you've said it on the record, the judge could allow it in trial."

Lars rushed over. "What's going on?" Padma had wanted him there for support, but now she regretted that he had to hear the whole sordid story.

"Well?" Sharon said, tapping her foot impatiently.

Padma took a deep breath, recalling the memory that had haunted her for decades. "Julia Kim was admitted with severe abdominal pain and blood in her stool," she said dully. "I was responsible for administering her medication under supervision. I mistakenly gave her a higher dose of the anticoagulant than I should have. It could have been fatal had my supervising not caught and corrected it."

"Oh Christ," Sharon muttered, rubbing her forehead.

Padma struggled to breathe through the shame crashing over her. Her mind spiraled back to those dark days—constant anxiety, slipping grades, nights spent drowning in alcohol. "I was under immense stress, overwhelmed. And yes, I drank too much to cope." Lars gripped her shoulder for support. "Being dismissed from medical school was the lowest point of my life," she admitted, voice raw. "But I got help. I've been sober for twenty-six years. I went back to school, worked harder than ever, and have never made another mistake like that." She met Sharon's eyes, pleading. "You have to believe me."

Sharon sighed. "It's not about me believing you. It's about the jury."

"I'm so sorry," Padma said, burying her face in her hands.

"How bad is this?" Lars gripped her hand.

Sharon shook her head. "It's not good, that's for sure." She gave a tight smile. "For now, let's get the rest of this over with. Don't answer anything unless I tell you to, understand? I'll file a motion to strike the other line of questioning, but there's no guarantee it'll be removed."

The rest of the deposition passed in a haze, with Padma sticking only to her Sharon-approved, cut and dried answers. Once it was over, she met Lars in the hallway, leaning on him as he helped her to her car.

"They knew everything," she said bitterly when they reached her parking spot. "The whole story about Julia Kim, me getting kicked out of school. And I just—panicked." She couldn't believe how stupid she'd been. What a mess she'd made of things.

"But how?" he said, his face creased with confusion.

"I don't know," she wailed. "I've only ever told you and—" She gasped, the truth hitting her like a brick wall. She felt the sharp pain of betrayal like a knife, followed immediately by a hot surge of embarrassment. How could she have been so stupid? Of course that's how they'd found out.

She locked eyes with Lars. "Dana," she breathed.

Shock flickered across Lars's face. "But would she really..." His voice trailed off, the question answering itself.

"She's suing me," Padma said bitterly. "So apparently, everything's fair game." She wiped her hand across her face, angry at herself for crying, angry that she'd let Dana hurt her this deeply.

Lars pulled her into his arms. "I'm so sorry, sweetheart," he murmured.

For a brief moment, Padma let herself sink into his comfort, but then she stepped back, offering a small, rueful smile. "I thought this would blow over," she admitted. "I never thought it would get this far."

Lars's face darkened. "I know. But it has." He paused, his expression grim. "And I think you need to be ready for it to get worse. Dana seems... determined."

A shiver ran through her, and Lars rubbed her arms, trying to ease the tension.

"Let's talk at home," he suggested. "I'll drive and we can come back for your car later." He'd driven straight from work to meet her.

Padma hesitated. She knew she should go with him, let him hold her, help her gather the shattered pieces of the mess she'd made—pieces of the life she was slowly breaking apart. But a deeper, more urgent need took hold. She shook her head. "I think I'm going to call Jamie," she said. "Maybe go to a meeting."

He nodded, his expression relieved. "That's a good idea." He pulled her into a tight embrace, then stepped back. "I'll see you at home after."

She got into her car, turning the radio on, flipping through the stations aimlessly as she watched Lars pull out of the lot. Once he was gone, she waited another minute before starting her car. But instead of driving toward the church where her meeting was held, she turned in the opposite direction.

A few minutes later, she pulled into the parking lot of a strip mall, where a gym she used to belong to was located. She parked, walked briskly past the gym, and slipped into the liquor store.

TWENTY-NINE
MAEVE

Thirty-six days after

Maeve stood in the hospital stairwell, waiting for Ian's text. It was midday Saturday and she'd been at home trying to do homework but mostly scrolling her phone when he'd first messaged.

Hey. My mom's at work, wanna come see Izzy?

Your dad?

He's leaving soon.

Be right there.

Now she stood waiting to hear that the coast was clear. Atlanta was having a late-November cold snap, and the stairwell was overheated. Maeve peeled off her puffy jacket, regretting not wearing a T-shirt under it instead of the gray and purple NYU sweatshirt from last year's family trip to the city. NYU was one of Izzy's target schools, and Maeve was also considering applying. Or she had been. Lately her future felt up in the air. She'd assumed she and Izzy would go to college together, or at least nearby—maybe Vassar and Bard. Izzy was planning to major in Political Science and then go to law school. Maeve was undecided, but with Izzy's encouragement she'd been considering pre-med since she was good at Chemistry. Now, though, everything felt on hold, like she was waiting for her own dreams and motivations to surface in the absence of Izzy's.

While waiting, she scrolled to Izzy's latest TikTok, a video of herself modeling her half of their Halloween costume: the red overalls with spice bottles glued on. *Guess my costume*, she'd captioned it, while the song "Wannabe" played in the background. It had been viewed over ten thousand times and flooded with comments since word of Izzy's coma spread at school.

So sad, how could this have happened to you????
You're so full of life, I can't believe this
Stay strong, Izzy, we're rooting for you!!!!!
Such a tragedy, I can't believe it. Sobbing.

Maeve paused on one comment: *Get better soon*, from username tayandrewso8. Irritation flared as she clicked on Taylor's profile picture—him kissing a football. How dare he comment like he actually cared? He never even looked at Maeve at school, despite her being the only one who knew he and Izzy were hooking up. She'd always thought Taylor was an arrogant jerk—though an undeniably attractive one—but never judged Izzy's crush. Maeve understood the intoxicating pull of wanting someone who ignored you... and the thrill when they finally didn't.

A text notification appeared on her screen.

Meet you in the hall.

Pocketing her phone, Maeve pushed open the door and

scanned the hallway, her pulse quickening. At the far end, Ian peeked out of a door, glancing around until his eyes met hers. He beckoned, and her heart sped up. Since he'd helped her sneak in to see Izzy earlier that week, they'd been texting —not the flirty, evasive messages he usually sent to girls. She knew this because Izzy had once swiped his phone, and together they had impersonated him in several ongoing conversations.

"*Hey, you up?*" Izzy had said, reading from Ian's phone and rolling her eyes. "Seriously?"

The messages between him and Maeve felt more like a long conversation they were constantly in the middle of. Maeve hoped it would never end. She felt a rush of pleasure every time Ian's name popped up on her screen.

> Made me think of you

He'd written yesterday afternoon, sending a link to a video of a four-year-old playing flawless Mozart on the piano.

> I don't play piano

> Not the piano, the look on his face. You look like that a lot.

> Like I'm constipated?

> No like you're deep in thought. Sometimes I see you at school and wonder what you're thinking about.

> Boring stuff probably.

> Like what?

> Idk like what to have for lunch or how I did on the calc quiz.

> What did you have for lunch?

Skipped it. The cafeteria feels weird lately, like I
don't know where I belong.

Welcome to my life. Come eat with me next
time.

In the parking lot??

It's way less weird than the cafeteria, promise.

Then that morning there was a text from him waiting when
she woke up.

What do you think it's like for her?

Maeve had known immediately what he was talking about.

Like can she see or hear or feel anything?

Yeah

Idk. I mean if she's not with us, maybe she's
somewhere else, like somewhere in between.
Maybe waiting to come back.

Like a waiting room?

Yeah but nicer. No muzak or gross old
magazines.

Maybe more like a green room, like with little
bottles of water and pretzels and mints and
stuff.

Mints???

Yeah Izzy likes them.

Maeve smiled to herself now thinking of this exchange as
she approached Ian in the hallway.

"Hey," Ian said, grinning. He stepped toward her, and for a

moment Maeve thought he was going to hug her, but he shuffled awkwardly to the side. "Come on in." He gestured to the door.

Inside, Maeve looked around. "Wow, upgrade," she commented, noting the cushier furniture and mass-produced watercolor prints on the walls.

"Yeah, very fancy," Ian agreed. "I might not have a college fund anymore—my parents are already arguing about the cost of a private room, which insurance doesn't cover—but my college options are slim anyway."

Maeve frowned as she approached Izzy. "Your brother needs to stop underestimating himself," she said, hopping onto the bed next to her. "His whole 'I'm such a fuckup' act is getting old."

"Wow." Ian raised his eyebrows.

"What?" Maeve crossed her arms.

"Nothing, I've just never heard you swear before."

"Is that what it takes to get your attention?" She lowered her eyes, and when she looked back up at him, the room crackled with new energy.

An earnest, almost shy expression appeared on his face. "You've always had my attention," he said.

Heat rose on Maeve's neck as she turned back to Izzy. "So, how are the mints in the green room?"

The old Izzy would have laughed, been in on the joke, but this Izzy just lay there, mouth open, arms slack. It had only been five days since Maeve last saw her—the day Ian walked her to her car, a thought that sent a shiver of pleasure through her—but already, Izzy seemed smaller, her cheeks hollower, her collarbone more pronounced.

Ian shifted and licked his lips. "Do you want, um, a minute with her?"

Maeve nodded, hoping he couldn't see the tears in her eyes. She held her breath until the door clicked shut behind him, then scooted up next to Izzy, leaning on the headboard and swinging her legs onto the bed.

"It is so inconvenient having a crush on your brother," Maeve said, glancing at Izzy. "Did you know? I always wondered if you'd figured it out. I know you kept trying to set me up with Rogan from orchestra, but it's always been Ian." She sighed, eyes flicking to the monitor and then back to her friend's face. "So, is this it, Iz? Like, forever?" She waited for the tears, but they didn't come. "It's hard to imagine life without you," she murmured. "Like, who even am I on my own?" She leaned back, cool fabric pressing against her cheek. "That sounds pathetic, doesn't it? Like I have no identity outside my best friend. But honestly, I'm starting to realize... I'm not sure I do."

Maeve peeked at Izzy's still face, biting her lip. "I don't want to hurt your feelings, but I think it's time for me to figure out who I am without you. What I want for myself." Her voice trembled and she reached for Izzy's hand, feeling its warmth, its limpness. "You get it, right? I mean, we're going to be seniors next year, and I don't want to go to college not knowing who I am. You're set on the East Coast, but I really like California. Maybe I'll apply to Berkeley or UCLA. We'll still talk, obviously, and visit each other."

She paused, then laughed. "Oh my God, I'm making it sound like we're breaking up—which we're not. You'll always be my best friend." She hesitated. "I just might need a little space."

A bolt of guilt shot through her. "Not like I need you to be in a coma," she added quickly, gripping Izzy's hand. "Just... not forever."

Sighing, she leaned back. "OK, good talk."

Her eyelids felt heavy. She'd been up late texting Ian, then tossed and turned all night, shifting to find a cool spot in the bed as she drifted in and out of dreams—playing her violin in a huge auditorium with only Izzy in the audience.

"Hey."

Maeve opened her eyes to find Ian standing next to the bed. Her mouth felt dry as she wiped a small trail of drool from her cheek. She reddened with embarrassment. "Oh my God, I'm sorry," she said. Clambering down from the tall bed, she tripped and collapsed forward. Ian caught her, electricity shooting through her body at his touch, jolting her fully awake.

He laughed. "Easy. If I'd known all you needed was a nap, you could've stayed home and I'd have sung you a lullaby over the phone."

"Sorry," Maeve mumbled again. "I didn't realize I was so tired." She glanced at Izzy, then smiled. "But I'm glad I came. We had a good talk."

Ian cocked his head. "Oh yeah? About what?" He hadn't released his grip on her upper arm, and his fingers tightened slightly. Maeve felt her insides fizz, like a cork had popped inside her.

"Oh, you know," she said lightly. "Girl stuff."

Their faces were inches from each other now, and Maeve's own voice echoed in her head. *It's time for me to figure out what I want for myself.*

This. She wanted this.

She leaned forward, or maybe he did, and an instant later they were kissing.

THIRTY

DANA

Thirty-eight days after

Dana stripped the sheets from the pullout bed, folding them neatly before collapsing the bed back into a chair. It was Monday, and her watch read 6:30 a.m. If she didn't leave now, she'd be late to shower and get ready for her deposition. Ben had been thrilled they got it scheduled before Thanksgiving. Crossing to Izzy's bed, she bent down and kissed her daughter's pale cheek.

"I won't be gone long," she murmured, ignoring the tightness in her chest. The thought of Izzy lying here alone gnawed at her. With Eric back at work full-time and Dana splitting her time between the hospital and the shop, there were long stretches when Izzy had no one by her side. Could she sense their absence? Did she feel lonely in the silent abyss of her coma?

Pushing the thought aside, she squeezed Izzy's hand one last time and headed out.

At home, Eric was in the kitchen, freshly showered, blending powders and oat milk into his signature smoothie. The sight made Dana's blood boil. How could he just continue his routines as if they hadn't been cleaved apart by Izzy's coma? All the rhythms of her life—her morning Starbucks runs, evening power walks, even her regular salon visits to keep her roots from showing—were relics of the "Before." She'd given them all up, surrendering her days to the sterile coffee and harsh lighting of the hospital. How could Eric still find time for his leg days and bullet coffee?

"Hey," he said, glancing up as she walked in. "I was hoping to catch you this morning."

A small arrow of hope pierced her resentment. She'd asked him to accompany her to the deposition for moral support, but he'd already used up all his time off. Maybe, though, he'd found a way to make it work.

"Oh?" she said.

"Yeah." He fidgeted with the blender buttons though it wasn't even plugged in. "I was hoping we could... talk."

A knot formed in her stomach. "Sure," she said warily, leaning against the counter.

Eric looked away, then back, his brow heavy above unreadable eyes. "It's been almost six weeks since Izzy went into the hospital," he said, his voice uneven. "And, well"—he swallowed hard—"we've put our lives on hold."

Dana stiffened. *At least I have*, she thought bitterly.

"I think it's time for us to start living again," Eric continued, his voice soft and pleading. "Or at least, some version of living."

Her eyes narrowed. "What are you talking about?"

He held her gaze for a moment, then sighed. "I want to move forward with the separation."

The words struck like a hammer, shattering the air between them. Dana felt everything inside her tilt, the ground pulled out from under her.

"What?" she whispered. Then anger surged, hot and sharp. "Our daughter is in a coma!" she cried, her fury so palpable Eric took a step back. "What kind of person walks out on their family now?"

"I'm not walking out," Eric said, crossing his arms. "But we can't stay frozen, waiting for a miracle. I want to start my life again. Neither of us wants to admit it, but Izzy may never wake up." His voice cracked. "And you—you're never home. You're always at the hospital—"

"Izzy needs me," Dana snapped, nails digging into her palms. She wanted to scream, to throw something, to hurt him like he was hurting her.

"Oh please, spare me the bullshit," Eric shot back.

"Excuse me?"

"You're using Izzy as an excuse," he said, his tone cutting. "You've put your entire life on pause—indefinitely. It's not healthy. For you. For Ian. For us."

Dana opened her mouth to argue, but the truth of his words sat heavy in her stomach. How many decisions had she avoided these past weeks? About Ian. About the shop. About her marriage.

"I want to live again, Dana," Eric said, his voice trembling. "Don't you?"

For a long moment, the only sound was the hum of their ancient fridge. Then, without a word, Dana turned and walked past him, leaving before he could see the tears burning in her eyes.

The deposition was at Ben's office. He met her in the lobby, dressed in a dark gray suit with razor-sharp creases.

"Coffee?" he offered as he led her to the conference room.

Dana shook her head. Her stomach was already churning.

Ben opened the door, revealing the room's occupants. A wave of panic crashed over Dana, and she recoiled.

"Dana?" Ben asked questioningly, following her back into the hall.

"She's here," Dana hissed.

Ben cocked his head, confused.

"*Padma,*" Dana clarified.

Ben nodded. "Yes, it's Dr. Paulsen's right to be here during your deposition, as we discussed."

"But I didn't go to hers," Dana said.

She vaguely remembered Ben asking if she wanted to attend Padma's deposition, but the idea had made her so nauseous that she'd immediately declined. She couldn't face looking Padma in the eye, unsure what she'd find there. Anger? Sadness? The deep, shared ache of navigating a world without the best friend you once believed would be by your side as you grew old together? Dana felt all those things.

Ben straightened his cuffs impatiently. "Just because you didn't attend her deposition, that doesn't negate her right to attend yours."

Dana put a hand on the wall to steady herself. "I just—need a minute."

"Of course," Ben said, glancing at his watch. "Take all the time you need."

Dana inhaled deeply, willing her hammering heart to slow. "OK," she said after a moment. "I'm ready."

Dana kept her eyes down as she and Ben entered the room and took their seats across from Padma's lawyer, who, Dana noticed when she glanced up, bore a resemblance to a younger version of her own mother, with red lipstick and a firm jawline. Padma sat farther down the table, slightly removed from her lawyer's side.

Dana focused on steadying her breath while Ben and the other attorney exchanged the typical formalities. The opposing lawyer, whose name was either Sharon or Sarah—Dana had had trouble focusing during introductions—turned to her.

"Mrs. Blair," the lawyer began, "let's discuss the initial ER visit when Dr. Paulsen examined your daughter, Isabelle. Can you recount that for us?"

Dana's chest tightened as her mind traveled back in time. "I met Izzy and her cross-country coach at the ER. The coach brought her in for severe leg pain, and Padma—Dr. Paulsen—examined her."

"Did Dr. Paulsen take a full medical history during that visit?" the lawyer asked.

Dana glanced at Ben, who nodded. "Not that I recall."

"Why do you think that might have been?" the lawyer pressed.

"Mrs. Callaway, my client is here to provide facts, not speculation," Ben cut in.

Dana noticed Padma shift in her chair but still couldn't bring herself to look at her friend.

The lawyer softened her tone. "Mrs. Blair, was Dr. Paulsen aware that your daughter was on birth control? Had you ever mentioned this to her during your time as friends?"

"Mrs. Callaway, please," Ben interrupted sharply. "Stick to relevant events from the ER visit."

"Like you did?" Padma's lawyer muttered caustically.

Dana shot a questioning glance at Ben, whose face remained placid.

"It's relevant to establish what Mrs. Blair may have shared with Dr. Paulsen regarding Isabelle's medical history," Padma's lawyer continued.

Ben nodded at Dana. "I didn't mention it," she said, "because I didn't know." Her face flushed, thinking of her failure as a mother.

"But if you had known," the lawyer pressed, "is that something you would have shared with Dr. Paulsen, as her friend?"

"Don't answer that," Ben said, casting a warning look at Dana. "Mrs. Callaway, you're overreaching."

For the first time since entering the room, Dana looked at Padma. Her dark hair was swept back into a low bun, with more gray woven through it than Dana remembered. She wore the dark red silk blouse Dana had urged her to buy on their girls' weekend in Savannah last year, insisting she needed some color in her all-neutral wardrobe. Padma, laughing, had acquiesced. At her throat, the thin gold chain she always wore glinted under the harsh overhead lights. Deep lines of exhaustion framed her eyes, and her mouth was set in a tight line. Suddenly their gazes met, and for a fleeting second, the tension in Padma's face softened into a small, sad smile. Then, just as quickly, it vanished as she looked away.

"Yes," Dana said, voice steady.

Padma's lawyer blinked. "Yes, what?"

"Yes, it's the kind of thing I would have told Padma," Dana admitted. "We talked about everything." Guiltily, she thought of her financial troubles. "Well, almost everything," she added.

Padma turned sharply to look at Dana, her eyes questioning. Dana felt a pang. If only she could talk to her about what had just happened with Eric, how hurt and abandoned she felt. Her eyes filled with tears and she blinked them away.

"Strike that from the record," Ben said, waving his hand. "Irrelevant."

Padma's lawyer heaved a sigh. "Mr. Ricard, is there any line of questioning you plan to permit during this deposition?" she asked with a withering look.

"I'm simply trying—"

"Never mind," Padma's lawyer cut in, exasperated.

Ben smiled with feigned innocence and gestured for her to proceed.

The rest of the deposition moved quickly with straightforward questions. Dana kept her eyes fixed ahead, focusing on the lawyer, but her gaze kept drifting to Padma. Each time, Padma met her eyes with a blank, distant look, as though Dana was just another face. A dull ache settled in Dana's chest. *It's still me,* she wanted to say.

"That concludes my questions. Thank you," Padma's lawyer said, snapping her file shut.

Ben stood and nodded at Dana to do the same. "We'll be in touch," he said.

"I'm sure," the lawyer replied dryly.

Dana glanced at Padma, who remained seated, eyes averted. She hesitated, wishing for an instant that the room would empty and leave them alone. But what would she say? *My life is unraveling, and I miss my best friend? I trusted you, how could you let this happen to Izzy?* The tangle of emotions knotted inside her. With a final, wistful look, Dana followed Ben out of the room.

THIRTY-ONE

IAN

Forty days after

Ian scanned the crowded hallway, hoping to spot Maeve before the bell rang. It was Wednesday, the day before Thanksgiving, and the building buzzed with manic pre-holiday energy. Ian vibrated with his own kind of euphoria, having taken a handful of pills in the parking lot earlier. Around him kids shouted to be heard over the chatter and lockers slammed shut. Teachers patrolled the halls, looking exhausted as they tried to keep the chaos in check—and it was only second period.

Hefting his backpack higher on his shoulder, Ian wove through the crowd toward Maeve's locker, which was all the way on the other side of the building. He hadn't been able to stop thinking about her since Saturday. He couldn't shake the image of her asleep on Izzy's bed, her wavy hair fanned out like a halo. How she'd opened her eyes—those silver eyes—and looked at him like she was really seeing him for the first time. How suddenly they'd been kissing, tentatively at first, then clinging to each other like a flash flood was barreling down on them. The feeling had been even better than the rush he got when the pills kicked in.

Now, hurrying through the hall to class, Ian smiled at the memory. Out of nowhere, he slammed into something, his phone flying from his hand and skidding across the linoleum. "Dude, watch it!" he exclaimed, looking up into the face of Taylor Andrews.

White-hot rage shot through Ian, and before he could think, he dropped his backpack and charged, his fist connecting with Taylor's chin.

"The fuck, man?" Taylor shouted, his hand flying to his face. He lowered his broad shoulder and slammed into Ian, sending a sharp pain through Ian's chest as he hit the floor.

"What the hell were you doing with my sister?" Ian hissed, scrambling to his feet, his heart hammering like a machine gun, just as Taylor moved to push him again. In the split second before his hand made contact with Ian's chest, confusion and then recognition flickered across Taylor's face.

"Shit," Taylor muttered, jerking his hand back before it slammed into Ian. "You're Ian. Jesus, man, I'm sorry. I didn't realize—" Taylor stopped, looking embarrassed. He shifted uncomfortably. "Dude, I'm really sorry about your sister."

"Like you actually care," Ian snapped. "Stay the hell away from her." He was panting and shaking—what the hell? Maybe he shouldn't have taken that extra Addy that morning.

"What's going on here?" came a voice.

Ian looked up to see Mr. Riley approaching. "Nothing," he said quickly, trying to calm his rapid breathing. "We're good." The last thing he needed was the one teacher who had any faith in him to see him getting in a fight.

Mr. Riley eyed both boys suspiciously, then pointed at Taylor. "Get to class," he said. But when Ian turned to go as well, Mr. Riley put up a hand to stop him. "No, Ian, you come with me."

Ian's heart sank as he trailed after Mr. Riley, shooting a bitter glance in Taylor's direction. Why was he always the one getting into trouble? Maybe it was just who he was, part of his DNA, like his dad seemed to believe.

Mr. Riley led him into his empty classroom and gestured to a student desk. Ian sat down warily as Mr. Riley took a seat across from him. Ian braced for the lecture he knew was coming, but instead, Mr. Riley just studied him.

"You OK?" he asked.

Ian blinked, caught off guard. "That wasn't my fault, I swear. Taylor started—"

"I don't want to talk about... whatever that was," Mr. Riley interrupted, waving a hand dismissively. "I want to know how you're doing."

"Uh, fine," Ian said, the word landing awkwardly.

"Be specific," Mr. Riley replied. "I'd dock you points for saying 'fine' in an essay."

"I'm pretty sure you have," Ian muttered.

Mr. Riley smiled faintly. "So?" he pressed.

"I'm..." Ian hesitated, searching for the right word. The last few days had been a blur of nonstop texts with Maeve since their kiss at the hospital. His chest buzzed with a nervous excitement he wasn't used to, like fireworks he couldn't quite control. And, for once, he might not be failing English, which felt like a small victory. For the first time in forever, he realized, he felt... happy.

"I'm good," he admitted, a small smile tugging at his lips. Then guilt crashed over him. How could he feel good when Izzy was still unconscious? "I mean, I'm OK," he corrected quickly, shrugging. "My sister's still in the hospital, so that sucks."

And shouldn't he be worried about his parents barely speaking? Or the way his anger flared out of nowhere, spiraling over the smallest things? He swallowed hard, shoving the thoughts aside.

"That's got to be hard, everything going on with Izzy," Mr. Riley said. "But it's OK to feel good sometimes, too, Ian. Being sad or angry all the time won't change anything with your sister. It doesn't mean you care about her any less."

His teacher's words hit him like a sudden dodgeball to the chest. Spoken aloud, they were so simple, so obvious—but somehow, he hadn't let himself think them.

"Yeah," Ian said slowly. "I guess I do feel kind of guilty about being, like, happy about other stuff."

"That's normal. But don't you think your sister would want you to be happy?"

"Yeah," Ian agreed. Just maybe not with Maeve.

Mr. Riley stood and walked to his desk, returning with a stapled packet. "I graded your last exam," he said. "I'm not due to post grades until after Thanksgiving, but I thought you'd want to see this now."

Ian's heart thudded. He'd actually put effort into studying for this test, more work than he ever had before, carefully titrating his pill intake so that his head was clear enough to focus. If all that effort still wasn't good enough, he didn't know what that would mean.

He stood and took the paper, holding his breath as he glanced down. A large red A stared back at him. Relief rushed out of him in a long exhale.

Mr. Riley smiled. "Your overall grade is now officially up to a B. Which means you can register for my Advanced Placement Language and Composition class next semester."

"AP?" Ian said, shaking his head. "Nah, I don't think so." AP classes were for kids like Izzy, not him.

Mr. Riley raised an eyebrow. "I already talked to the guidance counselor, and she's happy to rearrange your schedule. Think about it, will you?"

Ian nodded, still stunned.

"Now get to class," Mr. Riley said firmly.

As Ian walked out, the A grade still clutched in his hand, a small flicker of pride began to stir inside him. Maybe, just maybe, he wasn't such a screwup after all.

The minute the bell rang at the end of the day he texted Maeve.

Hang out after school? Could meet at the hospital or you could come over.

He pressed send, hoping his words didn't give away how nervous he felt. He and Maeve had never hung out just the two of them at home. Was it weird that he'd asked to? Also, why was he overthinking this so much? This was not his usual MO.

His phone screen lit up with Maeve's reply.

Will your parents be home?

No.

As far as he knew his mom would still be at the shop and his dad would be with Izzy.

Kk see you after school.

A rush of anticipation shot through him.

Later, at home, when the doorbell finally rang, Ian shot off the couch, his socks slipping on the hardwood as he skidded to the door. He caught himself on the handle, heart thudding, and wiped his palms on his jeans before opening it.

He'd taken a pill about an hour ago—OK, two, just enough to smooth out the static in his chest. But not the three pills he might've taken on a regular day, when his brain buzzed like a swarm of bees and pills were the only way to quiet it. Because being with Maeve was different. She made him forget, all on her own, the constant ticker of worry in his head. He didn't want to be high around her—not really high, anyway.

He ran a hand through his hair and gave himself a quick check in the mirror by the door—*you look fine, idiot, open the door already*—and then he did.

Maeve wore an oversized hoodie and her wavy hair was pulled up into a messy knot on top of her head with a few tendrils trailing loose. He had to stop himself from reaching out to touch them. She smiled, and Ian's chest did a weird stutter-step.

"Hey," she said. Just like that, the noise in his head quieted, like someone sliding a heavy glass door closed.

"Hey," he said, grinning.

She stepped inside, her familiar tangerine-vanilla scent swirling around him, almost knocking him off balance. *Be cool*, he told himself.

"Do you, um, want a drink?" he asked, shifting awkwardly.

She bit her lip, hesitating. "Um, I don't really drink."

"No, not like that," he said quickly, flushing. "I meant, like, a seltzer or something."

She laughed, her own cheeks turning pink. "Oh, yeah, duh. Sorry, I just assumed, since you..." She trailed off, looking at her feet.

He frowned. "Since I what?"

She met his eyes. "You kind of have a reputation as a partier."

A wave of disappointment hit him. Was that really how she saw him still—just some mindless party boy?

"I do, huh?" he said, trying to keep the sarcasm out of his voice, though he knew it was true.

Maeve flinched. "I mean, at least people talk about you," she said, a touch of sadness in her voice. "I'm basically invisible."

He let his eyes trace the constellation of freckles on her

nose, down to the collar of her sweatshirt. "Not to me, you're not," he said softly.

For a moment, time froze, and they drifted closer. Then Maeve closed the gap, standing on tiptoe to kiss him. He wrapped his arms around her waist, pulling her tight, as if trying to erase any distance between them.

A dog barked outside, and they jumped apart.

"Do you want to—" he began, but Maeve had already grabbed his hand and was leading him toward the stairs.

At the top, they paused, looking at Izzy's closed bedroom door. "Is this weird?" Ian asked. His sister's presence felt so strong, like she might be behind the door, studying or sprawled on the bed asleep.

"A little," Maeve admitted. "But not in a bad way."

They stepped into Ian's room, and he suddenly felt self-conscious. He'd tried to clean up, smoothing the comforter, tossing the empty snack wrappers. But now he saw the pile of dirty clothes in the corner, the sweatshirt draped haphazardly over the doorknob. Still, Maeve wasn't looking at the mess. She was staring right at him.

"How are you?" she asked, stepping closer.

The kindness in her eyes broke something inside him, like a sheet of ice falling off a glacier. A lump formed in his throat, and he choked on a sob. He tried to swallow it back, but it was too late. Tears streamed down his face.

"Hey," Maeve said softly, wrapping her arms around him. He buried his face in her hair, letting it soak up his tears.

He hadn't cried since Izzy was hospitalized. He'd come close, but always managed to hold it back, like a curtain dropping to shut off the world—the pills also helped with that, providing a welcome numbing effect. Now, though, the tears poured out, like they'd been lying in wait to ambush him the minute he let his guard down.

"God, I'm sorry," he mumbled, pulling away, suddenly

embarrassed. He sank onto the bed, wiping his face with a corner of the blanket.

Maeve sat next to him, their thighs touching. "It's OK," she said softly. "You looked like you needed it."

He turned to her, his eyes red and swollen. "Am I that pathetic?"

"It's not pathetic to feel things," she said. Her eyes were deep, endless, like he could dive in and never reach the bottom. She raised an eyebrow. "You might want to try it more often."

He ran a shaky hand through his hair. "I promised her I'd change if she woke up," he said, voice barely audible. "That I'd be good—for her."

Maeve took his hand, sending a jolt through him. "You're already good," she said. "You just have to show people."

He felt a stab of shame as he thought of his shoebox of pills at the top of his closet. If Maeve knew, there was no way she'd be saying that about him. For the first time, the pills didn't feel like a lifeline, but like an anchor around his legs, dragging him under.

Before his thoughts could take over, he leaned forward and kissed her.

They tipped back onto his bed, kissing deeply, the feel of her body against his making him feel like he might explode with happiness. "Is this OK?" he whispered, sliding his hand under her shirt and pausing with it on her stomach.

"Mm." She nodded, shifting to let him slip his hand higher up to cup her breast.

He felt dizzy with joy, but the sound of the garage door rumbling open jolted him upright. "Shit," he breathed, "someone's home."

Maeve's eyes widened, and she quickly pulled her shirt down.

A door creaked downstairs. "Ian?" his dad called. "You home, buddy?"

"Uh, yeah, just... studying," Ian called, frantically scanning the room for somewhere to hide Maeve.

Ian heard footsteps on the stairs, then heard his dad's phone, the ringtone blaring at full volume. Maeve winced, and Ian stifled a laugh.

"Hello?" his dad said, walking back down the stairs. "Yes, this is Eric Blair. Ah, thanks for the call back." The footsteps retreated and Ian heard the door to the study close.

"You have to go," Ian whispered, kissing Maeve one last time.

"How?" she whispered back, her eyes wide.

Ian peeked out of the room, then motioned for her to follow. They crept down the stairs, the muffled sound of his dad's voice drifting from the other room.

They slipped across the living room to the front door, adrenaline buzzing in Ian's veins.

"Can I see you tomorrow?" he whispered.

"It's Thanksgiving," Maeve reminded him.

Ian groaned softly and Maeve shushed him. He'd completely forgotten that his grandparents—his dad's folks—were coming in from Florida, and Grandma Cora would be joining them. The idea of being stuck at home all day with them made his skin crawl. He could already hear his Grandpa Bob's gruff voice asking about college plans, his Grandma Joan slipping in a dig about how much better Izzy always did in school, and Grandma Cora's sharp gaze, catching every small mistake he made.

"Friday, then?" he asked.

She smiled, her face glowing. "Friday."

Watching her walk out the door, Ian felt a flicker of hope that maybe, just maybe, things were changing.

THIRTY-TWO

DANA

Forty-one days after

Dana dabbed blush onto her cheekbones, watching her reflection in the mirror. She'd forced herself to blow-dry her hair and put on something other than leggings and one of Izzy's old sweatshirts. Since SueEllen's resignation last week, dragging Dana back into running the shop full-time, she'd struggled to find a balance between looking presentable and letting the hollowness inside her show. Somehow, looking too polished felt like a betrayal—like she wasn't grieving Izzy properly.

Today, though, it mattered more. It was Thanksgiving. Dana had been caught off guard by the arrival of the holiday, buried under the weight of her exhaustion from keeping Haven and Hearth open and Eric's decision to move forward with their separation. By the time she'd realized the holiday was approaching, it had been too late to cancel Eric's parents, already en route in their RV from Florida.

"We can tell Ian and the rest of the family after Thanksgiving," Eric had said, his voice tinged with sadness. Dana wondered if he genuinely felt bad or was simply counting the days until he could escape their fractured life.

"Fine," she'd agreed, too drained to argue. All her energy was consumed by Izzy's care, the shop, and the mechanics of the lawsuit. She barely had anything left for herself, let alone for Eric.

Eric had reluctantly agreed to celebrate Thanksgiving at the hospital. "We can't do it here without Izzy," Dana had pleaded. "It feels wrong, like we're giving up on her." She wished she could communicate to him how most days, she felt like she was balancing on a tightrope, inching forward because she had to, but never daring to do more than the bare minimum. Anything more might signal to God—or whatever force was out there—that she was ready to move on without Izzy. And a full Thanksgiving celebration, without a place set for her daughter, seemed like tempting fate.

That morning, she'd found herself staring blankly at the shower wall for an indeterminate amount of time, reliving her deposition. Across the sterile conference table from Padma, she'd felt a maelstrom of emotions: guilt for betraying her best friend, sadness for all they'd lost, anger at Padma's mistake, and desperation to do right by Izzy. For a fleeting moment—perhaps several—she'd wanted to call it off, to beg Padma for forgiveness. But Ben's calm assurance echoed in her mind: *"This is about securing Izzy's future. You're doing the right thing."* Dana clung to his words, repeating them like a mantra. Still, doubt lingered, gnawing at the edges of her resolve. Could any amount of winning ever feel like justice?

Dana finished applying her makeup just as the doorbell rang, followed by loud, persistent knocking. She made it downstairs just as Eric opened the door to a large-bellied man with silver hair, wearing striped pajamas and battered slippers.

"Dana, honey," her father-in-law said, stepping in. "Lovely to see you. Sorry we missed you last night."

"I was with Izzy at the hospital," Dana said defensively.

But Bob was already hurrying to the half-bathroom. "We'll chat in a sec, nature calls."

Eric glanced at the enormous RV parked outside. "I thought you had a bathroom in there?"

"Yeah, but the plumbing's shit for number two," Bob called back. "No pun intended."

As he closed the door, Dana shot Eric a look.

"At least they're staying in the RV," he said with a sigh.

Dana grabbed her purse. "I'll meet you at the hospital later. I need to swing by the shop."

"On Thanksgiving?" Eric frowned.

"Black Friday's tomorrow," she reminded him. "I have to be ready."

At Haven and Hearth, Dana inhaled the cinnamon and spice aroma of the holiday candles. It was comforting and cruel all at once, a reminder of better years. She busied herself rearranging displays and tagging merchandise, avoiding the office as long as she could. Eventually, she sat at the desk and faced the stack of bills. Rent and electricity couldn't wait; insurance and overdue notices would have to. Shifting funds between accounts, she managed to buy herself another week—a tiny reprieve, but all she could manage.

Later, when she picked up her mother from the retirement home, she felt another wave of anxiety wash over her as she prepared herself to try to keep her terrible secret hidden from the one person who always managed to see through her.

Cora, as always, was impeccable in crisp navy trousers, a goldenrod tunic, and her signature pearls. Next to her, Dana felt frumpy and inadequate.

"You're late," her mother said, kissing the air near Dana's cheek to avoid smudging her lipstick.

"Sorry," Dana murmured. "I was at the shop."

"Black Friday." Her mother nodded knowingly. "Big day."

"Bob and Joan are looking forward to seeing you," Dana said, steering the conversation to safer ground. She hadn't yet told her mother about SueEllen's resignation.

Her mother pursed her lips with distaste. "They've parked that awful thing in front of your house again, haven't they?"

Dana laughed weakly. "Yes, but we're celebrating at the hospital this year. For Izzy."

Dana saw a flash of emotion cross her mother's normally stoic face. She hesitated, then reached over to lightly pat Dana's arm.

At the hospital bright paper leaves and small pumpkins lined the nurses' stations and patient doors were adorned with cut-out turkeys bearing their names, giving the whole floor the feel of a primary school or a dorm. Dana paused outside Izzy's room, surprised to see her mother's eyes brimming with tears.

"I'm sorry I haven't gotten here sooner," her mother whispered.

"It's OK, Mom," Dana said gently. "I didn't want you to see her like this. But now... well..." She trailed off, leaving her worst fears unspoken—that the unresponsive Izzy lying in that bed might be all she had left.

Dana opened the door, taking in the sight of Eric arranging paper on a long folding table, draped in a white plastic cloth. At the center sat the vase of dried sunflowers from their foyer. It was far too big, blocking the view across the table.

"Hey there," Eric said, noticing her gaze. "I grabbed it last minute. I know you like a... whatever it's called."

"A centerpiece," Dana said, feeling a bittersweet ache. "It's perfect, thank you."

"Cora, good to see—" he began, turning toward her mother. But Cora had already drifted to Izzy's bedside, her hand pressed to her mouth.

"Hello, my darling," she whispered, gently brushing a

strand of hair from Izzy's forehead. She glanced at Dana. "Can she...?"

"Maybe," Dana murmured, stepping beside her.

"My sweet girl," her mother breathed.

"—only one slice of pie, and no whipped cream, remember what the doctor said." Dana's mother-in-law's loud, nasal voice pierced the quiet.

"Oh, lay off, Joan, it's Thanksgiving, for crying out loud," grumbled her father-in-law as they came in, followed by Ian, who looked like he'd rather be anywhere else.

"Dana, sweetheart, happy Thanksgiving," Joan said, sweeping Dana into a hug and pressing a kiss onto her cheek. Dana gently pulled back, dabbing at the smudge of coral lipstick Joan had left behind. Joan's face fell as she looked at Izzy. "I mean... not *happy*, of course, but... well, Thanksgiving." She nodded to Cora. "And Cora, dear, hello."

Dana's mother stiffened as Joan pulled her into an overly enthusiastic hug. "Good to see you both," she managed.

"It's good to be seen," Bob boomed, then let out a laugh that quickly faded as he glanced at Izzy. His expression sobered as the three grandparents gathered around the bed like mourners at a gravesite.

"A damn shame," Bob said after a moment, his voice thick. "A damn shame."

"Shall we sit?" Eric motioned toward the table, where he'd set out Tupperware containers of roast turkey, two kinds of potatoes, green beans, and cranberry sauce. There was even a bottle of the sweet red wine Joan favored.

Dana nodded, relieved to move things along.

"So, Ian," Joan asked as they began to pass food around, "how's school? Are you thinking about college yet?"

"Notre Dame, right?" Bob added, puffing out his chest at any chance to bring up his alma mater.

"Um, I haven't decided," Ian muttered, looking down. Dana

noted how narrow his shoulders looked under his hoodie—had he lost weight?

"He's got to get his grades up if he's going to have a shot at college," Eric said, frowning.

"So no chance at honor roll like your sister?" Dana's mother asked pointedly.

Bob cut in, waving a forkful of turkey. "Got yourself a job yet, young man? Never too soon to learn the value of a paycheck."

Dana watched Ian shrink into his chair, and her heart clenched. "Let's talk about something else," she suggested with a forced smile, trying to steer the conversation away from her son's unraveling confidence. "Bob, Joan, what would you like to do this weekend while you're in town?"

Joan's face lit up. "We thought we'd hit the Black Friday sales at the outlet malls tomorrow," she said brightly. "They open at five a.m."

Bob groaned, turning his weary gaze to Dana. "You're not opening the shop at some ungodly hour, are you?"

Dana mustered a tight smile. "Normal hours," she replied evenly.

"I'd like to come do my shopping there," her mother interjected. "What time can you pick me up?"

Dana pressed a hand to her temple, where a headache had begun to throb. "I can't, Mom. I'll be at the shop all day."

"Surely SueEllen can handle it alone for an hour or so," her mother said, frowning.

"SueEllen's not there anymore," Dana said, realizing too late the mistake of mentioning it.

"Not there anymore? Whatever do you mean?" Her mother's voice shot up an octave.

Dana hesitated, then gave a resigned sigh and reached for her wine. "She quit."

"Good gracious," her mother exclaimed. "How thoughtless

of her. Have you found a replacement? It's the busiest time of year!" She clucked her tongue in disapproval.

"I'm not planning to replace her," Dana said, tipping her wine glass back to get the last swallow.

Her mother's thin, penciled eyebrows shot skyward. "Why ever not? You can't—"

"I'm trying to cut costs," Dana interrupted, swallowing. The overly sweet wine was far from comforting, but it was something.

"That's ridiculous," her mother said sharply. "Surely things aren't so bad that—"

"I can help, if you want." Ian's voice broke through, so quiet Dana almost missed it.

All eyes turned to him.

"Like after school or on the weekends or something," he added, rubbing his eyes, which looked tired and red.

Dana blinked, startled by the offer. Why hadn't she thought of this before? It made perfect sense. She needed the help, and this way, she could keep an eye on Ian during the weekends and ensure he stayed on track. Plus, he'd cost far less than hiring someone new.

She gave him a grateful smile. "I think that's a wonderful idea, sweetheart."

"Seriously?" Eric frowned. "You're going to put him in front of customers?"

"Surely business isn't so bad you can't find someone other than Ian," her mother scoffed, to Dana's horror.

"He'll need a haircut for sure," Bob muttered, shaking his head.

"Izzy would've been a natural," Joan sighed. "Everyone likes her."

Dana's chest tightened as she saw hurt flash across Ian's face. "I think he'll do great," she said firmly, meeting her son's eyes. "Right, kiddo?"

"Sure," Ian said, his voice subdued.

For a few moments, the room fell into painful silence, the only sound the scrape of forks against plates. Then Dana's phone rang, the sound slicing through the quiet like a siren.

"Sorry," she said, jumping up to grab it from her purse. She glanced at the screen. Ben's name. Her stomach tightened. Hesitating, she answered, "Hello?"

"Mrs. Blair, I'm sorry to disturb you on a holiday," Ben said, his tone brisk but apologetic. "I wanted to make you aware of a... situation."

Dana frowned, glancing at her family. "A situation?" she repeated.

Ben cleared his throat. "Yes, well, it appears your case—your daughter's case—has garnered some media attention. They're requesting a statement from you."

"A statement? Today?" Dana asked, her voice rising in frustration. Eric gave her a questioning look.

"I'm afraid it can't wait," Ben said firmly. "Things are already in motion, and it's to our advantage to control the narrative."

Dana felt irritation bubble to the surface. "What do you mean, already in motion?" she pressed, her patience thinning. Why couldn't he just get to the point?

"Channel 5 News is currently setting up outside the hospital," Ben said.

THIRTY-THREE
PADMA

Forty-one days after

"The table looks beautiful," Padma said, watching as Maeve straightened the Thanksgiving centerpiece she'd made with pinecones, fall leaves, and mini pumpkins. While Padma relished the design and plan of houses, Maeve had a creative touch with their décor that Padma lacked.

Maeve shrugged. "It's just some decorations."

Padma frowned. "What do you mean?" She gestured at the table. "I could never put something like this together. I don't have a creative bone in my body."

Maeve let out a short laugh, but there was no humor in it. "Yeah, well, it's not like I'm saving lives or anything."

Padma studied her daughter. "Not many people are," she said lightly, trying to gauge what Maeve was getting at. After a beat, she softened her tone. "What's on your mind, sweetheart?"

Maeve sighed, rolling a mini pumpkin between her hands. "Nothing, never mind."

Padma held her daughter's gaze. Finally, Maeve exhaled heavily. "Fine. It's just... everyone seems to have their *thing*, you know? And I still have no idea what mine is. I keep waiting for something to come along that'll be my everything, like you have."

A pang of guilt twisted in Padma's chest. Maeve was right—her career had been her everything. And for years, she'd been proud of that, proud that she'd built something meaningful, that she'd dedicated herself so fully to a career that helped people. But now, for the first time, she wasn't so sure.

She cleared her throat, choosing her words carefully. "I don't think having something be your everything is necessarily a good thing."

Maeve blinked, caught off guard. "You don't?"

Padma shook her head, pressing her fingers to her temples. "No. I used to think if I just worked hard enough, if I poured everything into my career, I'd feel... fulfilled. Like I was enough." She let out a hollow laugh. "But now, with everything that's happening, all of it could go away. And if it does... I'm not sure I'll know who I am without it."

Maeve's face softened. "Oh, Mom." Then she brightened. "Well, I can always teach you how to do tablescapes."

Padma laughed, wiping at her eyes.

"When are Nana and Nani coming?" she asked, using the Indian terms for her grandparents.

"Any minute," Padma said, forcing a smile. Though she loved her parents, she always felt a pang of dread before seeing them. They lived just an hour away, but as they'd aged, the hassle of Atlanta traffic meant they visited less often. Padma knew they loved her, and also that she should feel guiltier about seeing them so infrequently, but their love often showed up in the form of suggestions on how she could work harder and achieve more.

"OK, I'm going to change," Maeve said, giving the centerpiece one last tweak.

"Sweetheart, you look fine," Padma said, taking in Maeve's

leggings and NYU sweatshirt. "It's not like William and Kate are coming to dinner," she teased. Maeve had an interest-bordering-on-obsession with the royal family.

Maeve rolled her eyes and nodded at Padma's sweatpants. "You'd probably still wear those if they were," she said.

"I probably would," Padma agreed, grinning.

Maeve sighed, giving a small shake of her head. "Dressing up can be fun, you know."

"Speaking of dressing up," Padma ventured, seizing the moment, "Winter Formal is next week—are you still going with your friends?" As a junior, it was the first big dance Maeve was eligible to attend, and she and Izzy had been excited about it, buying their dresses together months ago.

Maeve's face drooped. "I don't know. Without Izzy, it feels..." She trailed off with a shrug.

Padma squeezed her shoulder gently. "You know, there is life without Izzy."

"I know," Maeve sighed. Her phone dinged, and she glanced down. A shy smile, the kind Padma had never seen before, lit her face.

"Who's that?" Padma asked casually.

Maeve blushed. "Just—a friend." Then she turned and hurried up the stairs.

Padma's stomach growled as she followed the mouthwatering aromas from the kitchen. Lars was tenting foil over a perfectly browned turkey, while a pot of lamb rogan josh—her father's favorite—simmered on the stove. The counter overflowed with traditional Thanksgiving sides alongside biryani and naan.

"You do know there are only five of us, right?" she asked.

Lars shrugged. "So, we'll have leftovers."

"For two years," she teased. "Thank you for all this. I feel guilty—I haven't lifted a finger."

"I didn't want you to," he said, leaning in to kiss her. "I know it's been tough lately."

Padma tensed, recalling the fleeting look she'd shared with Dana across the conference room table—the brief moment when the distance between them seemed to vanish. But then Dana had turned away, silently following her lawyer out of the room, and the sting of betrayal hit all over again.

The doorbell rang, making her jump.

"Beta!" her mother exclaimed as Padma opened the door, using the Hindi term of endearment. Dressed in gray wool pants and a light green embroidered kurti, she carried several plastic shopping bags.

"Hi, Mom," Padma said, taking the bags and peering inside. "You know Lars is cooking, right?"

"Of course," her mother scoffed. "And thank goodness—no one expects you in the kitchen, jaan. But I couldn't come empty-handed."

"She's been cooking since dawn," her father added in a loud whisper, stepping forward in his usual white button-down and baggy jeans. Though they'd lived in the US for decades, traces of their lilting Indian accents remained.

"Hi, Dad." She kissed his cheek, feeling the roughness of his salt-and-pepper beard.

In the kitchen, her mother clucked approvingly over the rogan josh. "When will you let your Swedish husband teach you proper Indian cooking?" she asked.

Lars smiled as Padma rolled her eyes.

"Nani, Nana!" Maeve jogged downstairs, now wearing a long red sweater flecked with glitter and dangly earrings.

"My beautiful granddaughter," Padma's father said, opening his arms. Padma swallowed a lump in her throat as she watched them embrace, her parents' usual reserve melting for Maeve. They fussed over her, smoothing her hair, their affection effortless in a way it had never quite been with Padma.

Lars slid an arm around Padma's waist. "Can I get anyone a drink?"

Her father raised his hand. "I'll have one of your famous Old Fashioneds."

"Only one," her mother warned. "You have to drive us home later."

As Lars set out glasses, Padma's gaze drifted to the bottle of bourbon. Usually, alcohol was just background noise, like the football games Lars played at low volume during the weekend. But today, her eyes tracked the amber liquid as he poured.

She could slip upstairs, retrieve the unopened bottle hidden in her dresser drawer. No one would know. A quick sip of vodka might help her relax around her parents. It had been a rough week, like Lars said. Didn't she deserve a little reprieve, just like everyone else?

"Sweetheart?"

Padma blinked. Lars was watching her.

"Can I get you a seltzer?" he asked.

She forced the thought away and smiled. "Sure, thanks."

They gathered in the living room as her parents questioned Maeve about school, beaming over her selection as first violin and honor roll achievements.

"And your nice friend next door?" Padma's mother asked. "The runner. How is she?"

The room fell silent. Lars glanced at Padma, his brows lifting.

"You didn't tell them?" he murmured. Heat crept up her neck.

"Tell us what?" her father asked, brow furrowed.

"Izzy's... in a coma," Maeve said, her voice small as her gaze flicked between them.

"A coma?" her grandmother gasped. "That poor girl!" She turned to Padma. "What happened?"

"Did you help her find a good doctor?" her father demanded. "You must know someone. Such a nice family."

"And isn't the mother your friend?" her mother pressed.

Padma closed her eyes, nodding. "Yes. But it's... complicated."

Her mother's sharp gaze shifted to Maeve. "Please. Tell us what is going on."

Padma opened her eyes. Maeve's face was caught between surprise and uncertainty, like the squirrels frozen in the glare of their security camera's floodlight.

"Um, Mrs. Blair is suing Mom. For malpractice," Maeve said, barely above a whisper.

"Oh my God," Padma's mother breathed.

"Beta," her father said, looking straight at her. "Is this true?"

Padma glanced at Lars for support, but his face held only disappointment. She cleared her throat. "Yes, unfortunately, it's true."

"But why?" her mother cried.

"It's complicated," Padma said again, sweat beading along her back. She glanced at Maeve. "Maybe now isn't the best time."

"No," her father insisted. "Tell us everything." His tone—demanding, critical—was the same he'd used when questioning her grades or when her MCAT scores hadn't qualified her for Harvard.

Padma felt herself shrinking under her parents' scrutiny, just as she had as a girl, just as she had in the Dean's office years ago when she'd been expelled from medical school—a humiliation her parents still didn't know about.

She'd grown up feeling the distance between her immigrant parents and her friends' American families, knowing that, unlike her friends' parents, hers would never automatically take her side. Instead of assuming that any goal not scored or test not aced must be due to outside factors, Padma's parents turned first to her, believing that taking responsibility and accountability for her shortcomings would drive her to work harder and be better.

"Dinner is ready," Lars interjected gently, casting a concerned glance her way.

Padma endured the meal as her father's relentless questions pressed down on her like a stone. She retold the story—every painful detail—while he prodded further: Had she done this? Why hadn't she done that? What exactly had she said? Sweat pooled at her nape and slid down her spine. She was only grateful she hadn't mentioned the potential promotion to her parents—it would only have given them more ammunition.

"I think that's enough for now, Aswath," Lars said firmly, breaking the tension as he slid a slice of chocolate pecan pie— her father's favorite—onto the table with a worried glance in Padma's direction.

Her father pursed his lips, clearly dissatisfied, but let the conversation shift.

Hours later, after her parents left, Padma retreated upstairs to change for her shift. Holidays had long been her preferred time to work—if she could convince Lars to let her. The ER was usually quieter, giving her time to catch up on charts.

Standing in front of her dresser, she hesitated. Her hand drifted to the top drawer, sliding it open. Reaching toward the back, her fingers coiled around the bottle hidden there.

She knew she was treading dangerous ground. Yet, the bottle's presence brought her a warped sense of comfort, an anchor as the rest of her life unraveled. It was what she needed right now, she told herself.

Downstairs, she kissed Lars quickly on her way out. "Don't you dare wash those," she said, nodding toward the pile of pots and pans in the sink. "Just soak them—I'll do it later."

"I can't believe you're abandoning me with this pie," he said, pointing at the half-eaten dessert on the counter. "Who knows what I'm capable of?"

"Hey, I'm still here!" Maeve piped up, popping her head out of the pantry.

Lars grinned. "Then it's you, me, and the pie, kid."

Padma laughed, blowing them both a kiss as she headed for the door.

In the car, just as she backed out of the driveway, her phone rang. Toby's name flashed on the screen.

"Hey," she said, one hand on the wheel. "I'm on my way in. Everything OK? Don't tell me you're working today, too."

"Unfortunately, yeah," Toby replied, his voice tight. "Lyle called me to come in." The unease in his tone sent a chill down Padma's spine.

"What's going on?" she asked, her stomach knotting.

"There's a news van parked outside," Toby said. "And they want to talk to you."

THIRTY-FOUR

MAEVE

Forty-two days after

The pale light sneaking around Maeve's closed curtains told her it was too early to be awake, especially on a school vacation day. She rolled over, trying to drift back to sleep, but her mind was already whirring with anticipation—it was Friday, and she'd get to see Ian again.

After a few minutes, she sighed and pushed back the covers. Slipping her feet into the fuzzy white Ugg slippers Izzy had given her last Christmas, she headed to the bathroom. On the way, she caught her reflection in the full-length mirror. Izzy had always been the pretty one, with her sleek hair, flawless skin, and big blue eyes. But now, as Maeve studied her own wavy hair, warm skin, and odd-colored eyes, they seemed unexpectedly alluring. Ian seemed to think so, at least.

She pressed her hand to her lips, remembering his kisses, and ran the other slowly along the side of her breast, remembering his hand under her shirt. A shiver of pleasure ran through her. She'd long been embarrassed about being so inexperienced, a feeling heightened when Izzy started hooking up with Taylor. But now, she'd been kissed—by Ian no less. Wrapping her arms around herself, she smiled at her reflection, giddy. She couldn't wait to see him again, to kiss him again—and maybe more. The thought sent a fizzy rush of excitement through her.

She reached for her phone and saw a new message from him, sent late the night before after she'd gone to sleep.

Still up for hanging out tomorrow?

Yes

Maeve hit send before she could overthink it, clutching her phone to her chest as a smile spread so wide it hurt her cheeks.

Her stomach growled, but the thought of facing her parents after yesterday's awkward Thanksgiving dinner tightened her throat. The meal had unraveled after Maeve let it slip to her grandparents that Mrs. Blair was suing her mom. Their barrage of questions—pointed, accusatory—had taken Maeve by surprise. She'd assumed her mom was blameless, but could she have been wrong? Her grandfather's grilling had made her mom look small, defeated, almost fragile. It unsettled Maeve deeply; she'd always thought of her mom as invincible. Worse, her dad's disappointed look when the conversation spiraled made her stomach churn. She couldn't bear the thought of him being mad at her.

Steeling herself, Maeve pulled on a sweatshirt over her tank top and padded downstairs to the kitchen. She hesitated at the bottom of the stairs, spotting her dad at the island, coffee in hand, scanning his iPad. He glanced up, his worried expression smoothing into a tired smile.

"Hey, sweetheart," he said. "You're up early."

"Yeah." Maeve stifled a yawn, her eyes darting around. "Is Mom up?"

Her dad sighed. "Not yet. I don't think she slept well."

Sliding onto a stool, Maeve hooked her feet around the legs, guilt gnawing at her. "I'm sorry about what I said to Nani and Nana," she ventured. "They seemed mad at her."

Her dad set the iPad aside, his tone careful. "Not mad, exactly," he said, as though choosing each word deliberately. Maeve recognized the cautious way her parents talked when they thought she wasn't ready for the full truth. "Your mom's relationship with them is... complicated. They love her, but they show it by pointing out mistakes, thinking it'll help her avoid bigger ones."

Maeve frowned, struggling to reconcile this. "That's messed up," she said. Her parents never criticized her, though she rarely gave them reason to. As a straight-A student who practiced violin without being told, Maeve had always kept her path clear of parental disappointment.

"It is messed up," her dad admitted. "And it's hard for your mom. Maybe don't tell her we talked about this, OK?"

Maeve nodded, stealing a strawberry from his plate. "But... the lawsuit," she asked hesitantly. "Mom didn't do anything wrong, did she?"

Her dad's gaze flicked briefly to his iPad. "Your mom did her best," he said. "Sometimes things just... happen."

"Mm," Maeve murmured, noticing he still hadn't answered her question.

Her dad brightened, shifting the mood. "Mickey Mouse pancakes? How about it?"

She rolled her eyes. "Dad, I haven't eaten those in years."

"All the more reason to see if I've still got it," he teased, flexing his bicep.

After breakfast, Maeve checked her phone again. Ian had texted:

> Sadie's having a party later, would you wanna go? We don't have to stay long if you don't want to.

A jolt of nervous energy ran through Maeve. She didn't go to parties—not the kind Sadie Kemp hosted—and she didn't think Ian did, either. They were the domain of glossy, popular kids. And while Ian wasn't unpopular, he wasn't Sadie's crowd.

> Didn't know you were friends with Sadie

> I'm not

Then the three little dots appeared, dancing on her screen like they were trying to tease out her patience. Finally, his next text came through:

> Just need to stop by for a min.

> Yeah sure

If she was being honest, the thought of walking into a party with Ian sent a thrill through her. Would people look at her differently? She liked that idea. She pictured the scene: heads turning as they walked in, first to him, then to her. Would it change the way people saw her? Part of her hoped so.

Izzy would never have gone to one of Sadie's parties—not that she'd ever been invited, but she avoided any hint of underage drinking that could threaten her place on the cross-country team. Maeve bit her lip, realizing with a flash of guilt that she liked the idea of doing something Izzy never would.

> Cool

> We can get pizza first if you want.

Maeve felt the grin stretch across her face again. This was shaping up to be an actual date.

"All good over there?" her dad asked, glancing at her smile and then her phone.

"Mm-hm," she said, pushing her plate away. "I'm going to start my homework."

Upstairs, she glanced at her backpack but knew she couldn't focus. On any other day off, Izzy would've already texted her with plans: a Starbucks run, studying with any of the *Princess Diaries* movies—their favorite—on in the background, or dragging their wider friend group to do something totally random, like disco roller skating. But today there was no Izzy.

Maeve flopped onto her bed, staring at the ceiling. *What do I want to do?* she asked herself.

Run. The idea surprised her. Running was Izzy's thing, not hers. But right now, she needed to direct her restless energy somewhere, and she craved the sting of cold air and the burn in her muscles—something physical to remind herself she was alive, even if Izzy wasn't.

She pulled on leggings and a sports bra, pausing to take in her reflection. The curve of her hips, the weight of her chest— did Ian like her body? Would she let him take off her shirt tonight? Her skin flushed at the thought.

"I'm going for a run," she called to her dad as she tied her sneakers.

Outside, the air stung her cheeks. Stretching in the driveway, she scanned Ian's house. His grandparents' RV was parked on the curb, but the windows were dark. As she turned to start, the Blairs' front door opened. Maeve froze as Mrs. Blair stepped out, wrapped in a white puffy coat over a sweater dress.

"Oh," Mrs. Blair said, noticing Maeve. She hesitated, then continued toward her car, her face tight with exhaustion.

"How's Izzy?" Maeve blurted, her throat tightening. It had been nearly a week since Ian had snuck her in to visit Izzy—a record for how long they'd been apart.

Mrs. Blair stopped, her back to Maeve, then slowly turned. Her face was etched with pain, her mouth parting as if to respond, but no words came. She climbed into her car, reversed down the driveway, and drove away, glancing at Maeve only once.

A surge of hurt and anger rose in Maeve. The woman who'd taught her to French braid, who'd proudly displayed her school photo on the fridge alongside her own children, had just driven off without a word.

Maeve broke into a run, chasing the direction of the car. She sprinted until her lungs burned and her legs quaked, stopping only when the SUV disappeared around a distant corner. Panting, she leaned against a tree, her body trembling with exertion and anger. When her breathing steadied, she turned and jogged home.

Inside, the house was still, her parents' bedroom door shut. She could hear their muffled voices, the tension palpable even through the walls. She shook it off. She had a date tonight. For once, she wanted to focus on herself.

"Where's Mom?" she asked her dad later, realizing she hadn't seen her all day.

"In bed," he said with a tired smile. "She's not, um, feeling well."

A small pit of unease formed in her stomach. Her mother was never sick. She tried to push the feeling aside as she got ready to go out, carefully applying a coat of mascara and shimmery pink lip gloss, something she rarely bothered with.

She told her dad she was going for pizza and a movie with friends. Rather than his usual probing for details, he'd simply looked relieved she was going out at all. If Maeve weren't so excited, the thought might have hurt. Did her parents think she had no life outside of Izzy? Embarrassing.

Ian was already at the pizza place when she arrived. Without discussing it, they'd agreed to drive separately—neither wanted to explain if their parents caught them getting into a car together.

"Hey," Maeve said as she approached.

Ian looked up from his phone, standing so fast he knocked into the table. His water glass toppled, spilling across the surface and onto the chair. "Shit," he muttered, his face reddening as he grabbed a napkin to mop up the mess. "Now your chair's all wet."

"It's fine," she laughed, raising an eyebrow. "I'll just have to sit here." She pulled a chair from another table, positioning it right next to his.

"Yeah," he said, his eyes sweeping over her before meeting her gaze with a grin. "Much better."

They sat close, shoulders nearly touching, as they looked over the menu. When their pizza arrived—half pepperoni for him, half mushroom for her—they talked easily, both of them smiling between bites. Maeve forgot to feel nervous and even let herself laugh with her mouth wide open at one of Ian's jokes, something she only ever did with Izzy or her family.

"So, um, how was Thanksgiving?" Ian asked as their server cleared the table. His face had turned serious and his voice was cautious.

Maeve sighed, twisting her paper napkin into a tight cylinder. "Mm, I've had better," she admitted. "It got a little intense."

"Oh yeah?" Ian gave her a searching look.

The pit of dread stirred in her stomach again, but Maeve forced it down. "Just family stuff," she said, pasting on a smile. She hesitated, then slid her hand onto his thigh. Her own boldness made her dizzy, but when Ian covered her hand with his and exhaled sharply, her nerves gave way to exhilaration.

"Should we get out of here?" he asked, his voice low. She nodded.

They left Maeve's car at the pizza place and parked Ian's down the block from Sadie's house. Maeve's whole body hummed, desperate for him to lean over and kiss her. They locked eyes, the intensity of his gaze making her feel like one of the tightly wound strings of her violin.

They didn't ease into it like before. Their mouths opened, tongues meeting, and Maeve slid her hands under Ian's shirt, her fingers skimming the warmth of his chest. His hands mirrored hers, moving under her sweater, fingers brushing her stomach before slipping into her bra.

"Oh," she gasped, a spark of heat racing through her. His lips pressed harder against hers, his hands exploring. Ian pulled her closer, trying to lift her onto his lap. Maeve wasn't sure how the mechanics of that were going to work but she didn't care. She only cared that she felt good, really good. Better than she had in a long time.

Then his phone buzzed and he paused to look at it.

"Shit," he said. "We should go in."

"Sure." Maeve shrugged, trying to sound breezy. In truth, she wanted to stay in the car with him.

Ian wiped his hands on his jeans, as though trying to calm himself. "We don't have to stay long," he said. "I just have to do one quick thing." He squeezed her hand, and her insides liquified.

Inside, the house was packed. A Sabrina Carpenter remix thudded through the speakers, and the sharp tang of weed hung in the air. Maeve recognized faces from school, but she felt out of place.

"There you are," Sadie said, her fake lashes fluttering. "Max was looking for you. He's about to leave."

Maeve felt Ian tense next to her. "I'll be right back," he said to her, squeezing her arm before disappearing into the crowd.

Maeve nodded and tried to smile like she was comfortable standing there alone.

Sadie tilted her head, her eyes narrowing. "Maeve Paulsen, right?"

Maeve nodded. "We have Chemistry together."

Sadie smirked. "And you're here with... Ian?" The disbelief in her voice prickled at Maeve's nerves.

"Yeah," Maeve said, lifting her chin. "Why?"

Sadie shrugged. "Just, you're so... straight. And Ian's only here to buy drugs from my brother."

Maeve blinked, confusion washing over her. Sadie's smirk deepened.

"You didn't know?" Sadie said, laughing. "Ian's one of his best customers."

Maeve felt her stomach drop.

Sadie's eyes sparkled with sudden recognition. "Wait, is your mom a doctor?"

"Uh, yeah," Maeve replied warily, scanning the room for Ian, hoping he'd hurry up with whatever he was doing.

Sadie's face lit up. "Oh my God, is your mom *the* doctor? The one who put Izzy Blair in a coma?"

Maeve's throat constricted.

Sadie turned, calling to her friend. "Mia! Maeve's mom is the coma doctor!"

A tall blonde girl looked up and came toward them, her face twisting in surprise. "You poor thing," she said, scrolling on her phone. "We were just looking at this."

She handed her phone to Maeve, who stared at the headline: *Atlanta Doctor's Negligence Puts High School Athlete in Coma.*

Maeve's breath caught. "Where did you get this?" she whispered, handing the phone back.

Mia shrugged. "It's everywhere."

Without another word, Maeve turned and bolted out the door.

THIRTY-FIVE

IAN

Forty-two days after

Ian had woken that morning to his mom gently shaking his shoulder. "It's time to get up, sweetie," she'd said softly.

He'd groaned, pulling the pillow over his head. "There's no school today."

"You're helping at the shop, remember? It's Black Friday."

He'd winced as the memory resurfaced—his bright idea at Thanksgiving dinner to pitch in at the store. It had seemed like a good plan at the time, fueled by his vague desire to prove he wasn't totally useless and the pleasant Adderall wave he'd been riding. Squinting at the clock, he groaned again. *What was I thinking?* At least he was seeing Maeve later, something to look forward to and get him through the day.

Less than thirty minutes later, he was at Haven and Hearth, rubbing sleep from his eyes as his mom walked him through the basics of retail survival: ringing up purchases, searching inventory, processing special orders.

"OK, OK, I've got it," he grumbled after the third demonstration of the point-of-sale system. She patted his shoulder and left to grab breakfast sandwiches, leaving him instructions to restock the candle display.

When she returned, she eyed the shelf critically. "Not half bad," she said, handing him a bacon, egg, and cheese melt.

The smell of eggs hit him hard, and he turned away quickly, swallowing the nausea rising in his throat.

His mom tilted her head. "You OK?"

"Yeah," he lied, shoving his hands into his pockets to hide their trembling. "Just not super hungry."

Once she disappeared into the office, Ian darted for his backpack, relief flooding him as he pulled out the pill bottle hidden in an inner pocket. But when he shook it, only two pills fell into his palm. His stomach sank. *How have I burned through it so fast?* He racked his brain for answers but came up empty. Resigned, he swallowed them both and texted Max.

The morning blurred in a haze of ringing up customers, restocking shelves, and wrestling with the ribbon dispenser at the gift-wrapping station. His phone stayed silent, and as the hours passed, his anxiety grew. Finally, around lunchtime, his phone dinged. Max.

> I'm stopping by Sadie's party tonight. Meet me there.

Ian sighed, slamming the register drawer closed. The last thing he wanted to do was drag himself to Sadie's party. He texted back quickly.

> Can I meet you earlier?

> Can't

"Put your phone away," his mom murmured as a customer set seven candles on the counter, each needing individual wrapping. Ian barely suppressed a groan as he reached for the scissors.

Later, during a lull, Ian finally ate his sandwich, leaning against the counter as his mom straightened a display of blankets. "Is it always this busy?" he asked.

She gave a tight smile. "Sadly, no. But Black Friday's a big deal—lots of stores turn their yearly profit today."

"What about Haven and Hearth?" Ian asked, licking his fingers as he popped the last bite of his sandwich in his mouth.

She hesitated, tucking her hair behind her ear. "I hope so. It hasn't been a great year—or a great couple of years," she admitted dryly. "Sometimes I think I'm not very good at this."

"At what?"

She gestured toward the shelves. "Running the shop. This was Grandma's world—she was so good at it. I'm... not her."

"I always thought you loved it," he said. "I mean, you and Grandma talk about it pretty much nonstop. Like, seriously, who loves linen napkins *that* much?"

His mom laughed, then her face tightened. "I don't think we have much else to talk about."

"Oh," Ian said.

She added, "I took over to keep it in the family, but it was really hers. Sometimes I feel like I'm just pretending."

Ian crumpled his napkin and tossed it perfectly into the trash. "Seems like you're doing great," he said, surprising himself with how much he meant it.

Her smile was small but real. "Thanks, sweetie." Then her face grew serious. "Ian," she said cautiously, "I know you're still... figuring things out. What you want your life to look like and all that. And I want you to know that's OK. I mean, I'm forty-six, and most days I'm still not even sure."

There was a quiet sadness in her voice that made Ian sit up and look at her. He wasn't used to thinking of his mom as vulnerable. She was the person who held everything together. But now, with the tired lines around her eyes and the slump in her shoulders, she seemed human in a way that made his throat tighten.

"OK," he said awkwardly. "Thanks."

Hours later, as the sky darkened, his mom flipped the sign to *Closed.* Ian let out a sigh of relief. "I can't wait to go home," he said, his feet aching, his stomach growling.

His mom glanced around. "We still need to clean up and reconcile the register," she said, nodding at the rifled displays and the mess of ribbon and wrapping paper scraps.

Ian moaned. How did she do this every day? But when he glanced over, she was smiling at him.

"I couldn't have managed today without you," she said. "And you picked up the inventory system so fast."

A flicker of pride warmed his chest. *Take that, Grandpa Bob,* he thought. *Maybe I don't suck at everything after all.*

Back home, Ian collapsed onto his bed, drained. *Just five minutes,* he thought, closing his eyes.

When he woke, the room was dark. Disoriented, he rubbed his face until the realization hit: It was time to meet Maeve. Excitement jolted through him, chasing away the last of his grogginess. He smoothed a hand over the rumpled sheet, the memory of her beside him earlier that week rushing back—the feel of her lips, the faint scent of her shampoo lingering in the air.

But more than the kissing, it was the way she'd looked at him, the way she'd listened. Their conversations had felt effortless, her laugh the brightest sound in the room. He couldn't remember ever feeling like that with anyone. He liked her so much it was almost terrifying.

Sitting up, his headache hit him, along with the dry, cottony feeling in his mouth. Instinctively he reached for the pill bottle in his backpack, then remembered it was empty. Panic shot through him and he felt himself begin to sweat.

It's OK, he told himself, trying to slow his breathing. *You'll see Max in a few hours. You can do this.*

Maeve wasn't there yet when he arrived at the pizza place, so Ian fired off a quick text to Max.

> Be there soon. It's gonna be a big order.

Max sent back a thumbs up.

"Hey."

Ian looked up to see Maeve approaching, her hair pulled back into a ponytail with soft tendrils escaping around her face. Her silver-gray eyes sparkled as she smiled, and for a moment, everything else fell away. He tried to push any thoughts about pills out of his mind.

During dinner, Ian got lost in Maeve's laugh and the brush of her leg against his under the table. By the time she placed her hand on his thigh, all he wanted was to take her somewhere quiet—but his head was pounding, and he felt like he might crawl out of his skin. He had to get to Sadie's.

"We'll be quick at Sadie's," he assured Maeve after they'd pulled apart in his car. He told himself it wouldn't take long: He'd slip away once they were inside, deal with what he needed to, and get right back to her. Then they'd pick up where they'd left off.

Ian found Max in the kitchen, leaning against the counter like he owned the place. Sadie's older brother had the same cocky smirk she did, but his felt sharper, more calculating. Ian shifted nervously, glancing around to make sure no one was paying attention. The party noise drowned out most conversations—a bass-heavy song rattled the floor, and someone shouted about a spilled drink in the living room.

"You need something?" Max asked, already knowing the answer.

"Yeah. Adderall," Ian said, keeping his voice low. He hesitated. "And, uh, maybe some Xanax. Just to help me sleep."

Max raised an eyebrow but didn't comment. Instead, he motioned for Ian to follow him down the hall to one of the bedrooms, where he pulled a pill bottle from his jacket pocket, shook out a mix of blue and white pills, and handed them to Ian in a small plastic bag. "You know the deal."

Ian slipped him the cash without counting it. His hands trembled as he popped one of the Adderall pills into his mouth, dry swallowing like it was second nature. Relief hit instantly, even if he knew it was just in his head.

"Thanks," Ian muttered before heading for the door.

Back in the crowded main room, Ian scanned for Maeve but couldn't find her. He checked the kitchen, the backyard, the patio, all with no luck. Just as he turned to head inside again, he almost collided with Sadie, who was walking and filming herself on her phone.

"Watch it," she snapped, then glanced up and immediately pasted on a pouty smile. "Oh, hey, Ian."

"Have you seen Maeve?" he asked, his voice edged with urgency.

Sadie flipped her hair over one shoulder, her eyes glinting with mischief. "Mm, I think she left."

Ian's stomach dropped. "What? Why?"

Her lashes fluttered in mock sympathy. "I'm so sorry. I didn't realize she hadn't seen the news story about her mom." She placed a perfectly manicured hand over her chest. "I never should have brought it up."

Ian's hands balled into fists at his sides. Maeve hadn't said anything about the news story at dinner, so he'd assumed she hadn't seen it. He hadn't wanted to ruin the mood by bringing it up.

Sadie tilted her head coyly. "Also," she added, her voice dropping conspiratorially, "I might have mentioned why you were really here tonight." She leaned closer, her fingers grazing his arm. "I didn't know your girlfriend was so... naïve." Her lips curved into a smirk. "I thought everyone knew about your... habit."

Ian shook off her hand, his voice tight. "Thanks a lot, Sadie."

"Hey, man, I got you a beer." Jenner appeared at his side, a bottle in one hand. He slung the other arm around Sadie's shoulders.

"I have to go," Ian said abruptly, brushing past them. Outside, he pulled out his phone and dialed Maeve. It went straight to voicemail.

THIRTY-SIX

DANA

Forty-five days after

Dana sat on the edge of her bed, her phone vibrating relentlessly beside her. The news story had spread like wildfire since Thanksgiving, and by now—the Monday after—everyone she'd ever crossed paths with seemed to have an opinion. Former clients, neighbors, even a college roommate she hadn't spoken to in twenty years were reaching out with texts and emails that ranged from supportive to curious to outright intrusive.

She skimmed one message after another:

> OMG I saw the story. To think you and Padma were so close! Here for you.

> I never thought you were the kind of person to do something like that to a friend.

> I heard your awful news. Call me—let's catch up!

The last one was from a woman Dana could barely remember, someone who'd once tried to sell her essential oils.

Eric walked into the room, holding a cup of coffee. He took one look at her phone and frowned. "Still going?" he asked.

Dana let out a weary laugh and flipped the phone over to silence the notifications. "I can't believe how fast this spiraled. The whole neighborhood seems to be taking sides like it's a football game or something."

Eric leaned against the doorframe. "It will die down. People have short memories."

"I don't know." Dana rubbed the back of her neck. "The media circus, the people taking sides. Is this really what's best for Izzy?" Dana felt a familiar pang of guilt and frustration rising in her chest. She didn't have an answer to her own question—not one that felt complete or convincing.

"But Ben said media attention was a good thing, right?" Eric said.

Dana let out a dry laugh. "Of course he did. For him, it probably is. But we're the ones who have to live with the fallout."

Eric shook his head and sighed. "This is temporary," he said, though his tone carried more hope than certainty. He hesitated, then added, "Have you seen the hospital bills that have started to come in?"

Dana's stomach lurched. She stood, brushing past him to grab her coat. "I'm meeting with Ben this morning before work," she said. "I'll see what else he has to say."

As she walked out the door, she could hear her mother's voice in her head, the sharp, disapproving tone on Thanksgiving when she'd discovered what was going on with the news coverage.

"Dana, this hullabaloo you've stirred up—it's unbecoming. You should have kept this private. You're a business owner! What will people think?"

She clenched her jaw as she got into her car. Her mother's concern was always about appearances, never substance. Izzy was in a coma, and all Dana's mother cared about was how Dana's actions reflected on the family business.

At his office, Ben greeted her with his usual brisk efficiency. His tailored suit and polished shoes made him look like someone who belonged in a glossy ad for legal services.

"This is good," he said, sitting across from her. "The judge has agreed to fast-track the case, citing the public interest. The media attention is working in our favor."

Dana stared at him, feeling a mixture of relief and unease. "How fast is fast?"

"Months instead of years," Ben said. "It's a win, Mrs. Blair."

She hesitated, twisting her wedding band around her finger. "I never wanted it to be like this," she said. "The cameras, the headlines—Padma's face plastered everywhere like she's a criminal." Her voice wavered. "She's my best friend."

Ben's expression softened slightly, though his tone remained matter of fact. "Mrs. Blair, let me remind you that this isn't personal. It's legal. And public opinion matters. The more people are paying attention, the more pressure there is for a favorable settlement—or a strong outcome if we go to trial."

"But at what cost?" Dana asked, the words tumbling out before she could stop them.

Ben leaned back in his chair, folding his hands. "At the cost of ensuring Izzy gets the care she'll need for the rest of her life. That's why you're doing this."

Ben's reference to the rest of Izzy's life landed like a blow. It was clear he meant Izzy's life as it was now—unresponsive, unreachable, locked away even from those who loved her most. The doctors had been trying to gently prepare Dana for the possibility that this might be her daughter's future. But Dana wasn't ready to give up hope. She didn't think she ever would be.

Leaving Ben's office, Dana felt more conflicted than ever. Was she doing the right thing? Padma *had* made a mistake. And Izzy had suffered for it—would continue to suffer, if the doctors' predictions were right. Dana's body went cold at the thought. Plus, though she'd avoided Eric's mention of it, she had seen the stack of medical bills they'd begun to receive. The sums listed only added to her constant feeling of despair.

She had never wanted any of this. At a red light, Dana closed her eyes, imagining a different version of her life—one where she hadn't let Izzy push herself so hard, where she'd been a better, more present mother. The kind whose daughter would talk to her about boys and birth control. Who wouldn't let Ian fade into the background, outshone by his sister and judged harshly by his father.

A honk behind her jolted her eyes open. The light was green. Swallowing the hopelessness rising in her throat, she eased forward. She couldn't undo it. Years spent drifting, letting life carry her along, had led here: a crumbling marriage, a career she wasn't suited for, and a daughter she might lose forever.

The only bright spot lately—amazingly—had been Ian. He'd spent Thanksgiving weekend helping at the shop, unexpectedly patient with customers and quick to restock shelves. Even the older women adored him. "Such a nice boy," one had said warmly, making Ian duck his head, his face flushing with embarrassment—but not before Dana saw a flicker of pride.

"You're a natural," she'd told him as they locked up Sunday evening.

Ian shrugged. "It's not that hard," he said, but his voice held a warmth she hadn't heard in weeks. For the first time in a long while, she felt a glimmer of hope that their relationship might be mending.

Pulling into her driveway, Dana glimpsed Padma coming out her own front door. Her heart sank. Padma stood waiting as Dana rolled to a stop, her face etched with exhaustion and fury.

For a brief moment Dana considered staying in the car—possibly forever—but then sighed and climbed out.

"Padma," she began, but Padma raised a hand.

"No," Padma said, her voice tight with restrained anger. "You don't get to justify this. Not to me."

Dana swallowed hard. "I didn't want it to turn into this. The news vans, the headlines—it's not what I wanted."

"But it's what happened," Padma snapped. "Do you know what it's like to walk into my own hospital and feel everyone staring at me like I'm a monster? My career, my reputation, my shot at getting promoted—Dana, you've put everything I've worked for at risk."

Dana's eyes filled with tears. "I didn't want to hurt you," she said quietly. "I'm just trying to do what's right for Izzy."

Padma shook her head, disbelief in her eyes. "By ruining my life?"

"You still have Maeve," Dana blurted, her voice trembling. "And Lars. You have so much, Padma. It's just work—just a job. I've lost my daughter. Eric is moving out this week. Everything that matters to me is gone—don't you see that?" Her voice cracked, her words unraveling in the chilly evening air.

Padma's shoulders sagged, and for a moment, sympathy softened her features. "I'm sorry about Eric," she said quietly. But then her expression hardened. "But it's not my job to comfort you anymore, Dana. You made your choice—and it wasn't me." Without waiting for a reply, she turned and walked to her house, leaving Dana alone in the driveway, the silence heavier than words could ever be.

Later, Dana sat in the stillness of Izzy's hospital room, the rhythmic hum of the ventilator blending into the background. The sound that had once unnerved her now felt oddly soothing. Tears streaked her cheeks. As a rule, she tried not to cry in front of Izzy. She'd always made an effort not to cry in front of the kids, believing it was her job to appear competent and unflappable—just as her mother had. But now she wondered if that had been a mistake—if they'd needed to see her falter, get angry, or feel pain. What had her façade of strength achieved? Izzy hadn't trusted her enough to talk about birth control, and Ian had drifted away until recently.

"I'm so sorry," she whispered to Izzy, her voice breaking. "For all of it." If she could do it all over again, she'd make different choices—though what exactly, she wasn't sure. The thing was, she'd never really let herself think about what *she* wanted, never let herself imagine or dream. Her future had always been assumed. She'd take over the shop. She'd marry Eric, who had treated their relationship like a foregone conclusion from the day they met in her senior year of college.

A nurse bustled in, and Dana quickly wiped her tears. She needed to stop fantasizing about having a different life and start focusing on fixing the one she did have. Leaning over, she pressed a kiss to Izzy's forehead. "I'll be back tomorrow, love," she murmured.

Driving home, dread pooled in her stomach like lead. Tonight, she and Eric would tell Ian about the separation. She'd begged for more time—her fragile connection with Ian felt like a tender shoot just beginning to grow—but Eric had been firm. They couldn't live in limbo anymore.

At the kitchen table, Ian's eyes darted nervously between them. Dana saw the question in his furrowed brow, the tension in his hunched shoulders.

"Is it Izzy?" he asked, his voice tinged with fear.

"No," Dana said quickly. She looked at Eric. This was his news to break.

Eric took a deep breath, his voice steady but heavy with finality. "Your mom and I have decided to separate."

Ian froze, his eyes wide. "For how long?" he asked after a beat.

Dana's throat tightened. "We don't know yet," she admitted softly. "But we need you to understand—this isn't your fault."

Ian let out a bitter laugh. "Right. It's never the kid's fault." He stood abruptly, his chair scraping against the floor. "I've got homework."

"Ian, wait," Dana started, but Ian was already halfway up the stairs. His door slammed shut, the sound a heavy thud that shut Dana out all over again.

THIRTY-SEVEN

PADMA

Forty-six days after

On Tuesday morning, Padma rolled over in bed, keeping her eyes closed for one more precious minute. She wasn't ready to face the fallout from the long holiday weekend.

Thanksgiving night at Midtown Hospital was generally quiet; the ER typically experienced a holiday lull aside from food poisoning cases or turkey carving accidents. But the moment she pulled into the parking lot after Toby's call, Padma realized this year would be different.

A Channel 5 News van sat near the entrance, its satellite dish towering like an ominous beacon against the night sky. A reporter checked her reflection in her phone while a cameraman hovered beside her. Anxiety tightened in Padma's chest. The employee side door was locked after hours, so she had no choice but to walk past them to get to the ER.

Climbing out of her car, she wrapped her coat tightly around herself, wishing she could disappear. The reporter's head jerked up. "Dr. Padma Paulsen?"

Padma quickened her pace, the hospital doors sliding open

just as the reporter's voice followed her: "Can you comment on the allegations—"

Inside the ER, the tension was worse. Nurses whispered by the reception desk, casting uneasy glances her way. Padma's cheeks burned, but she walked briskly to check the patient list.

As though sensing her presence, Toby emerged from his office and beckoned to her, his face grim, his usual white coat replaced with jeans and a faded Yankees sweatshirt. "You saw them?" he asked as she followed him into his office.

"They're hard to miss," Padma replied tersely.

Toby rubbed his temples. "Lyle isn't happy," he began. "The media attention—it's not a good look for the hospital."

Padma bristled. "None of this is my fault."

"I know," Toby said gently. "But perception matters. And right now, the perception is..." He let the words hang.

Padma crossed her arms. "Say it."

He sighed. "That you made a mistake, and now the hospital is paying for it."

Her stomach roiled with anger and humiliation. "How do I fix it?" she said, hearing the desperation in her own voice. "Out there"—she jerked her head toward the ER—"I always know what to do. But I don't know what to do right now." She gave him a pleading look.

Toby looked defeated. "Lyle wants you to consider a leave of absence. Until things settle down."

"No." The word came out fast and sharper than she intended. She took a deep breath, lowering her voice. "Please, Toby. I'm in the running for your job. If I step away right now, how does that look?"

"I'm not saying I agree with him," Toby said, rubbing his hand over his forehead. "But you have to see the position this puts everyone in."

"What about the position this puts *me* in?" Padma shot back. "I've worked here for fifteen years. I've earned that job."

Toby's face softened. "You're still being considered, Padma," he said. "But this... this isn't helping your cause."

She set her jaw. "Is Lyle asking me to take a leave, or telling me?"

Toby heaved a tired sigh. "Asking." He raised an eyebrow. "For now."

She nodded. "Then I need to get back out there to work."

The rest of her shift that Thanksgiving night had been miserable. Her colleagues kept their distance, avoiding the usual camaraderie of griping about slow lab results and joking about difficult patients. She tried to focus on her charts, but the weight of too many eyes on her made it impossible to concentrate.

Back home the next morning, she climbed into bed and stayed there until Sunday, claiming the flu. Lars didn't buy it— she was rarely sick, let alone bedridden—but he brought her tea and toast anyway, murmuring, "I'm here when you want to talk." She'd nodded, feeling too raw with hurt and humiliation to accept his sympathy.

Padma's excuse for staying in bed gained some credibility when Maeve woke Monday morning saying she didn't feel well enough for school, though she had no fever or visible symptoms. They let her stay home anyway, Maeve sequestered in her room, Padma in hers.

Now it was Tuesday, and Padma couldn't hide anymore. She opened her eyes with a groan, muttering, "Fucking Lyle."

There was no way she was giving in to his suggestion of a leave of absence. She was a better doctor and worked harder than anyone else in her department; Toby's job should be rightfully hers. Nothing—not a lawsuit, not media scrutiny, not even her colleagues' frosty behavior—was going to take it away.

The house was empty. Lars and Maeve had already left for work and school—at least Maeve was feeling better. In the kitchen, toast crusts and Lars's half-empty coffee cup sat abandoned on the counter, relics of another time. Guilt pricked at

Padma for avoiding her family all weekend. Tonight, she'd make it up to them—pizza so Lars wouldn't have to cook, and maybe she could convince Maeve to skip homework for a family movie night. She owed them that much.

She arrived at the hospital early and, before heading to the ER, took the elevator to the fifth floor. She knew she shouldn't be here, especially after the news coverage, but it was a habit she couldn't break.

Sunlight streamed through the open blinds in Izzy's room, softening her pale face, making her look more alive than she had in weeks. Izzy lay motionless, the ventilator's steady rhythm the only movement. Padma noted the absence of Dana's coat or bag. Izzy was alone.

That was good, she told herself—Dana needed to reclaim some semblance of a life. Yet a pang of something—sympathy, understanding—tugged at her. She knew how grief could consume, how hard it was to keep going when everything felt broken. But Dana's absence meant Padma could be here. It gave her a small, selfish comfort to know she could still care for Izzy in these quiet moments.

"I'm sorry, honey," she whispered, brushing a strand of hair from Izzy's forehead. "I wish I could fix this."

She stayed a few minutes longer, then slipped back to the ER before her shift began.

By the end of her shift, Padma was drained. The commanding confidence she once carried in the ER had been replaced by relentless self-doubt. She second-guessed every decision, triple-checked every test and diagnosis. It was exhausting, but with Lyle and the higher-ups deliberating Toby's replacement, she was determined to be beyond reproach. After that, she told herself, she'd ease up. Maybe.

Walking into the kitchen at home, the first thing she saw was the bottle of vodka from her dresser sitting on the counter. Lars stood next to it, looking grim.

Her stomach twisted. "Lars—" she began, her voice trembling.

"How long?" he interrupted, his tone flat. "How long has this been going on?"

"It's not what you think," she said quickly. "I haven't even opened it."

"Then why is it in our house? In your drawer?"

"How did you—" she began faintly.

"I do your laundry, remember?" His voice rose. "Wash it, fold it, put it away." He ticked off on his fingers. "I also do the grocery shopping, cook dinner, plan our vacations, plan our date nights—which, by the way, you cancel half the time because of work."

She flinched.

"So, tell me again," he said, voice softer but cutting. "Why is there a bottle of vodka in your dresser?"

"I needed... something," she admitted, voice faltering. "I don't even know what. But I haven't touched it. I swear."

"You're shutting me out," he said. The disappointment in his voice was worse than anger.

"I'm not," she insisted, but even as she said it, she knew it wasn't true. She had been withdrawing, retreating into work because it was the one thing she could control, the one thing she knew how to do well. It had always been that way.

"Yes, you are," he said, shaking his head. "You work all the time. And even when you're here, you're not here."

"You know I have a chance at Toby's job." She grasped for the one defense she had. "Once that's settled, I'll—"

"You'll work more," he cut in, throwing up his hands. "You'll keep working until there's nothing left for your family. But it's fine because you'll have this." He jerked his thumb toward the bottle.

He turned and walked out, leaving Padma burning with shame. She stared at the bottle, her reflection warped in the glass. Then, after a long moment, she grabbed it and poured its contents down the sink, the sharp smell of vodka stinging her nose.

When the bottle was empty, she set it down and gripped the counter, knuckles white, tears pricking her eyes. She had to fix this. If only she knew how.

THIRTY-EIGHT

MAEVE

Forty-six days after

Maeve walked into school on Tuesday morning, her stomach churning. The hallways felt tighter than usual, the air heavier, like the entire building had been holding its breath. The whispers started before she even reached her locker. She could feel eyes following her, voices dropping to murmurs as she passed. She kept her gaze fixed on the dull gray lockers in front of her and her arms tight against her sides.

After she'd left Sadie's party in tears on Friday night, her phone had buzzed relentlessly with calls and texts from Ian.

> Where'd you go?

> Are you OK?

> Please answer.

But she hadn't responded. Not right away. She'd gone home, crawled under her covers, and stared at the darkness until the first threads of dawn snaked through her blinds. Then, unable to hold it in any longer, she'd sent him a single message with a link to the article about her mom:

Did you know about this?

Despite the early hour, he started to reply immediately, the gray dots dancing on her screen for what felt like an eternity. Then a single word appeared.

Yes

Where did you go at the party?

She asked, her fingers trembling as she typed.

There was a long pause before the three dots appeared, then disappeared, then appeared again.

I'm so sorry, I screwed up. Can we talk?

She turned off her phone and rolled back over in bed, tears wetting her pillow.

When she woke up again hours later, she made her way downstairs. In the kitchen her dad took one look at her red eyes and wild hair and pushed aside the bread he'd been kneading.

"What's going on?" he asked, though his face told her he already knew.

"Have you seen it?" she asked, her voice hollow. "The news story?"

Her dad sighed and rubbed his knuckle across his forehead, leaving a trail of flour. "I did." He nodded. "It's not the whole story, sweetheart. You know that, right? People like to jump to conclusions."

"They're calling her negligent," Maeve whispered. "They're saying she hurt Izzy." Her voice cracked on her friend's name, and the tears she'd been holding back broke free.

"Hey, hey," her dad said, wiping his hands on a towel and pulling her into his arms. "Your mom loves Izzy. She's a good doctor. She's just... in a tough spot right now. But it'll be OK, I promise."

"How do you know?" she demanded, pulling back from his embrace. "How can you say that?"

"I just do," he said firmly, though his eyes betrayed his own uncertainty.

Her mom hadn't come downstairs all weekend.

"The flu," her dad explained, though Maeve wasn't sure she believed him. Her mom never got sick. She was invincible. Or she had been.

On Monday morning Maeve decided that she, too, wasn't ready to face the world. Though her parents looked skeptical, they'd let her stay home. Now, as Maeve grabbed her books from her locker and shoved them into her bag, she wished she was still there.

She headed in the direction of her first period class, trying to tune out the voices around her.

"She's the coma doctor's kid," someone said, not even trying to lower their voice.

"Did you see the article? I would literally die if that was my mom."

"Yeah, you actually might," someone else joked.

Maeve kept her head down, her cheeks burning.

At lunch, she tried to sit at her usual table, but the awkward silence that greeted her was worse than the whispers. Even her friends didn't seem to know what to say. She picked at her sandwich for a few minutes before standing abruptly and leaving.

She had just rounded the corner of the hallway near the library when she heard his voice.

"Maeve, wait!"

Ian jogged toward her, his face pale and drawn. She stopped, folding her arms tightly across her chest.

"What do you want?" she asked, her tone icy.

"Maeve, I didn't mean for any of this to happen," Ian said, his voice raw. "I didn't know Sadie would—"

"Show me that article? Or tell me that you only brought me to her party so you can get drugs from her brother?" she interrupted.

He flinched, and for a moment, she thought he might deny it. But he didn't.

"I'm sorry," he said again. "I was—"

"Just leave me alone," Maeve said, brushing past him.

By the time she reached her next class, her hands were trembling, and it was all she could do to keep herself from bursting into tears. She never should have let herself get pulled into Ian's orbit. The rumors had been there, but she'd convinced herself she knew him better—knew the real Ian. After all, they'd grown up together. She gave a short, bitter laugh. She was so naïve. So stupid. The same things she'd accused Izzy of when it came to Taylor. Turns out, Maeve wasn't any different.

The whispers followed her throughout the day, growing louder and crueler. In the hallway toward the end of the day a boy named Caden smirked at her as he passed her locker.

"Hey, Maeve," he said. "Does insurance cover comas? Or does your mom charge extra for that?"

Laughter rippled around her and Maeve's face flamed. She opened her mouth to say something, but her voice wouldn't come.

"What the hell is your problem, Caden?" Ian's voice cut through the laughter like a knife, shoving another kid out of the way as he approached.

"Just making conversation," Caden said with a shrug, though he looked less smug now.

Ian closed the gap between them in a long stride, grabbed Caden by the front of his shirt and slammed him against the lockers. Caden's head snapped back and hit the metal lockers with a thud.

"Say it again," Ian snarled. "I dare you."

"Ow!" Caden cried, his hand flying to the back of his head. "Chill, dude!"

"You two," a teacher shouted. "Break it up, now."

Ian gave Caden a final shove, then released him, but his glare never wavered.

"To the principal's office. Now," the teacher ordered.

Maeve saw Ian's face fall. His eyes flickered up, his face unreadable as they locked on hers for a split second before he was led away.

THIRTY-NINE

IAN

Forty-six days after

Ian perched on the edge of the principal's stiff, overstuffed chair, his fists clenched so tightly his nails bit into his palms. His heart hammered against his ribcage, each beat so fast and forceful he half-expected it to crack. His mind ricocheted between thoughts, chaotic and impossible to pin down. He tried to steady himself with a deep breath, but his lungs refused to cooperate. Was this the pills? Or was he just a mess all on his own?

He was so stupid. Things had just been starting to turn around for him at school, and now this. Though he didn't totally regret throwing Caden against the wall. What he regretted was the look on Maeve's face when he did it—embarrassment, maybe even regret.

When his dad arrived, his face was stony, his eyes blazing with disappointment.

"Assault?" his dad said in a low, tight voice. "You assaulted another student? I had to leave work for this?"

Ian didn't answer, staring at the floor like it might open up and swallow him whole.

Thirty minutes later, Ian walked out of the building with a suspension notice in his hand and his father trailing behind him. The silence in the car on the way home was almost unbearable, broken only by the sound of his dad gripping the steering wheel so tightly his knuckles whitened.

His dad finally spoke once they'd pulled into the driveway. "What were you thinking?" he asked, his voice tight with frustration. "Do you have any idea how serious this is? Colleges look at this stuff, Ian!"

Ian shrugged, feigning indifference, though he could feel the tears gathering behind his eyes. "Maybe I'm not going to college."

"Oh, that's a great plan," Eric said. "Throw your future away. Perfect."

"Why do you even care?" Ian shot back, his voice rising. "You're leaving anyway."

Eric froze, blinking in surprise. "What?"

"You and Mom are separating. Why do you care what I do? You'll be gone."

"That's not fair," Eric said, his voice quieter now but no less intense. "I'm still your father."

"Could've fooled me," Ian muttered.

"What the hell does that mean?" Eric demanded.

"You have no idea what's going on with me," Ian said, his voice cracking. "You haven't for years."

Eric looked wounded, then his face hardened. "This isn't about me, Ian. You need to stop screwing up or eventually there will be real consequences that Mom and I can't bail you out of. You need to start focusing on your future."

Ian shook his head, getting out of the car. "Whatever."

A little while later, a knock sounded on Ian's bedroom door as he lay staring at the ceiling, his mind spinning with anger.

Why couldn't his dad just accept that Ian wasn't like him or like Izzy—that he wasn't perfect, he didn't have everything figured out, and maybe never would?

"What?" he barked.

"It's me," his mom said softly. "Can I come in?"

Ian sighed and rolled onto his back. "Sure."

His mom stepped into the room and moved to sit on the edge of his bed.

"What happened?" she asked.

"Didn't Dad already tell you?" Ian said sarcastically.

She nodded. "Yes, but I want to hear it from you."

"I got in a fight." He shrugged. "They were harassing Maeve and—"

"Maeve?" his mom interrupted, her tone sharper now. "What does this have to do with Maeve?"

Ian hesitated, avoiding her eyes. The air in the room seemed to shift, charged with an energy that made his skin prickle.

"Ian," his mom said, her voice pitching higher. "Is there something going on between you and Maeve?"

He felt his throat tighten. His eyes flickered up to hers, then dropped back down to his hands, fidgeting in his lap. The sharp intake of her breath cut through the silence like a knife.

"Ian," she said, her voice strained. "You can't... do you have any idea how complicated that makes things?"

"I don't care," he said stubbornly. "I like her." He tried to push away the thought that Maeve may no longer like him, now that she knew the truth about him.

His mother's face twisted with a mix of frustration and disbelief. "This isn't a joke, Ian. Your sister is in a coma because of Maeve's mother."

"You don't know that," Ian shot back. "What if it's not her fault?"

His mother's shoulders sagged, and her eyes took on a

pleading look. "I'm trying to protect our family, Ian. Don't you see that?"

"It doesn't feel like it," he said bitterly. "It feels like you and Dad are just ripping it apart."

His mom stood abruptly, her hands trembling. "You don't understand now," she said, her voice quieter but no less intense. "But someday you will. And I hope you never have to make a choice like this."

She turned and left, closing the door softly behind her. For a moment, Ian stared at the door, his chest tight and his fists clenched. He wanted to call her back, to ask her not to leave him alone, to tell her that he needed her—that he didn't have anyone else. But the words wouldn't come.

Instead, he brushed the tears from his eyes, feeling like he was being pulled in a thousand directions, but every tether unraveling faster than he could hold on.

That night he did his best to fall asleep without taking a Xanax to counteract the Adderall. He was going to stop the pills. He had to. He lay in bed, replaying moments with Maeve: their first kiss in Izzy's hospital room, her laugh when he said something funny, the shy smile at the pizza place, the feel of her hand on his chest in the car—and the look of betrayal on her face that morning at school.

He hated himself for taking her to Sadie's party. He didn't want to be that version of himself anymore, but he'd dragged her right into it. She was the first person in forever who looked at him like he was worth knowing, and he'd screwed it up.

Before he could second-guess himself, Ian swung his legs out of bed. His parents were asleep, their room dark down the hall. Moving silently, he slipped outside. The cool night air hit him, and he stood barefoot in the grass, staring at Maeve's window.

The house was quiet, lights off. He considered going back, but the pull toward her was stronger. Crossing the yard, he picked up a rock and gently lobbed it at the glass. The faint tap broke the stillness.

Nothing.

Ian frowned and picked up another. He hesitated, suddenly feeling ridiculous—like some desperate, lovesick teenager in an old rom-com. But then again, wasn't that exactly what he was? He threw the second rock, this time a little harder. It hit the glass with a soft clink.

For a long moment, there was no movement. Ian's chest tightened, and he started to turn away. But then the curtain shifted. Maeve's face appeared in the window, pale in the moonlight, her hair falling in loose waves over her shoulders. For a second, Ian thought she might just close the curtain again. But then she raised the window.

"What are you doing?" she said in a loud whisper.

"I needed to see you," he said, his voice thick.

She frowned, a mix of confusion and hurt in her expression.

"Can we talk? Just for a minute," he pleaded.

Maeve bit her lip but disappeared from the window. Moments later, the front door opened and she stepped outside in flannel pajama pants and a tank top, arms crossed.

"What are you doing?" she said, voice low and tense.

Ian shoved his hands in his pockets. "I messed up," he admitted. "I shouldn't have taken you to the party. Not when I was there for... other reasons." He shook his head. "I'm done with all that. I promise."

Maeve's face softened slightly, but anger lingered in her eyes. "You didn't even warn me about the news story. You let me walk into that blind."

"I didn't know how," Ian said. "I didn't want to ruin the night."

"Well, you did," she said flatly.

He stepped closer, testing the space between them. "I'm sorry," he said softly. He reached for her hand, and she let him take it. A spark of hope flared in him. "Maeve, I like you. More than I've ever liked anyone. I don't know how to fix this, but I'll do whatever it takes." He brushed a tear from her cheek, their faces so close their lips nearly touched. Then a voice cut through the night like a blade.

"Maeve!"

They jumped apart as Dr. Paulsen appeared in the doorway, her tone sharp. "What the hell are you two doing?"

Maeve's body went rigid. "Mom, I—"

"Inside. Now," her mother ordered.

Maeve hesitated, then she gave Ian a final look before disappearing into the house.

Padma turned to Ian, her eyes blazing. "Stay away from my daughter," she said coldly.

"But I—" Ian began, his voice faltering.

"Whatever this is," Padma said, gesturing toward the house, "it's over."

Ian squared his shoulders. "That's not your decision," he said, his voice steadier than he felt.

Padma's expression darkened. "Your mom is capsizing my career, and you think this is a good time to start something with Maeve? Did you see the news story your mom planted about me?" she asked.

Ian froze. Wait, *planted?*

Padma folded her arms tightly across her chest. "Now my lawyer wants *me* to go public, to point out that your mom's lawsuit looks like a desperate money grab, with all Izzy's medical bills." Padma's gaze hardened. "Do you think I should do that?"

"No," Ian said quickly.

"Then don't make me," Padma said, her tone softening briefly, almost pitying, before turning cold again. "Stay away from Maeve."

FORTY

PADMA

Forty-seven days after

Padma barely slept. The image of Ian and Maeve on the porch, her hand in his, their heads close in the darkness, looped in her mind like a film she couldn't shut off. Maeve—her quiet, responsible Maeve—with Ian Blair, of all people. What could Maeve possibly see in him? A boy stumbling through school, with a reputation for trouble. Padma knew too much about Ian's struggles from Dana to ever approve of Maeve dating him.

And then there was the lawsuit. The last thing Padma needed was Maeve hanging around with someone who was tied to everything threatening their peace. How could Maeve not see how dangerous and disloyal her connection to Ian was?

Turning over in bed, Padma stared at the dark ceiling, guilt gnawing at her. When had her best friend become her enemy? They'd shared everything once, but now their friendship was unrecognizable. Padma told herself she had no choice but to protect her family and career. Her thoughts twisted in her mind as she rolled over again, chasing sleep that refused to come.

The next morning, she was brewing coffee when she heard

Maeve's hesitant footsteps on the stairs. When Maeve entered the kitchen, her hair mussed and eyes wary, Padma set a mug on the counter.

"Good morning," Padma said evenly.

Maeve didn't respond, walking to the fridge and yanking it open. She poured herself a glass of orange juice and leaned against the counter, her eyes focused somewhere in the middle distance.

"We need to talk," Padma said.

Maeve's eyes snapped to hers, glinting with anger. "How could you do that to me last night?" she demanded.

"You were outside in the middle of the night," Padma said, her voice tightening. "With Ian Blair."

"So?" Maeve shot back. "We weren't doing anything wrong."

"I know exactly what you were doing," Padma said. "And you can't see him anymore." She heard the sharpness in her voice, knew it would only widen the rift between her and Maeve. But with everything else crumbling around her, this was the one thing she could still control.

Maeve slammed the plastic juice glass onto the counter. "I'm not a little kid. You don't get to decide who I see."

"Maybe not," Padma said, trying to steady her voice. "But I know Ian better than you do. He's bad news, Maeve." Hurt and anger swirled in her chest, along with a healthy dose of guilt. She'd never kept Maeve from anything she loved. But how could her daughter not see how betrayed Padma felt that she'd chosen Ian, of all people?

Maeve's expression twisted. "No, you don't. You don't know him at all." She paused, her voice cold. "You just don't want me to see him because of the lawsuit."

"It's not exactly convenient," Padma admitted with a sigh, "but that's not why—"

"You're so selfish!" Maeve burst out, stamping her foot like she used to as a toddler. "First it was work, and now it's this lawsuit! It's all you think about and it's ruining my life!"

Before Padma could respond, Maeve stormed out, her footsteps pounding up the stairs, followed by the slam of her bedroom door.

Padma stood in the kitchen, the air knocked out of her. She poured coffee but didn't drink it, staring out the window at Dana's house. Was Maeve right? And Lars? Was she guilty of putting work before her family? Or was she simply fortunate to be so passionate about her career? Shaking her head, she dismissed the thought. Maeve was just being a moody teenager. And Lars—well, they needed to talk.

Later that morning, the chaos of the ER provided a familiar rhythm. The buzz from the news story seemed to have eased; fewer heads turned her way, and colleagues made polite conversation.

She moved quickly through her first few patients, assessing, diagnosing, treating. For a moment, it felt like any other shift. She walked briskly to exam room four, which, her notes told her, held a seventy-two-year-old man who'd suffered a fall.

"Mr. Bennett," she said warmly, pulling back the curtain to reveal a large man with a shock of white hair. "Let's take a look at your arm and then get some X-rays."

As she removed his makeshift sling, he grunted in pain. "Press down on my hand," she instructed.

He winced, then froze, his eyes narrowing. "Wait," he said. "You're the doctor from the news."

Padma stiffened. "Excuse me?"

"You're the one who put that kid in a coma," he said, his tone accusatory.

Padma flushed. "I can assure you—"

"I watch the news," he snapped. "I want a different doctor."

"Sir, I—"

"I said, I want a different doctor!" His voice rose. Turning to the nurse, he said, "Get me someone else."

Padma felt her face burn. "I'll have another doctor take over your care," she said tightly, turning on her heel and leaving the room.

In the hallway, Padma pressed her back against the wall, her chest rising and falling in sharp, shallow breaths as a wave of humiliation crashed over her. She gripped the stethoscope hanging around her neck like an anchor, willing herself not to cry.

"Everything OK?"

She looked up to see Gary Ackerman's sardonic expression.

"All good," she said, her voice tight, and walked away before he noticed the tears welling in her eyes.

The rest of her shift passed in a numb haze. When she closed out her last chart, she found herself at Toby's office door, her hand trembling as she knocked.

"Come in," Toby called, his smile fading as he saw her face. "Rough shift?"

Padma gave a brittle laugh. "You could say that."

Toby gestured for her to sit. She sank into the chair, letting out a shaky sigh, feeling utterly defeated. The vision of the future she'd once had for herself danced at the edges of her mind, mocking her with how far out of reach it suddenly felt.

Padma swallowed hard. "I think it's time for me to take that leave of absence."

FORTY-ONE
DANA

Forty-seven days after

Dana sat by Izzy's bed. With December finally here, she'd dug out their old box of Christmas books and begun reading them aloud to Izzy. When Ian and Izzy were little, they'd eagerly awaited the return of these stories each year—*The Polar Express, A Snowy Day*—a tradition that had faded as they grew older and lost interest. Now, though, Dana hoped hearing the familiar stories might stir something deep in Izzy's unconscious mind, a spark strong enough to guide her back.

It had been nearly seven weeks since Dana found Izzy in the shower. Seven weeks of waiting, wondering if her daughter would ever come back. The doctors still performed their routine evaluations—shining lights into Izzy's pupils, pressing her nail beds, testing her gag reflex. The results were always the same: Izzy's brain was active; there was no medical reason she shouldn't wake up. But she didn't. The urgency of CT scans and EEGs had faded as the weeks stretched into months.

Dana stroked Izzy's arm, her thoughts drifting to parents whose children were kept alive by machines but without hope of waking. She shuddered, imagining the excruciating decision they faced. And yet, a small, shameful part of her wondered if that might be easier. Hope was supposed to sustain her, but instead, it felt like it was slowly killing her. How many more mornings could she survive waking up with the fragile thought *maybe today*, only to crawl back into bed crushed anew when nothing changed?

Her phone buzzed on the chair beside her, cutting through her dark thoughts. It was Ben. Her stomach twisted. The trial had only been fast-tracked two days ago—what now?

"I have good news," Ben said when she answered.

Dana's pulse quickened. "What is it?"

"The judge reviewed the depositions and is allowing the Julia Kim incident and Dr. Paulsen's dismissal from medical school into evidence," he said, his voice laced with satisfaction. "This strengthens our case significantly."

Dana gripped the phone tighter. She should feel triumphant—this was a win, wasn't it? Instead, the knot in her stomach tightened. Her mind leapt back to the night Padma had first shared that story.

They'd only known each other a few months, but already Dana knew they'd be best friends. Curious why Padma never drank, she had asked, "Is it a health thing?"

Padma hesitated. "No," she admitted. "I used to... have a problem with it." Then she had told Dana about Julia Kim, the spiraling shame, the nights spent questioning whether she was meant to be a doctor at all. Her voice had been measured, but Dana had heard the pain beneath it.

"What an awful thing for you to go through," Dana had said —and she'd meant it.

Now, Padma's past would be laid bare, dissected for everyone to see—because of her. Guilt stabbed through Dana's chest.

"Right," she said flatly. "Thanks for letting me know." She hung up before Ben could reply.

Leaving the hospital to drive to Haven and Hearth, Dana felt heavier as she got closer to the shop. As she navigated the morning traffic, she allowed herself to fantasize about selling the shop, escaping the endless cycle of dwindling sales and overdue bills. But what would her mother say? And what would she even do next? Shaking off the thought, she pulled into the parking lot. She wasn't walking away. She had responsibilities. Flipping the sign to *Open*, she prepared for another long day.

Later, Ian arrived, his expression stony. She'd made it clear he wouldn't spend his one-day suspension for getting in a fight sitting at home. But seeing his closed-off demeanor, she wondered if it would have been better to let him stay in his room, doing whatever it was he did.

"Hey," he said, his tone short and chilly. "What do you need me to do?"

Dana felt an ache at the iciness radiating off him that had replaced the fragile rapport they'd begun to redevelop. The talk Dana and Eric had had with Ian about the separation had left him distant again, and he showed no signs of having forgiven her order to put an end to his relationship—or whatever it was—with Maeve.

"You can restock the candle display by the front," she said. "And wipe down the glass shelves."

Ian nodded tightly, his resentment palpable.

The chime of the front door interrupted her thoughts. She looked up to see Rhett Randolph, her landlord, stepping inside. His blazer strained over his portly frame, his polite smile tight.

"Dana, how are you?" he asked, his voice too loud in the empty store.

Dana forced a smile. "Rhett, what a nice surprise."

"I need a minute of your time, if you can," he said, his tone formal and distant.

"Of course," she said, her voice steady despite the warning bells sounding in her head. She turned to Ian. "Cover the front for me?"

He nodded and she led Rhett to the small office in the back of the shop.

He sat heavily across from her desk. "Your rent is three months overdue," he said without preamble. "I've been patient, what with the situation with your daughter, but I can't let this go on."

Dana's face flushed. "I'm trying to catch up," she said quickly. "But with everything going on..." Her voice faltered, and she turned away, blinking back tears of despair. Why couldn't anything go right? It felt like life kept knocking her down, over and over—had she done something to deserve this?

"I sympathize," Rhett interrupted, his tone clipped but not unkind. "I truly do. I know your daughter's situation is..." He trailed off awkwardly, clearing his throat with a harsh, wet sound. "Delicate. But sympathy doesn't pay the bills." He leaned forward slightly, his hands bracing his knees. "If I don't receive the full balance within thirty days, I'll have no choice but to post an eviction notice."

Her stomach sank. "Thirty days?" she whispered.

"I'm sorry, Dana. I like you, and I liked Cora. But this is business." He stood and smoothed the front of his blazer.

Dana sat frozen as he left the office. The air in the small room felt suddenly suffocating. She exhaled shakily and buried her face in her hands. How could she possibly come up with three months' rent in thirty days? The thought of an eviction notice taped to the shop's window filled her with shame. It would ruin them financially—and the whispers around the neighborhood would pile on top of the lawsuit.

A sound at the door startled her. Ian stood there, worry creased on his face. "You're being evicted?" he asked.

Dana stared at him, torn between wanting to shield him

from the truth and knowing the clock was running out on her lies. "Yes," she admitted finally. Fear gripped her. "But please, don't tell your father—not yet."

Ian nodded slowly, his expression unreadable. Then he turned and walked back to the front of the store, leaving Dana alone with the suffocating weight of her failure.

FORTY-TWO

MAEVE

Forty-eight days after

The final bell rang Thursday afternoon, and Maeve hovered by Ian's locker, scanning the hall. That morning, she'd woken with the memory of his warm hand closing around hers on the porch two nights ago. The moment he touched her, her anger had started to unravel, his pleading expression chipping away at her hurt. He'd screwed up—yeah—but didn't everyone deserve another chance after a mistake? He'd sworn he was done with the pills. Didn't that count for something?

A flicker of embarrassment crept in as she thought about how many times she'd warned Izzy that Taylor wasn't going to change. That no matter what he said, he was still the same arrogant jerk who would only hook up with her in his basement, safely out of sight. Izzy never listened. But Ian wasn't Taylor. He wasn't like anyone else. He could change. She believed that.

That certainty had fueled her as she'd texted Ian the day before, her need to be with him outweighing whatever anger still lingered.

> When you said you really liked me… I really like you too. And I don't care what my mom says, whatever this is, I don't want to stop.

Her thumb hovered over the send button before she finally tapped it. Relief swept through her as the message whooshed away. It felt good to be honest, to lean into her feelings for Ian despite the chaos around them. To trust that when he promised things would be different, he meant it.

Except there had been no reply.

At first, she reasoned, maybe his phone was dead, or he'd left it at home. Then she heard he'd been suspended for the day, which only made things worse. If he wasn't at school, he should've seen her text. By the next morning, when there was still nothing, unease gnawed at her. What if he'd changed his mind? What if, after everything, he'd decided she wasn't worth it?

Now, on Thursday, she knew he was back at school. She needed to see him, to have him smile at her, reach for her hand, erase the doubt pooling in her chest.

The hallway buzzed with students heading to the parking lot or after-school clubs, but Ian was nowhere. Leaning against the cold metal lockers, she tightened her grip on her backpack, her nervous energy shifting into dread. She checked her phone. Still nothing.

Fifteen minutes passed, and the hallway emptied. She sighed, hoisting her backpack over her shoulder, late for orchestra practice.

Then, suddenly, there he was.

At the far end of the hall, Ian walked alongside Jenner, laughing at something he said. Relief flooded her, and she moved toward him.

"Ian!" she called, lifting her hand in a tentative wave.

His eyes flicked toward her and he froze.

For a second, she thought he might smile back, but instead, his gaze darted away. Quickly. Deliberately. He muttered something to Jenner, then turned sharply, pushing through the double doors to the parking lot without a backward glance.

Maeve stood still, her hand still half-raised, breath caught somewhere between her chest and throat. He hadn't smiled. Hadn't waved. Hadn't even acknowledged her.

Her heart cracked, sharp and sudden. What just happened?

Tears pricked her eyes as humiliation and confusion set in. Lowering her hand, she turned and stumbled toward the refuge of the girls' bathroom.

At home that night, after practice, Maeve sat cross-legged on her bed, scrolling through old messages from Ian, trying to untangle the knot of emotions choking her. Anger and sadness battled it out in her brain, but mostly she just felt hollow. She couldn't remember ever feeling so alone.

She switched over to her texts with Izzy, rereading the last ones they'd exchanged. The timestamp felt like a relic from another life. How had it been seven weeks since she'd been able to talk to her best friend? She ached to talk to her now. Not that she could have told Izzy what was going on with Ian—*awkward!*—but the simple comfort of knowing Izzy was there, that she'd listen, was what Maeve needed most. Maybe she still could? Her fingers hovered over the screen, hesitating, before she began to type.

> Hey. I miss you. I wish we could talk. Everything feels so messed up right now. Did you know our moms aren't even friends anymore? I can't believe it. We would never let that happen to us, right? Never let anything come between us. Which means you can't be mad when I tell you I'm kind of hanging out with your brother. Or I was… until he totally ghosted me. I feel so stupid. I was ready to give him another chance. I told him how much I like him. And he straight up looked right through me. I feel like shit. So there's that. Anyway, I don't know if you'll ever read this (maybe it's better if you don't lol). I just wish I could talk to you. Love you.

Her phone buzzed in her hand as she hit send, and a message from Ian popped up. Maeve's heart pounded as she read it.

> Hey. I don't think we should see each other anymore. It's not a good idea.

Her breath hitched as she typed a reply.

> Why? What happened? Is this because of my mom?

Dots appeared, showing that he was typing—then vanished. She stared at her screen, waiting for a response that never came.

Tears stung her eyes. She bit her lip, trying to keep them in, but the ache in her chest felt too big to contain. Clutching a pillow to her chest, the first sob broke free.

A soft knock sounded at her door. Maeve ignored it, pressing her face into the pillow, but the door opened, and her mother stepped inside.

"Maeve?" Her mom's voice was gentle, concerned. "Sweetheart, what's wrong?"

Maeve wiped at her face but refused to look up. "Nothing. I'm fine."

Her mom hesitated near the door. "You don't seem fine."

Maeve tried to summon the anger she'd felt toward her mother two nights ago when she'd showed up on the porch during Ian's visit, but her need for comfort outweighed it. "He doesn't want to see me anymore," she said, her voice cracking.

Her mom sighed, stepping closer. "Oh, sweetheart." She sat down on the bed.

Maeve turned to her, tears streaming. "Why would he say that? Two days ago, everything was fine. He *liked* me. And I... I feel the same way. I don't understand." She looked sharply at her mom, suspicion flaring. "Did you *say* something to him?"

Her mom pressed her lips together. "I know this is hard, but when someone shows you who they really are, you have to believe them."

"No." Maeve shook her head. "You don't know him like I do."

Her mother's face tightened, but she didn't argue. Instead, she pulled Maeve into a hug. And despite everything, Maeve let her.

"It'll get better," her mom whispered. "I promise."

But Maeve had no reason to believe her.

FORTY-THREE

PADMA

Fifty-five days after

Padma had been home on leave for a week. The first morning, she jolted awake at 6 a.m., still wired for hospital shifts, only to stare at the ceiling, disoriented by the silence. No beeping monitors, no charts to review, no colleagues needing answers. By noon, she'd rearranged the living room twice, organized the pantry, and abandoned a YouTube yoga video after nearly toppling over in tree pose.

Lars came home that evening to find her hunched over her laptop, scrolling through Zillow listings.

"Didn't the couch used to be on the other side of the room?" he asked, scanning the space.

"The flow is better this way," Padma said.

"And my favorite armchair is...?"

"It looked better in the guest bedroom."

Lars scratched his head. "Should I be scared to go upstairs?"

Padma waved a hand, still scrolling. "I haven't gotten to the upstairs yet. Tomorrow."

"Tomorrow," he echoed. "Great." He sat beside her, resting

a hand on her leg. "I think," he said carefully, "it might be time for a new hobby." He sniffed the air. "What's that smell?"

"Shit!" Padma shoved her laptop aside and bolted to the kitchen. "Dinner!"

Lars followed her to the kitchen, where she pulled a baking sheet of charred potatoes out of the oven. "Also," he said as he regarded it, "I don't think that hobby should be cooking."

Padma sighed, fanning away the smoke. She wasn't ready to laugh about it yet.

The next few days felt just as aimless. Each morning, she got up early and made breakfast for Maeve before she left for school. The first day, Maeve eyed the yogurt parfait Padma placed in front of her like it might bite. Her eyes were puffy, her expression raw.

Padma's chest ached at the sight of her daughter's heartbreak, realizing she hadn't fully understood how much Maeve liked Ian. Still, she was relieved he seemed to be holding up his end of the bargain.

By the fourth morning, Maeve sat down without hesitation and started eating. Between bites, she glanced up shyly. "This is really nice," she said softly.

"What is?" Padma asked.

"You being here more."

Padma tilted her head and smiled. "It is," she agreed. But while part of her enjoyed the slower pace, another part itched for more than making breakfast, cleaning the fridge, and calling her AA sponsor daily. She'd told Toby she was taking at least a week off, but now she wasn't sure how long she could stay away from the hospital.

She started browsing job postings—other hospitals, other cities. "How do you feel about Seattle?" she asked Lars one night, scrolling through listings while half-watching a detective show.

"Like for a vacation?"

"Like to live."

Lars glanced at her, then paused the TV. "Honey," he said gently, "it feels like you're trying to plan your escape."

"I'm just looking," Padma insisted. "Seattle also has great real estate."

Lars sighed, rubbing his face. "We're not buying a Victorian fixer-upper in Seattle. Maeve has one year of high school left. We're not uprooting her."

"OK, maybe not Seattle," Padma conceded. "But..." She hesitated. "Maybe another neighborhood."

Lars was quiet for a moment. "Is that really what you need?" he asked.

Padma's throat tightened. "I don't know. Maybe it's not sustainable to live next door to Dana." She looked out the window at the fence between their yards. It had never felt like a barrier before, but now it seemed insurmountable. "I guess I just wonder if this will ever be over. If there's a world where..." She trailed off.

"Where you're friends again?" Lars supplied.

"It's a stupid thought." Padma shook her head, embarrassed. How, after everything Dana had done, could she even consider that possibility? But despite everything, she missed her best friend. She missed how they used to be.

"Maybe," Lars said. "But maybe not. Life is long."

Padma nodded, unsure if the sadness washing over her was because she didn't believe she and Dana could ever fix things— or because she wasn't sure she even wanted to try.

On the sixth day of her leave, Padma's phone buzzed mid-Zillow scroll. Toby's name flashed on the screen. She answered immediately.

"Hey," she said, trying to sound upbeat.

"Hey," he replied. "How are you holding up?"

"Oh, you know," she said, twirling a strand of hair. "Keeping busy."

"Good, good," he said distractedly. Something in his tone made her sit up.

"What's going on?" she asked.

There was a pause. Padma knew Toby well enough to sense he was choosing his words carefully. "I wanted to tell you before you heard it from someone else. The board made their decision about my replacement."

Her chest tightened. "And?"

"They went with Gary Ackerman."

She waited for the crushing disappointment, but instead, she felt... nothing. "Gary," she repeated, as if saying it aloud might help it sink in.

"I fought for you," Toby said quickly. "But given the circumstances..."

"Right. The lawsuit. The news story." Her tone was sharper than she intended. She sighed. "It's fine, Toby. Really."

"It's not fine," he countered. "You're more qualified than Gary by a mile. Everybody knows that. But he's got less... baggage."

"Toby, do you think I'm a good doctor?"

"One of the best," he replied without hesitation.

She nodded, though he couldn't see her. "I guess I'm trying to figure out how to be less of a doctor and more of a... person—whatever that means."

He gave a rueful laugh. "You and me both. The elusive work-life balance."

"Balance," she echoed, the word foreign on her tongue.

"You have a wonderful family, a whole life outside the hospital," Toby said gently. "Maybe it's time to lean into that for a while."

She swallowed hard, wanting to tell him that she loved her job, but that sitting there, scrolling through pictures of homes in cities hundreds of miles away—and her own—she realized she didn't know who she was without it. "Maybe," she murmured.

"But you're coming back, right? We need you." A note of panic crept into his voice.

"Of course," she said, straightening. "I'll be back next week."

After they hung up, she set the phone on the coffee table and stared out the window. Gary Ackerman had her job. The one she'd spent years working toward. And yet, all she felt was emptiness. Maybe Toby was right. Maybe it was time to figure out who she was without a title, without the long hours and constant pressure.

She picked up her laptop again, the glow of the screen lighting her face as she resumed her Zillow scroll.

FORTY-FOUR

IAN

Fifty-five days after

Ian rang up the customer's purchase, a green glass vase that was hand-blown—whatever that meant. "Would you like it gift-wrapped, ma'am?" he asked, forcing a smile to mask the nausea rolling through him.

"That would be wonderful, thank you," the woman said, her Christmas ball earrings swaying as she nodded.

"Of course. It'll just take a minute. We have some holiday napkins on sale near the front, if you're interested," he said.

Her eyes lit up. "Ooh, I'll take a look. You can never have too many napkins." She chuckled like she'd just delivered a punchline, and Ian forced himself to chuckle back even as his head throbbed.

As she browsed, he carefully wrapped the vase in tissue paper, trying to steady his hands. He was almost out of pills, and Max was out of the country until next week. He'd been rationing them, taking half-doses in an attempt to cut back. But as his hands shook and his stomach churned, he'd felt his resolve to quit them entirely weakening. Besides, Maeve had fallen for him while he was *on* the pills. Maybe he was better that way, more interesting and laid back. Or at least able to function like a normal human.

Yesterday, he'd hit three open houses and come up with nothing but a bottle of Viagra. If he didn't score today, he'd be completely out, and he had no idea what that would do to him.

Wiping clammy sweat from his brow, he glanced around Haven and Hearth and wondered—again—why he was even here. Sure, helping out had been his idea, but he'd felt like a different person when he made that offer weeks ago. Someone better. Someone who wasn't shaking and sweating because he didn't have enough drugs in his system.

He'd tried to do things right—working harder at school, helping his mom, spending more time with Maeve, raiding fewer strangers' medicine cabinets. And for what? He'd still gotten suspended, pissing off both parents: his mom, because it involved Maeve, and his dad, because it was "the last straw" in Ian being a screwup. He'd also missed an essay test in Mr. Riley's class that he'd actually studied for, probably tanking his grade. Now, he couldn't even look his teacher in the eye, instead slinking into class as the bell rang and bolting the second it ended. No way would Mr. Riley let him stay in AP next term, now.

But the worst part? It had all been for nothing—things with Maeve were over. That was what really hurt. She'd been the one person who believed he could be better, and he'd let her down. She probably thought he was a total jerk for ending things the way he did. Which, fair—he was. A cowardly, selfish jerk. But he couldn't risk their relationship screwing with his mom's lawsuit.

Ian glanced toward the office, where his mom was typing, the faint scrape of her roller chair the only sound. A week had passed since the landlord's visit, but the fear in her eyes that day was burned into his mind. She'd told him not to worry, but eviction sounded really bad. If she lost the shop, then what? His dad was a teacher—not exactly raking it in—and Izzy's medical bills had to be piling up. The dark circles under his mom's eyes, the haunted look she wore all the time now—he couldn't stop thinking about them.

That was why he stayed away from Maeve. Why he kept coming to the shop after school and on weekends. His mom needed him, and for once, he wasn't going to let her down.

The woman with the Christmas earrings returned, a stack of red napkins in her hands. "I'll take these as well," she said brightly.

The shop's door dinged as she left, and Ian pulled out his phone.

Hey man

Anyone else I can hit up while you're gone?

Max replied immediately.

I don't refer my customers to other people.

Anger surged through Ian. He set his phone down harder than he meant to, the clunk echoing through the quiet shop.

"Everything OK?"

He jumped, spinning around. His mom stood behind him, arms crossed. He hadn't even heard her come out of the office.

"Yeah, fine," he muttered, brushing his hair back.

"I'd appreciate it if you weren't on your phone at work," she said.

He rolled his eyes, frustration boiling over. "It's not like there's anyone in here but us. No wonder business is so bad."

The words were out before he could stop them. The flicker of hurt on his mom's face made his stomach twist.

The bell above the door dinged. Two women in matching puffy vests walked in.

"What a cute little shop!" one of them exclaimed.

His mom straightened, pasting on a smile. But when she turned back to him, her voice was tight. "Maybe you should leave for the day," she said. "I don't want your mood putting off customers."

Ian blinked. "But don't you need me to—"

"No." She shook her head firmly. "Not like this, I don't."

His shoulders stiffened. "Fine." He stuffed his phone in his pocket and grabbed his backpack.

"I'll see you at home later," his mom called. "Start on your homework, OK?"

"Yeah, whatever," he muttered, resisting the urge to smash a shelf of porcelain Santas as he stormed out.

In the parking lot he took his phone back out and pulled up a real estate site.

The first two open houses he hit yielded nothing, and his body became increasingly rigid with desperation, his pulse deafening in his ears. The third one, a gut renovated Cape Cod house—so said the listing—was in a neighborhood west of his own.

He flashed a wide smile at the real estate agent near the door, a middle-aged woman with cat's-eye glasses and a clipboard.

"Good afternoon," he said smoothly. "Just taking a look for my mom. She's running late but really interested in the neighborhood."

She eyed him briefly, skepticism flickering before she returned his smile. "Of course. Feel free to look around. Let me know if you have any questions."

"Thank you," Ian said, dipping his head politely.

He wandered the first floor, heart hammering, eyes scanning for the staircase. The kitchen gleamed with new appliances, and a couple stood chatting about school districts and square footage. Ian slipped past them, keeping his pace casual as he found the stairs.

Upstairs was empty. The hall bathroom yielded nothing. He ducked into the master bath, pulse spiking. Opening the medicine cabinet, he scanned the rows of bottles—aspirin, antacids... Oxy. His breath hitched at the orange bottle, the label stark:

CONTROLLED SUBSTANCE.
DANGEROUS UNLESS USED AS DIRECTED.

He'd never taken Oxy, not even when Max had offered to let him try it for free. He wasn't stupid; he knew what it could lead to. Now, though, his fingers closed around the bottle, a grim satisfaction settling in his chest.

But as he turned, the real estate agent appeared in the doorway, arms crossed, face stony.

"What do you think you're doing?" she demanded.

Ian froze. "Uh..." His mind scrambled. "Just checking out the space. It's really nice."

"Emptying the medicine cabinet isn't part of the tour," she snapped, grabbing her phone. "I'm calling the police."

Panic surged through him. This couldn't be happening, not now. He pictured his father's fury, the harsh judgment in his eyes. And his mom—God, what would it do to her? She already had one kid hooked up to machines. Now she'd have another in handcuffs. How could he be so stupid?

The agent's finger hovered over her phone, her glare sharpening.

"You don't have to do that," Ian blurted, desperation raw in his voice. "It was a stupid mistake—I'm sorry!"

"Excuse me," came a voice from the hallway. "I was wondering if the washer and dryer are included?"

Ian's stomach dropped as Dr. Paulsen appeared over the agent's shoulder. In one swift glance, she took in his panicked face, the pill bottle clenched in his hand.

"Ian," she breathed.

The agent turned sharply. "Do you know this boy?"

Dr. Paulsen's eyes narrowed. "I do."

Ian's pulse pounded. After she caught him outside with Maeve, this had to feel like karma to her. Seeing him like this—busted, pathetic—probably felt like victory. Could this get any worse?

"I'm his mother," Dr. Paulsen added.

The agent blinked, her eyes darting between Ian's pale face and Padma's dark skin. "You're... his mother?" she said, her skepticism clear.

Dr. Paulsen's expression didn't waver. "Yes. I'm sure you're aware families come in all colors? Perhaps you've seen a Cheerios commercial."

The agent flushed. "Oh, I didn't mean—"

Dr. Paulsen cut her off. "We just lost my husband—his father," she said, voice softening. "It's been a difficult time, and he's acting out in ways that aren't like him." She stepped closer, placing a firm hand on Ian's shoulder. He wondered if she could feel how hard he was shaking. What the hell was she doing?

"Ian," she said sharply. "This is unacceptable. We'll discuss it at home." To the agent, she offered a look of quiet embarrassment. "I'm so sorry for the trouble. Grief affects people in different ways."

The agent hesitated, her anger visibly cooling. "I... I'm sorry for your loss."

Dr. Paulsen nodded. "Thank you. We're just taking things one day at a time."

The agent sighed, lowering her phone. "I won't call the police, but you both need to leave."

"Of course," Dr. Paulsen said smoothly, steering Ian toward the stairs. "And thank you for understanding."

They walked down the stairs together, Ian afraid his legs might give out with a combined sense of relief that he wasn't going to be arrested and renewed fear of what Dr. Paulsen might have in store for him.

The moment they reached the sidewalk, she turned to face him, her expression unreadable.

Tears burned his eyes. "Please," he whispered. "Don't tell my mom."

FORTY-FIVE

DANA

Fifty-five days after

Dana had come home from work to find Eric in their walk-in closet, stuffing clothes into a garbage bag. Her heart quickened. "Are you leaving?" she asked, trying to keep the hurt out of her voice. Since telling Ian about their separation, she knew Eric had been looking at apartments, but she hadn't imagined he would just pack up and go without saying anything.

"What? No," Eric said, shaking his head. "Not yet, I mean." He held up a Marie Kondo book. "I just finished this and thought I'd, um, streamline things a bit. So, when I do move out, it's not such a hassle."

Dana fought the urge to roll her eyes. Was there a self-improvement book Eric hadn't read?

He glanced sheepishly at the pile of clothes on the floor. "We've been in this house a long time—I think I've maybe become a bit of a pack rat."

Dana snorted. "Maybe? You still have T-shirts from college."

"Only the good ones," he said defensively.

"And every back issue of *National Geographic* since 1992. Plus two broken DVD players."

"I use those magazines for my classes," Eric said. "And I'm sure I can fix the DVD players if I just tinker a little."

"Honey, no one uses DVD players anymore," Dana said, then flushed immediately at the term of endearment that had slipped out. The atmosphere in the small closet shifted as Eric's gaze settled on her.

"It's nice to hear you call me that," he said softly.

She crossed her arms. "Don't," she said, her tone icy.

"Don't what?"

"Don't act like we're not splitting up."

"We're not splitting up—"

"You're moving out!" she snapped, frustrated by the tears welling in her eyes. All she ever seemed to do was cry.

Eric held up his hands. "You're right," he said. "You're right. Start as you mean to go on."

Dana fixed him with a hard stare. "I remember when you used to talk like a normal person, not in inspirational quotes."

Eric's eyes narrowed. "Great. Here we go," he said, his tone sarcastic.

Dana's stomach churned. This wasn't how she'd intended the conversation to go. Not when she had something so big to tell him. She took a deep breath, forcing her shoulders down and away from her ears. "We need to talk," she said quietly.

"I told you, I just haven't found the right apartment yet," Eric said sharply. "Anything even remotely nearby is really expensive."

Dana leaned against a shelf of shoes, steadying herself for what she knew she had to say. "You might not be able to afford to move out," she said.

Eric turned back to his shirts, rifling through the hangers. "Of course I will," he said. "I just need to keep looking."

"No, I mean..." Dana inhaled deeply, her heart racing. "I mean, I might be losing the shop."

Eric turned sharply, confusion on his face. "Haven and Hearth? What are you talking about? It's almost Christmas—business must be great."

"It's not. It hasn't been. I'm being... evicted." Her voice broke on the last word, and she watched as Eric's face paled.

"What?" he asked. "No. How is that even possible?"

She shrugged helplessly. "A lot of things are possible when you haven't paid your rent in three months."

"Three months? What the hell, Dana? How could you forget to pay rent?"

She waited for the hot sting of shame to settle over her but instead felt the cool flood of relief. She'd said it. She'd said the thing she'd been too scared to say for months. The world hadn't stopped turning. "I didn't forget," she said. "I couldn't pay it."

Eric's face turned splotchy with anger. "Then pay it now!" he exclaimed.

Dana let out a bitter laugh. "Please. If it were that simple, don't you think I already would have? But I can't pay because I have a bank loan in default, vendors sending my account to collections, and sales that have nosedived compared to last year." She gave a sharp, oddly gleeful laugh, feeling unhinged. "It's a mess!" Sliding down the wall, she collapsed onto the floor, her laughter turning to tears.

"I fail to see how this is funny," Eric snapped, his tone sharp. "This is a disaster. How did you let this happen?"

"It turns out," Dana said, lying flat and staring at the ceiling, "I'm really bad at this. Like, terrible." She turned her head to the side and noticed a colony of dust bunnies near the laundry hamper. Her housekeeping had definitely suffered these last few months.

The splotches faded from Eric's face, and it turned a sickly shade of white. "But if you lose the shop, I don't make enough to cover the mortgage, not to mention the other bills."

"I know," Dana whispered. "I know."

"Why didn't you tell me?" he demanded.

Propping herself up on her elbows, Dana met his eyes. "I thought I could fix it," she said softly. "Like I always think I can fix everything. Ian. Izzy. Our marriage. But it turns out I can't fix any of it."

Eric sank to the floor beside her, his head in his hands. "We're so screwed," he murmured.

"We are," Dana agreed, wiping her eyes. The starkness of the truth sat between them. It was raw and ugly, but at least now it didn't belong to her alone.

The doorbell rang, sharp and insistent. Eric pulled out his phone, glancing at the security camera app.

"It's Padma," he said, frowning, "and Ian."

Dana's stomach dropped. Instinctively, she flew down the stairs, dread tightening her chest. Something was wrong. She barely registered Eric following her as she reached the foyer just as the door swung open.

Ian stepped inside, his eyes bloodshot, his skin pale and damp with sweat. Without a word, he crossed the room and sank into one of the dining room chairs, slumping forward, his elbows braced on his knees, his face buried in his hands. Padma hovered in the doorway, her expression grim.

Dana rushed to Ian's side, gripping his shoulder. "Ian, honey, are you all right? What happened?" she asked, her voice trembling.

Ian didn't answer. Instead, he leaned forward, wrapping his arms tightly around her legs, his body convulsing as he began to sob.

"What the hell's going on here?" Eric demanded.

"I'm sorry," Ian gasped, his voice breaking. "I'm so sorry."

Padma stepped inside, her movements hesitant. "I found him at an open house," she said, her voice low.

Dana blinked, confused. "What?"

"Real estate," Padma clarified. She paused, shifting uncomfortably. "He was stealing prescription drugs from the bathroom." She drew in a breath, her lips pressed tightly together. "Oxy."

The word ricocheted through the room like a gunshot, and Dana felt as though the floor had given way beneath her. Reaching for the chair beside Ian, she sank into it, her legs too weak to hold her. Ian still clung to her, his sobs shaking them both.

"What did you just say?" Eric's voice was tight, like he was struggling to breathe. He turned to Ian, his face pale. "Ian, is that true?"

Ian lifted his tear-streaked face from Dana's lap, his expression broken, and gave a miserable nod. "She was going to call the police," he choked out between sobs.

Eric whirled to face Padma. "The police? How dare you—"

"Not her," Ian cut in, his voice hoarse. "The realtor."

Dana's gaze snapped to Padma, their eyes locking. Slowly, Padma nodded.

"I asked her—she agreed not to," Padma said, shifting on her feet. Her eyes flicked to Ian, then back to Dana. "But he needs help," she said firmly, pulling a piece of paper from her pocket and holding it out. "Dr. Garcia is an addiction specialist. She's excellent, and—"

"Addiction?" Eric's voice sliced through the air. "What the hell are you talking about?"

Padma gave him a long look, sadness playing around her lips. "I think you should ask your son," she said. Then she turned and walked back out the door.

FORTY-SIX
PADMA

Fifty-seven days after

On Saturday morning, Padma sat at the kitchen counter, sipping coffee that had gone lukewarm while she scrolled through her laptop.

"Good morning," Lars said, padding into the room. "You're up early for a Saturday." He yawned, running a hand through his bedhead. Catching sight of her screen, he raised an eyebrow. "More real estate listings?"

Padma laughed. "No, vacation ideas, actually."

Lars placed a hand on his chest in mock disbelief. "A vacation? You? Willingly?" He leaned over and touched her forehead. "Are you feeling OK?"

"Very funny." She swatted his hand away. "And, yes, I think I deserve a little R&R. Maybe the Bahamas over New Year's?"

He leaned in, scanning the screen. "Book it. Right now. Before you get a sudden attack of practicality." Wrapping his arms around her shoulders, he pressed a kiss to the crown of her head. "I think it's good you're focusing on something other than... you know," he said softly.

She leaned into him, closing her eyes at the comfort of his touch. They'd been careful with each other lately—too careful, as if walking a tightrope, their politeness stripping away their usual easy intimacy.

"I'm still thinking about it," she admitted, her voice low. "All the time." She hesitated, choosing her words. "But I think I'm finally realizing why it's so hard."

"Because your best friend betrayed you?" Lars asked.

She turned, wrapping her legs around his. "Yes," she said. "But also because... if I'm not a doctor—a good doctor—then who am I?" Saying it out loud made the question feel even heavier.

His hands framed her face, his thumbs brushing her cheeks. "You're the love of my life, that's who," he said, his voice steady and certain.

She pressed a hand on his chest and pulled back. "I didn't get the job," she said, the confession a lump in her throat. "They gave it to Gary."

Lars's face melted into sympathy. "Oof, honey, I'm so sorry. And Gary, of all people." He grimaced. "When did you find out?"

Padma swallowed. "Thursday."

The muscle in Lars's jaw twitched. "Thursday as in two days ago? Why didn't you tell me?"

She pressed her lips together, swallowing the anguish that threatened to spill over. There was so much she hadn't told him —how the thought of returning to work felt unbearable now that she was out of the running for the job that had once seemed hers for the taking. And yet, if work no longer consumed her, what was left? She wasn't sure she even knew how to exist without it taking up so much space in her life.

Lars shook his head, the tension melting from his face as he saw her distress. "Never mind," he sighed. "It doesn't matter. Are you all right?"

Padma felt a pang, knowing exactly what he was asking. "No." She met his gaze, determined to be honest this time. "But I will be. Eventually."

"Have you—"

"I've talked to Jamie," she cut in before he could finish. "And I'll see him at my meeting on Monday." She saw the tension in his shoulders ease slightly. For a moment, she wanted to resent the constant vigilance, the questions that implied doubt. But who could blame him?

"I'm sorry," Lars said. "I just care about you. About us. You have so much to lose."

Her lips curved faintly. "Yeah. I think I'm finally starting to see that."

He bent to kiss her, and this time she didn't pull away. She met him halfway, the warmth of his lips sending a ripple of pleasure through her body.

"Ew, you guys are so gross!"

Padma looked up to see Maeve standing behind them wearing a stricken expression.

Lars rolled his eyes, but grinned and squeezed Padma's hand. "Who wants pancakes?" he asked.

Later that morning, Padma perched by the front door, lacing up her sneakers when Maeve appeared, eyeing her mother's footwear curiously.

"Where are you going?" Maeve asked.

"For a jog," Padma replied.

Though there was still a layer of frost between them, the chill was slowly thawing. Maeve's eyes weren't perpetually red and puffy anymore, though Padma sometimes still noticed signs she'd been crying.

"Like, for exercise?" Maeve's eyebrows shot up in disbelief.

"Well," Padma said, straightening up, "so far this week, I've learned I hate yoga, Pilates, and Zumba. Jogging feels like the next logical option."

"Oh, you'll definitely hate that, too," Maeve said knowingly.

"Gee, thanks for the vote of confidence."

"But why?" Maeve pressed.

"Why what?"

"Why are you doing all that stuff?"

Padma paused, tugging at her jacket zipper as she tried to find the words. "I'm trying something new," she said finally. "Being a whole person, outside of work." She hesitated, then sighed. She might as well say it. "Sweetheart, I'm sorry if I've ever—not been there for you."

Maeve frowned in confusion but remained quiet, listening.

"I work a lot," Padma said slowly, gathering her thoughts. "Maybe too much. Or I think too much about work when I'm not at work—like when I'm with you and I should be thinking about you. I'm sorry if you've ever felt... let down."

Maeve studied her mother, then nodded. "Thanks."

"That's not to say that I'm apologizing for having a successful career," Padma hastened. "Women should *never* have to apologize for that. God knows men are never expected to."

Maeve rolled her eyes. "OK." Then she chewed her lip and nodded at Padma's shoes. "Can I come?"

Warmth flooded Padma's chest. "Of course," she said.

They settled on a brisk walk instead of a jog, which Padma had to admit was probably the smarter choice. The mid-December sun was bright and warm, even for Atlanta, and Padma soon tied her fleece jacket around her waist.

"So," Padma said, searching for neutral conversation topics, "your dad and I were thinking maybe we'd take a family vacation after Christmas. Maybe the Bahamas."

"Really?" Maeve turned to her, her face bright with surprise. "Cool. We never go anywhere."

"Well, we're going to start," Padma said with quiet resolve.

They walked in companionable silence until Maeve spoke

again. "I'm still mad at you, you know." She didn't look at Padma, her gaze fixed straight ahead, her jaw set in determination.

"I know," Padma replied softly.

"But also, I kind of think maybe you were right."

Padma kept her expression steady, though the admission startled her. According to Maeve, Padma hadn't been right about anything since she turned thirteen. "Oh?"

Maeve's shoulders rounded forward. "I just feel stupid for being so into him, you know? I mean, I've known Ian practically my whole life. I've seen how he is with other girls—I should have known better."

A boulder of guilt pressed against Padma's chest, recalling the desperation on Ian's face after she'd stopped the real estate agent from calling the police. There was terror, but beneath that was something deeper—something achingly familiar. Sadness. Despair. The hollow, lost expression of someone who didn't recognize the person they'd become. It was the same look she'd seen on her own face in the mirror all those years ago following her devastating conversation with the medical school Dean. It was a look that wordlessly asked, *How did this happen? How did I become this? And how do I make it stop?*

Looking at Maeve now, Padma gave a sad smile. "You're not stupid, sweetheart. And maybe I was too hard on him. I don't think Ian is a bad person—I think he's just going through a really hard time."

"Because of Izzy?"

Padma hesitated. "Because of a lot of things."

Maeve looked at her frankly. "Like the pills?"

Padma stopped abruptly and stared at her daughter. "You know about that?"

Maeve gave a small nod and looked away. "I know he does them. I just thought maybe he would stop... because of me." She chewed her lip, and when she looked back at her mother, there were tears in her eyes. "He wanted to change, you know? And I thought I could, like, help him."

"Oh, sweetheart." Padma leaned forward to embrace her daughter. "It's not your job to help anyone change. Your own life is the only one you can control."

"Yeah," Maeve said, her wet cheek pressed against Padma's. "I think I finally get that."

FORTY-SEVEN

MAEVE

Fifty-seven days after

Maeve returned from the walk, turning over her mom's apology in her head. For as long as she could remember, her mom hadn't been the one reading *Green Eggs and Ham* as the class Mystery Reader or bringing cookies to the school holiday party. That had been her dad's gig. He'd done his best, but it wasn't the same. While other kids had their moms there, Maeve had been stuck with the reminder that her mom's job was too important, that saving lives mattered more than chaperoning field trips. Which made sense—until it didn't. Until Maeve realized how much it had hurt to always feel second place, even when she knew she had no right to complain. But hearing her mom say she was sorry; it was like Maeve suddenly had permission to feel all these things. And in a weird way, she suddenly felt lighter than she had in a long time.

Flopping onto her bed, Maeve unlocked her phone and opened her messages. Automatically, her thumb hovered over Ian's name, and just like that, the ache in her chest flared up again. She'd done this too many times—rereading old texts she'd already memorized, searching for clues about what went wrong. But this time, she stopped herself. Her grip tightened on the phone as she took a deep breath, swiped left on the message chain, and hit delete before she could talk herself out of it.

The silence after the texts disappeared felt loud, like something enormous had shifted. She scrolled through the rest of her messages: the short, factual ones from her parents, the long, rambling one she had sent Izzy with no hope of a reply. And then there were the messages from her other friends: friends she and Izzy had shared, Maeve's own orchestra friends, people who had checked in, invited her to things, tried to pull her out of the darkness. At first, Maeve had answered politely but distantly, feeling like she had a monopoly on grief. She was Izzy's best friend, after all. How could they understand what she was going through? But after she'd turned down enough of their invitations, they stopped asking her. Now, even at school, there was a distance. Her friends had moved on. Maeve, still stuck in limbo, was just the sad girl whose best friend—her only real friend—was in a coma.

Staring at her phone, a wave of anger toward Izzy surged through her. Maeve had handed Izzy the keys to her entire life, not realizing she was locking herself out of the driver's seat. *Thanks a lot, Iz.* The thought was cruel, but at least for the first time in weeks Maeve felt something besides sadness.

She dropped her phone onto the bed and rolled over, catching sight of herself in the mirror on her closet door. Her eyes were faintly red, her thick, wavy hair tangled. She thought about Ian running his hands through it, then stopped herself. *No more,* she told herself. She was done being the sad girl. Done with retreating into herself and watching her life pass her by. If Izzy were awake, she'd never let Maeve wallow like this. Izzy didn't sit around; she did things. And now it was up to Maeve to do things for herself.

She picked her phone up and opened a text to three of her and Izzy's mutual friends.

Hey, you guys around this weekend? Dying to get away from my family, lol.

One of them responded immediately.

Same!! Painted Pin is doing disco bowling later —wanna go?

There was a knock at her door, and her mom poked her head in.

"Hey, sweetheart," her mom said. "I was thinking of seeing a movie this afternoon. Any interest?"

Maeve glanced down at her phone, then looked back up at her mom. For the first time in days, her smile felt like something she didn't have to force.

"No, thanks," she said. "I have plans."

FORTY-EIGHT

IAN

Fifty-nine days after

Ian rolled over and checked the clock. Four p.m. Monday. He'd slept most of the day, his body recovering from the brutal withdrawal of the last few days. Thursday night was a blur—he remembered falling into his mother's arms, sobbing, as Dr. Paulsen brought him home. As terrified as he'd been of his parents' reactions, having the truth out felt like cracking open an ice-cold soda after an afternoon at the beach.

But the relief had been short-lived. Friday morning hit like the flu times a million—aches, chills, and a mind racing so fast he spent several desperate hours curled on the bathroom floor before his parents could get him in to see Dr. Garcia that afternoon.

Dr. Garcia spoke to him first with his parents and then alone. It was the first time he'd been honest with anyone in months. He admitted how long he'd been taking pills, and how much he used. To his relief, she didn't judge—she just listened, then told him she could help. After seeing his parents' frightened faces, he needed that.

When he told her how sick he felt without the pills, she spoke frankly.

"The next forty-eight hours will be even worse," she warned him, "so let's do what we can to get you through it. You're lucky, there are several good inpatient rehabilitation programs in the Atlanta area that accept teenagers. I can make some calls."

"Rehab?" he'd sputtered. "No way."

Dr. Garcia raised an eyebrow.

"I don't want to go anywhere," he said, feeling the tears forming. "My sister is in the hospital and my mom—just, please."

Dr. Garcia clicked her pen open and shut, then nodded. "Only if your parents agree. You'll need strict supervision for the next forty-eight hours, at least—withdrawal can trigger intense depression. I'll prescribe something to help you get through the worst of it."

Now, three days later, Ian had finally managed to get out of bed and make his way downstairs where his mom was sitting at the kitchen table with her laptop.

Ian's chest tightened as he took in her furrowed brow and hunched posture, how exhausted and worn she seemed. She looked like she was carrying the weight of the world, and now he'd added his own breakdown to her already-overloaded shoulders. If Dr. Paulsen hadn't intervened the other night, his mom might be sitting in a police station right now, dealing with yet another crisis. She didn't deserve that—not after everything she'd already been through.

"Sweetie, hi," his mom said, jumping up when she saw him. "How are you feeling?"

"OK, I think," he said, though his head still pounded and his body ached. The Valium Dr. Garcia had prescribed had helped to slow his racing thoughts, at least.

His thoughts drifted back to the moment Dr. Paulsen had walked in at the open house, seeing the bottle of Oxy in his hand. Shame crashed over him, followed by intense gratitude. He'd expected her to walk away, to leave him with the furious realtor. Instead, she'd marched him outside into the cold.

"Are you going to call my mom?" he'd asked, voice barely a whisper.

"Ian," Dr. Paulsen said slowly, her face unreadable, "are you taking those pills?"

"No," he said quickly. "Not Oxy. Just... other stuff. But I'm stopping. I swear."

She looked at him—*really* looked at him—then gently asked, "Do you need help?"

The world seemed to stop as her words swirled in his head, pulling him under like a rip current. He fought against it, but the effort left him exhausted, too tired to resist. Finally, desperate, he whispered, "Yes."

Shaking the memory from his head, he saw his mom studying him. "Can I get you anything?" she asked.

He flushed, remembering her sitting by his bed all weekend, pressing a cool cloth to his forehead like when he was a kid. He swallowed. "I was wondering... would it be OK if I went to see Izzy?"

His mom's eyes softened. "Of course," she said.

Ian entered Izzy's hospital room, the familiar sounds of the ventilator and heart monitor greeting him like old acquaintances. His mom hovered in the doorway, clearly torn. "I'll give you some space," she said, though the doubt in her voice made it sound more like a question.

Ian tried to remember how to smile. "Thanks."

She hesitated. "You're not going anywhere else?"

"Mom," he said, exasperation softening into reassurance. "No one here is going to give me drugs. I'm just going to sit with Izzy and try not to fall even more behind in school." He held up his backpack, as if it might help convince her. Dr. Garcia had agreed that he should take a few days off while his body adjusted to being clean, so long as his parents kept a close eye on him. What Ian couldn't explain to his mom was how much easier it felt to be here—with the hum of machines and nurses' chatter in the hall—than at home in his own room, where the silence only made his shame echo louder.

"OK," she said finally, stepping forward to smooth his hair with her hand. "I'll be back in a little while."

Ian nodded, waiting until her footsteps faded down the hall. He had barely sunk into the chair by Izzy's bed when the soft sound of movement behind him made him turn. Standing in the doorway was Dr. Paulsen.

She shifted on her feet, glancing over her shoulder. "Ian, hi," she said hesitantly. "Is, um, your mom here?"

Ian shook his head. "She just left." His mouth grew dry. He hadn't seen Dr. Paulsen since the night of the open house, and he wasn't sure what to expect—a lecture? Another warning about steering clear of Maeve?

The tension eased from her shoulders as she stepped into the room. "Sorry, I hope I'm not intruding." Her gaze drifted to Izzy. "I... visit her sometimes."

"Nah, it's cool," Ian said, knotting his hands together in his lap.

She pulled up a chair beside him, and Ian's mind raced, grasping for the right words—to say he was sorry for what he'd done, that he was grateful she'd saved him, that he was scared of what lay ahead.

"How are you?" Dr. Paulsen asked softly, her eyes staring straight ahead at Izzy.

"Fine." He shrugged.

She turned to eye him skeptically. "You know what 'fine' stands for in addiction recovery?" she asked. "Fucked up, insecure, neurotic, and emotional."

Ian blinked, startled. He'd never heard her swear before.

She smiled. "There's plenty of other zingers where that one came from."

A laugh escaped him, more like a cough, and it caught him off guard.

"I'm just saying," Dr. Paulsen went on, her voice gentle, "it's OK to be honest. I've been where you are, and I know you can do better. It sucks and it's one of the hardest things you'll ever go through." Her voice caught for a moment. "But it's worth it. I promise." She turned back toward Izzy, but not before Ian noticed her eyes glistening.

His throat grew thick, his chest tightening. "Yeah?"

She nodded, firm and certain. "Definitely." Standing, she brushed quickly at her eyes. "I should go." She paused. "Just... Ian, I'm here if you need me. I know you have your mom, but I think I understand. So, if you need someone—anytime—reach out, OK?"

She placed her hand lightly on his shoulder and gave it a reassuring squeeze.

Ian nodded, his eyes filling as she headed for the door. By the time he swiped away his tears, she was gone. He sucked in a ragged breath as a small flicker of hope ignited in his chest. Then he turned back to the bed, staring for a long moment at his sister. Her face was as still as always, her skin pale against the white pillow.

"Hey, Iz," he said softly. "How's it going?" Her face was as still as always, her skin pale against the white pillow.

"I was going to say I'm fine," he said, as though she'd replied. "But, uh, yeah. Surviving is more like it." He ran a hand through his hair and let out a shaky breath. "Barely."

He sat back, staring at the ceiling tiles, then at the machines keeping his sister alive. His fingers traced the stitching on the chair's armrest as he spoke. "So, I guess you're wondering what all that was about with Maeve's mom." He nodded toward the door through which Dr. Paulsen had just left. "See, a few days ago, I was at this open house. And I was... well, I was doing what I do. I know you know." He glanced down at his hands, shame pooling in his chest. "Anyway, the real estate agent busted me cold. But then Maeve's mom showed up." He let out a dry laugh, shaking his head. "I figured that was it for me since I was pretty sure she had it in for me because of—" He hesitated, stealing a glance at Izzy's still face. "Yeah, I guess you don't really know about me and Maeve, huh? But maybe it's better that way, now that... well, now that it's over." He rubbed a hand over the back of his neck, trying to shove the image of Maeve's eyes, Maeve's lips, out of his mind. "But yeah, Dr. Paulsen talked the agent out of calling the cops."

He fell silent, Dr. Paulsen's words just now gnawing at the edges of his thoughts. *You can do better.*

Ian exhaled, letting the phrase settle into his chest. When he'd tried to do better before, it had always been for someone else: for his mom, to make her proud; for Maeve, to feel like he deserved her. But what if he stopped trying to live up to what other people thought he could be? What if he started doing it for himself?

He exhaled. "Anyway, if you were awake right now, you'd be so pissed at what I've gotten myself into," he said to Izzy. "You'd definitely call me a dumbass. And you'd be right."

Ian's gaze fell to her hand, resting limp on the blanket. He reached out and gently took it, his thumb brushing over her knuckles. "I'm gonna try, Iz. I don't know how, but I'm gonna try. For real this time. For me."

A soft rustling sound made him glance up—and his breath caught in his throat.

Izzy's eyes were open, staring at him. Her face was pale, her expression blank, but her gaze was locked on his. Ian froze, unable to process what he was seeing.

"Izzy?" he whispered, his voice cracking.

Her lips moved, but no sound came out.

The machines beeped steadily, oblivious to the seismic shift in the room. Ian leaned closer, gripping her hand tighter. "Izzy? Can you hear me? Can you—say something?"

Her eyelids fluttered, her lips trembled.

Ian's heart thundered in his chest as he pressed the call button by the bed, then jumped from his chair and sprinted to the door. "Help, please!" he yelled into the hallway. "Please, someone, my sister's awake!"

FORTY-NINE

DANA

Fifty-nine days after

Back home, Dana found Eric in the kitchen measuring out cauliflower pasta for dinner. When she told him she'd left Ian at the hospital alone, his face darkened.

"Is that a good idea?" he asked, his tone tinged with disapproval.

Dana bristled. "I checked his location. He hasn't gone anywhere." She hated how Eric questioned her instincts, as if she couldn't be trusted to make the right call. Ever since Padma had shown up with Ian, Eric had morphed into some hyper-involved, good-cop dad, spouting things like *We'll get through this together, son* while taking veiled jabs at her: *I should have been more involved* or *You clearly had too much on your plate to really be there for the kids*. It was obvious who he thought was to blame for Ian's troubles.

Eric gave a tight nod, leaving Dana to second-guess herself. Everything about their new normal felt precarious, full of invisible trip wires. Should they interrogate Ian about his feelings? Search his room? Hover over him? Give him space? It had been four days since their world had imploded—again—and already, she felt like she was failing.

Eric, of course, acted like he had all the answers.

"I still think he should go to rehab," he said, leaning against the counter.

"The doctor said he could do treatment at home," Dana reminded him. "She said he has the right mindset for it. And rehab is expensive."

"The doctor Padma recommended," Eric countered, his mouth twisting skeptically.

"You met Dr. Garcia, too," Dana said, crossing her arms. "You thought she was great."

"That was Friday," Eric argued. "Right after everything blew up. Anyone would've seemed good then."

"If Padma says she's the best, I trust her."

Eric's face darkened. "And look where trusting Padma got us with Izzy."

There it was. The accusation, sharp and unforgiving. Dana's pulse spiked, fury rising in her chest.

"Oh, so Izzy's coma is on me? And Ian's drug problem, too?" she shot back. "Funny how every parenting failure lands on my shoulders, but none of the successes. When did I become the sole bearer of blame?"

"Grow up, Dana," Eric said, exasperated. "You don't have to keep score all the time."

She let out a bitter laugh, setting her glass down before she could throw it at him. "Maybe I wouldn't feel like it was if you hadn't made it that way," she said. "Look, Ian doesn't want to go to rehab. He doesn't want to be away from Izzy. The least we can do is let him try at home."

Eric's jaw clenched. "And what if that's the wrong choice? What if something happens?"

Tears welled in her eyes, frustration and guilt crashing together. "I don't know, Eric!" she burst out. "I've never done this before—I never thought I'd have to. And reading a couple of WebMD articles and Reddit threads doesn't make *you* an expert either." She took a breath. "Ironically, the only real expert here is Padma—because she's a doctor *and* because she's been where Ian is. So yeah, I'm trusting her on this."

Eric held up his hands. "Fine. We'll do it your way." He turned back to the counter. "I should finish dinner."

Dana eyed the gray cauliflower noodles with distaste. "Fine. I'll get Ian. But I'm picking up pizza. That stuff tastes like glue."

Grabbing her purse, Dana headed to the car. Just as she slid into the driver's seat, her phone buzzed. Ben's name flashed on the screen. She hesitated, her hand hovering over the phone. He was the last person she wanted to talk to—a sharp reminder of the lawsuit and the tangled mess she'd created.

When Padma had shown up with Ian, the lawsuit had been the furthest thing from Dana's mind—though she suspected it had been on Padma's. Had she weighed Dana's betrayal against the chance to help Ian? Or had she simply chosen compassion? A wave of shame rose in Dana's chest. If their roles had been reversed, would *she* have done the same?

She exhaled sharply and answered Ben's call just before it went to voicemail.

"Mrs. Blair, hope I'm not catching you at a bad time," Ben said, his voice brisk.

"I'm just heading to the hospital," she said, backing out of the driveway as the call synced to her car's speaker.

"I'll be quick, then. The judge set a trial date."

Dana stomped on the brake. The car lurched, and she forced herself to breathe. "When?"

"January fourth."

"That's three weeks from now," she said, her knuckles whitening on the steering wheel.

"Yes," Ben said, a note of triumph in his voice. "It's great news. And still plenty of time to prepare. Call the office tomorrow, and we'll set up a meeting to go over next steps."

"But we've had some—family things come up," she began, her voice thin.

"Understandable. Let's discuss tomorrow," Ben cut in. "I'm getting another call. Talk soon." The line went dead.

Dana stared at the screen, dread tightening around her ribs. *Three weeks.* This was what she wanted, wasn't it? A swift resolution. Justice for Izzy.

And yet, the thought of stepping into a courtroom, of facing Padma, made her stomach twist. The lawsuit had always been a double-edged sword. She wanted accountability—but at what cost? Their friendship was already in ruins. Dragging Padma's past into court, exposing her to public scrutiny, felt like a cruel final blow. Yet, she also couldn't shake the image of Izzy lying still in that hospital bed, the future she'd dreamed of for her daughter slipping further out of reach with each passing day while their medical bills mounted.

The screen on her car's dashboard lit up with another call. Ian. *Is this how it's going to be now?* she wondered. *Every time he calls, I expect the worst?*

She answered quickly. "Ian?"

"You have to come," he said, his voice shaking. "She's awake, Mom. Izzy's awake."

For a moment, Dana couldn't process the words. "What?"

"Izzy's awake. You have to come. Now."

Her heart slammed against her ribs as she dropped the phone into the cupholder, fumbling to shift the car into drive. The streets blurred past in streaks of red lights she barely obeyed, her fingers gripping the wheel, her mind racing—was it real? Was it possible?

At the hospital, Dana sprinted to the elevator. The doors took an eternity to close, and she stabbed at the button for Izzy's floor as if sheer force could make it move faster.

When she finally reached Izzy's room, her knees went weak.

The room was crowded with medical personnel, including Dr. Roberts, the neurologist, speaking calmly to a nurse. Machines beeped loudly, but Dana barely heard them over the rush of blood in her ears. Ian stood in the corner, his eyes wide with a mixture of disbelief and joy. And there, sitting up in the bed, was Izzy.

Her eyes were open.

Dana pressed a hand to her mouth, tears spilling over. "Izzy," she whispered, her voice breaking.

Izzy's gaze shifted toward her, glassy and confused. "Mom?" she croaked, barely audible.

Dana rushed to her side, gripping her hand in both of hers. "I'm here, sweetheart. I'm right here."

FIFTY

PADMA

Fifty-nine days after

Padma stepped into the hospital that evening for her first shift after her leave, the familiar antiseptic smell wrapping around her like a second skin. Her veins pumped with a strange mix of relief and dread. She'd missed this—missed the rhythm, the problem-solving, the quiet satisfaction of being useful. And yet, a part of her was afraid. She felt the doubts and insecurities that had driven her to take a leave lying dormant, waiting to ambush her the first time she faltered.

Her badge clicked against her lanyard as she passed through the ER doors. Before she could even drop her bag, Toby appeared, as though he'd been waiting for her. That couldn't be good.

"Padma," he said, his voice urgent. "Can we talk for a minute?"

She nodded, her pulse quickening. "Of course."

In his office, Toby gestured for her to sit. She braced herself for whatever he had to say. Was she being asked to extend her leave? Fired?

"I wanted you to hear this from me," he said, leaning forward, his voice tinged with awe. "Isabelle Blair woke up a few hours ago."

The words landed like a jolt. Padma stared at him, stunned. She sat back in her chair, trying to form her scrambled thoughts into words. She had to keep herself from sprinting from Toby's office straight to Izzy's room. She needed to see for herself that Izzy had been returned to them, that Padma's medical treatment all those weeks ago hadn't condemned the girl to an endless, silent void.

She forced herself to stay put. "How—how's her prognosis?" she managed, trying to stay rooted on the medical side of things. It was easier than thinking about the emotional weight of it all.

Toby sighed. "There's still a lot we don't know. But according to Roberts, she's oriented and can follow simple commands. There could be lasting deficits, obviously, and she'll need extensive rehab, both physical and cognitive. But right now, it's pretty damn miraculous she's where she is."

Padma nodded, absorbing the information. Her heartbeat accelerated as she thought of Dana, despite her effort not to. She knew Dana well enough to imagine the whirlwind of emotions she must be feeling, the fragile line between hope and fear she must be walking.

Toby leaned back in his chair. "Anyway, I don't know if this changes anything for you, but I wanted you to hear it from me first."

"You mean instead of seeing it on the news," Padma said flatly.

He grimaced. "Yeah, there's always that possibility, I guess."

She nodded. "Thanks, Toby."

"How are you feeling?" he asked, tilting his head. "Ready to be back?"

Padma hesitated, then nodded. "I think so. I hope so."

Toby smiled. "You'll be fine. Go get 'em, kid."

The ER was even busier than usual that night and Padma quickly found herself bouncing from a man with chest pain who ended up needing a cardiac cath, a middle school soccer player with a broken wrist, and an older woman with a stubborn UTI. Padma quickly lost herself in the flow of the work. Despite her fears, her self-doubt remained dormant and her instincts, dulled by anxiety during the weeks leading up to her leave, felt sharper, like everything had come back into focus.

When she double-checked a patient's chart, it wasn't out of an obsessive need to confirm she hadn't missed anything—it was simply part of the process. It felt good, natural, like coming home to a version of herself she'd been convinced she'd lost.

At one point she rounded a corner and came face to face with Gary Ackerman.

"Oh, hey, Padma," he said, his familiar self-important grin setting her teeth on edge.

"Hey, Gary," she said, moving to step around him. He shifted to block her way.

"I just wanted to say I hope there won't be any hard feelings about me getting Toby's job," he said, his tone pointed—making it clear he knew she'd been in the running and had lost out to him.

She forced a smile and pictured herself clobbering him with the clipboard she was carrying. "No hard feelings, Gary."

"I'm told it was a very objective process," he said. "That they just wanted the best man for the job."

Padma raised her eyebrows. "I'm sure." She stepped around him and caught the eye of another ER doctor passing.

"Just not the best woman," the doctor said, rolling his eyes in Gary's direction, and Padma suppressed a laugh.

When her shift ended in the early morning hours, instead of heading to the parking garage, Padma made her way upstairs, her feet carrying her almost involuntarily to Izzy's floor. She hesitated outside the door, peeking in. There was no sign of

Dana. The pullout bed looked slept in and hadn't been put away yet, but the room was quiet, the soft beeping of monitors the only sound.

Izzy lay in the bed, her eyes fluttering open as Padma approached.

"Dr. Paulsen," Izzy said, her voice hoarse and low.

"Hi, Izzy," Padma said, feeling a lump appear in her throat. A thousand memories flashed through her mind in the space of an instant: seven-year-old Izzy splashing in their backyard kiddie pool with Maeve. The girls' matching neon sweatshirts on the first day of middle school. Izzy showing up at their front door with a handmade get-well card for Maeve the year she'd had mono, the glitter glue on it still sticky.

"How are you feeling?" Padma asked Izzy now, forcing herself back into the present.

"Tired," Izzy rasped. "And my throat really hurts."

"That's from the breathing tube," Padma explained. "It will feel better in a day or so. Do you need some ice chips to suck on?"

"I think my mom just went to get me some," Izzy said.

Padma's pulse quickened at the thought of Dana so nearby, but she didn't move to leave.

"What happened to me?" Izzy frowned. "The doctors told me, but I didn't really get it."

Padma took a deep breath, choosing her words carefully. "You had a blood clot that traveled to your lungs and blocked an artery. It made your brain—parts of your brain—shut down."

Izzy closed her eyes. "I don't remember," she said, her scratchy voice barely audible.

"That's normal," Padma assured her. "Your brain has been through a lot. It'll take time to piece things together."

Izzy nodded slowly, her eyes re-opening. "How long was I... like this?"

"Two months, give or take," Padma said gently.

Izzy's eyebrows knit together. "Where's Maeve? When is she coming to see me?"

Padma's chest tightened. "I think you'll need to ask your mom about that," she said.

"OK," Izzy agreed, her eyes drifting closed again. "I'm sorry, I'm really tired."

"It's OK," Padma said, feeling tears slip down her cheeks, grateful Izzy couldn't see them. "Rest."

She bent to pat Izzy's arm, then turned and slipped out of the room.

FIFTY-ONE

IAN

Sixty-three days after

Ian ducked into the classroom, the sound of his sneakers scuffing against the tiled floor echoing in the quiet. After a week of detoxing under the close watch of his parents, he was finally back at school for the last few days of the semester.

He hadn't admitted it to his parents, but he'd liked being at home. It wasn't just that his body was too wrung out to handle much else; it was all the other stuff: helping his mom decorate the Christmas tree. Baking her signature candy cane cookies, which he used to devour as a kid. Watching old Schwarzenegger movies with his dad, who had a running commentary for each one.

"Wait, this guy was governor of California?" Ian had asked during *Pumping Iron*, incredulous. "He can barely speak English."

"A true American success story," his dad had replied, grinning as Ian's mom appeared in the living room bearing a bowl of popcorn mixed with Raisinets, Ian's favorite.

During the days Ian had been home before Izzy woke up,

he'd had his parents to himself. Most of that time, he lay in bed, nauseous and exhausted, his body wrecked by withdrawal while his mind raced too chaotically to let him sleep. But even through the misery, their presence steadied him. His mom was there with a cool washcloth when he was sweating, an extra blanket when the chills set in. His dad brought him freshly squeezed orange juice, sitting beside him on the couch as they watched TV in easy silence. It was a quiet, steady care that seeped into his bones—a deep comfort he hadn't felt in a long time. For once, Ian felt like the main event, not just his sister's backup dancer.

But now Izzy was awake.

He was happy, of course. Overjoyed. Relieved. But he also felt himself hoarding his parents' attention like a desert plant storing water before a drought. Because deep down, he knew it wouldn't last. Izzy would come home eventually, and everything would shift back to the way it had always been—the old normal, where Ian was an afterthought.

The hallway at school emptied at warp speed as kids slammed lockers and called out to each other, funneling toward the cafeteria. And though according to Dr. Garcia Ian was physically done with withdrawal, the thought of facing the cafeteria—the crowded tables, the stares, the whispers—made sweat spring up on the back of his neck.

That morning, returning to school, Ian was an instant celebrity. Word had spread that Izzy had woken from her coma, and everyone clamored to talk to him. Even kids he swore he'd never seen before suddenly knew his name. Thankfully, no one seemed to question why he'd been absent the past week, probably assuming it was tied to Izzy's recovery. But Ian knew it was only a matter of time before the truth came out.

"It's a miracle," said a girl he didn't recognize, tucking limp, brown hair behind one ear as her fingers toyed with a wooden cross on a leather strap around her neck.

There was a twenty-five to forty percent chance she'd wake up, he wanted to say—he'd done extensive research on this fact. *Which doesn't make it a miracle.*

The attention continued to build as the morning went on. The editor of the school paper wanted to interview him about his "trauma experience." The president of the yearbook club asked him for baby pictures of him and Izzy so they could do a full-page spread dedicating the issue to her.

Ian shuddered, his gaze darting down the nearly empty hallway as he searched for a quiet corner to eat his lunch in peace.

"Hey," someone purred. He turned to see Sadie lounging against his locker, as if she'd materialized out of thin air like an unwelcome genie.

"So, we're nominating Izzy for prom queen," she'd said, looking proud of herself. "You have to help spread the word. Be Izzy's voice."

Ian didn't even bother to hide his eye roll. "You know she can talk again, right?" he said. "She doesn't need me to be her *voice*." He made air quotes.

Sadie huffed, tossing her hair in annoyance, but before she could reply, Ian turned and walked away, his pace quickening. Everyone's voices from that morning echoed in his head—telling him how thrilled, grateful, over the moon he should be.

And part of him was. Of course he was relieved Izzy had woken up, relieved she was back. But another part, a dark, slinking part of him, felt resentful.

I just figured out how to live without you, he thought bitterly, *and now you're back.*

OK, maybe "figured out" was an overstatement. His so-called new life was a shaky work in progress, stitched together by meetings with Dr. Garcia, hours in the kitchen baking cookies, and endless cycles of nausea and headaches as he detoxed.

It wasn't pretty, but for the first time in months, he'd started to feel human again—which wasn't all good.

And now, with Izzy awake, all the air seemed to rush out of the space he'd begun carving for himself. How could he compete with a sister who had literally risen from a coma? How could anyone?

Rounding the corner, Ian peeked into an empty classroom and slipped into a chair at the back. He felt like he'd been hit by a truck, flattened by the emotional chaos of the past week. He found himself on a dizzying roller coaster of shame, guilt, gratitude, despair, and hope, unable to predict how he would feel from one minute to the next. But at least he was feeling something after months of numbing himself out.

At least that's what Dr. Paulsen had told him.

He'd gotten up the courage to text her after seeing her in Izzy's hospital room. She'd replied immediately, assuring him that everything he was experiencing was normal.

> Take it one day at a time. And if that's too much, just one minute at a time.

Her words played on repeat in his head now, grounding him as he stared out the classroom window, forcing himself to breathe.

"Hi, Ian."

Ian startled at the sound of his English teacher's voice. Mr. Riley stood in the doorway, holding a can of Coke and a manilla folder.

"Oh, uh, hey," Ian mumbled, sitting up straighter. "Sorry to, um, barge in. I was just looking for a place to eat. Is that OK? I won't, like, bother you or anything." Despite his embarrassment at letting Mr. Riley down by getting suspended and then disappearing from the face of the planet for a week, his classroom still felt like the only place in school where Ian could fully exhale.

Mr. Riley spread his arm in welcome. "Be my guest."

Ian pulled out the sack lunch his mom had made him. She'd started packing his lunch again like she'd done when he was little. Today's included a pepperoni and butter sandwich—his favorite—chips, apple slices, and three candy cane cookies.

"How are you holding up?" Mr. Riley asked, sitting at his desk. His tone was even but his eyes were watchful.

"Fine," Ian said automatically.

"I heard the news."

Ian stiffened with embarrassment. Great, so his favorite teacher knew he was a drug addict.

"About your sister," Mr. Riley clarified.

"Oh, yeah, that," Ian said. He braced himself. Here it came —the "miracle" talk, the same praise and platitudes he'd been hearing all morning.

"It made me think about our last talk," Mr. Riley said, leaning back in his chair. "About what it's been like for you, having Izzy as a sister." He paused, giving Ian space to respond. "We don't have to get into it if you don't want to, but just in case, I'll ask again: How are you?"

Ian kept his eyes fixed on the desk, tracing the grain of the wood with his finger. Finally, he looked up, meeting Mr. Riley's steady, compassionate gaze. The kindness in his teacher's eyes undid him, and he felt a hot prickle of tears threatening to spill.

"I'm, um... you know," Ian began, his voice unsteady. "It's a lot." He shrugged. "Things without Izzy were... different. And now they won't be anymore."

Mr. Riley nodded thoughtfully. "Some things will change, sure," he said. "But not everything has to. A lot of it is up to you, Ian. And from what I've seen, you're more than capable of charting your own path—a path you choose, one that you're proud of."

Ian rubbed at his eyes with the heel of his hand and let the words sink in. "Yeah," he said softly, the word filled with a cautious kind of hope. "Maybe I can."

FIFTY-TWO

DANA

Sixty-three days after

Dana sat by Izzy's bed, her hands resting on her lap as she studied her daughter's face.

Izzy had been awake just moments ago, nodding as Dana spoke cheerfully to her about innocuous topics—decorating for Christmas, how much her friends had missed her—before she'd drifted off again. Every time Izzy's eyes closed, Dana felt a tight grip of fear in her chest. What if she didn't wake up again? Dr. Roberts had assured her repeatedly that once a patient remained conscious for this length of time, the likelihood of slipping back into a coma was extraordinarily rare. Still, Dana couldn't shake her trepidation. After months of waiting for Izzy to wake up, she wasn't ready to trust the relief.

Now she tried to savor the rare quiet. In the three days Izzy had been awake, her room had become a hive of activity. The nurses came and went, performing an endless string of tasks: checking vitals, adjusting monitors, drawing blood. Izzy's recovery had already involved a slew of tests: a CT scan, an EEG, pulmonary function tests, and more still to come. The activity unsettled Izzy, whose eyes darted nervously every time a new face entered the room.

"Why is this happening?" she asked, her voice thin and hoarse, each time someone approached her bed.

Dana often scrambled for words, trying to keep her tone calm and reassuring, though even she struggled to track the deluge of medical procedures. The first time a nurse came to clean the area around Izzy's feeding tube, Izzy had stared with wide-eyed fear at the tube protruding from her abdomen. Panic filled her voice as she tried to scoot away. "What is that? Mommy, why is that thing in me?"

Dana had been too choked up to respond, helpless as tears filled Izzy's eyes. Thankfully, the nurse, an older woman with a soothing demeanor, had stepped in to explain the feeding tube and its purpose.

"We'll be able to take it out as soon as you show us you can eat enough calories on your own," the nurse said in a comforting voice. "It's still early days, sweetie."

"I want ice cream," Izzy muttered, the petulant edge in her voice making Dana's lips twitch into an involuntary smile.

The nurse had smiled back at Dana. "She sounds just like my grandson."

By the second day, she had managed to swallow small sips of water and eat a few bites of pudding. "Disgusting," she'd declared, scrunching her nose.

Dana and Eric had laughed, and the sound startled Dana. It had been so long since either of them had laughed—it felt foreign, almost unnatural.

Dana glanced at the clock on the wall now. It was early on Friday morning, with only one week to go until Christmas. Beside her Izzy slept, the room oddly quiet without the hiss of the ventilator to help her breathe.

Eric appeared in the doorway, bearing a Starbucks cup for

her along with the miniature vanilla scones that were her favorite.

"Good morning," he said. He handed her the coffee, then stood behind her with his hands on her shoulders, massaging them lightly.

Dana felt torn between leaning into his touch and pulling away. Since Izzy had woken up, Dana and Eric had reverted back to acting like husband and wife. They often sat close together at Izzy's bedside, their chairs touching, their fingers intertwined. It was like they'd been granted permission to be a family again now that Izzy, the missing piece of their puzzle, had returned. Still, Dana knew this wasn't their true reality. Each gesture that echoed their old intimacy left her questioning whether she truly wanted it back—or whether that was even possible.

"How was dropping Ian at school?" Dana asked quietly, careful not to wake Izzy.

Ian had seen Dr. Garcia twice more over the past week to monitor his withdrawal symptoms. He seemed to be improving —eating more, with some color returning to his face—but the haunted look in his eyes hadn't faded. After a week, though, Dr. Garcia suggested that returning to school might help him ease back into a routine.

Today was his first day back at school. Dana's chest had tightened as she watched him walk to the car with Eric, Ian's once broad shoulders appearing slight and hunched under his backpack.

"It was fine," Eric replied. He moved to pull the blanket more fully over Izzy.

"How did he—seem?" Dana fiddled with the plastic top on her coffee.

"Sober," Eric said with a tight smile, answering the question she'd really meant to ask—the only one that mattered lately.

They were each treading carefully with Ian—maybe too

carefully, it was so hard to know—watching for any sign that he wasn't himself.

"We watched a movie together last night while you were here with Izzy," Eric added, lowering himself in the chair next to her. "Well, I watched a movie and he played on his phone, but we sat in the room together, like Dr. Garcia recommended."

"Down time can be hard," Dr. Garcia had said, "especially if Ian is trying to stay out of situations where he would previously have taken pills, like around certain people. New routines can be helpful, such as family dinners or movie nights, and regular AA or NA meetings."

"NA?" Eric had asked.

"Narcotics Anonymous," Dr. Garcia clarified, and the swirling sense of failure in Dana's stomach deepened. "In the folder I gave you I included a list of young adult and teen twelve-step meetings in the area. Early recovery is very important, and it's truly a one-day-at-a-time situation. Over half of all patients relapse at some point."

Ian's eyes had widened with fear and Dana felt nausea rise up.

"Dr. Garcia seems good," Eric said, shifting in his chair next to Dana so that his leg brushed hers. She didn't move away. "I shouldn't have been so judgmental before." He gave her an apologetic smile.

Eric had taken another leave from work—unpaid since he'd already used up all his time off, but Dana was trying not to think about that. And Dana had done the unthinkable and asked her mother for help with the shop.

"Of course I'll do it," Cora had said briskly, her voice heavy with uncharacteristic emotion. "Anything you need. This is wonderful news about Izzy, my dear. Simply wonderful."

"Thank you," Dana had said, her throat tight. "Eric will pick you up tomorrow morning."

"Don't be ridiculous," Cora had scoffed. "He should be at

the hospital. I'll take an Uber—one of the ladies here showed me how to use it. I'll come to visit Izzy first. I need to see my granddaughter."

Dana closed her eyes and shook her head. Having her mother underfoot was the last thing she needed, but what other choice did she have, with each of her two children acutely needing her attention? Her chest ached at the thought of Ian. Would there ever be a time when both her children were happy and whole at the same time? Could the universe not grant her even one day of unmarred joy?

Izzy's eyes fluttered open just then, and she turned her head slowly toward them. Eric was on his feet in an instant, his hand reaching for hers.

"Hi, sweetheart," he said, his voice full of tenderness. "How are you? Do you need anything?"

Izzy blinked at him, her lips parting. "Thirsty," she mumbled, her voice thin.

Eric immediately grabbed the hospital-issued cup from her bedside table, the kind with the bendy straw sticking out of the lid, and brought it to her lips. Dana watched as Izzy took small, halting sips. It reminded Dana of when Izzy was a baby, her little body learning to work in harmony, the liquid moving through her tiny throat as she drank from a bottle. Now, it seemed they were back at the beginning, rebuilding from scratch.

When Izzy leaned back against the pillow, her eyes scanned the room. "Where's my phone?" she asked.

"The doctor said using your phone might not be the best idea right now," Dana said gently. "Your brain is still healing."

Izzy's face twisted with sudden fury. "Well, he's a fucking jerk," she snapped. "I want my phone."

Dana flinched, her mouth opening to reprimand Izzy, but she stopped herself. Dr. Roberts had warned them that as Izzy's brain adjusted, emotional outbursts were normal. Mood swings, irritability, and an inability to filter emotions were all potential lingering effects of the coma, he had said. Still, it was one thing to hear the clinical explanation for Izzy's moodiness, but another to see it take shape in her daughter's sharp edges.

"When can I go home?" Izzy asked suddenly, her voice shifting from anger to plaintive sadness in the space of a breath. It was as if the outburst had drained her, leaving a much younger version of herself in its place.

Dana moved closer, perching on the edge of Izzy's bed. She smoothed a stray wisp of hair from Izzy's forehead, her touch as gentle as her voice. "It will probably be a while, sweetie. There are things you'll need to relearn first—things like getting dressed on your own, using the bathroom."

Izzy groaned, rolling her eyes in frustration. "Obviously I can do those things if you guys would just let me get out of bed."

"Soon," Eric promised.

"Where's Maeve?" Izzy asked abruptly.

Dana froze. She glanced at Eric, whose face was as blank as a sheet of paper. Neither of them spoke.

Izzy's eyes darted between them. "Why won't anyone tell me where she is?" Izzy demanded, her voice rising with agitation. On the monitor beside her bed, Dana saw her blood pressure spike. "Dr. Paulsen said I should ask you."

Dana blinked, thrown off guard. "Dr. Paulsen? When did you see her?"

Izzy's face relaxed slightly, her gaze drifting to the chair beside the bed. "Last night—or maybe a few nights ago? I don't remember exactly. But it was dark and she was sitting right there."

Dana's heart twisted. Padma had been here to see Izzy. The idea felt like both an intrusion and a gift.

Before she could respond, her phone buzzed on the bedside table. She glanced at the screen and saw Ben's name.

"I need to take this," Dana said quickly, grateful for the

excuse to exit the conversation. She slipped out of the room, her head spinning.

In the hallway, a cart laden with breakfast trays rolled by, the mingled smells of scrambled eggs and orange juice making Dana's stomach churn. She leaned against the wall, staring at Ben's name glowing on the screen. The thought of speaking to him, of diving back into the chaos of the lawsuit, felt unbearable in that moment.

With a deep breath, Dana hit the button to send the call to voicemail. Then she let her head fall back against the wall and closed her eyes, willing the confusing tide of emotions inside her to recede.

FIFTY-THREE

PADMA

Sixty-six days after

The late-afternoon sunlight slanted through the car windows, casting a golden glow over the interior. Padma sat in the passenger seat, scrolling through photos of the house they'd just toured. Lars drove with one hand on the wheel, the other resting casually on the center console.

"So," she began, clicking to a close-up of the backyard. "The deck will definitely need to be replaced. And that avocado-green tile in the upstairs bathroom? That has to go."

Lars glanced at her with an amused smile. "We haven't even made an offer yet, and you're already planning a full-scale renovation."

Padma smiled back and gave a playful eye roll. "It never hurts to be prepared."

"Maybe let's just get through Christmas, first," Lars teased. As the road curved toward their neighborhood, his smile softened into something more serious. "Are you sure you want to do this, though? Move, I mean. You've put so much into our house."

Padma's grip tightened on her phone. "It's a good house," she said carefully. "And it's nearby, so Maeve wouldn't have to change schools."

"That's not what I'm asking," Lars said gently. "Is this really about the house? Or is it about Dana? About everything that's happened?"

Padma looked out the window, watching as familiar houses came into view as they neared their street. Lars always knew how to cut through her layers of logic to the emotions beneath. It was infuriating and comforting at the same time. "It's everything," she said after a moment. "The lawsuit. The way the neighborhood has taken sides. Every time I walk out the front door, I feel like people are watching me, like I'm on a bad reality TV show."

"Maybe it will die down now that Izzy is... you know," he said. "And with the trial date pushed back."

Padma's lawyer had called earlier that week with the news that Dana had requested the trial date be pushed back due to everything her family was dealing with. Padma wasn't sure what that meant, or whether it meant anything at all.

"Things will just start up again whenever there is a trial," Padma replied, suddenly feeling exhausted. She dropped her phone back into her purse and leaned her head back in the seat.

Lars reached over and squeezed her hand. "It's just still all so... unbelievable. That we went from seeing them all the time to... this."

"I know." Padma closed her eyes. "No matter what, I don't think I can keep living next door, pretending nothing happened. It feels like trying to rebuild a house after a hurricane. Even if you fix the walls, the foundation's never the same."

Lars was quiet for a moment, his brow furrowed in concentration as he turned into their driveway. "If moving feels right to you, then let's do it," he said finally. "But I just want to make sure you're doing this because it's what you truly need, not because you feel like you need to run away from anything." His mouth tightened. "If anything, Dana should be the one to run away."

Padma's heart twisted at his words. "I'm not running away," she said softly. "I'm trying to start over."

As Lars parked the car in their driveway, Padma's eyes drifted to Dana's house. Ian's car was outside, and she made a mental note to check in on him. She'd been urging him, gently but persistently, to attend a twelve-step meeting. He'd so far brushed her off, assuring her he was making good progress, but she knew recovery wasn't a straight line. It was a thousand small steps forward and backward. Despite everything that had happened between their families, she felt a responsibility to help him keep moving in the right direction, just like so many people had done for her.

Lars unbuckled his seatbelt. "Come on," he said. "Let's go inside. I'll make dinner and you can try to convince me that these renovations will be quick and painless."

She smiled faintly, following him into the house. He headed for the kitchen while she lingered near the front window, shrugging off her coat. As she hung it on the hook, movement outside caught her eye. A car was pulling into Dana's driveway.

Padma froze as Dana stepped out of the car, her face weary. Dana looked up, and their eyes met through the glass. For a moment, neither of them moved. Then, to Padma's surprise, Dana lifted her hand in a tentative wave.

Padma's instinct was to turn away, to retreat into the safety of her home and the painful distance she'd carefully cultivated. But something stopped her. Before she could overthink it, she raised her hand and waved back. It was a small gesture, barely more than a flicker of acknowledgment. But as she turned away from the window and walked toward the kitchen, she couldn't ignore the ache of longing for her best friend.

FIFTY-FOUR

MAEVE

Sixty-six days after

Maeve lingered outside Izzy's hospital room, her fingers brushing the edge of the doorframe. It was Saturday morning, and she could hear muted voices inside—Izzy's mom, maybe a nurse—but she hesitated, her feet anchored to the floor. It had been a week since Izzy had woken from her coma, and Maeve had finally gotten the green light from her mother to visit.

"She's too fragile," her mom had insisted at first. "She may have sustained brain damage; it's too early to say. Let them run the tests they need to, let Izzy spend time with her family."

Finally, though, Maeve had insisted she was going to the hospital.

"Fine," her mother had sighed. "Just, I don't know how Dana—Mrs. Blair—will react to you being there. Things between us are still..."

"You mean she's still suing you?" Maeve asked dryly, then immediately regretted it, seeing the hurt on her mother's face. "I'm sorry, Mom," she said. "I just really want to see my best friend."

Now, though, she couldn't bring herself to walk into the room. She wasn't sure what she was afraid of. Seeing Izzy again would be incredible—of course it would—but things weren't as simple as they used to be.

Izzy had been a constant in Maeve's life since kindergarten. But for weeks now, Maeve had been figuring out how to exist without her—learning to be the center of her own universe instead of a satellite orbiting Izzy. And in that time, she'd discovered pieces of herself she hadn't known were there.

She'd started meeting up with a couple of orchestra friends to experiment with improvisational pieces—way outside her comfort zone, but surprisingly fun. At the urging of another friend, she'd signed up for a hip-hop dance class, where she felt goofy and uncoordinated but also exhilarated. She'd even scheduled a meeting with the school guidance counselor to talk about applying to colleges in California. Maybe she'd learn to surf.

But this new person she was becoming still felt fragile, like the tiny tomato plants her dad planted in their garden each spring. What if the old Maeve—Izzy's shadow—reappeared the moment they were back together?

But it was Izzy. Her Izzy. Maeve couldn't stay away any longer.

Squaring her shoulders, she knocked lightly before pushing the door open.

Izzy turned her head toward the sound, her face lighting up when she saw Maeve. "Hey!" she said, her voice hoarse but clear.

"Hey yourself," Maeve said, stepping inside and letting the door click softly behind her. She dropped her bag on the chair and crossed to the bed, hesitating for only a second before leaning down to hug her. Izzy's arms wrapped around her, weaker than Maeve remembered, but warm. Solid. Real. Maeve felt a rush of emotion somewhere between relief and joy, along with a faint pang of uncertainty.

"You look good," Maeve said as she straightened, tucking a strand of hair behind her ear.

Izzy rolled her eyes. "I look like shit. Do you know no one bothered to shave my legs for the whole two months?" She shuddered and pointed to the blankets covering her lower half. "It's gnarly down there."

Maeve laughed and sank into the chair by Izzy's bed. For a moment, they just looked at each other, and some of Maeve's nervousness melted away. No matter what had changed, this part felt the same: the unspoken understanding, the way they could fill the air between them without saying a word. Best friends forever.

"How are you, um, feeling?" Maeve asked tentatively.

Izzy groaned dramatically. "I hate it here. They won't let me sleep through the night, they wake me up, like, every hour for one thing or another. And Mom keeps taking my phone. Like, seriously?" She gestured to the bedside table, where her phone sat like a caged bird with a timer app glowing on the screen. "She gives me ten minutes per day. Ten. Minutes. It's barbaric."

Maeve smiled. "You're suffering, clearly."

"I am!" Izzy leaned her head back against the pillow, and Maeve caught the flicker of humor in her friend's eyes. But then Izzy's face turned serious. "The worst part is that I can't do anything. Like, literally, anything. It's like my body forgot how to work. I peed by myself yesterday for the first time and the nurse cheered." Her eyes filled with tears and her voice dropped to a whisper. "It's so embarrassing."

"You'll get there," Maeve said.

Izzy's jaw clenched. "What if I don't?" she said softly. "What if things never go back to the way they were before?"

Maeve reached out to grip Izzy's hand. "They won't," she said honestly. "Not for any of us. But that doesn't mean things won't be good again. They'll just be... different."

Izzy stared at her for a long moment, then nodded. "I

guess." She sighed, glancing at her phone. "You know who *hasn't* texted me? Taylor. Not once. Not even to see if I was, like, alive."

Maeve sighed and willed herself not to say *I told you so.* "He knows you're alive, believe me. It's all anyone at school is talking about—well, until today, anyway, when we all found out that Ms. Boswell and Coach Davis are dating."

Izzy raised an eyebrow. "The guidance counselor and the gym teacher? Huh. That actually kind of makes sense on so many levels."

Maeve laughed and relief swelled in her chest at the return of their easy banter.

"Anyway," Izzy said, her face falling slightly. "Screw Taylor. I'm done with him, for good." She shifted in the bed and pressed her lips together, fixing Maeve with a knowing look. "But speaking of boys, it seems like you've been busy with them —specifically with my brother."

Maeve felt her heart stop and she released Izzy's hand. "How do you—?"

Izzy nodded toward her phone. "Your text."

Maeve's heart sank as she remembered the rambling, confessional text she'd sent Izzy the night she'd felt so alone. The text she was sure Izzy would never read. Her face flamed at the realization. "I didn't—we didn't, I mean, I would have..." She trailed off and let out a soft groan. "I'm really sorry, Iz," she said softly. "It just kind of happened."

Izzy gave a short, raspy laugh. "Whatever, it's fine," she said. "At first, I was mad. Like, really mad. I mean, Ian?" She made a face. "I just don't know why you'd want to be with him."

Maeve clasped her hands together in her lap and gazed down at them. "It doesn't matter," she said, her voice tight. "It's over. He ended it. Over text." She rolled her eyes and looked up at Izzy.

Izzy frowned. "Oh my God, what a shithead."

Maeve tilted her head, wondering for the first time if anyone had told Izzy about the lawsuit between their mothers. Whether she knew their friendship was over. She opened her mouth to ask, then closed it again. "Yeah," she agreed. "Anyway, it's probably for the best." She shrugged, trying to brush it off, though the ache in her chest lingered.

Izzy yawned. "God, I'm so tired, like, all the time. It's the worst."

"I'll let you sleep," Maeve said, rising from her chair.

"Come back later?" Izzy mumbled. Her eyelids were already drooping.

Maeve nodded and reached out to squeeze her hand again, but Izzy had already faded into sleep.

Maeve turned to leave just as the door opened and Ian walked in. Her heart dropped into her stomach. He looked somehow taller and leaner than the last time they were in the same room, and his eyes seemed shadowed by exhaustion.

"Hey," he said awkwardly, hovering near the doorway. "Sorry. Is it OK if I—?"

"Yeah, sure." Maeve shifted on her feet, her pulse thudding in her ears. She'd done her best to avoid running into him at school for the past three weeks, afraid the sight of him would break her heart all over again. And now, here he was, so close she could reach out and touch him. His hair was even shaggier than usual, curling at the edges, and when he brushed it out of his eyes, something in her chest ached.

But along with the ache came a voice, clear and certain. *Not for you. Not right now.*

Ian approached, his gaze on Izzy. "How is she?" he asked quietly, sinking into the chair Maeve had just vacated.

Maeve tucked her hands into the pocket of her hoodie. "Mad your mom locked her phone," she said, raising an eyebrow.

A small grin tugged at his lips. "That sounds like Izzy."

They sat in silence. For a moment there was the kind of silence that felt heavy but not awkward. Finally, Maeve broke it. "Why weren't you at school last week?"

Ian rubbed the back of his neck, then ran a hand through his hair. His shoulders hunched, like he was bracing for something. "Because of Izzy," he said, and then, after a long pause, "and... other stuff."

Maeve studied him, noticing the dark smudges of circles under his eyes, the way he seemed weighed down by something bigger than he could carry. "You can be honest with me, you know," she said quietly. "I'm not going to judge you. I never judged you."

He looked away, his jaw tightening, and for a second, she thought he wasn't going to answer. But then he turned back, his eyes meeting hers. "Things got bad... with the pills," he admitted, his voice low and raw. "But I'm off them now. I have a doctor and everything. It's been... hard. Really hard." He swallowed, his throat bobbing. "Your mom has been great, though."

Maeve blinked, confused. "My mom? What do you mean?"

His face flushed. "It's a long story," he said, shifting in his seat. "But I want to tell you... someday."

Maeve inhaled, her mind spinning. How had she missed how bad things had gotten for him? Had he been on drugs the whole time they'd been talking, texting, kissing? The thought made her chest tighten with anger. But then she looked at him again, really looked at him—the rawness in his gaze, the pain, the tiny glimmer of hope—and something softened inside her.

"I'm glad you're getting help," she said quietly, and she meant it.

Ian nodded, then took a deep breath, like he was bracing himself. "Maeve, about us, about what happened—"

She held up her hand. "You don't have to—"

"No, I do," he interrupted. "What I did... breaking things off like that... it was shitty."

"It's fine—"

"It was shitty," Ian repeated, his voice insistent. He met her gaze, his eyes wet. "I could have fought for you. I could have been honest with you. And instead, I—I didn't, I wasn't. I'm sorry."

Maeve nodded, a lump rising in her throat. For a moment, the weight of everything unsaid settled between them, thick as fog. Maeve glanced at Izzy, her chest tightening. Izzy was the constant, the anchor between them, even now.

Footsteps echoed faintly in the hallway, and Maeve turned toward the door. "I should go," she said. She glanced back at Izzy, then at Ian, and felt the ache of the in between: caught between who she had been and who she wanted to be, between holding on and letting go.

"Tell her I'll be back later, OK?" she said. She hesitated, then leaned over and brushed her lips against his cheek for the briefest moment. Before he could say anything, she slipped out of the room.

FIFTY-FIVE

DANA

Sixty-seven days after

Dana glanced over at Ian, slouched in the passenger seat, his gaze fixed out the window. It was the Tuesday before Christmas, and she'd just ferried him to one of his now frequent medical appointments.

"How was your appointment with Dr. Garcia?" she asked, trying to keep her voice light and conversational, masking the undercurrent of fear that rippled through her words. She wasn't just asking about the appointment; she was asking if he was still holding on, if the temptation to slide backward into old habits was creeping in.

"Fine," Ian said with a shrug, still looking outside.

It had only been twelve days since Padma had brought Ian home and laid bare the harsh truth of just how bad off he was. As she'd ushered both him and Padma inside, she hadn't stopped to think about how long it had been since Padma had entered her house, until she saw her hesitate on the threshold, as if crossing into Dana's space might be a betrayal of the invisible wall that had sprung up between them. But in that moment, none of it mattered to Dana—not the weeks Izzy had spent unconscious, not the lawsuit and who was or wasn't at fault, not their fractured friendship. Padma had come to help Ian, and Dana had trusted her, instinctively falling back into the comfort of their shared history.

Now, though, Dana felt like she was navigating Ian's recovery on her own. Eric was there, of course—they spent their nights dissecting Ian's every move, analyzing his mood, his eating habits, his schoolwork, his sleeping patterns. But she and Eric were in survival mode, their interactions limited to discussing Ian's wellbeing. It reminded her of when the twins were babies and all they could talk about was how to get them to sleep, to eat, to stop crying, to stay alive. Except this time, the stakes felt even higher. It wasn't just about keeping Ian alive; it was about helping him find his way back to himself.

"Dr. Garcia seems very knowledgeable," Dana ventured again, hoping to draw Ian out.

Ian shifted in his seat and shrugged. "Yeah. She's good."

She allowed herself a small smile. For a teenager, that was practically an effusive endorsement.

"I have to go by the shop for a few minutes," she said, trying to gauge his reaction. "Will you be OK at home?" Translation: Will you use drugs or otherwise screw up your life again while I'm gone?

Ian turned to her. "I can come with you. If you want."

Dana tried to keep the surprise off her face. For the past twelve days Ian had shown little enthusiasm for going anywhere but the hospital.

"Are you sure?" she asked, wary of pushing too hard.

"Yeah," he said. "It's weird, but I kind of like it there."

"Well, good," Dana said, her voice softening. "I like having you there." She reached over and gave his arm a quick squeeze. He didn't pull away.

The shop smelled woodsy and fresh from the scented

candles Dana's mother had placed near the door. Cora stood at the register, her snow-white hair smooth from a recent blowout, a deep green scarf tied in a crisp knot at her neck, chatting animatedly with a customer about a porcelain tea set.

"There are some papers in the back that need to be shredded if you want to start on that," Dana said to Ian. He nodded, and with a wave to his grandmother, headed toward the office.

Dana exhaled as her mother wrapped up with the customer, steeling herself for whatever off-handed judgmental comment would come her way once they were alone. For the past week Cora had been running the shop almost singlehandedly while Dana focused on Ian and Izzy. She knew her mother had started to piece together just how dire things had gotten with the business. There was no hiding it now.

A few minutes later, Cora approached the counter, smoothing the silk scarf at her throat. "He looks better," she said, nodding toward the back office where Ian had disappeared. Her voice was even, but Dana heard the weight of unsaid questions beneath it.

"He's getting there," Dana replied, keeping her tone neutral.

Cora tilted her head, her perceptive gaze cutting through Dana's defenses. "And you? How are you holding up?"

Dana hesitated, caught between the impulse to brush off the question and the need to finally tell the truth. She fiddled with the edge of her sweater, inhaled deeply, and said, "Mom, there's something I need to tell you."

Cora's expression remained unreadable. Dana straightened her spine, reaching for her last shred of courage.

The words, which had cost her so many sleepless nights to arrive at, spilled out more easily than she expected. Almost immediately, relief washed over her, followed by a bracing apprehension as she searched her mother's face for a reaction.

Cora pursed her lips, her signature red lipstick still pristine after hours of work. "I figured as much," she said matter-of-factly.

"You did?" Dana blinked, startled.

Her mother's gaze softened, though her tone remained crisp. "Well, you can't very well go on like this, now, can you?"

Dana felt something halfway between a laugh and a sob rising in her chest—she seemed to exist on the verge of both these days. "No," she admitted. "I suppose I can't." She leaned back against the counter, studying her mother. "Are you upset?" she asked, her voice quieter now.

"Upset?" Cora frowned, her hands hovering in the air in front of her. "Of course. I know how hard this must be for you."

Dana tilted her head, suspicious. "No, I mean upset because I destroyed the business you created. The one you ran for so many years—your legacy."

Her mother snorted, a sound so out of character it startled Dana. "My legacy? Darling, don't be dramatic. I'm not dead yet, and I don't plan to be anytime soon. Whether you like it or not, I've got plenty of years left in me." A wry smile danced on her lips. "It's true, I started Haven and Hearth, and it served me well for a long time." The smile faded, her tone growing more contemplative. "But I let it go years ago, and good riddance."

Dana's eyes widened. "What do you mean? You loved owning this place."

Her mother's smile deepened, but there was something bittersweet in it now. "I did. I loved knowing I'd built something successful on my own. I loved proving everyone wrong, especially your father. After Haven and Hearth took off, I never had to ask him for permission to buy anything again, for myself or for you and your brothers. I was finally in charge of my own life." She sighed and appeared to wilt slightly. "But it's damn hard work being the boss, darling. There were days—months, even—when I'd have traded it all to go back to being a simple housewife. By the time you were ready to take over, I was done. And to be honest, I almost sold the business instead of passing it to you. I had several offers."

"You should have," Dana said, embarrassment rising in her cheeks. "I clearly wasn't suited to it."

Her mother gave a sharp shake of her head. "It wasn't about your ability. It's that I didn't want to saddle you with the stresses and burdens of it all. I thought you might find something of your own, something you really wanted to do. Not this."

Dana's throat tightened, guilt swelling alongside relief. "And obviously, I should have," she said. "Instead, I'll be lucky to break even once everything's sold off."

Her gaze swept around the store, her mind painting a picture of shelves emptied, displays dismantled, the space echoing with absence. The thought was both painful and oddly freeing.

Her mother reached out and patted Dana's arm with brisk affection. "It's only money, dear. You're a smart girl. You'll figure something out."

Dana blinked, warmth blooming in her chest at her mother's rare expression of confidence in her. She smiled shyly, a flicker of hope glowing through the fog of her failure. "Maybe I will."

At home later she and Ian ate leftover pizza standing up at the counter together while he showed her TikTok videos of a middle school teacher trying to explain Gen A slang.

"I still don't get it," Dana said, her brow creasing as she chewed. "Is skibidi good or bad? And what's wrong with Ohio?"

Ian laughed, spraying crumbs of pizza onto the counter in front of them. Dana smiled. It was so good to have him back.

Later that evening, Dana drove to the hospital to swap with Eric, who had been with Izzy that afternoon. When she walked into the room, an old episode of *Gossip Girl* was playing on the

TV, and Eric was perched on the edge of a chair, engrossed, while Izzy dozed in the bed.

"I didn't know you were a fan," Dana said lightly as she approached him.

Eric turned, flashing a sheepish grin. "She wanted to watch it after dinner but fell asleep a couple of episodes in. Now I'm hooked."

Dana raised an eyebrow and set her bag down. "Careful, it's a slippery slope. Next thing you know, you'll be quoting Blair Waldorf."

He stood, reaching for her hand. "Come, sit. I want to talk to you."

Dana allowed herself to be guided to the small couch. He sat close beside her, their legs touching, his hand warm around hers.

"What's going on?" she asked, suspicious. "Oh God, you don't have cancer or something, do you? I can't handle another crisis right now."

Eric smiled. "Nothing like that. No, it's good news."

She tilted her head, waiting.

"These last few weeks have been a roller coaster," Eric began slowly. "But I think we've really banded together. We've acted as a team, showed up for the kids, and supported each other in a way we hadn't in years. Despite how hard everything's been, it's felt... good. Like we're a family again."

Dana chewed her lip, unsure where he was going.

"I hate that it took such terrible circumstances to bring us closer, but I'm grateful it happened. I've realized some things," he continued, his voice soft but resolute. "Dana, I'm so proud of you. Letting go of the shop—it was a hard decision, but the right one. You're making space for what's next, and I can see you're coming into your own. I want to be here for you, to support you." His free hand slid to her thigh, a familiar gesture that sent a small, unwanted thrill through her. "I'm here now," he said, his voice thick with emotion. "This is where I want to be. With you. Always."

Dana stiffened as his hand stroked her leg. He leaned in, his lips brushing hers. For a moment, her body melted instinctively into the kiss—but then she pulled back.

"Wait. I'm sorry—what are you saying exactly?" she asked, her voice sharp.

Eric reached for her hair, smoothing it back, his expression tender. "I'm saying I want to be with you. To grow old together. To build a big, beautiful future, together."

Dana sat back, stunned. "So, you don't want to separate?" she asked, her voice rising despite herself. "You're taking it all back?"

Eric's cheeks reddened. "Yes. I've realized how much I want this—how much I want us. You've shown me that."

Dana stood, pushing his hand away. "Unbelievable," she said. "No, that's not how this works. You don't get to call all the shots in this marriage. You don't get to decide whether it's over or not, whether we're staying together or not."

"Honey, shh." Eric gestured toward Izzy, who stirred slightly in her sleep.

"No," Dana said more quietly but no less heated, her words cutting through the dim hospital room. "You don't get to dictate this. I exist, too, Eric. I get to weigh in on what happens to me, on what I want. In fact, I'm the *only* one who gets to decide that."

Eric rose from the couch, his face etched with confusion and hurt. "But I thought you—"

"All you do is think, Eric," Dana snapped, cutting him off. "You never ask. You never ask me what I want."

He paused, clearly thrown. "OK," he said finally, his voice almost plaintive. "What do you want?"

Dana swallowed hard, the answer rising to her lips before she could stop it. "I don't entirely know yet," she admitted. She gestured between them. "But for the first time in a long time, I'm pretty sure it's not this."

FIFTY-SIX

PADMA

Sixty-eight days after

Padma pulled the stethoscope from her ears and addressed the middle-aged man perched on the edge of the exam table. His protruding belly strained against his paper gown, and his nose hair quivered with indignation.

"Mr. Fontaine, I assure you, your heart is perfectly fine," she said, her tone calm but firm. "You're not having a heart attack."

"Run the tests again," he demanded. "My arm is tingling. I looked it up, and that's one of the signs."

"It can be," Padma agreed. She resisted the urge to sigh. She knew exactly where this was headed. "When did the tingling start?"

"I was lying on the couch, watching TV," he said, pausing to add a dramatic flourish to the story. "And all of a sudden, my arm went numb. Just like that!"

"Were you, by any chance, lying on your arm while you were on the couch?" Padma asked, tilting her head, her lips twitching with the effort to keep her expression neutral.

He nodded.

"Mr. Fontaine, is it possible that your arm fell asleep?"

He opened his mouth, closed it again, then rubbed his arm sheepishly. "Maybe," he muttered.

Padma nodded, placing a hand on the edge of the table. "I'll get started on your discharge papers. If you're still concerned, you can always follow up with your primary care physician."

She pulled the curtain aside, stepping into the bustling corridor, dodging a nurse pushing a stretcher in her direction.

With two days to go until Christmas, the ER hummed with a barely contained chaos that felt as familiar to Padma as her own skin. The holiday touches the staff had added—red and green garlands strung along the cabinets, the table near the nurses' station laden with plates of cookies for the annual bake-off—gave the place a festive feel.

"Busy night," Toby remarked, joining her near the crowded cookie table, where staff were already debating which plate would win the coveted blue ribbon.

"Looks like everyone's squeezing in their emergencies before the big day," Padma agreed.

Toby plucked a sugar cookie decorated with green and red frosting from the table and pointed to the gingerbread men on the far side. Their lopsided arms and smudged features stood in stark contrast to the more polished entries. "Avoid those. They look like someone's toddler made them. Probably sneezed in the frosting, too."

Padma raised an eyebrow. "Those are mine."

Toby laughed, then caught her deadpan stare and winced. "Seriously?"

"Seriously," she said, crossing her arms. "I'm trying to be more of a joiner." She couldn't resist the tiniest eyeroll.

"Well, in that case." Toby picked up one of the gingerbread men and took a large bite. "Huh," he said, chewing appreciatively. "They may look like the cookie factory rejects, but they're pretty good."

Padma snorted. "Gee, thanks."

Toby shrugged and picked up a peanut butter cookie topped with a Hershey's Kiss. "I forget, are you working Christmas?" he asked.

"Not this year," she said. "I think I'm done working holidays for a while."

He raised his eyebrows. "Really? Good for you."

"Personal growth, or whatever," Padma said with a shrug. She selected a menorah-shaped sugar cookie from a plate. "So, I got my invite to your retirement party," she said, glancing at him.

Toby groaned. "I told Monica I didn't want a party. I just wanted to leave quietly. No fuss."

"Monica lives for fuss," Padma said. "And anyway, you deserve a party."

Toby shrugged, his gaze shifting out toward the busy floor. "I'm going to miss this place," he said quietly.

Padma followed his gaze to the nurses hurrying by, the doctors barking orders, the stretchers lined up in the halls as the less critical patients waited for exam rooms to become available. She couldn't imagine walking away from it all. Not yet, anyway.

She wondered how Toby would do in retirement after decades of building his whole identity around being an ER doctor and then the Director of Emergency Medicine. Her eyes drifted toward his office at the end of the hall. For years, she had pictured it as her future: stepping into his role, pouring even more of herself into this place she loved so much. But now, staring down the path she'd once thought inevitable, she found herself wondering what she would truly have at the end of it all.

Unexpectedly, a wave of gratitude washed over her. She closed her eyes and imagined a different kind of future, one she hadn't considered before. A future where she still took pride in her work but didn't make it her whole personality. Where she showed up more for her family, rekindled friendships she'd let fall away, traveled, and explored interests she hadn't even discovered yet. For so long, she had defined herself solely by her job, but now she saw a sliver of hope that she could become someone outside of it.

She was surprised at how liberating the thought was. The weight of the lawsuit still hung over her, but the stakes didn't feel as dire as they once had. The trial might take its toll, but for the first time, she realized she wouldn't lose everything—even if she lost the case. Because work wasn't everything. Not anymore.

When her shift ended just before dawn, Padma was too wired to head home right away. The night had passed smoothly, a satisfying rhythm of diagnosing and treating without the crushing pressure she used to put on herself to triple-check everything out of fear of making another mistake.

As she walked toward the exit, her feet turned instinctively toward the wing where Izzy's room was. Maeve had resumed visiting Izzy, and at first, Padma had worried about her daughter being sucked into Izzy's recovery and making it her entire world. But Maeve's schedule now also seemed full of plans with other new friends and activities. It filled Padma with a quiet relief and pride, seeing her daughter step out of Izzy's shadow and into her own light.

She paused outside Izzy's door, her hand hovering near the frame. She was about to knock when the murmur of voices stopped her. One was soft and raspy—Izzy. The other was unmistakable, a laugh that was loud, throaty, and achingly familiar: Dana.

Padma froze, her fingers curling into her palm. The small wave they'd exchanged two days ago flashed in her mind, tentative and full of unspoken questions. Was she ready for this? For seeing Dana again—not across a driveway, but here, face to face?

Something felt like it had shifted in the past few days, though nothing tangible had changed. The trial still loomed over them, unresolved. Their circumstances were the same. And yet, everything felt different. Or maybe *she* was different. She remembered hearing in one of her early AA meetings that letting go didn't happen all at once. It came in waves, chipping away at the anger, the pain, the need for control. Had she reached that point, standing outside this hospital room?

Padma's hand hovered by the door a moment longer, her heart thudding in her chest. Then, slowly, she lowered it. She wasn't ready—maybe she never would be. Turning on her heel, she headed back toward the elevator, her footsteps quieter than before.

Padma headed for the parking garage, the fluorescent lights overhead casting harsh reflections on the dirty concrete. Sliding into the driver's seat, she reached for her phone and noticed a missed call and a voicemail from her lawyer. The timestamp indicated it had come in just after her shift had started the evening before.

Her stomach tightened. Voicemails from lawyers rarely bore good news—or so her experience over the last few months had taught her. With a deep inhale, she pressed play.

"Padma, hi," came Sharon's voice, brisk and professional. "I'm calling with some fantastic news. The Blairs are dropping the lawsuit. There won't be a trial. It's over." A brief pause, punctuated by the soft rustling of papers, followed. "Anyway, call me when you get this. Merry Christmas."

Padma's phone slid from her hand into her lap as her mind scrambled to catch up. Dropping the lawsuit? No trial? It was over? For a moment, she simply sat there, motionless as her thoughts cartwheeled at increasing speed. This thing that had consumed her for months, hollowing her out and leaving her second-guessing every moment of her career, was simply gone? The storm that had loomed on the horizon for so long, threatening everything she'd built, had dissipated in an instant.

She sat, stunned, waiting for the weight she'd carried for so long to lift—but it didn't. Instead, it seemed to settle more heavily into her chest, as if demanding one last acknowledgment of its presence. She felt the tears prick at the corners of her eyes and swallowed hard.

The lawsuit had nearly destroyed her—not just her career but her sense of self. It had shaken her marriage, created a chasm between her and her best friend, and left her questioning whether she'd ever been the kind of doctor—or person—she'd once believed herself to be. It had pushed her to the brink of picking up a drink for the first time in years. And now, suddenly, it was over.

She took a deep, shaky breath and looked out the windshield at the empty garage. Somewhere a car alarm echoed faintly, a sharp sound cutting through the silence. *What now?* she wondered. How did you rebuild yourself after surviving something that had nearly broken you?

Turning the key in the ignition, Padma started the car and let the familiar hum of the engine steady her. Then slowly she pulled out of the parking garage and headed home to her family.

FIFTY-SEVEN

IAN

Sixty-eight days after

The bell rang, echoing through the classroom like the starting gun of a race Ian wasn't sure he wanted to run. Around him, backpacks zipped, and sneakers squeaked on linoleum as his classmates hurried to the door, chattering with excitement about winter break. Ian moved slower, his hands deliberate as he slid his books into his backpack and double-checked his desk.

Two weeks off school. Before, the idea would have thrilled him—two weeks of sneaking out with Jenner, going to parties where he could obliterate himself, then sleep it off until noon the next day. Rinse, repeat.

But now, the thought of the long stretch of unstructured time made his shoulders tighten. What would he do with himself? Helping his mom wind down Haven and Hearth would fill some of the hours, but not all of them. The nights stretched out in his mind like dark, empty tunnels. Jenner had texted him about a party that night, the promise of easy fun hanging in the air like bait, but Ian knew better than to take it. He didn't trust himself to go anywhere near his old scene, not yet. He sighed. The physical part of quitting the pills had been easy compared to figuring out how to completely remake his life.

He stuffed his hands into the pocket of his hoodie and shuffled toward the front of the room. "Have a good break," he mumbled to Mr. Riley.

"Hold on a sec," Mr. Riley said, opening a desk drawer. He pulled out three worn paperbacks and handed them to Ian.

Ian turned them over in his hands: *The Kite Runner*, *Pride and Prejudice*, and *1984*. His heart leapt as he glanced up at Mr. Riley. "Are these for..."

"My AP Language class next term," Mr. Riley said with a grin. "You're in. I submitted your grades yesterday, including the essay test you made up. You barely squeaked by, but you earned it."

For a moment, Ian could only stare. His chest felt too tight to reply, his eyes too wet. "Wow," he managed, swiping an embarrassed hand over his face. "Thanks."

Mr. Riley nodded. "I thought you might want to get a jump on the reading list. These are my copies for you to borrow over winter break. And I'll email you the full reading list in case you finish those and want to pick up some of the others."

"Yeah, cool," Ian said, feeling a wide, stupid grin spread across his face. "Thanks."

He put the books in his backpack, did a last swing by his locker, then slammed it shut and headed for the parking lot.

As he made his way down the hall, Jenner's voice called out.

"Hey, man!" Jenner jogged to catch up. "Long time no see," he said with an easy smile.

Ian shrugged. "Been busy."

Jenner's smile faltered. "Yeah, I heard... you know." He shifted awkwardly. "You doing OK?"

Ian looked down and kicked at a smudge on the linoleum. The reason for his absence last week had finally trickled out and made the rounds in the high school rumor mill. "Yeah, I'm all right."

Jenner looked relieved. "Good, man. I was worried for a minute there." He paused. "So, Xander's party tonight, you in?"

For a moment, Ian wavered. He could see it so clearly—the darkened rooms, the swirl of laughter and music, the comforting haze of alcohol smoothing out the jagged edges of everything. He could feel the tug of it, the promise of oblivion as opposed to the emotional soup of anxiety and self-loathing with the occasional faint glimmer of hope that he experienced most days.

He reached behind him, feeling the weight of the books Mr. Riley had given him in his backpack, then looked up at Jenner. "Sorry, man, can't make it. I have plans."

"No worries," Jenner said. "Next time. Later, bro."

Ian headed in the opposite direction, the pull of the party fading with every step he took toward his car. Outside in the parking lot, his phone buzzed as he slid into the driver's seat.

Hi, checking in. How are you?

Dr. Paulsen's texts always seemed to pop up like little lifelines just when he needed them. She had a way of asking questions that made him want to answer them, even when he didn't feel like talking to anyone else.

Fine

No, really?

He sighed. She never let him get away with non-answers.

Nervous about winter break

Too much time to kill.

You could try a teen NA meeting

He made a face. He'd heard about Narcotics Anonymous meetings from Dr. Garcia, too, but the idea of sitting in a circle confessing his sins to strangers made his skin crawl.

I'm good

Anyway, those are for people with real addictions.

So you're saying yours is fake?

Ian groaned but couldn't help smiling.

Yeah, OK I'll think about it.

Good. I'm here if you need me.

Thanks

Putting down his phone, he navigated out of the crowded parking lot and headed toward the hospital. Stopping by to see Izzy after school had become a routine, a place to be where he could put his own swirling thoughts on hold for a little while.

Nearly ten days had passed since Izzy had woken up, and she was growing stronger. She stayed awake and alert for longer stretches, and her voice, once hoarse and tentative, had regained its familiar edge as she complained about the hospital food and relentlessly pressed the doctors for a release date. More than once, Ian had caught his parents exchanging the same "what are we going to do with her?" glance they used to save for him when he was the one pushing boundaries or making demands.

The elevator doors opened on the hospital's third floor, and Ian stepped out into a hallway humming with holiday cheer. Nurses bustled past wearing Santa hats and reindeer antlers, the faint strains of "Jingle Bell Rock" playing from a portable speaker someone had set up.

Izzy's voice greeted him before he even reached her room.

"I'm telling you, I need a new PT—this one barely has me doing anything! He doesn't get it, Mom. I mean, does he know I'm a varsity athlete?"

Ian leaned against the doorframe, watching as Izzy crossed her arms, her glare fierce despite the hospital gown and IV line. Their parents looked exhausted.

"Whoa," Ian said, stepping inside. "Diva much?" He tried to hide his smile. There was something deeply satisfying about not being the problem child for once.

"Sweetheart," his dad said to Izzy, "you have to trust the process. These are professionals, and—"

"Then get me new professionals!" Izzy cried, pounding the mattress in frustration.

Ian caught his mom rolling her eyes. Exasperated, she stood from the chair. "I'm going to get some air," she said. His dad followed, leaving Ian and Izzy alone.

Ian dropped into the chair by Izzy's bed. "You done scaring away the staff?" he asked with a playful smirk.

Izzy's lips twitched. "Probably not." She crossed her arms, clearly fuming.

They sat in silence for a minute, then Ian cleared his throat. "They've been through a lot, you know," he said quietly. "And they're doing the best they can. Maybe you could give them a break."

Izzy's mouth gaped in anger, then she gave a sharp laugh. "God, when did you start sounding so rational?"

Ian shrugged. "I'm working on it."

She leaned back on her pillow. "Did you bring me any good gossip from school?"

"I got into Mr. Riley's AP Lang class," he offered.

She rolled her eyes but smiled. "Not what I meant. But, hey, congrats. I think Maeve's in that class, too, right?"

"Mm, not sure," Ian said, trying not to give away the tiny backflip his heart had just done. "Other than that, I have zero gossip, probably because I've become a social outcast. Apparently having a mental breakdown because you're a drug addict is uncool."

Izzy waved her hand. "Being cool is overrated."

"You would know," Ian cracked, and she laughed.

They were quiet for another minute, then he leaned forward with his elbows on his knees and looked at her. "I'm glad you're back," he said.

She smiled. "I'm glad you're back, too."

FIFTY-EIGHT

DANA

Seventy-six days after

Dana flipped through the channels, landing on a shot of a television host wrapped in an expensive-looking overcoat, his too-white teeth flashing in a high-wattage smile as he rubbed his hands together for warmth. Behind him, the screens of Times Square pulsed like a futuristic neon city.

"The crowd is building, the excitement is through the roof, and we are inching closer to midnight," he announced, his breath curling into the cold air like a frosty ghost. "So, stick with us as we bid goodbye to the old year and welcome in the new one. This is one celebration you're not going to want to miss!"

Dana clicked the remote, thinking how she'd never in her life been so ready to bid goodbye to a year.

The streaming menu flickered onto the TV screen, a list of half-watched shows she'd abandoned months ago, before Izzy's accident. She scrolled through them, recognizing some of the titles but unable to recall a single plotline. Had she really once had the luxury of time to binge entire seasons? The memory of that life felt as distant as a faded photograph—

an outline of the person she used to be. How had she even passed her time when she wasn't spending all her waking hours at the hospital while also trying to save her failing business?

With Padma, of course.

A prickle of guilt crept down Dana's spine. She had come so close to facing down her best friend in a courtroom, to potentially destroying the career Padma had spent a lifetime building. Maybe she *had* destroyed it. Since Izzy had come back to them, Dana felt like she'd shrugged off blinders: the lawsuit no longer feeling like the only way forward, the only way to be a good mother to Izzy, the only way to keep their family afloat.

Now, though, Izzy was not only awake, but making remarkable progress. She was regaining her strength at an amazing pace, which her doctors chalked up to her athletic training. She could feed herself now, use the bathroom, brush her teeth. The doctors spoke in hopeful tones, crediting her youth, her brain plasticity. No signs of lasting damage. No reason to believe she wouldn't make a full recovery.

The more Dana let that truth settle, the more confident she felt about her decision to withdraw the lawsuit. There was no need for justice when the world—God?—had already shown them so much mercy. To keep pursuing it would only keep Dana shackled to the darkness that had consumed her for months.

She shivered and pulled the fleece throw onto her lap, sinking deeper into the couch. She never wanted to go back there. Yes, life was still uncertain, but for now, both of her children were safe, and that was enough.

She thought of Izzy, who had been sleeping soundly when Dana left the hospital an hour earlier. She'd pressed a kiss to her daughter's forehead and whispered, "Sleep well, sweetheart. See you in the morning." And Ian—when she'd paused at his bedroom door to invite him to watch a movie with her, he hadn't even looked up from the book he was stretched out reading on his bed.

"Yeah, maybe later," he'd murmured, flipping a page.

Dana had just smiled.

"Hey."

She looked up from the couch to see Eric standing in the doorway, dressed in sweatpants and the fleece zip-up she'd gotten him for Christmas last year.

"Hey," she said. "I see we both really went all out for New Year's Eve." She gestured to her own pajama pants.

He chuckled, then hesitated as he scanned the room. There was space beside her on the couch, but she didn't offer it, so he sat in the armchair instead.

"What are you up to?" he asked.

"Mindless screentime." She picked at a stray thread on the blanket. Any other year, she might have felt obligated to make plans—host a dinner party, have Padma and Lars over for fondue and charades. But this year, this was all she had the energy for, and she was letting herself be OK with that. "You?"

Eric rubbed his chin. "I was journaling. Reflecting on the year and setting some intentions for the future." He drummed his fingers against the chair's arm. "This year, I want to be more... attuned."

Dana raised an eyebrow. "Attuned?"

"Yeah, like, more in harmony with what our family needs from me." He shifted uncomfortably. "And I want to be the self-actualized partner you deserve." His voice softened, and when he looked up, his eyes were uncertain, as if bracing for her response.

Once, she might have found this uncertainty endearing. But now, she only felt a flicker of impatience. "Great," she said, turning back to the TV. "But instead of setting intentions about me, maybe set some about Ian. He's the one who actually needs you right now. I'm going to be fine."

She had no evidence for that last part. She was in the process of closing her business—the only job she'd ever had—and had no idea what she'd do next. The medical bills were piling up and Izzy was going to need hours of pricey therapy as they prepared to bring her home. Ian was still in the fragile days of early recovery. But somehow, in a way she couldn't explain, she knew they were going to be OK.

She was going to be OK.

Across the room, Eric swallowed, his eyes wet. "I'll be there for Ian. I promise. We're going to have a fresh start, and I'm going to make sure he gets through this."

Dana hummed in acknowledgment, already turning back to the TV. A fresh start.

That sounded just about right.

FIFTY-NINE

DANA

Four months later

Dana called up the stairs. "Izzy, the Uber will be here in five minutes, and we still haven't taken pictures!"

"Just a minute!" Izzy called back, her tone somewhere between excitement and exasperation.

"You said that five minutes ago," Dana muttered, but any hint of annoyance evaporated the moment Izzy appeared at the top of the staircase.

Her daughter descended slowly, first her feet, clad in bright white Converse high tops, followed by her long legs, strong and shapely again after four months of painstaking physical therapy. The flared skirt of her dark teal, strapless dress skimmed the tops of her thighs, its knotted bodice containing a small cutout on the upper part of her stomach, through which a patch of her pale skin peeked. Izzy's cheeks were pink, her eyes glowing with excitement.

For a moment, Dana couldn't breathe. Gratitude wasn't a big enough word for what she felt. It was awe, relief, love, all tangled together in a staggeringly powerful emotion that threatened to spill over into tears at the sight of her daughter, healthy and whole once more—her beautiful daughter, who'd spent the last several hours giggling with her friends as they got ready for prom, an occasion Dana had once taken for granted. Never again.

Dana had spent the afternoon delivering snack trays to Izzy's room and refilling glasses of sparkling cider, cherishing every squeal of laughter and complaint about curling irons. Now, seeing her daughter this way—alive in every sense of the word—was more than she'd dared to hope for.

Izzy had been home for nearly four months, and back at school full-time for three. Her return to normalcy had been anything but seamless. The outpatient rehab sessions were grueling, and her frustration boiled over daily. She yelled at her parents, her therapists—anyone within earshot—venting the anger and disappointment that came with her body's betrayal. Progress came in excruciatingly small increments, a maddening pace for someone as driven and Type A as Izzy. Her relentless personality was both her greatest asset and her greatest obstacle; she attacked her occupational and physical therapy exercises with an almost militant determination, but when her recovery lagged behind her impossibly high expectations, both she and Dana would spiral into tears.

Now, though, life had settled into a more predictable rhythm. Izzy thrived on the structure and social interaction of school. She'd even started training again, carefully and under supervision, with the cross-country team. Her runs were shorter and slower than they'd been before, but Dana could tell she relished the feeling of lacing up her shoes and finding her stride again. Slowly, her familiar routines were returning, and with them, the light in her eyes that Dana hadn't seen in far too long.

"You look gorgeous," Dana said, her voice catching. "Stunning, all of you."

Behind Izzy, her friends followed like a colorful procession.

Skyler, a curly-haired redhead from the cross-country team, grinned and said, "Thanks, Mrs. Blair," as the girls gathered at the bottom of the stairs, their dresses forming a vibrant mosaic of jewel tones.

The front door burst open, and Eric stepped inside, breathless. "Did I miss it?" he asked.

"We're still here, Dad," Izzy said with an amused smile.

"Why don't you girls line up in front of the fireplace for pictures?" Dana suggested. "Then we can do some outside if there's time."

"I hit construction traffic," Eric said to her. "Sorry."

Dana raised an eyebrow. "You could've knocked," she murmured.

He flushed. "Sorry," he said. "Habit."

Eric had officially moved out a month ago, taking an apartment a few miles away. Izzy had not taken the news well.

"You decided to split up while I was in a *coma?*" she wailed. "How could you?"

Dana and Eric had exchanged a stricken glance. When put like that, it did sound bad. But how could they explain the long, tangled road that had led them here? One of them hesitating, the other holding the pieces of a broken heart, until finally, they'd agreed that the only way forward was apart. Izzy didn't need the messy details. She just needed to know they'd tried.

Now, they'd settled into a rhythm that resembled normalcy. The kids stayed mostly with Dana during the week to keep things stable for school, occasionally spending weekends with Eric. At first, his frequent presence at weeknight dinners had seemed like a good idea—a way to maintain some semblance of family unity. But as the weeks went on and Dana adjusted to the quiet rhythm of being on her own, she found herself wishing they could phase out the awkward shared meals. They both needed to move on, and it was hard to do that when Eric's cauliflower pasta still lived in her pantry.

Dana smiled as she snapped what felt like a hundred photos of the girls from different angles and in different permutations.

"Now one with my parents," Izzy said, and Dana and Eric stood stiffly on either side of Izzy while Skyler manned the camera.

"Say cheese," she said, grinning.

Dana's phone buzzed, signaling the arrival of the Uber. "Time to go," she announced, trying not to sound as emotional as she felt. She pulled Izzy into a tight hug. "Have fun, sweetheart. I love you so much."

"Love you, too, Mom," Izzy said, squeezing her back before rushing out the door with her friends.

Dana and Eric stepped onto the porch and watched as the girls climbed into the car, the taillights fading down the street. Eric broke the silence.

"She looked so grown up," he said. "I guess I'm used to seeing her in sweatpants—or a hospital gown." He winced at the memory.

"She's doing well," Dana said softly.

"What about you?" Eric said, his voice suddenly hoarse. "How are you doing?"

"I'm fine," Dana said lightly, hoping to deflect. She was working to close the door on the part of their relationship where he had the right to ask questions like that. While it had taken time to adjust to his absence—she'd had to learn how to change the batteries in the smoke detector on her own, for one—she'd discovered she didn't mind the empty space he'd left behind. At first, it had felt unbearably lonely, especially on the nights when the kids weren't with her. But now, the quiet had softened, taking on a texture of possibility. The emptiness no longer felt like a void; it felt like room to breathe, to stretch, to imagine something new.

The front door creaked open behind them. Ian stepped out, adjusting the slim, satin lapels of his tuxedo jacket. He looked dashing, the cut of the suit hugging his frame perfectly. Dana felt her heart swell.

"Oh, sweetheart," she breathed. "You look—" Her voice cracked. "So handsome."

Ian rolled his eyes, a small smile tugging at his lips. "Can you guys please not cry? Just this once?"

Dana looked over to see Eric also had tears in his eyes.

"Sorry," they said in unison, then laughed, cutting through the tension.

"You look great, son," Eric said, pulling Ian into a hug.

"I should get going," Ian said, glancing at his phone. "I don't want to be late picking Maeve up."

The *For Sale* sign next door had gone up three months ago, and the house had been scooped up almost immediately by a young family with two kids whose training wheels still scraped along the pavement during their wobbly bike rides. Through Ian, Dana had learned that Padma, Lars, and Maeve had settled just one neighborhood over, into a house they were renovating, including, Ian had noted with excitement, putting in a pool.

As far as Dana could tell, Maeve and Ian had only recently started seeing each other again. She wasn't entirely sure of the details, and knew only that he and Maeve spent a lot of time together "studying" for their AP Language class. Otherwise, Ian kept things vague, which was both infuriating and oddly reassuring teenage behavior. What Dana did know was that Ian seemed happier lately, more grounded. He was still seeing Dr. Garcia and also, he'd let slip, occasionally talking to Padma. For now, that had to be good enough for Dana. She had to learn to trust him again, the same way he was learning to trust himself.

"You'll take pictures at their house?" Dana called after him. "Have Lars do it—Padma's a terrible photographer."

Ian grinned. "Yeah, OK." He started to walk down the front steps, then turned back, leaning down to kiss her cheek. "Love you, Mom."

"Love you, too," she said, her throat tight.

She stood a minute longer with Eric as Ian climbed into his car and backed down the driveway, turning to offer his parents a brief wave before he pulled into the street.

When she glanced at Eric, she saw him studying her.

"Any big plans for the evening?" he asked.

Dana hesitated, then smiled. "Actually, yes."

He tilted his head, clearly waiting for her to say more, but she didn't elaborate. She had a first date of sorts, and it was too early to say where things would go.

Eric nodded, and after a beat, he turned and walked toward his car. Dana went back inside, her phone buzzing in her pocket with a text.

Still on for later? 7 p.m. at the Thai place?

She felt a shot of nervousness as she read it. It had been so long since she'd done this. Would it be awkward? What would they talk about?

Perfect

FYI, Ian's on his way over. Send pictures?

Don't worry, I'll make sure Lars takes them

I have to be honest, I'm really nervous about seeing you.

Me too

But I'm glad we're going to try.

Same.

Dana slipped her phone into her pocket and let her gaze drift around the living room. The photos on the mantel told the story of Ian and Izzy, a timeline of missing teeth, first days of school and other milestones that seemed both distant and impossibly close. Each picture showed them growing older, stepping closer to the adults they would one day become. Her wish for them—her only real wish—was that they would know themselves fully, deeply, much sooner than she ever had.

She was only beginning that work herself, and it felt both exhilarating and terrifying. But most days now, she felt content —happy, even. She'd closed the shop two months ago, and while her financial life was a disaster and she had no clue what came next, she was sleeping better than she had in years.

The past six months had taken so much from her: her marriage, her career, nearly both her children. Yet in the wreckage, she'd found something unexpected: peace. A quiet, tentative sense of self she hadn't known she was missing. And while the path ahead was still unclear, she trusted, for the first time in a long time, that she would find her way.

A LETTER FROM THE AUTHOR

I want to say a huge thank you for reading *Who We Used to Be*. I hope you enjoyed reading about Dana, Padma, and their families as much as I did writing about them. If you'd like to join other readers in hearing all about my new releases and getting access to giveaways and bonus content you can sign up for my newsletter—I promise not to bother you too often.

www.stormpublishing.co/caitlin-weaver

If you enjoyed this book and could spare a few moments to leave a review that would be hugely appreciated. Even a short review can make all the difference in encouraging someone else to discover my books for the first time. Thank you so much!

Dana is a woman who has spent her life letting others dictate her path—until everything unravels and she's forced to ask herself the hard questions: What does she truly want? Who is she beyond her roles as wife and mother?

Her journey of self-discovery is one I think many of us can relate to. Sometimes, it's only when life falls apart that we're given the chance to rebuild, stronger and more fully ourselves. Dana's journey is messy, painful, and full of those "what if" moments, when one decision has the power to change everything.

But Dana's story is just one part of the narrative. It's also about Padma, Ian, and Maeve, each of them trying to release the old identities that have held them back in order to make room for new ones. Often, that means taking the scary step of letting go before truly knowing what comes next, but trusting that growth will happen.

At its core, this book is about motherhood, friendship, forgiveness, and finding the courage to move forward, even when the path ahead is unclear. It's about the complicated nature of life's turning points—the messy, unexpected moments that challenge us to grow and redefine who we are. I hope it resonates with you as much as it has with me!

Thank you for joining me on this journey and I hope you'll stick around. I have many more stories to entertain you with!

With love and gratitude,

Caitlin Weaver

www.caitlinrweaver.com/contact
www.threads.net/@caitlinrweaver

ACKNOWLEDGEMENTS

First and foremost, a heartfelt thank you to the entire Storm Publishing team for their unwavering support. A special mention goes to my brilliant editor, Vicky Blunden, whose guidance never fails to make me a better writer.

I'm also deeply grateful to my amazing writing group—Amanda Vink, Ojus Patel, and Renee Ryan—for their constant moral support and the invaluable feedback that made this book so much stronger.

A huge thank you to Dr. Patrick Meloy for his help reasoning out the medical scenario on which the book is based. In addition, his patience in answering my (many!) questions and giving me a window into life as an emergency room physician helped (I hope!) bring authenticity to the book. Any mistakes are entirely my own.

I'm equally thankful to Martha Thompson, whose insights into medical malpractice law were crucial in shaping the legal aspects of the story. Again, any errors are mine to claim.

To Brent Thompson, thank you for the casual conversation over lunch that sparked the idea for this book!

To my mom, thank you for your keen eye during the copyediting process, and to both of my parents for their enthusiastic support of my work.

A big shout-out to my Atlanta Literati crew for always being my biggest cheerleaders and eagerly awaiting my next book. And to Virginia Highland Books—thank you for being the best local bookstore an author could ask for!

I'm forever grateful to my husband, Marcus, and our sweet boys, Elijah and Sam, for their pride in me and constant love and affection. You make everything possible, and I am so lucky to have you by my side.

And finally, thank you to **you**, dear reader. With so many books out there, you chose mine—and for that, I am truly grateful.

If you've read my other books, you might have noticed a recurring theme: the power of female friendship. There's nothing like the steadfast support of good friends. To all of my incredible friends, near and far—I love you, and I couldn't do this without you.